STALKERS

Paul Finch is a former cop and journalist, now turned full-time writer. He cut his literary teeth penning episodes of the British TV crime drama, *The Bill*, and has written extensively in the field of children's animation. However, he is probably best known for his work in thrillers, dark fantasy and horror.

Paul lives in Lancashire, UK, with his wife Cathy and his children, Eleanor and Harry. His website can be found at: www.paulfinch-writer.blogspot.com.

PAUL FINCH

Stalkers

AVON

AVON
A division of HarperCollins*Publishers*
1 London Bridge Street
London SE1 9GF

www.harpercollins.co.uk

A Paperback Original 2013

A catalogue record for this book is
available from the British Library

ISBN 978-0-00-749229-9

Typeset in Sabon by Palimpsest Book Production Limited,
Falkirk, Stirlingshire

Printed by CPI Group (UK) Ltd, Croydon, CR0 4YY

MIX
Paper from
responsible sources

FSC **FSC™ C007454**
www.fsc.org

For Mum and Dad,
whose encouragement never flagged

ACKNOWLEDGEMENTS

There are many without whom this book would not have been possible. I owe a debt of thanks to lots of people in my two former professions – police work and journalism – for passing on their expertise, advice and friendship in the most generous fashion. I'm not going to name-check you guys because you all know who you are, and you can rest assured, you did one hell of a job.

The same applies to my many editors, publishers, producers, directors and fellow-writers, who have been such a rock for me over so many years, not just in their assistance and support, but in their ideas and opinions which have never been less than instructive, and more than anything in the enthusiasm they have shown for my work ever since I first embarked on this rocky road in the late 1980s. I can't possibly draw up a list for fear that I may inadvertently miss someone out, and that would never do. Suffice to say, as before – you folks know who you are and how much you have contributed to my writing, and for that you have my undying gratitude.

I'd also like to thank my agent, Julian Friedmann, who has been the strongest of allies over the last decade, and my editor at Avon Books, Helen Bolton, who championed my cause so tenaciously that even Mark Heckenburg would pale in comparison.

Above all, I want to thank my family:

My dad, Brian, for providing the original spark. My mum, Margaret, whose support has always come straight from the heart. My sisters, Katie, Caroline and Charlotte, who have been among my biggest fans. My parents-in-law, Stephanie and John, who allowed their daughter to buy into this strange world I inhabit. My children, Eleanor and Harry, for putting up with all my 'artistic' stresses and moods. My late-companion of 14 years, Mollie, who co-wrote with me from the end of her lead simply by allowing me to walk her for tireless miles while I dictated. And my beloved wife, Catherine, who has shared every up and down, listening patiently to each draft, offering criticism and congratulation in equal measure; living the dream (and sometimes the nightmare) right alongside me. I owe her more than I can ever say.

Chapter 1

There was something innately relaxing about Friday evenings in London.

They were especially pleasant in late August. As five o'clock came and went, and the minute hand progressed steadily around towards six, you could feel the city unwinding beneath the balmy, dust-filled sky. The chaos of its streets was as wild and noisy as ever – the rivers of traffic flowed and tooted, the sidewalks thronged with bustling pedestrians – yet the 'grump' was absent. People were still rushing, yes, but now they were rushing to get somewhere where they wanted to be, not because they were on a time-clock.

In the offices of Goldstein & Hoff, on the sixth floor of Branscombe Court in the heart of the capital's glittering Square Mile, Louise Jennings felt exactly the same way. She had ten minutes' worth of paperwork to finish, and then the weekend officially began – and how she was anticipating it. She was out riding on Saturday morning, and in the afternoon was shopping for a new outfit as they had a rotary club dinner that evening. Sunday would just be a nice, lazy day, which, if the weather reports were anything to go by, they could spend in the garden or on a drive into the Chilterns.

Louise was a secretary by trade, but that job-title might have been a little misleading. She was actually a 'senior secretary'; she had several staff of her own, was ensconced for most of the working day in her private office, and answered directly to Mr Malcolm Forester, who was MD of Goldstein & Hoff's Compliance department. She turned over a neat forty thousand pounds per annum, which wasn't bad for an ex-secondary school girl from Burnt Oak, and was held in high esteem by most of the company's employees, particularly the men – though this might have owed as much to her shapely thirty-year-old figure, long strawberry-blonde hair and pretty blue eyes as to her intellect. Not that Louise minded. She was spoken for – she'd been married to Alan for six years now, and had dated him for three years before that. But she enjoyed being attractive. It made her husband proud, and so long as other men restricted themselves to looking, she had no gripes. If she was honest, her looks were a weapon in her armoury. Few in the financial sector, of either sex, were what you'd call 'reconstructed'. It was a patriarchal society, and though the potential was always there for women to wield great power, they still had to look and behave like women. When Louise had first been interviewed for a job with Goldstein & Hoff, she'd been under strict orders from Alan to make the best of herself – to wear a smart tight skirt, high heels, a clingy, low-cut blouse. It had got her the job, and had remained her official uniform ever since.

Okay, on one hand it might be a little demeaning to consider that you'd only advanced through life because you were gorgeous, but that was never the whole story. Louise was highly qualified, but so were numerous other women; in which case, anything that gave you an edge was to be embraced.

4

It was just after six when she got away, hurrying across the road to Mad Jack's, where Simone, Nicola and Carly, her three underlings – all of whom had been released at the generous 'Friday afternoon only' time of four-thirty – would be waiting for her.

Mad Jack's, a onetime gin palace dating from Dickens's day, had been refurbished for the modern age, but still reeked of atmosphere. Behind its traditional wood and glass entrance was a dimly-lit interior, arranged on split-levels and filled wherever you looked with timber beams, hard-wood panelling and exposed brickwork. As always at this time of the week, it was crowded to its outer doors with shouting, besuited revellers. The noise level was astonishing. Guffaws echoed from wall to wall; there was a clashing of glasses and a banging of tables and chairs on the solid oak floor. It could have been worse of course: Louise had started at Goldstein & Hoff before the smoking-ban had been introduced, and back in those days the place was fogged with cigar fumes.

The four girls made a little enclave for themselves in one of the far corners, and settled down. They ordered a salad each, though with a central order of chips accompanied by mayo and ketchup dips. Louise made sure to drink only a couple of Chardonnays with hers. It wasn't just that she was the boss and therefore had a responsibility to behave with wisdom and decorum, but she had to drive some of the way home. Nevertheless, it was a part of the week that they all looked forward to; a time for the sort of rude quips that were strictly forbidden during company hours (at least, on Louise's watch). Occasionally other colleagues would drag up stools and join them, men to drunkenly flirt or women to share tasty snippets they'd just picked up. At some point that evening it would assume the dimensions of a free-for-all. By seven-thirty, Carly was onto her sixth Southern Comfort and coke and Nicola was in a deep conversation with a handsome young chap from Securities. The ornately glazed doors crashed open as yet more City guys piled in. There were further multi-decibel greetings, increased roars of laughter. The place was starting to smell of sweat as well as alcohol, and, checking her watch, Louise decided that she'd soon be on her way.

Before heading for home, she went downstairs into the basement, where the lavatories were. The ladies was located at the end of a short passage, alongside several other doors – two marked 'Staff Only', one marked 'Gents'. When she entered, it was empty. She went into one of the cubicles, hiked her skirt up, lowered her tights and sat down.

And heard someone come into the room after her.

Louise expected the normal 'click-click-click' of heels progressing to one of the other cubicles or to the mirror over the washbasins. But for the briefest time there was no sound at all. Then she heard it – the slow *stump* of flat shoes filled by heavy feet.

They advanced a couple of yards and then halted. Louise found herself listening curiously. Why did she suddenly have the feeling that whoever it was had stopped just on the other side of her door? She glanced down. From this angle it was impossible to see beneath the door, but she was suddenly convinced there was someone there, listening.

She glanced at the lock. It was fully engaged.

The silence continued for several seconds, before the feet moved away.

Louise struggled not to exhale with relief. She was being absurd, she realised. There was nothing to worry about. She was only seven or eight feet below the brawling bedlam that was Mad Jack's on a Friday evening.

Once more the feet halted.

Louise listened again. Had they entered one of the other

6

cubicles? Almost certainly they had, but there was no sound of a door being closed or a lock being thrown. And now that she was listening particularly hard, she fancied she could hear breathing – steady, regular, but also deep and husky. Like a man's breathing.

Maybe it was a member of staff, a caretaker or repairman? She was about to clear her throat, to let him know that there was a woman in here, when it suddenly struck her as a bad idea. Suppose it *wasn't* a member of staff?

The breathing continued, and the feet moved again across the room; more dull heavy thuds on the tiled floor, getting louder. Whoever it was, they were backtracking along the front of the row of cubicles.

Unconsciously, Louise raised a knuckle to her mouth. Was he going to stop outside her door again?

But he didn't.

He *stumped* heavily past, veering away across the room. A second later, she heard the lavatories' main door open and close. And then there was silence.

Louise waited. Still there was silence.

Eventually she stood, pulled her tights back up, pushed her skirt down, cautiously disengaged the lock, and peeked out. She couldn't see everything, but she appeared to be alone. She took a breath, then rushed across to the door, opened it and went out into the passage – and stopped in her tracks. Halfway up it on the right, one of the other doors was ajar. It was one of those marked 'Staff Only' and a thin slice of blackness was visible on the other side. Louise stared at it hard. Was that faint movement she could see through there? Was someone partly concealed but staring back at her?

The door crashed open with a violent bang.

But the man who came through it was young and wearing the pressed black trousers and olive-green t-shirt of the bar-staff. He was carrying a plastic tray filled with gleaming wet

7

crockery. When he saw her and realised that he'd made her jump, he grinned apologetically. 'Sorry love.'

He sauntered away up the stairs, towards the bar area.

With one hand on her heart, Louise ventured forward and glanced through the door as it swung slowly closed. Beyond it, a darkened corridor with boxes down one side connected with a series of lit rooms, and at its far end, with a door opening out into one of the service alleys behind the building. Several other members of staff were moving around down there.

Feeling foolish, she hurried on upstairs and rejoined the others.

Louise finally left the premises, briefcase in hand, just before eight. It was a five-minute walk down to Bank, where she took the Central Line to Oxford Circus. There, she changed to the Bakerloo.

She rode down the escalator to the northbound line, and when she got to the bottom found that she was alone. This might have been odd at any other time of day, but it was now Friday evening and most travellers would have been headed into town rather than away from it. The arched passageways were equally deserted, yet Louise had only walked a few yards when she thought she heard footsteps somewhere behind her. She stopped and listened, but now heard nothing.

She strolled through onto the platform. Again, no one else was present. A gust of warm wind blew a few scraps of waste paper along the gleaming tracks. And then she heard the footsteps again – apparently drawing closer. Discomforted, she gazed back along the passage, seeing nothing but expecting someone to come into view.

No one did. And now the footsteps stopped. It was almost as though whoever it was had sensed that she was waiting for him.

A train groaned into the station behind her.

Relieved, she climbed aboard.

At Marylebone, back among commuters, she bought an evening paper and had a coffee before boarding an overland train to High Wycombe. It was now close to eight-thirty. There was no real rush – Alan, who owned his own insurance company, spent his Friday afternoons on the golf course and would be in the clubhouse bar until well after eleven, but it was always good to feel you were almost home. She glanced through the window as she sped along. In the smoky dusk, the drear West London suburbs gradually blended with the woods and fields of the Home Counties. Darkness was encroaching fast; twenty-five minutes later, when she left the train at Gerrards Cross, it had fallen completely.

She was alone again, and it was very quiet. But she wasn't worried – this was entirely normal. Gerrards Cross was a typical South Bucks country town, so small that it was actually more of a village. Being the most expensive postcode outside London, it was way too upmarket to have a lively night-life, even on Fridays. Its main street, which ran through it from one end to the other, boasted a few bars and restaurants, but these were quality establishments; pub-crawlers and binge-drinkers never darkened their doors.

Louise left the station, which was unmanned at this hour, and followed a hedged side-path down towards the parking area. Gerrards Cross railway station was built in a deep cutting, on a much lower level than the town itself, so its car park was a dark, secluded spot at the best of times. Now, as she descended the steeply sloping path from the station, she noted that several of its electric floodlights were not working. What was more, as the car park came into view she thought that her car was missing.

She stopped, surprised, but then spotted it. It was the only vehicle left and it was down at the farthest end, under the low, leafy boughs of a very ancient chestnut tree. Thanks to the damaged lights, that particular corner was deep in gloom. She set off walking.

And heard footsteps again.

She halted and glanced over her shoulder.

The path curved away behind, so she could only see twenty yards along it. There was no one in sight, and the footsteps abruptly stopped.

Louise continued to peer behind her. The slope of the station roof was visible over the hedge. Beyond that, higher up, there were lights along the balustrade of the bridge – it was possible she'd heard someone crossing it on foot. But again, there was no sign of anyone.

She started out across the car park, which was perhaps two hundred yards long by fifty wide and was bordered on its right-hand side by thick undergrowth. Louise now imagined she could hear movement in this undergrowth: a persistent crackling of foliage, as if something heavy was pushing its way through. An animal, she told herself. This part of the county was alive with badgers and foxes, especially at night.

Then she saw the figure sitting against the trunk of the chestnut tree.

She stopped short, a cold chill down her spine.

Was it a tramp, a hobo of some sort? You rarely, if ever, saw anyone like that in this exclusive district. He was slumped and ragged, and wearing what looked like a dirty old coat, tatters of which were moving in the breeze.

But then she realised what she was actually seeing.

The ragged, bundled object 'seated' against the tree-trunk was nothing more than a bin-bag stuffed with rubbish and waste paper.

Again feeling ridiculous, Louise hurried on.

The car was still half-hidden in murk. Its near-side, where the driver's door was, was up against the undergrowth, and the narrow gap this afforded was completely hidden in shadow. But now Louise just wanted to get home. She was spooking herself with all these daft, pointless worries. So she went deliberately and boldly around to the driver's side, acutely aware of the deep undergrowth at her back as she fiddled with the key-fob. But she could no longer hear movement in it, and even if she could, so what? It was summer. Birds would be roosting in there. She was only a few hundred yards from the Packhorse Common, where wild deer had been sighted. In any case, there was no sound now.

She unlocked the car, threw her briefcase into the back and climbed in behind the wheel. A moment later, she'd gunned the engine, and was on her way out.

She left Gerrards Cross via the B416, heading south towards Slough. At Stoke Poges she turned right and continued west along narrow, unnamed lanes. It was a breezy but warm night, so she had her window partially wound down. Moths and other bugs fluttered in her headlights. The eyes of a cat sparkled as it slid across the road in front of her. At Farnham Common she swung south towards Burnham. Belts of trees growing on either side of the road hemmed her in a tunnel, their branches interlacing overhead like fingers.

Louise had relaxed again. She was only three miles from the snug comforts of home.

But with a thunderous *bang*, she lost control of the vehicle. It lurched violently downward and slewed across the road, the steering wheel spinning in her hands. She jammed her brakes on, skidding to a halt with a fearsome screech.

When finally at rest against the verge, she sat there, stunned. The only sound was the engine ticking as it cooled. She jumped out.

What she saw left her astounded: her front two tyres hung in shreds around their wheel-trims. It was the same with her rear tyres. They'd literally been ripped to pieces; spokes of broken ply-cord poked out from them. She walked around the vehicle in a circle, scarcely able to comprehend the misfortune of it. One blow-out would have been bad enough; she'd never changed a wheel before and thought she could probably do it, but here – in the middle of the woods, at this time of night? Not that it mattered now, because she didn't have spares for all four of them.

She fumbled in her jacket pocket for her mobile phone. She'd have to call Alan. Okay, he was at the golf club and would probably have had too many drinks to drive, but there might be someone who could come and pick her up. If not, he'd know what to do.

Then Louise spotted something else.

The phone was now in her hand, but her finger froze on the keypad.

About forty yards behind the car, something glinted with moonlight as it lay across the road. She walked slowly towards it, but stopped when she was only halfway.

It was a 'stinger' – at least, that's what she thought they were called. One of those retractable beds of nails that police use to stop getaway cars after bank robberies. Someone had deliberately left it across the road.

Louise realised that she was shaking. She backtracked towards the car. Had some hooligans done this, some idiotic bunch of kids who had no better way to waste their time? Or was it something more sinister? Not allowing herself to think about the latter option, and certainly not glancing into the unlit reaches of woodland on all sides, she scrambled back to the car and yanked open the driver's door.

She paused briefly to consider: she couldn't drive on her hubcaps of course. But she *could* lock herself in. Yes, that was what she'd do. She'd lock herself in and call for help. She climbed behind the wheel, closed the door and made to apply the locks when she sensed the presence, just to the left of her.

Slowly, she twisted around to look.

He was in the front passenger seat, having clearly climbed in while she'd been distracted by the stinger. He was of heavy build and wore dark clothing: a bulky leather jacket and underneath that a 'hoodie' top with the hood actually pulled back. His hair was thinning and he had a pair of huge, jug-handle ears. But he had no nose – just a gristle-filled cavity – and no eyelids, while the rest of his face was a patchwork of puffy, raddled scar tissue.

Louise tried to scream, but a thick hand in a leather glove slapped onto her mouth. A second hand, also gloved, fastened around her throat.

And began to squeeze.

Chapter 2

It was typical Bermondsey – scrap yards, wasteland, litter, graffiti running over everything.

Heck drove through it with a jaundiced eye, thinking only that his battered old Fiat Brava matched this decayed environment perfectly. To his left somewhere lay the river, delineated by the occasional crane or wharf-tower. He passed a row of boarded-up buildings on his right. A bag-lady sat on the kerb, her knees spread indecently wide as she drank from a bottle of cheap wine. Directly ahead, derelict tower blocks – bleak edifices of stained concrete and broken glass – were framed on the slate-grey sky.

He drove on, too weary to be oppressed by such a scene.

The appointed meeting-place turned out to be a crossroads close to a low railway arch. Corrugated steel fences hemmed it in from all sides and there was a single streetlight, its bulb long smashed. On the left, a mound of flattened brick rubble provided sufficient room for parking. However, Heck cruised on past, surveying the place carefully. There was nobody there, which, checking his watch – it was now ten minutes to six – was not surprising. He was early for the rendezvous, but at this hour on a Sunday morning there was unlikely to be anyone about in this desolate neck of the woods. He passed under the arch and drove another three hundred yards until a broken fence and a patch of scorched ground afforded him a turning-space. After that, driving slowly this time, he made his way back.

At the crossroads, another vehicle was now present. A maroon Bentley had parked, and a tall, lean man was standing against it, reading the *Sunday Sport*. He wore a black suit and had short hair bleached a shocking blonde. When Heck saw the car and the man, he groaned with disbelief. In truth, he hadn't expected a great deal from this meeting. The voice on his office answering-machine had been abrupt and to the point, stating simply that it had information he might find useful. It had then given a time and place, and had rung off. When Heck had traced it, the call had been made from a payphone somewhere in South London. He'd received dozens of similar things over the last few months, but on this occasion, perhaps because he was so dog-tired, he'd started thinking irrationally; he'd wondered if maybe he'd get a break simply because he was due one.

Not so apparently. It was another false dawn.

He pulled up on the opposite side of the crossroads and climbed from his Fiat. He knew that he looked like shit: he was groggy with fatigue, sallow-faced, unshaven. His jacket and tie were rumpled, his shirt stained from drips of late-night coffee.

Heck idled across the road, hands in his trouser pockets. The tall, blond man, whose name was Dale Loxton, glanced up over his newspaper. This close, his otherwise smart appearance was belied by the ugly, jagged scar down his left cheek and the fanged snakehead tattoo on the side of his neck. He wore black leather gloves.

Heck sensed that another figure had appeared from a concealed position to his right. It was Lennie 'the Loon'

Asquith: he was burly, almost ape-like. He too wore a black suit and black leather gloves, but he had long, greasy red hair and a brutal face pock-marked with acne scars. Neither of the men was smiling.

'Regular double-act, you two, aren't you?' Heck said.

Loxton folded his paper. 'Mr Ballamara would like a word with you.'

'And I'd like to get home and find Jessica Alba making my breakfast wearing only an apron and high heels. What are the chances of that, do you reckon?'

'It's just a little chat,' Loxton said, opening the Bentley's rear off-side door.

Asquith had advanced until he was very close and now stood there like a rock, his big arms folded across his barrel chest. Heck knew he had no option. Not that he fancied it. Even 'little chats' with Bobby Ballamara had a habit of turning nasty.

He climbed in and Loxton closed the door behind him. The car's interior was plush, all fragrant leather and varnished woodwork. Ballamara, as always, immaculate in a pinstriped suit with a shirt and tie of pink silk and a pink handkerchief peeking from his breast pocket, was engrossed in a copy of *The Times*. He was an elderly man, maybe sixty, rat-faced, with close-cropped white hair and a white, pencil-thin moustache. To all intents and purposes he looked like an ordinary businessman, until you saw his eyes; they were dead, flat, ice-grey in colour.

'Ah,' he said, in his only slightly noticeable Cockney accent. 'Heck.'

'My friends call me "Heck". To you it's "Detective Sergeant Heckenburg".'

Ballamara smiled to himself and closed the newspaper.

'What do you want?' Heck asked.

'How's it going? You making any progress?'

Heck reached up to loosen his tie, only to find that it was already loose; it hung at his throat in a limp knot. 'Do I look like I am?'

'You've certainly been putting the hours in. There's no question about that.'

'Been keeping tabs on me, have you?'

'Now and then. As a scrupulous tax-payer, I like to know my money's being well-spent.'

Heck feigned surprise. 'They tax drugs and prostitution now, do they?'

'Let's try and keep this friendly, Heckenburg.'

'You asking me that, or telling me?'

Ballamara's smile faded a little. 'You know, these snappy comebacks may win you kudos with the secretaries in the CID office. But I'd remind you that my daughter has now been missing for two years.'

'And I'd remind you that a large number of other people's daughters have been missing for a similar period of time, if not longer. And I'm no more personally answerable to them than I am to you.'

'You still the only officer on the case?'

'You know I can't divulge information regarding an ongoing enquiry.'

Ballamara nodded thoughtfully. 'Which means you *are* the only officer on the case. In the whole of the Metropolitan Police only one detective is working on my daughter's disappearance.'

Heck sighed. He felt like they'd been over this ground umpteen times. 'I'm not in the Metropolitan Police anymore, Mr Ballamara. I'm with the National Crime Group, as you well know. That means we have less manpower and we're not only investigating crime in London, we're investigating it in the whole of England and Wales. However, the point is a good one. So why don't you lodge your complaint with

Commander Laycock at New Scotland Yard? Believe me, I'd like nothing better. Now, if that's all there is, I've been on a surveillance operation all night, I have about six hours of paperwork still to do, and after that I'm off to bed.'

He opened the door and made to climb out, but Asquith was standing on the other side, and slammed it closed again. Heck pulled back sharply, only just managing to avoid smashing his face on the window.

'Heckenburg, there's something you should know about me,' Ballamara said. It was said casually; a simple statement. But the gang leader's flat, grey eyes had now hardened until they were more like coins. 'I have personally used the foundations of motorway bridges to bury coppers who were much tougher, much cleverer, and much, much higher up the food-chain than you. You think I'm just going to sit back and let some low-rank pipsqueak keep fobbing me off while my daughter is suffering God knows what?'

Heck rubbed his forehead. 'I'm doing what I can.'

'It isn't enough.'

'There's no case, alright?' Heck stared at him as earnestly as he could. 'I've told you this before. Your Noreen went missing. I'm sorry about that, but she was nineteen and a big girl. She had money, she had her independence – she's hardly what you'd class as a vulnerable person. You need to accept the possibility that she might have disappeared because she wanted to.'

'She was out with her mates in the West End,' Ballamara reminded him. 'It was their usual Saturday night get-together. All she had with her was her handbag and the very skimpy clothes she was standing up in. The next day I searched her flat, myself. The wardrobes were still full. All her suitcases were there, her passport was in the fucking drawer, for Christ's sake.'

Heck didn't really know how to reply. They'd had this

18

conversation over and over, and in any case the gangster was preaching to the converted. Heck also believed that Noreen Ballamara had fallen victim to foul play, and, in that respect, his toeing the 'official' line was becoming thankless and tiresome.

'Look Ballamara,' he finally said, 'you need to understand . . .'

'*Mister* Ballamara, while we're insisting on formalities.'

'Mr Ballamara, it's not me you've got to convince. But with no body, no crime scene and basically no evidence of anything at all, I'm pissing in the wind. At present, all we can do is class Noreen as a missing person.'

'And what about all the others?'

'The same thing. There's no proof that any of these disappearances are connected.'

'You don't think it's a hell of a coincidence?'

'Look at the bigger picture. Thousands of people drop out of sight every year, but only a fraction of them in suspicious circumstances.'

Ballamara nodded at this and smiled. 'In which case, why are *you*, an officer in the NCG's Serial Crimes Unit, looking into these particular forty cases?'

'That's what my gaffers are wondering.'

'It isn't good enough, Heckenburg. I want answers.'

'What do you think I want?'

'*I don't give a flying fuck what you want!*' The gangster leaned across and peered into Heck's face with lupine intensity. He'd now blanched to a very unhealthy shade of white and was so close that his breath filled the cop's nostrils with a reek of peppermint. When he spoke again, it was in a low, menacing monotone. 'Now you listen, my son. I've had it up to here with this bullshit. So from now on, you aren't just working for the police – you're working for *me*. Consider the fact that you're still walking around with an intact spine your salary. Now get out and get back on the job, or I'll personally rearrange your face so your fucking mum wouldn't recognise it.'

Right on cue, the car door opened again.

Heck found himself being helped out by Asquith, though, with a bunched fist gripping him by the back of his collar, it was the sort of help he probably didn't need. The door closed with a *thud*, and then Heck was standing in the road watching as Asquith sidled around the vehicle to the front passenger door, and Loxton made to climb behind the steering wheel.

'Don't suppose you lot have been looking for Noreen, have you?' Heck asked them.

Loxton eyed him as though he couldn't believe a copper could ask so stupid a question. 'Course we fucking have.'

'Any leads you'd care to share?'

'Dale!' Ballamara shouted from inside the car. 'Stop jawing with that fucking waste of space. He hasn't got time for idle chat.'

Heck stood back as the Bentley swerved off the rubble and drove away in a cloud of dust and debris. In truth, there was any number of things he could have charged Bobby Ballamara with. That morning alone he was good for wasting police time, threatening to kill, unlawful imprisonment, and so on. But these were Mickey Mouse offences, arrests that would only distract from the main story, which was the thirty-eight missing women that Heck had been looking for since the beginning of 2010. What was more, Bobby Ballamara and his boys who, by their own admission, were keeping their ear to the ground, had a potentially useful role to play in this, so alienating them even further would be self-defeating. Besides, for all his bravado, Ballamara was unlikely to whack a copper. He was strictly old school. A vicious, violent racketeer, he wouldn't hesitate to have a fellow lowlife's brains beaten out of him if he felt like it. But his traditional gangland ethics made him seem anachronistic in this age of crazy, gun-toting killers who'd think nothing of massacring school-kids should they get in the way.

Heck walked back to his car, only to spot that its front nearside tyre was flat. For an angry moment he assumed that either Asquith or Loxton had got bored while he'd been in conversation with their boss. But then he saw the rusty nail sticking out of it, almost certainly picked up on the patch of burned ground that he'd used as a turning-space earlier. Irritated with his own carelessness, and feeling way too tired for the physical effort now required, he went to the boot for his spare.

That was when it began to rain.

Chapter 3

Each time Louise woke up it seemed like she was emerging from a horrific nightmare, only to discover that it was reality.

She was in the boot of a vehicle – she'd realised that much from the rumbling of the engine and the constant jolting and bumping. Her hands were secured behind her back in what felt like a pair of plastic cuffs, which were pulled so tight that they burned into her flesh. Her legs were crooked painfully beneath her because she couldn't lie full-length in such an enclosed space. It was pitch-black and stiflingly hot; her clothes were damp with sweat, and yet her body was utterly frozen with terror. She didn't know how long she'd been in here. It seemed like days, though surely it couldn't have been that long – a day and a night maybe, possibly a little longer? Either way, she was parched with thirst, hunger was gnawing her insides out and the atmosphere was unspeakably foul as she'd urinated on herself at least twice. Yet none of that compared to the mind-numbing fear of what might lie ahead.

A piece of duct-tape had been smacked across her mouth and wrapped around the back of her head so she could barely whimper, let alone scream. A blindfold made of cloth was bound around her eyes. The memory of what had happened on the quiet country road was only vague. Whoever the man was who'd attacked her – if it had been a man (that diabolical face was still imprinted on her mind) – he'd choked her into unconsciousness. But at least that brief instant of agony and dread had been swift. She'd have swapped the merciful oblivion it brought for the prolonged, torturous ordeal that she was going through now. She'd been enclosed in this metal coffin for so long that she'd even slept once or twice, though that was mainly because each time when she'd woken she'd thrashed about frantically until she was exhausted. Louise struggled again, futilely, wailing beneath her gag. The problem was that the boot was claustropho-bically tight and confined; its lid was only a couple of inches above her, and she had no leverage with which to kick against it.

For the thousandth time, her thoughts raced chaotically as she tried to recall the contradictory advice she'd heard over the years about what a woman should do if she was attacked by a rapist. She was sure a police officer on televi-sion had said that you should fight, scratch, bite – but what if this antagonised the assailant? Someone else had said that you should plead with him, humanise yourself by talking about your family, your children. But again – what if he was a sadist, and that gave him even more pleasure?

Of course, at the end of the day all this was theory. It had never occurred to Louise that she might at some time be in a position to put such horrors to the test. Even now they barely seemed real. Some thirty-six hours later – it was at least that long, she decided, which made it sometime on Sunday morning – she was still numb with shock, still faint, still nauseated by fear. Fresh sweat seeped through her clothes as she pondered the many possibilities behind her abduction. Above all, Louise clung to the fact that she was still alive so many hours later. She *hadn't* been raped yet, or beaten, or murdered. In addition, the car had stopped once – quite a few hours ago now, it seemed – the boot had opened, her gag had briefly been removed and someone who never spoke had forced a plastic straw between her lips, allowing her a few sips of water. Surely all this meant she was more to them than a mere plaything? It seemed increasingly likely that they needed her alive, though she hardly dared anticipate such. Alan was a wealthy guy and Goldstein & Hoff were major players on the international banking scene: obvious targets for ransom demands. In addition, her kidnapper had gone to great trouble to snare her in the first place: she hadn't just been dragged into an alley. That slow pursuit all the way from the City, the stinger across the country road – clear evidence of deliberation, of forward planning. In some ways that made it even more frightening, but it also gave Louise hope that she was merely a pawn in a larger game. What game that might be, she had no clue; it wasn't necessarily financial – heaven knew what the top brass in the City sometimes got involved with – but as long as this was not a personal attack against her surely she stood at least a reasonable chance of being released unharmed . . .?

Very abruptly, the vehicle slid to a halt.

There was a squeal of tyres, and a loud *clunk* as the handbrake was applied.

Louise lay shuddering as the engine was switched off and two car doors opened and closed simultaneously. This had already happened several times during the course of her imprisonment in here. There was the incident when she was given water, but on the other occasions no one had come to her. Hours had then passed, during which she'd squirmed and wrestled with her bonds, and again had tried to cry out – to no avail. Whoever had taken her was clearly moving her from place to place and, on the few occasions when they'd left her, they chose somewhere very private where not a sound could be heard. In due course, they'd always returned and the car had started up again.

However, that didn't happen this time.

Icy fingers scurried all over Louise as she listened to the sound of heavy feet approaching. A key was fitted into the lock, there was another *clunk*, and light spilled down on her; it was so bright after her long hours of confinement that it poured through her blindfold, searing her retinas. When the cloth strap was torn away, she snapped her eyelids shut and averted her face, but rough hands took hold of her. She moaned and went dizzy as they hauled her upright and left her in a sitting position. Blinking rapidly, she tried to adjust her vision, but only after several seconds did everything swim into focus. What she saw proved just how long she'd been peering into empty blackness: it wasn't glaring sunshine that had half-blinded her, but the gloomy twilight of an underground car park.

Her eyes darted fearfully around, seeing water-marks on concrete pillars, loops of corroded chain hanging from over-head. About twenty yards in front was the hulk of a burned-out vehicle. Beyond that lay deep shadows, cross-cut with occasional shafts of dull, grimy daylight. Then she saw the two men looking down at her.

Both wore dark overalls and gloves, and knitted ski-masks with holes cut for their eyes and mouths. One ski-mask was purple, the other day-glo orange. She stared helplessly back, eyes bulging, as they appraised her.

'She's a fucking sight,' the one in the purple mask said.

But it was the reply from the one in the orange mask which sent a deeper, more paralysing chill through Louise than she'd ever known. 'Aren't they always.'

'I suppose she'll scrub up,' Purple added.

Orange continued to stare at her. He was taller than his comrade. Narrow circles of skin were visible around his eye-sockets, and, by the looks of these, he was black. When he'd spoken it had been without an obvious accent, though the other one, who looked to be white, sounded as though he was from the Midlands somewhere.

'Nice legs on her,' Purple remarked.

Belatedly, Louise realised that her skirt and shoes had been removed, though her tights, torn full of holes, were still in place.

Purple leaned down and squeezed her left breast. 'Firm tits too. Keeps herself in shape for her old fella.'

Louise barely noticed the personal violation. With each passing second, this ordeal was becoming ever more real. Suddenly it seemed terribly, terribly certain that she'd never see Alan again, or their lovely house in rural Buckinghamshire.

Purple chuckled. 'Least she's not shit herself. Hate it when they do that.'

'P-please,' she stammered. 'Let me go, let me go, just let me go . . . I won't say anything . . . how can I say anything, I don't know anything!' But it was a spittle-slurred mumble that was barely audible outside the duct-tape. The men paid no attention anyway.

'How we doing for time?' Orange asked.

Purple glanced at his watch. 'No problem.'

Orange nodded, bent down to a haversack and fumbled around inside it. Louise watched, hair stiffening, not knowing how she'd react if he took out a knife. She was bewildered rather than relieved when he produced a bottle of water and what looked like a ham roll wrapped in cellophane.

Before doing anything else, Orange regarded her intently with his liquid brown eyes. At last he spoke again, and this time it was to *her*, not to his henchman.

'Listen love, and listen good. I'm going to take that gag off. You can scream and shout all you want. No one'll hear. But it'll piss us off royally, and what's going to happen to you is still going to happen. The only difference is if we're pissed off we might decide to beat the fucking shit out of you first. You understand?'

Louise returned his gaze helplessly, before vaguely nodding. She was in no doubt that he was absolutely serious.

'Now you be a good girl and keep things nice and quiet,' he added, reaching out and slowly peeling back the duct-tape.

It snagged on her dry lips and when he tore it loose from the back of her head, yanked out several strands of hair, but at that moment she didn't mind, she was too thankful to have it taken off her. It was so good to be able to breathe properly.

She sucked the air in great lungfuls, but despite the promise she'd just made, couldn't stop herself speaking. 'Look . . . whatever it is you want, my husband'll get it for you. Or my company. I don't know who you are or why you're doing this – I don't even want to know, but look . . .'

Orange glared at her. 'I thought I told you to keep your mouth shut?'

'Just let my husband know I'm alright,' she begged. 'That's all I ask . . .'

'Alright?' Purple said casually. 'Who said you're alright?'

She glanced from one to the other, trying to be bold, trying to look as if she wasn't frightened, but knowing that she was little more than a scared rabbit in their unblinking gaze. 'You just . . . you just should know that whatever you took me for, whatever you've got planned . . . you can make money out of this. Good money. All you need to—'

Orange leaned menacingly towards her. 'I said shut – the – fuck – up.'

The edge to his voice was so hard, the maniac gleam in his eye so intense that this time, desperate as she was, Louise clammed up.

He watched her closely for several seconds, and then,

satisfied, unscrewed the cap from the water bottle and offered it to her. At first, Louise felt inclined to refuse – as if such an act of miniature defiance would be a victory over them – but it just as quickly occurred to her that it was ludicrous to think it would ever matter to men like these how dry her throat became. She had to remain clear-minded and level-headed; any action she took must be geared towards survival – that was the only way she was going to get through this. So when she finally drank, she drank deeply, thirstily.

After that, they presented her with the sandwich, holding it to her mouth, though despite her hunger pangs she was still so sick with fear that she could do no more than nibble at it. As she did, she eyed her surroundings again, wondering if there was any possible means of escape. Far to her right, what looked like an exit/entry ramp sloped down from above, but now that her vision was fully attuned, there were other shattered cars on view: mangled masses of burned or rusty metal, dumped in forgotten corners and thick with dust and cobwebs. It had entered her head that, wherever she was, someone might unknowingly venture down here and prove her accidental saviour, but the more dankness and dereliction she spied, the less likely this seemed. In addition, there was nowhere for her to run to, even in the unlikely event she got free. God knew how many exit ramps she'd have to scramble up before she reached the surface, and she was so weak from her confinement that she doubted she could even stand. Once again, that sense of horror and despair overwhelmed her.

Giving up on the sandwich, Orange scrunched it in its wrapper and tossed it. He screwed the top back onto the bottle and shoved it into his pocket. 'Now for dessert,' he said, delving into the haversack again and taking out a small steel box.

He opened it to reveal two slim objects, one of which he handed to his compatriot, the other which he kept hold of himself. Louise felt her heart miss a beat when she saw that the objects were hypodermic syringes. The fluid in the one in Purple's hand was transparent, whilst the one in Orange's hand was a dark, brackish red.

'We're going to inject you,' Orange said matter-of-factly. He showed her his syringe. 'As you can see, this one's dirty. It's been used loads of times, and currently contains blood that was recently extracted from a heroin-addicted prostitute. However, the one my mate here's got is sterile and contains a medically-approved sedative. It's up to you which one we use?'

There was a brief silence, during which Louise tried to speak but could only gag. Once she'd dry-heaved a couple of times, she glanced up again, but said nothing. She inclined her head slightly to indicate that she'd give them no trouble.

'Smart move,' Orange said, replacing his blood-filled syringe in the box and putting it away, then clamping a hand across her mouth and pushing her back down into the boot. 'I knew you'd be sensible.'

Behind him, Purple removed the cap from the sterile needle and flicked steadily at it with his gloved finger.

'Just lie still,' Orange added, 'and think of England.'

Chapter 4

Deptford Green Police Station was built in the 1970s, and, typically of that soulless era, was a monolithic structure of grey, faceless cement. It was three floors high and sat with its back to the Thames on a toe of land jutting out into the part of the river that looped south around the Isle of Dogs. From the front it had a relaxed air: there was a blue lamp over its tall, wide entrance and blinds in its windows.

However, the appearance of life at Deptford Green and its reality were two different things. At the rear of the station, its three impounds, which were crammed to bursting with vehicles recovered after theft or use in crime, and the official personnel car park, were surrounded by nine-foot-high steel fences that were covered in anti-climb paint and had security lights located at regular intervals along their parapets. Also around the rear of the station, offensive, anti-police graffiti was much in evidence (the local commander only insisted on its prompt removal when it appeared at the front), alongside a litter of bricks and broken bottles, which had all been used as missiles on various occasions. There were even bullet-holes in some parts of the station's exterior, though these too tended to be repaired quickly.

Deptford, once a thriving dockland, had gone through various incarnations in its past. In the present post-industrial era it had become an urban waste, and even though at the same time it had developed a lively arts and cultural scene, crime and poverty were rampant behind its colourful façade. As a result, though things had improved a little since the dawn of the twenty-first century, there was still an aura of 'Fort Apache' about Deptford Green nick, and this was reflected inside as well as out. Even by normal London standards, it was an extraordinarily busy police station. Both uniform and plain clothes officers tended to scramble about its cramped rabbit-warren of passages and rooms as though in a 'life or death' hurry. There was a constant trilling of telephones and barking of orders. The custody suite was never less than full of prisoners waiting to be processed.

Of course, Sunday morning could be an exception. Even the bleakest corners of the inner city tended to be quiet in the soporific hours following the weekly Saturday night booze-fest.

For this reason, when Heck drove in just after ten that morning, he was surprised to see several more cars parked up than usual, and one in particular – a white BMW Coupe. He stood looking at it for a moment, before going wearily in through the personnel door. The first person he met on entering was Paula Clark, his civilian admin assistant. She was a short, buxom lady, a local lass – bleached-blonde and busty, very much in the Barbara Windsor mould – who'd been loaned to him from local CID Admin.

'What are you doing here?' he said, surprised to see her at the weekend.

Paula appeared to be on her way out. She was carrying her coat and a handbag under one arm, and a bundle of reports, which she presumably intended to type up at home, under the other. She didn't smile when she saw him – not that she smiled very much – though on this particular occasion she looked even more irate than usual.

'I had to come in and sort some papers out because you weren't answering your phone,' she said.

He filched his mobile from his jacket pocket and saw that it was dead. 'Bastard thing's on the blink again.'

'Superintendent Piper's here,' she added.

'I know. I've just seen her car outside. What does she want?'

'*You.*' Paula gave him a long, meaningful look, then bustled past on her spike-heels and exited the building.

Heck ascended to the second floor via the back stairs. The office he currently worked from was located in what he was sure was the most under-used and least accessible corner of the building. Local officers here still referred to it as 'the spare parade room' even though Heck had now occupied it for over two years.

He headed down the corridor towards it, only stopping when he saw that the door was already open and the tall shape of Detective Inspector Des Palliser standing there. Palliser was fifty-five now and a hard-bitten cop of many years' experience, though his lean, grizzled appearance – he was leathery skinned and had sported a scraggy grey beard and moustache for as long as Heck could remember – belied a genial personality. He spotted Heck immediately and beckoned. Heck slouched on towards him, in no hurry. There was someone else in the office, pacing around behind Palliser. By the statuesque shape, pearl blouse, tight black skirt and mass of tawny hair (she wasn't known as 'the Lioness' for nothing), he knew it was Detective Superintendent Gemma Piper. Not atypically, she had a pile of documents in her hand and was discarding them irritably, one after another, as she read speedily through them.

32

'Morning at last,' Palliser said, when Heck reached him.

Heck didn't say anything. He'd just spotted a notice that someone had hung on the outside of the office door, which read:

> *WDFA Squad*
> *(We Do Fuck All)*

He could have done without that at a time like this, he thought.

Detective Superintendent Piper was now regarding him from the other side of the room. Locks of hair, which she tended to wear up during the day, had come loose and hung to either shoulder, making her look rather fetching. But she was pale in the cheek and her steel-blue eyes blazed.

'Do you know we've been waiting nearly two hours?' she said.

'Er . . . no, I didn't.'

'What do you think you're playing at, Heck?' she demanded. Heck was six foot, but Superintendent Piper wasn't a great deal shorter than him; even if she had been, her force of personality was colossal. She stalked the room in anger. 'You think I want to spend my Sunday mornings sifting through your chaotic trash?'

'My phone's not working.'

'Well get one that does!'

'I will . . . if I can include it on my expenses.'

She arched an eyebrow. 'You what?'

'I've worn it out on this job, so if I have to buy another one . . .'

'Are you deliberately winding me up?'

'No, it's just that . . .'

'Because I'm not in the mood.'

33

'I can see that.'

She jabbed a finger at him. 'And don't smart-mouth me either.'

'An apology might be in order, Heck,' Palliser said. 'You *have* kept us waiting.'

'I know, sorry. But I wasn't expecting you.'

'That's plainly obvious,' Superintendent Piper replied, gesturing at the piles of disorderly documentation stacked between the computer terminals, at the unwashed coffee mugs, at the overflowing in-trays. 'Look at this place; it's like a bomb site. And while we're on the subject . . .' She crossed the room and snatched the notice from the outside of the door. 'What's this supposed to be?'

Heck gave a wry smile. 'Wouldn't be a normal day without one of these appearing.'

'You been rubbing people up the wrong way?'

'I don't get close enough to rub anyone up any way,' he said. 'Not anymore. I'm pretty sure it was one of this nick's detectives who tipped off Bobby Ballamara that his daughter's disappearance is being treated as part of a series. Don't see how else he could have found out. He's made my life hell ever since.'

'Have you got proof of that?' Palliser asked, looking shocked.

'Course I haven't.'

'And in the meantime, what does this *mean*?' Superintendent Piper asked, still brandishing the notice.

Heck shrugged. 'You know what Division are like – they don't think anyone works as hard as they do. According to them, I'm on a very cushy number here.'

'Unfortunately, they're not the only ones who think that.' There was a brief silence. Superintendent Piper suddenly looked awkward, uncomfortable.

'Oh,' Heck replied. 'So that's how it is?'

'You must've known something like this was coming,' Palliser said.

'Rumblings at the Yard, are there?'

'Your comparative-case-analysis didn't have the desired effect,' Palliser explained.

Heck slumped into a chair, making no effort to disguise his irritation. 'Three bloody weeks I worked on that.'

'The effort was clearly there,' Superintendent Piper said, sitting opposite. 'But that's all. Considering the time put in, the evidence is too thin. How long have you been on this case now?'

'Two years, four months.'

'And ground gained – zero.'

'I need more men,' he protested.

'Well you've got one less from today.'

Heck sat up slowly. 'How can I have one less than none?'

'The one less is you, Heck,' Palliser said.

Heck glanced from one to the other, finally fixing on Superintendent Piper. 'You're not shutting it down?'

'It's not my choice.'

'Don't tell me,' he said. 'Laycock. What a surprise.'

'It's a nothing case,' she retorted. 'You've admitted that yourself.'

'In moments of frustration I may have admitted that.'

'There seems to be more frustration than anything else.'

He stood up. 'Look, what's the problem? I'm working every hour God sends, but most of it's for free. I haven't made any unreasonable requests for overtime.'

'The problem is you could be better used elsewhere,' she said. 'Crime doesn't stop just because you're involved in something you find more interesting.'

'"Interesting"?' Heck could hardly believe what she'd just said. 'We've got thirty-eight missing women here! Surely it's more than "interesting"?'

35

Superintendent Piper responded by rifling through a few files and print-outs, of which there were plenty strewn across the desk. 'Where's the evidence they're connected? Where's the pattern? Some of them are four hundred miles apart, for God's sake! Sorry . . . I've trusted you on this for nearly two years, but that's it. The trust's run out.'

'Look, ma'am . . .'

'Don't give me the usual blarney, Heck. You're one of the best detectives I've got, but these hunches of yours are proving an expensive luxury. And look at the bloody state of you! For God's sake, tidy yourself up!'

'Don't you even want to know why I'm in this state?' he wondered.

'No.'

'I've been on an all-night surveillance operation. And guess what, I had to do it all myself because there's no one else to help.'

Voices could now be heard out in the corridor; one of them had a distinct South London twang, distinguishing it as that of DCI Slackworth, who ran the CID office here at Deptford Green.

'I've got one new lead in particular, which is looking really good,' Heck added. 'But I haven't even had a chance to start following it yet.'

'Put it all on paper,' Superintendent Piper said, half-listening to the voice outside and looking again at the notice that had been pinned to her officer's door. 'Each case is being referred back to the divisional CID or mis-pers department that originally dealt with it. Your new stuff can go with them.'

'*Thirty-eight* missing women, ma'am.'

'You *think*,' Palliser said.

'But how can we just close it down?' Heck asked. 'We're the Serial Crimes Unit, for Christ's sake!'

Superintendent Piper stood up. 'We'll keep it under review. But at present we haven't got the resources.'

'How about if . . .'

'I'm not arguing with you, Heck. I've actually done you a courtesy coming down here to tell you in person. I could've sent Des, I could've told you on the bloody phone. Just deal with it, alright.'

She marched to the door, pulling on her suit jacket.

'You know, it's a miracle anyone stays in this job,' Heck said. 'And I'll tell you another miracle – that we ever catch anyone with some of the clowns we've got in charge.'

'Watch it!' She rounded on him fiercely. 'Just watch it, Sergeant!'

'I didn't mean you . . .'

'I don't give a damn! I won't have insubordination! Now your work here is done. So do us all a favour, get your paperwork in order and, following that, get your head in order. Then get your scruffy arse back to the Yard, pronto.'

And she was off, storming down the passage to catch up with DCI Slackworth – a burly, foursquare slaphead with flabby cheeks and pig-mean eyes – who was busy chatting up a pretty young female constable from the day-shift.

Heck watched her go, sourly.

'Do you think anyone'll mind if I light up in here?' Palliser wondered, edging out of view of those in the corridor.

'How should I know?' Heck replied.

'It's *your* office.'

'Not anymore.'

At the end of the corridor, Superintendent Piper was standing arms folded, yet still managing to wave the notice around, as she gave both barrels to Slackworth. The familiar whipcrack voice came echoing along the passage, and Slackworth, a tough-nut in front of his own crew, was soon shuffling awkwardly and looking abashed.

'"The Lioness",' Heck said. 'Talk about well named.'

'She has a softer side.' Palliser was now beside an open window, blowing smoke. 'If anyone should know that, it's you.'

'That was a long time ago.'

'She still cares about you though.'

'Yeah, right.'

'For one thing, she reckons you need some leave.'

'What?'

'You're in a state, Heck. You haven't had a break in two years.'

'I haven't been able to.'

'Beside the point.'

'No it isn't.' Heck indicated the empty desks and tables. 'I used to have six officers working for me in here, Des. One by one, I've watched them get shunted to other duties. All I've had for the last nine weeks is an admin assistant, part-time.'

Palliser shrugged. 'Understanding why you're knackered isn't really a solution to it. She's the gaffer and she reckons that your judgment's become impaired. You're losing sight of the wood for the trees.'

'So I'm a burn-out as well?'

'Not far off.'

'This is bollocks.'

'No, she's genuinely concerned.'

'I mean this whole thing.'

'Oh that, yeah. That's definitely bollocks.' Palliser suddenly glanced up at the ceiling, wondering belatedly if there was a smoke-detector present, and relaxing when he saw that there wasn't. 'You're a DS, Heck, that's all. Yet for two years you've been working under your own steam, authorising your own hours and resources. It was inevitable someone was going to whinge about it. It's politics, typical office bullshit. But it's not unimportant.'

38

'Especially not when someone like Laycock's involved, eh?'

While Superintendent Piper was head of the Serial Crimes Unit, her immediate supervisor, Commander Jim Laycock, was director of the National Crime Group and was, to all intents and purposes, God. Despite this, Heck had managed to bump heads with him on a number of occasions.

'Laycock's answerable to a higher power as well,' Palliser said, as if this was some kind of consolation.

'He's a pencil-pushing suit.'

'Which is all the more reason to fall in line for him. He has to balance the books somehow. Given the history you and him have got, it's a wonder he's let it drag on this long.'

Heck walked back to his desk, his head aching with frustration. He sat down heavily. 'At the end of the day, all I'm concerned about is these missing women. I can crack this, Des. I know it. I can find them, or at least find out what happened to them.'

Palliser chucked his cig-butt from the window. 'We've been through this already, mate. Wrap it up and get some rest. God knows, you need it.'

Chapter 5

When Louise came round, she felt ghastly: headachey and sick to the pit of her stomach.

Initially the awful memory of her abduction eluded her. All she could do at first was puzzle about why she was slumped in a ratty old armchair that smelled of stale urine. But then, when she looked around and realised that she was in a small, windowless room and that the throbbing pain in her right bicep was the result of an injection, everything surged back – and with it, a wild panic.

She tried to leap to her feet, but was still groggy and immediately overbalanced, her shoeless feet sliding on the white linoleum floor. She fell heavily, landing alongside an open cardboard box, which, when she looked inside it, was stuffed to the brim with lingerie: pairs of lacy knickers, silk stockings, suspender belts. She recoiled from it the way she would if it had been full of snakes. Struggling to her knees, she backed away, only to collide with something else: a steel-framed clothes rack, which again was loaded with garments. In this case they were dresses, camisoles and skirts of various sizes and colours, though in all cases they were slinky, flimsy, transparent, the sort of things glamour models would wear.

Again the tawdriness of it both revolted and terrified her – in no way could this be good.

Heart thumping, Louise tried to lurch back to her feet, but it wasn't easy. She'd evidently been sedated for several hours, and now felt as if she was recovering from a fever; every quick or ill-timed move brought on a new flutter of dizziness. But there was one thing at least – whoever had put her here, they'd left her unbound. Tender weals were impressed into her wrists, but thankfully the plastic cuffs had been removed, and, small and stuffy as this room might be, it had to be an improvement on the claustrophobic confines of that car boot. She pivoted around, looking for any means of escape.

The room was lit by a single unshaded bulb and was no larger than a shop fitting-room, but it contained two doors, both made of varnished wood. Louise blundered to the first. It had a lever-handle, which she pushed down. The door opened, but on the other side of it there was only a narrow, white-tiled cubicle, containing a toilet, a wash-bowl and a shower. There was also a mirror, and fleetingly she caught her own reflection – it was so different from any previous mirror image of herself that she jumped backward with a shriek.

Only after a split second of disbelief did she come forward again.

Then she started to cry.

Her face looked like it had been made up for a stage-show of the macabre. Her eyes were red with weeping; her hair hung in rat-tails; what remained of her make-up was smeared and blotched grotesquely; beneath that, her normal healthy complexion had paled to an ashen, almost greenish hue. Even though she'd only been in captivity for a couple of days at the most, she already looked to have lost weight: her cheekbones were painfully prominent. She glanced down at herself and saw that what remained of her clothing was in a disgusting state: stained with engine oil and body fluids. The vile stench of urine was suddenly explainable.

The shock of all this was simply too much. Louise had tried to maintain her composure, tried to rationalise her way through this entire kidnapping ordeal rather than keep surrendering to panic, but surely she was insane to think that remaining calm would serve any purpose now? Good God, she'd been in these animals' clutches no time at all, and she resembled a corpse already! Suppose they kept her for weeks, months, maybe longer?

There was no option. She had to escape from here, any way she could, whatever it cost her.

She backed into the main room again, turning frantically. She'd been correct in her first impression that there were no windows in here. She glanced up: the ceiling, which comprised bare wooden boards, was only about two feet above her head. She reached up and pressed it; it was unyielding. What she'd been expecting, she didn't know – that it would lift like a lid? Ridiculous. But for some reason she pressed again, even harder, exerting all her strength, then overbalanced, almost fell.

At first she assumed that she was having a relapse; that maybe the drugs were kicking in for a second time. But then she realised something bizarre: *she* wasn't the one who'd overbalanced – it was the room itself. The floor had tilted. It tilted again and she had to stagger to keep upright. The entire room was swaying – not hugely, but noticeably.

So what in Christ's name was this? Where the hell was she?

Panic once again nagged at her to get out of here, insisting that, whatever this horrendous situation was, she needed to get out – for Christ's sake, she just had to get out!

There was still the remaining door.

Louise had no doubt that this one would be locked. And indeed, when she pushed against it and tried the handle – in this case a brass knob – it wouldn't budge. She swore under her breath, struggling to suppress whimpers of despair. She tried again, but couldn't even get the knob to turn.

'Goddamn,' she moaned, thrusting her shoulder against the wood, but only succeeding in hurting herself. 'Goddamn it!' Her voice rose to a desperate cry. '*Goddamn it, someone please help me!*'

Abruptly, the handle turned in the opposite direction. There was a loud *click* as a lock was disengaged. Louise retreated. The door virtually flew open, and a man came through, closing it behind him. It was the tall black man in the overalls, gloves and day-glo orange ski-mask, an ensemble he was still wearing. He eyed her up and down. As before, it was not the way she'd been eyed by men in the past. There was no hunger there, no arousal – it was strictly professional; a cool, clinical appraisal. When he finally spoke, she was so astonished by what he said that at first she thought she'd misheard.

'I said you're size four, yeah? Your feet, I mean?'

Hardly knowing what to say, Louise nodded.

'Good. These are for you.'

He pushed a pair of shoes into her hands. With a sense of unreality, she looked down at them: heeled sling-backs, black patent with red trim, evidently brand new. Under normal circumstances, they'd be far too trashy for Louise's taste. Yet somehow she didn't think that they were intended as a gift for her.

'And for Jesus's sake, take a shower,' he added. 'You're stinking the entire place out.'

She glared up at him, the injustice of the situation finally firing her spirit. 'Surely that doesn't bloody surprise you?'

He pointed to the shower-room. 'In there. You'll find a

toothbrush and toothpaste in the cabinet next to the mirror, so clean your teeth as well. And freshen your breath.'

'*What?*'

'You've got two hours. Better do a good job.'

'What're you talking about?'

'Pretty yourself up, you silly tart!'

Perhaps the fact that they still hadn't killed her, proving that she was of more value alive, was giving her extra courage. Or maybe, in some basic animal way, she now realised they were approaching the main event and that all bets were off. Either way, Louise was suddenly angry rather than afraid.

'I'm not going to do any such thing,' she stated.

The man lurched towards her. 'Listen girl, you have no say here. You have no opinions. You have no views. You just do as you're told. Understand?'

'You're not going to get away with this!'

'No?'

'The police will be looking for me.'

'Occupational hazard for us, darling.' And he smiled, showing white, shark-like teeth. 'But I have to say, not much of one.'

She made a dash to get past him.

He caught her before she could even open the door, clamping one gloved hand to her throat and throwing her violently back across the room. She landed in the armchair with sufficient force to drive the wind from her. For all his size, he advanced like a cat – lithe, sinuous. He sprang onto her, thrusting his face into hers. This close, the whites of his eyes were red-rimmed; his breath reeked of garlic. She craned her neck to look away from him, but his weight pinned her down.

'You stupid bitch!' he hissed. 'I'm under orders not to mess you up until this is all over, but I won't hesitate to do it afterwards! So don't try that shit again!'

'My name is Louise Samantha Jennings,' she said in a quaking but determined voice. 'I am thirty years old. You may think my family are rich because I work in the City and live in South Buckinghamshire. But I was born in North London. My father is a taxi-driver, my mother a day-care worker. I have two older sisters and one little brother. We see each other all the time. We're a very close-knit family. I also have a niece and nephew, one on my side and one on my . . .'

'What am I supposed to do?' he snickered. 'Fall on the floor blubbing?'

'I'm a human being. I don't care what you think you're going to get from this, you can't treat human beings this way . . .'

He slapped her across the left side of her face – not hard; to humiliate rather than hurt. 'How about *this* way?' he wondered. Then he slapped her across the right side. 'How about *that* way?'

She mashed her lips together, determined not to cry out, trying desperately to show that she wasn't the crumpled wreck she must have appeared. But her mouth trembled and fresh tears brimmed from her eyes. 'I . . . I want to speak to your boss . . .'

'Really?'

'If I can't reason with the oily rag, I'll try with the engine driver.'

He gazed down at her for several long moments, licking his lips with a sharp, pink tongue. 'Well . . . who knows,' he finally said, 'you may get that chance.' He seemed excited by the resistance she'd shown: sweat greased the flesh around his eyes; he panted rather than breathed. But perhaps thinking that he was starting to enjoy himself too much here, he now released her and rose slowly, reluctantly to his feet. 'Not yet though . . . first you've got some business to attend to. These

45

clothes, these undies.' He pointed at the jumbled garb. 'Get yourself something sexy and pretty on.' While Louise watched in amazement, he reached down and pulled a foot-locker out from under the rack of dresses. 'There's make-up in here, perfume and what-not.' He kicked at a second locker. 'This one's jewellery. Help yourself. Just make sure you look and smell good.' He moved to the door, but turned to face her one more time. 'You've got two hours. Do not disappoint us.'

'Dis— disappoint you?' she stammered in near-disbelief. And then she laughed, though it was actually more like a deranged cackle. 'And . . . and if I do?'

'Ask the women all this stuff used to belong to.'

He closed the door behind him. And locked it.

Chapter 6

The National Crime Group was based at New Scotland Yard, where it shared several floors with the Metropolitan Police's Specialist Crime Directorate. Its own Serial Crimes Unit, whose remit was primarily to consult on nationwide crime sprees and, where necessary, to elicit and organise multi-force cooperation, was on the sixth floor, and basically comprised one corridor. The DO – or Detectives' Office, the hub of all activity – was located part way along it, next door to the admin room where the NCG's civilian secretaries worked. At this late hour on a Sunday afternoon its various desks and computer monitors were deserted, with half the unit off duty and the rest out on enquiries. In fact, the only person present when Heck began humping his sacks of paperwork and boxes of disks up from the car park was DI Palliser, who, given his age, was these days more a duty officer than an investigator, and tended to remain at base, working as coordinator for all SCU operations.

At present, he stood, hands in pockets, in the doorway to his own office which, like the offices belonging to the other three detective inspectors in the department, was separated from the main area by a glazed partition wall. 'That the lot?' he asked.

Heck dumped down the last heavy bag of documentation, and nodded. He mopped sweat from his brow. 'It's in no particular order, I'm afraid.'

'Don't worry. We'll sort it.'

There was a brief silence as they surveyed the immense pile of materials now spilling out all over the floor of the department's tea making area.

'You know, none of this work will get wasted,' Palliser said. 'All these cases will continue to be investigated.'

'Yeah, but as the lowest of low priorities.'

'Not necessarily.'

'You know they will,' Heck said glumly. 'I spent months zeroing in on each one of these, and now they'll just get thrown back in with the runaway teens and the absentee fathers.'

'Well . . . it's not your problem now.'

'The trouble is, Des, it won't be anyone's problem. Apart from the families who are missing their loved ones.'

Palliser didn't even try to argue with that assessment. 'Whatever . . . the Lioness wants to see you.'

Heck nodded and went out into the corridor. Detective Superintendent Piper's office was at its far end. He knocked on the door and when she called him, went in.

She was seated at her desk, writing what looked like a lengthy report. 'Take a seat, Heck. I'll not be a moment.'

There were two chairs to one side. Heck slumped down into one. He glanced around. It wasn't a particularly showy office for so senior a rank. In fact, it was quite small. With its row of filing cabinets, single rubber plant and dusty Venetian blind over the window, it was like something from the 1970s; the only concession to modernity being the quiet hum of the air-conditioning. It was a far cry from the palatial residence upstairs enjoyed by Commander Laycock and his PA.

'Our office at Deptford Green has now been closed down, yes?' she asked.

'Yes, ma'am.'

She continued writing. Heck waited, ruminating on whether or not, if he'd centred his investigation here at the Yard and had not set up a separate incident room down at Deptford, thus saving them some expense, it might have bought him a little extra time. The problem was that the first cluster of disappearances he'd linked together had all occurred, probably by coincidence, in South London – Peckham, Greenwich, Lewisham and Sydenham – and he'd wanted to be 'on-site'. At the time, of course, he hadn't realised the enquiry would soon widen to cover most of the country.

Not that any of this mattered now.

'Is that it, ma'am?' he asked.

She glanced up. 'You got somewhere else you need to be?'

He shrugged. 'Well . . . I presume I'm being reassigned.'

'Yes you are. You're being reassigned to Cornwall. Or the Lake District. Or Spain or the Florida Keys, or even your own back garden. Anywhere you fancy taking a long vacation.'

'I don't get you.'

'You're going on extended leave.' She pushed the top sheet of paperwork she'd been working on across the desk towards him. 'All I need now is your signature on the request form.'

Heck stood up as he read it. Only slowly did the reality sink in.

'December?' he said. 'That's three months off.'

'I don't want to see you back a day sooner.'

'But three months!'

'Heck, your willingness to work, work and work is well known. But it's hardly healthy.'

'I don't need three months.'

'That's entirely a matter of opinion, and mine carries more weight than yours. You've been under massive pressure this last year, and it's showing – in your work, your appearance, your general demeanour.'

'This is bollocks!'

'*Especially* your demeanour.'

'Gemma, please . . .'

'Can you honestly say, hand on heart – bearing in mind that, on occasion, lives may depend on how fit you are to work – that you don't need a decent break? That your batteries will go on forever without being recharged?' She waited for an answer. 'Or is it just that you think the Serial Crimes Unit will fall apart without you?'

Heck was lost for words. Then, very abruptly, he shrugged and took a pen from his inside pocket. 'No, it's okay. In fact it's great. Three months is extremely generous.'

He scribbled his signature on the form and handed it back.

She eyed him with sudden suspicion. 'So you're happy with this?'

'Sure.'

'Good. In that case . . .' though she still didn't seem convinced, 'bye for now.'

Heck nodded and moved towards the door.

'Mark, before you go,' she said – and that was a red-letter moment, because these days she hardly ever called him 'Mark'. He glanced back. She softened her tone, which was also highly unusual. 'Mark, for what it's worth, I'm sorry the case you were building didn't work out.'

'It's alright. I know it wasn't your fault.'

'It was nobody's fault. This job's about balancing time and resources, you know that. You're needed on other cases.'

'Which is why I'm being discharged from duty for the entire autumn?'

'You're no good to anyone running on empty. Least of all yourself.'

'No, I guess not.'

'So what're you planning to do?'

He mused. 'Fool around, I suppose.' Mischievously, he added, 'See if I can pull a bird.'

She didn't rise to that bait and began filing his completed paperwork in her out-tray. 'You could do with getting some sun on your back. And start eating properly; you look underweight to me.'

'You care?' he asked.

She glanced up again, almost looking hurt by the question. 'Of course I care.'

'I mean more than just because I'm part of your team?'

'Why should my personal feelings matter to you?'

Heck couldn't reply. She'd reversed the situation very neatly.

'Take yourself on holiday, Heck,' she said, resuming business mode. 'Relax, have a good time. Pull yourself a bird, if you must. But when you're back in this office on December first, I want you full of piss and vinegar, okay?'

'Yes ma'am.'

'Off you go.'

And he went.

Heck peeled his jacket off and strolled into the rec room to see if there was anyone to shoot some pool with. But it was empty. Instead, he got himself a coffee from the vending machine and stood by the window, looking down on Victoria Street. The hot drink had a soothing effect. Gemma had been right about one thing – at present he was running on empty, but even so, being forced to take a holiday for three months was the last thing he'd wanted. If anyone asked why, he'd tell them that this was because he was a workaholic, but in his more honest, introspective moments he'd admit that it probably owed more to there being nothing else going on in his life. There was no question that Heck *loved* the job. Catching criminals, putting them away, slamming cell doors on those who brought terror and misery to the lives of the innocent gave him a buzz that he didn't get anywhere else.

But on this occasion – on this *one* occasion – being ordered to stay away from the office for a few months might well be to his advantage.

Before he could ponder the situation further, someone else came into the room. He turned, and saw that it was Commander Laycock.

'Heck,' Laycock said with a grin. 'Glad I caught you.' He sauntered over.

Laycock's looks belied his age, which was somewhere in the early-to-mid forties. He was a big, burly bloke, tall and broad at the shoulder, yet trim at the waist. Even now he wore the shorts and sweat-dampened vest that he'd no doubt been working out in down in the gym. A towel was looped around the back of his bull-neck. At first glance he had the look of the archetypical man's man: he was fair-haired, square-jawed, handsome, and yet he had a rugged edge. You'd imagine he could easily go round for round with the lads – and this wasn't an inaccurate impression. He nearly always adopted a 'hail fellow, well met' approach when dealing with 'his troops', as he liked to call them, an attitude he'd inherited from his early days in the Royal Military Police.

Heck wasn't fooled by any of it.

'I just wanted to congratulate you on the time and effort you put in on the missing women case,' Laycock said.

Heck nodded. 'Thank you, Sir.'

'You understand why I had it wound up?'

'I've got a pretty good idea.'

'Your last CCA wasn't totally convincing, I'm afraid. Not considering the amount we've been spending on this.'

'It's alright, Sir. It's all been explained to me.'

'Okay. You don't seem very happy about it, though?'

Heck feigned surprise. 'What, I'm supposed to be happy as well? Sorry, I didn't get the written order for that.'

Laycock's smile faded. 'There's no being nice to you, is there?'

'I don't see any point in pretending we're friends, that's all.'

'Blunt as ever, I see. Okay, well let's cut to the chase. One of the problems of being a detective and having cases to investigate is that, now and then, you're expected to close a few – not widen them and widen them until every bloody person in the service is at your beck and call.'

'And why would that be, Sir?'

'Excuse me?'

'Perhaps you can explain it to me,' Heck said. 'Why do we – sorry, why do *you* – prefer cases we can close quickly and easily to cases that require a load of work?'

Laycock's eyes were now hard; his lips had tightened. 'You're going on leave, I understand. I suggest you go now, before you get on my wrong side.'

'You're not going to answer the question? Would that be because, as far as you're concerned, the National Crime Group's an ego-trip?'

'I'm warning you, Heckenburg . . .'

'Gold-plated job for a Bramshill brat-packer like you, isn't it? Very high profile, lots of TV interviews, regular briefings with whichever Home Secretary happens to be in power this week.'

Laycock looked as though he was about to explode, but his anger quickly abated and he smiled again. 'You know, I always had misgivings about having you in my outfit, Heck. And now I can see they were well-placed. You're a chancer, an adventurer – and that doesn't work in the modern police.'

'I'd have been delighted to be a team-player, if you'd actually given me a team.'

Laycock chuckled. 'Forget about a team. You should be more concerned now about whether you actually fit into this department. You know they've started calling the National Crime Group "the British FBI". And that's something I'm encouraging. It makes us sound like the slick, smart, modern organisation I want us to be. Oddballs won't have any place in it.'

'So who'll be running it when *you* leave?'

'Insubordinates won't either.'

'Ahh . . . you're saying you're kicking me out?'

'I'm saying you're not the sort of police officer I necessarily want working under me.'

'I'd never have guessed.' At last Heck allowed himself to show some emotion. 'From the very first day of that missing women enquiry, I didn't get one word of support from you, Sir. Not one.'

'I wasn't convinced by the evidence.'

'What would *you* know about evidence? You're not a copper, you're a politician.'

Laycock's lips tightened again. Consummate actor though he was, Heck always managed to bring out the beast in him. 'You're lucky no one else is present to hear this, sergeant.'

'If anyone else was present, I wouldn't be saying it.'

'I can still break you, Heckenburg.'

'Yeah, you're apparently an expert.' Heck knew he was going too far now, but suddenly all the frustration and annoyance of the last few months was pouring out. 'They tell me that when you were a uniformed inspector at Ladbroke Grove, after refusing to spare anyone to clear the yobs away from the war memorial, where they'd been drinking all day, you personally supervised the arrest and conviction of an old lady who'd hit one of them with her brolly.'

'If you've got a job to come back to in December, I'll be extraordinarily surprised.'

'It's a pity you can't divert some of that belligerence into standing up to the Home Office and demanding more money for our major enquiries,' Heck retorted. 'Or how about standing up to the CPS when they say we can't proceed with a prosecution because there's only a small chance of success?'

'You really think you're fireproof just because you used to shag your super?'

That comment caught Heck on the hop. He'd thought that only Des Palliser was aware he'd once had a romance with Gemma Piper; it was ancient history after all, when they were both young, newly made detectives.

Laycock chuckled again. 'Oh yes. You'd be amazed at some of the things I know. You see, that's the difference between you and me, Heckenburg. You're just a foot-soldier, a grunt. And I'm a five-star general. I'm running the whole show. It's my job to know everything. But by all means, if you really fancy it, try and take me on. I'd relish the contest, though it wouldn't last for long.'

Realising that he was on dodgier ground than he'd first thought, Heck said nothing. He grabbed his jacket from a chair and pulled it on.

'All my service I've been meeting coppers like you,' Laycock added, leaning so close that Heck could smell his sweat. 'Surly, resentful, jealous of those who've earned promotion, embittered that they have to take orders from people they consider themselves superior to. Determined that anyone who doesn't operate at their mediocre level is to be sneered at. Well I'm not going to stand for it in NCG anymore. We're an elite outfit. There'll be no dissent in *these* ranks. And if you think you're going to be the exception to that rule because you're protected, you – and your protectress,

I might add – could both be in for a big shock. Now get out of my sight.'

As Heck left, he realised that he should have gone earlier, before he'd let his mouth run away with him. It was just that, with three months of leave looming, he might not have got another chance to have a pop at the person most responsible for wrecking his case.

Not that some of the things said in retaliation hadn't stung him. To start with, his attitude to Laycock had nothing to do with Gemma Piper providing him cover. In truth, he'd never even considered her that way – until now. The real reason was that he'd always found his supreme boss so aggravating that open criticism of him was unavoidable. It wasn't even a personality clash; the wound went much deeper than that. To Heck, Laycock was a poster-child for the modern-day senior policeman; young, good looking, university-educated as well as being an ex-military man – and more than capable of kissing all the right buttocks. In short, he embodied everything that was turning British law-enforcement into a career opportunity rather than a vocation.

Not that going lip-to-lip with your commanding officer like Heck had just done, was well-advised. Okay, there'd been no witnesses, so there'd be no one to corroborate accusations at a disciplinary hearing. But he had no doubt that Laycock could and would fix it for him somehow, if he got the chance. There were times when Heck would say that he didn't care about stuff like that; that as far as he was concerned an idiot was an idiot, and he would always use that exact terminology because he couldn't abide being disingenuous. But there were other times when he regretted this impulsive nature. It wasn't as if he was innately rebellious or insolent. Fair enough, he resented having seventeen years in and still only holding the rank of sergeant, but he accepted his place in the pyramid of power. But there was something about Laycock and the number-crunching suits he represented that really stuck in Heck's craw.

Of course, whatever the reason for it, today's confrontation – and it was only one of several he'd had with Laycock, but it had been more explosive than most – might have more serious repercussions than usual. Until now Heck had always relied on his reputation for being a highly productive officer who'd sent way more than his fair share of slags and skags to prison, to guarantee his job security. In addition to that, aside from his differences with Laycock, he had a relatively clean shirt. So it wouldn't be easy ousting him. And it would be even harder to oust Gemma. She was probably the NCG's most prized asset: not only was she a woman, which was always a bonus these days, but she'd blazed her way through the male-dominated world of CID with skill, guile, determination and, above all, results, and had earned her high position because she deserved it rather than because of positive discrimination. On top of all that, she was eye-candy, so it looked particularly good when she was accepting her commendations on TV. But Laycock would still try to stick the knife in, possibly using the missing women enquiry, and how much cash had drained into it for so little return, as the main springboard of his assault.

Which, when Heck thought about it, made the plan he was now hatching for the next three months – extremely risky though it was – all the more important.

Chapter 7

Louise looked herself over in the mirror.

She'd had the shower as instructed, and had done the best she could with her hair and make-up, though it had hardly been a labour of love. The clothes she'd finally selected would never have been her normal choice, but there hadn't been much option. She'd put on dark stockings, a short, black, pleated skirt, a red silk blouse with ruffles at the front, and a smart black jacket. The trashy red and black shoes had come last, though in truth the whole thing was trashy, not to mention demeaning; it was the 'office look' perhaps, though a male fantasy version of it rather than the real thing. She hadn't been able to find a single item of underwear that didn't come straight from the advertising section of *Penthouse*, and after some searching had eventually opted for a matching set of black lace bra and knickers, though the knickers were so sheer that they might as well not have been there.

Not that this troubled her now. Briefly, as she stood rigid in front of the cold glass, wearing skimpy drawers seemed the very least of her problems.

She kept envisioning her house, her garden, Alan's tousled head and grinning face when he woke her up each morning with a cup of tea, the spare bedroom they'd tentatively begun to think of as a nursery, which she'd filled in her imagination with soft, pink and white furniture, with cuddly toys, with animal mobiles turning on strings, with Disney wallpaper – but no, no, *NO*!

It didn't pay to dwell on those things. She had to focus on the positives. She'd been a prisoner all this time, but they hadn't yet brutalised her; in fact they'd fed her, watered her, allowed her to wash. In some ways that was sinister, but in others it was good. And she had definitely been abducted to order – they hadn't just grabbed her off the streets; she wasn't a random victim. As such, the idea had coalesced in her mind that this kidnapping could only be some kind of plot against Goldstein & Hoff – which was less frightening than it being directed against her, but even so it could have a fatal outcome, so she had to play it smart and go along with them for the moment. She had no other choice.

At least, this was what she told herself as she assessed her reflection for the umpteenth time. Cheap – that was the only way to describe the version of Louise Jennings that her captors wanted; cheap and slutty, like a porno actress on set. It was such a different look from her normal tasteful preference that this in itself almost made her cry, but she resisted resolutely. They'd degraded her enough; she wasn't going to give them the satisfaction of breaking down. Besides, as she kept reminding herself, it was vital to keep a cool head. Cooperate but be cool – that was her plan. It was the only way to earn their respect. Never show a dangerous animal that you're frightened.

But of course, it was easier to say such a thing than to do it.

The jewellery for example – Louise had glanced into the jewellery box, and had been surprised by the quality of the stuff it contained: earrings, bracelets, brooches, rings, necklaces, all of real gold and silver, encrusted with gems. But after the rather large hint her jailer had dropped about where this high-class merchandise had come from, she couldn't bring herself to touch any of it, much less wear it. She doubted that she'd ever be able to wear jewellery again, not even her own – assuming she ever got home to it. Her bravado half-crumbled and fresh tears sprang into her eyes, though she hurriedly wiped them away with a tissue, determined to be brave.

As she did this, the door clicked open.

She spun around. Surely two hours hadn't passed already?

Nobody came in. Louise waited tensely, hands clasped in front of her. Then she heard a voice from the next room.

'Louise?' it said hesitantly. Incredibly, it sounded familiar. 'Do you want to come in here?'

At first bewildered, but then with sudden desperate energy, she dashed forward and pushed the door open. On the other side she saw a larger room, which was much more luxurious than her dressing-room-sized prison. There was a thick pile carpet on the floor, and soft fabric covering the walls. A shaded bulb cast a rosy glow over a double bed, its eiderdown folded neatly back on crisp, golden sheets. However, none of this amazed her as much as the person occupying the room.

He was a middle-aged man, but tall and well built, with grey at his temples and pale, handsome features. He was usually a very imposing figure; scrupulously neat, with a formal air and stern attitude which appeared to brook no nonsense, but at present, though he wore his normal pinstriped suit, his jacket and collar were unbuttoned and his tie hung in a loose knot.

Despite this, there was no mistaking him.

'Mr Blenkinsop,' she said, hardly able to believe her eyes – new tears now appeared there, tears of relief.

He gave a helpless shrug. 'Hi.'

Ian Blenkinsop was not part of Louise's department at Goldstein & Hoff, but a director in Commodity Finance, two floors above her. She didn't know him particularly well, but they'd been part of the same company long enough to be on speaking terms. He was now standing on the other side of the bed, in front of an oak-panelled door, next to what looked like a well-stocked drinks cabinet.

She slammed the dressing-room door behind her and rushed towards him, jabbering frantically. 'They . . . they grabbed me on my way home. I didn't realise until it was too . . . there was nothing I could do . . . I'm so, so sorry . . . honestly, there was nothing . . .'

He nodded patiently, but seemed rather nervous. He was breathing quickly; sweat glinted on his brow – which was not his normal form. Ordinarily, Ian Blenkinsop was a man of poise, a smooth operator from whose fingertips multi-million-pound deals flowed on a daily basis. But why was *he* here? The question hit Louise hard. He was a banker, for Christ's sake! Why was *he* the one who'd been sent to find her? Unless . . .

'Oh my God,' she breathed. 'Did they get you too?'

'Er . . .' He half-smiled. 'In a way, yes.'

'Oh . . . Jesus!' She put her fingers to her brow as it furrowed with disappointment. She wasn't saved after all. Still, if nothing else, at least here was a friend, an ally, someone to share the ordeal with.

'Who . . . who are these people?' she said, trying her damnedest not to start crying again. 'I mean . . . *who*?'

'I don't know. Listen, come and have a drink.'

To her bemusement, he turned to the cabinet. On its shelf there was a bottle of champagne, which he'd uncorked, and two glasses. He'd already filled one and now filled the other. He came around the bed and offered it to her.

'Are you serious?' she said, ignoring it. 'Don't you think we should be trying to get out of here?'

Still he pushed the drink towards her. 'I know this has all been a bit of a shock for you, Louise, but if you play along it'll be a lot easier.'

'"Play along"?' Confusion made her tone shrill. 'What the hell do you mean?'

He drained his own glass and placed hers on a sideboard, before sitting on the bed and patting the mattress next to him. 'Come here for a minute.'

'What? Mr Blenkinsop . . . what are you doing?'

'Louise, there's no point trying to resist. These people are professionals.'

'You *know* them?'

He stood up again, frustrated, pacing the room. 'You haven't guessed what this is about yet?'

'Am I supposed to have?' In the midst of her fear, she was completely bewildered.

'You should just accept the inevitable.' His voice had hardened, but he eyed her up and down as if noticing her attire for the first time and appreciating it a great deal. 'You look good, I must admit.'

She backed away from him. 'You're not a prisoner here at all, are you?'

'You want the truth?' He stared at her, glassy-eyed. Suddenly he'd dropped all pretence at friendship. He looked cold, indifferent. 'It's the first time I've done anything like this here in the UK. But why not? Every day I create wealth and jobs for others. Society owes me so very much, so if I see something I want, why shouldn't I take it? Because at the end of the day, I *will* have the things I desire and deserve. And if that means hurting a few little idiot-bitches who think it's alright to dress provocatively because it makes them feel good, but who scream "harassment" the moment someone

62

so much as looks at them . . . well, that's hardly my problem. On the subject of which, you *do* look good, Louise.'

He slid towards her. She continued to back away; the dressing-room door was close behind her, but of course that offered no escape.

'I've watched you every day for quite a few years now,' he added. 'Sashaying around Branscombe Court in those "fuck-my-wet-cunt" outfits.'

Despite everything, it was a chilling shock to hear such profanity from him. Louise couldn't suppress a gasp.

'Though you never looked as good then as you do now.'

'You bastard,' she whispered.

She'd now backed right up to the door. He didn't come straight up to her but stopped a few yards short, from where he continued to eye her in the sort of brazenly lustful way that nowadays could land a man in court.

'It's up to you how you play this,' he said. 'But if you comply, I reckon we'll both have a good time.'

Finally she understood. Several times in the office recently she'd suspected that Blenkinsop was furtively observing her. Evidently it hadn't just been her imagination. 'I . . . I . . .'

'I think the words you're looking for are "okay, let's do it."' Blenkinsop was clearly growing impatient; his mouth fixed in a half-smile/half-snarl. 'Look Louise . . . it's not like you've got a choice here. You've seen the sort of team I'm working with. They don't mess around. They've been watching you for weeks, noting your every move. They know who your friends are, where your family can be found . . .'

'My . . . my family?' she said, with a new sense of creeping horror.

'That's correct, Louise . . . your family. If this thing goes tits up, it isn't going to finish with you. I'm going to get what I want, and I don't care how. Of course it would be easier for all of us if we kept things nice and friendly.' He ogled her revealing outfit again. 'At least . . . as much as I'm capable of that. Your play, my darling.'

'I . . . I need a drink first.'

He looked surprised by that, and not a little pleased. 'That's a good girl. Well done.' He turned to the sideboard, collecting her champagne. 'This is a Bollinger 1990 by the way. I spared no expense, as you can see.'

She stepped forward to accept it, trying her best to smile, though it was difficult to keep her lips from trembling. Perhaps he sensed this as she took the drink from him – his expression suddenly changed, but it was too late. She hurled the drink into his face, glass and all. The glass broke with the impact, a shard slicing open his left cheek.

'You fucking bitch!' he squawked, flailing blindly at her.

She pushed past him and went straight for the door next to the drinks cabinet, praying that it wouldn't be locked – though of course it was. She wanted to scream as she pounded on it with her fists. Behind her, Blenkinsop was still swearing. She swung around to face him, expecting to have to ward off blows. But he hadn't followed her. Instead he was addressing someone else, gazing up at a corner of the ceiling where she now saw a small surveillance camera.

'Look what she's fucking done!' he shouted, clamping a handkerchief to his bloodied cheek. 'I told you I need her compliant. I've given her every fucking chance, but she doesn't want to know.'

There was a loud thumping of wood, and a *clunk* as a bolt was drawn. Louise toppled forward as the door burst open behind her. Two men came barging in: the black guy in the orange ski-mask and the white guy in the purple. Orange grabbed her by the wrists and threw her onto the bed. Purple, she could see, was already tapping another needle.

'*No!*' she shrieked, but her struggles were futile.

Orange held her down easily, pressing her on the mattress with his own body as his associate leaned forward and applied the injection. Blenkinsop stood to one side and watched in silence, though his face had gone a little grey; blood was turning his handkerchief crimson. When Orange got back to his feet, Louise lay still, limp as a rag doll. He casually flicked her skirt up, before turning to face Blenkinsop.

'Reckon you can manage now?'

Blenkinsop nodded nervously, unable to take his eyes off Louise's exposed underwear and the golden triangle of pubic hair visible through its filmy material.

'You might need this.' Orange pushed something into Blenkinsop's hand.

It was a jar of lubricant.

Chapter 8

The Raven's Nest at Hammersmith was the closest thing Heck had to a local. He'd lived in Fulham for fourteen years now, and had finally chosen 'the Nest' not just because it was small and homely – as opposed to being large and impersonal, like so many London pubs – but also because its landlord Phil Mackintosh was an Aussie, who regularly had the widescreen TV in his snug tuned to Australian rugby league. Heck, being a Lancashire lad by origin, also had a fondness for the thirteen-a-side rugby code, so this had proved a draw for him.

Unfortunately, that first Sunday evening of Heck's enforced leave there was no match on, Phil was off duty and, this being one of the quieter nights of the week, there wasn't really anyone else to talk to. Instead, Heck drank a few beers and sank a few whiskies – since leaving the Yard that afternoon, the idea of getting totally plastered had become very appealing. It was another warm August evening, so he spent his first couple of hours on the terrace watching the river glide by, then finally traipsed back indoors where he bought another beer with a whisky chaser, and moved into the pool room. He shot a few balls around, hoping someone would turn up and offer him a game, but no one did. Going into the bar again, he exchanged pleasantries with a couple of customers who he knew vaguely, but it was difficult striking up conversation purely for the sake of it.

Mid-evening had now arrived, so he bought yet another round and retreated back to the pool room. He was warming up inside and his vision was getting blurry, which was just the way he wanted it. The downside of course was that hitting targets accurately had become a complex process. It took an age working his way round to the black, and he then spent several minutes squinting along his cue, trying to focus on the final pocket, only to be distracted by a very shapely pair of crossed legs that he suddenly noticed on the other side of the table. He tried to concentrate on what he was doing, but those legs were brown, bare, very smooth, and went all the way up to the hem of an indecently short denim skirt. A backless white sandal with a stiletto heel dangled sexily.

Perhaps not surprisingly, the shot went wide.

'Oh dear,' said a sympathetic voice.

Heck glanced up at the girl to whom the legs belonged. She was seated on a high stool, from where she'd clearly been watching him for several minutes.

She was somewhere in her late twenties and a stunner – with dark eyes, full lips and perfectly symmetrical features, she almost looked like a young Halle Berry. Her thick black hair was held up with wooden pins, though it would probably fall to her shoulders in a slick of glossy curls if released. A tight green vest with an image of Jay-Z emblazoned on the front accentuated a trim waist and generous bosom.

Heck realised he was gawking. He clamped his mouth shut.

'See anything you like?' she asked innocently.

'Er, no . . . I mean yeah obviously . . . er, sorry.' He smiled awkwardly, placed his cue on the table and headed for the bar.

'Play with yourself here often?' she called after him.

He turned and looked back. She was smiling provocatively, as if dying to hear his response.

'I wouldn't usually,' he said. 'But I've never found anyone else who's up to the job.'

'That's a brave boast after what I've just seen.'

'You challenging me, miss?'

She leaned forward and rested her chin on her fist. 'It would be no contest at all.'

He indicated the vacant table. 'Rack 'em up.'

She did. And very gallantly, he let her take the first shot. Which proved to be a big mistake. She potted four stripes one after another, only missing a fifth by millimetres. In response, he potted a spot, but the white followed it down. She then embarked on another break, which only ended when she potted the black after bouncing it skilfully off two opposing cushions.

'You know, all that proves is you've had a misspent youth,' Heck said.

'My mum wouldn't need that proving to her.'

'I'll bet she wouldn't.' He couldn't help checking her out again, especially those shiny, shapely legs. 'Fancy a drink?'

'You offering?'

They went through to the bar, where Heck – still unable to believe his luck, because this sort of thing never, ever happened – ordered her a rum with coke, getting himself another pint of bitter and a double Scotch.

'You drinking to forget, or something?' she asked, as they settled at a table.

'I'm drinking because I'm on holiday.'

'You're on holiday?' She sounded surprised, which puzzled him a little.

'That bothers you?'

'No, it's just . . .' She smiled again. 'I'm on holiday too. Sort of.'

He shrugged. 'Good health.'

The glasses clinked; they both sipped.

'I'm Lauren,' she said. 'I'm from Yorkshire.'

He nodded. Her accent had already given that away – he guessed Huddersfield or Leeds.

'You're not a local either, are you?' she asked. 'Manchester, is it?'

'Near there. Bradburn.'

'You're a long way from home.'

He swilled more beer. 'Sometimes it feels like that. But I travel a lot, so it's as broad as long. My name's Mark, by the way. But friends call me "Heck".'

'I know. The barmaid told me.'

'She did?' Now Heck was really puzzled. The girl had been interested enough to ask someone his name? That had to be a first. He had a certain rugged appeal – he was aware of that, but he wasn't the sort of bloke that lookers like this moved in on. Unless? – abruptly his mood changed. He'd been right to remind himself that this sort of thing never, ever happened – because it wasn't happening now either.

'This your local?' she wondered.

'Suppose so. I don't get in too often. What can I do for you, anyway?'

'What do you mean?'

'Come on, love. You're not on the pull. If you were, you wouldn't choose me.'

She folded her arms – an unconsciously defensive gesture, he noted. 'Maybe I just fancied a chat with someone who looked pleasant.'

'Same as before. You wouldn't choose me.'

'You don't have a very high opinion of yourself, do you?'

69

'My opinion doesn't count for much, I'm afraid.'

'Listen, I'm just trying to be friendly.'

'No you're not. You're up to something. Now if I didn't know better . . .' he glanced again at her legs, and then much more closely at her arms, but couldn't spot any tell-tale needle-tracks, 'I'd guess you were the sort of lady who Phil Mackintosh doesn't normally allow into this establishment.'

She stiffened. 'I'm not a hooker, if that's what you mean.'

'So why're you acting like one?' He gave her the gaze he normally reserved for the interview room, his eyes boring into her. She became flustered, ill-at-ease.

'I just wanted some information?' she finally said.

'So it's not my amazing body you're interested in. Now there's a surprise.'

'About your investigation . . .'

'Ahhh.'

She now looked very uncomfortable. 'How – look, how's it going?'

Heck finished his beer. He shouted across to the bar for another, before turning back to her. 'So what is this? Mr Ballamara's decided that, as the rough stuff doesn't work, he'll try a gentler touch?'

'Eh?'

'Is that the deal? I deliver, and I get a night in the sack with some quality tail?'

She looked totally baffled.

He leaned forward. 'Go back to your boss and tell him to shove it. Not only do I not take orders from him, I don't take bribes either. And frankly I'm surprised anyone does. You know why? Because he's a walking-talking anachronism, a throwback – a gobshite who runs a few South London boozers and thinks he's Pablo Escobar. Another year and I dare say he'll be at the beck and call of some sixteen-year-old Romanian, and no doubt he'll be grateful for it.'

He pushed his chair back and stood up.

'For someone who doesn't rate himself, you don't half like the sound of your own voice,' she said.

'For someone who looks as good as you, you keep very trashy company. And just in case he decides to send the heavies round again, tell him not to waste his time. I'm off the case. It's finished.'

'Finished?' She sounded startled. But Heck had gone. He was over at the bar again, paying for his next round, when she reappeared. 'Finished, did you say?'

'Yes. It's been closed down. And if Mr Ballamara doesn't like that – as I told him before, he can take it up with Commander Laycock at Scotland Yard.'

'You mean no one's looking into it at all?'

'Someone will be somewhere.' He sipped his fresh pint, leaving froth on his top lip. 'But only if they haven't got something much, much more important to do. Like watch some paint dry.'

He tried to move away, but she grabbed his arm tightly. He turned to face her – and was surprised to see that she was livid with rage. Tears were welling in her eyes.

'I heard good things about you,' she said. 'I thought you were going to help me, but now I can see you're just another *FUCKING DICKHEAD*!' She banged money on the bar-top. 'That's for the drink I owe you. Stick it up your arse!'

And she stormed out of the pub, stopping only to grab up her handbag and sling it over her shoulder.

'You coppers really know how to make friends and influence people,' the barmaid, who happened to be Phil Mackintosh's eldest daughter, commented.

Heck was equally bemused. 'I'm guessing I've just cost her a decent commission.'

He went back to his seat, shaking his head. The lowlifes he had to deal with. Mind you, hookers didn't generally scream and cry when johns turned them down. Now that he looked back on it, the entire meeting had been a little surreal – but what the hell, this was London. Nothing should be a surprise here. He put it from his mind and the evening rolled on tediously. He managed a couple more rounds and a few more brief exchanges of mundane chat with other punters before the bell rang for last orders.

Before leaving, he went for a pee, and then stood looking at himself in the greasy toilet mirror. Considering he was now in his late thirties, he'd kept reasonably well. Some might say he was handsome but he was also rumpled; his black hair didn't have any grey in it yet but seemed to be permanently mussed, and he *did* look tired. He was unshaved and his normally piercing blue eyes were bloodshot, though that might be due to drink rather than fatigue. The rest of him was in okay shape. He certainly wasn't overweight, though that was because during the investigation he hadn't been eating properly or even regularly enough. But he was still reasonably solid and well-built; years of sports activities in his younger police days had served a purpose after all.

He yawned, scratched his grizzled cheek, then ambled back out and shouted his goodbyes to the bar staff. The muggy atmosphere outside did little to help with his semi-inebriated state, and he tottered across the pub car park to his Fiat. Even leaning against it, he had trouble inserting his key into the lock.

'You're not seriously thinking of driving in that state?' someone asked.

Heck turned around. At first he didn't recognise Gemma Piper. Her white Coupe was parked about twenty yards away. She'd got out and approached without him noticing. She was wearing jeans, trainers and a lilac running top.

'I, er . . . no, my jacket's in the back,' he said.

'Really?'

He opened the door and, with a flourish, pulled a light-weight leather jacket from the rear seat, where it had been dumped earlier. She eyed him sceptically, unconvinced.

'What's the matter anyway?' he asked. 'Why are you here?'

'I want to talk to you.'

'Yeah? Well tough. I'm off duty.'

He turned, stumbled across the car park and onto the pavement, though he hadn't walked more than thirty yards before he realised that he'd be lucky to make it home. He'd drunk far more that evening than he had in quite some time. The white Coupe pulled up alongside him, and Gemma powered down her window.

'Stop acting like a kid, Heck, and get in. At the very least, I can give you a ride home.'

Heck fumbled his way around the vehicle, and all but collapsed into the front passenger seat. Gemma leaned across him to check that his seatbelt was secure. As she did, he tried to nuzzle her neck. She pulled back sharply, glaring at him.

'Don't even go there. That's not what this is about, and you know it.'

He shrugged as she put the car in gear and drove them away from the kerb.

'What *is* it about?' he asked sulkily.

'I wanted to talk some business, but by the looks of it you're in no fit state.'

'I'll be the judge of that, thank you.'

'Will you, indeed.' She shook her head. 'It's difficult enough getting you to exercise good judgment when you're stone-cold sober. It'd be a laugh a minute watching you try to do it tonight.'

Chapter 9

Cherrybrook Drive was a cul-de-sac, with Heck's place situated at its far end, where a ten-foot-high wall of soot-black bricks separated the residential neighbourhood from a stretch of tube running overland. The houses, which faced each other in two sombre rows, were tall and narrow, and fronted straight onto the pavement. Heck occupied an upstairs flat in the last one, accessible via a steep, dingy stairway. When he'd swayed up to the top, he flicked a light on, revealing a threadbare carpet and walls stripped to the plaster.

'Nothing like living in style,' Gemma observed.

'I forgot . . . you haven't been to this pad, have you?' he replied. 'Well . . . doesn't matter, does it? I'm hardly ever here.'

The apartment itself was warm and not quite as gloomy as its entrance suggested. The kitchen was small but modern, and very clean – every worktop sparkled (though this might have been because food was rarely prepared here, as a bin crammed with kebab wrappers and pizza boxes seemed to suggest). There was a basic but surprisingly spacious lounge-diner, which would have been fairly pleasant had it not been for its window gazing down on the trash-filled cutting where the trains passed, a bathroom and a bedroom. The final room, separated from the hall by a sliding screen door, was box-sized and windowless. Its dim interior appeared to be scattered with disordered paperwork, but Heck closed the door on that before Gemma had a chance to check it out properly. It was his office, he said, though at present it was more like a junk room.

'Coffee?' he asked. 'Tea? Something stronger?'

'Coffee's fine,' she said.

He went into the kitchen, filled the kettle and prepared a single mug. As the water boiled, he took a tumbler and a bottle of whisky from a cupboard and poured himself three fingers. Walking back into the lounge, he threw his jacket across the armchair and hit the button on the phone-messaging system. There was only one message. It was from his older sister, Dana: 'Mark, when am I going to see you? It's been ages. I mean, if you're not coming up, you can at least call.'

He pressed 'delete'.

'You and Dana still not getting on?' Gemma asked.

'Everything's fine. I just can't be bothered.'

'Charming.'

Gemma glanced around at the lounge. It was neat enough, but very functional. The word 'minimalist' wouldn't cover it – 'Spartan' would be more accurate. The walls were bare of paintings, the sideboard and shelves empty of flowers or photographs. The red and orange flowered curtains, blue vinyl sofa, and mauve carpet were a tasteless mish-mash.

'Still no sign of a woman's touch,' she said.

'Surely that doesn't surprise you?'

'No, I suppose not.'

He swilled his whisky, and went back into the kitchen.

She took in the room again. A few books sat on a side-board, all recent titles from the bestseller list, covering various genres, which again was no surprise – it suggested Heck had neither the time nor inclination for a more specialised interest. DVDs occupied a wooden tower alongside the television, their cases thick with dust. It was clearly a while since he'd sat down and watched one of them. Next to the sofa there was a newspaper rack, but it contained only one item – yesterday's edition of the *Standard*. Periodicals and style magazines of the sort that cluttered most people's lounges were noticeably absent. Heck returned, carrying her coffee. She noticed that he'd poured himself another two fingers.

'Have you got a drink problem that I don't know about?' she asked.

He dropped into the armchair. 'The only problem I have is that I don't get enough time to drink. Until now of course. Cheers!'

She placed her coffee down. 'You know, there are times when a little gratitude wouldn't go amiss.'

'Okay . . . you're right. Thanks for the lift home.'

'You're as impossible now as you were . . .'

'As I was *then*?'

She bit her lip and shook her head, as if suppressing a response that she'd regret.

For some reason, this half-conciliatory act warmed Heck inside. He added to it by swilling more whisky. 'Well . . . I wouldn't want to disappoint you.'

Gemma sighed. 'Heck, I've defended your corner for a long time. But there's only so much even I can do if you insist on winding up Jim Laycock every time you meet him.'

'Oh, so that's what this is about . . .'

'No, it isn't. And don't start giving *me* attitude, Heck . . . because *I'm* not going to put up with it either.' She paused, picked her coffee up and took a sip. 'My God, that's foul. You know they call me "the Lioness"?'

'I'd noticed.'

'Yeah, well that's except where *you're* concerned. Where *you're* concerned, they call me "the Pussy Cat". Now what do you think that's doing to my self-esteem, eh?'

'Alright, I'm sorry.' He grabbed at his tie to loosen it, only to find that he wasn't wearing one. 'But he's got to get off my back . . .'

'For Christ's sake, Heck! He's a commander, you're a sergeant!'

'Yeah, and I close cases he wouldn't have the first idea how to approach.'

'That's not the point. History's written by the top brass, not the cannon fodder. So would you mind, now and then, just trying to make my job a little bit easier?'

'I said I'm sorry.' The thread of conversation was beginning to elude Heck. No doubt it was the booze. On the subject of which – he drained his glass, and lurched back into the kitchen for a refill.

'That's really going to help,' Gemma said, following him.

'It helps me,' he retorted, though the corners of his vision were fogging badly.

'Good Lord,' she said, as he filled his glass almost to the brim.

'It's not like I've got something to get up for in the morning, is it?'

'Well, that's a matter of opinion.'

Even in Heck's state, he detected meaning in those words. He swung round to face her. She was watching him carefully, suspiciously.

'Don't know what you're talking about,' he said.

'You accepted this enforced leave way too easily in my opinion.'

'Naw . . . the idea just grew on me, that's all.'

'Heck, this is *me* you're talking to. Give me some credit, eh!'

Her gaze was suddenly intense. Heck tried to return it, but doubted it would have much effect. He wasn't just tipsy anymore, he was properly drunk. Which might explain why he suddenly wanted to spill the whole thing, tell her everything about his plans. Not that it was purely because his inhibitions had fled. Partly it was because confiding in someone – anyone – about the worry and uncertainty accrued over so many months of tireless effort and soul-destroying frustration, not to mention the bitterness at the way his gaffers had treated him, would be a kind of release, a burden shared.

Gemma was still talking. 'You're planning to continue investigating while you're on leave, aren't you?'

'That would be against every rule in the book and completely unethical.'

'And you expect me to believe that would make a difference to you?'

'Do you want a drink yet?' he asked, reaching for the bottle.

'No.' She snatched it away. 'And you don't either.'

They stared at each other, Heck having to lean on the kitchen units to stay upright. He rubbed at his face. It was numb, damp with sweat.

'What's in that room?' she asked.

'Which room?'

'The room you didn't want me to look in when we first got here.'

'Have you come as a friend or a boss, Gemma?'

She looked surprisingly torn by the question. 'Heck, I can't be one or the other. Not when the stakes are as high as this.'

He nodded gravely, as if there was no point denying reality any longer, and levered himself upright, beckoning her to follow him out of the kitchen. In the hall, he yanked open the screen door he'd hurried to close on arriving. Again, a mess of heaped paperwork met their gaze. He switched the light on, bringing it into full clarity.

It was, as he'd said, an office. There was a desk, a swivel chair and a computer terminal. All were swamped with documents – official police documents by the looks of them, covered in typing and handwritten notes – but also maps, wanted posters, newspaper clippings. Two of the walls were occupied by noticeboards hung with further paperwork. A closer glance at this revealed witness statements, progress reports, criminal intelligence print-outs. The facing wall was more neatly arrayed with glossy photographs: the blown-up headshots of various different women. Lines and arrows had been drawn between them with a blue marker pen; captions and notations had been scribbled on the wallpaper.

'Jesus H. Christ,' Gemma said with slow disbelief. 'You've set up your own incident room.'

'Sorry boss, but I couldn't let this go. I don't care what anyone says.'

She picked a few documents up – gingerly, almost as if she wanted to check they were real but was hoping they weren't. 'You haven't done all this in one evening. I know you haven't . . . not when you were in the bloody pub getting wasted.'

Heck shrugged. 'I had a feeling this was coming. I've been making copies of everything and bringing them here for weeks.'

'You understand what this means, Heck?' She turned to look at him with an expression that was more fear than anger. 'This isn't just a bit of indiscipline, this is an actual *crime*. This is all Laycock will need to bounce you right out of the job.'

Heck offered her his wrists. 'You'd better take me in then, hadn't you?'

Gemma gazed back into the makeshift incident room, at the thirty-eight lovely, smiling faces on its far wall. Even now, after seeing them so many times, their effect on her was physically sobering. Each one didn't just represent a human life snatched away in its prime, but a devastated family: sorrowing children, tortured parents, a bereft spouse.

'You may recall I drew up this profile some time ago,' Heck said. 'Women who were never likely to go off under their own steam. Career women, graduates, young mothers. Girls who've all got a good family life, good prospects, that sort of thing. You'll notice there are no hookers or drug addicts here . . .'

'*Heck, I'm familiar with the facts!*' she snapped, sounding furious but still pale with shock. Her voice dropped to an intense whisper. 'What I'm not familiar with is a level of disrespect for the chain of command that knocks everything else you've ever done into a cocked hat! In God's name, what did you not understand about me telling you this case was closed?'

'Every part of it,' he replied brazenly. 'Every single word.' He wheeled around and tottered back into the lounge, where he slumped into the armchair. When she reappeared in the doorway, he picked up the telephone. 'Shall I call for prisoner transport, or will you?'

She shook her head. 'You have put me in some difficult situations, Mark Heckenburg, but this is . . .'

'I'm sorry, Gemma,' he slurred. 'But we are where we are.'

'Oh great. The philosophy of the drunk. That's all I bloody need.' She paced back and forth, rubbing at her brow with a carefully manicured finger. 'You know, Heck, when we were hotshot young DCs at Bethnal Green, you were always three or four steps ahead of the game. You ran rings round the scrotes, the guv'nors. You were a risk-taker, but you *so* knew what you were doing. That's what made it exciting to work with you. The angles and tangents we went off at – we never knew where we were going to finish up. It was like living in a high-octane cop movie. And then one day, DCI Jewson – remember him, fat belly, shaggy beard – we used to call him Grizzly Adams? A real old-stager, he was. He took me to one side and said: "Darling, you've got a great future. But you're too close to young Heckenburg for your own good. That lad's running before he can walk and he's got way too many tricks up his sleeve. Mark my words, when he goes down – and he will – he's going to take a chunk of the service with him." Those were his exact words, Heck. I've never forgotten them. How could I? Because that's when I decided that enough was as good as a feast, and that maybe me and you should cool things a little . . .'

A gentle snore from the other side of the room interrupted her.

She turned, to find Heck asleep in the armchair. She regarded him for several anguished moments, before shaking her head, taking him by the armpits and lugging him out of his seat, across his lounge and down the hall. Finally, with no little grunting and struggling, she deposited him on his bed, where she stared at him again for several long seconds. 'Damn it, Heck, why do you always do this to me?'

He didn't respond. So she switched the light out, before leaving the room.

Chapter 10

Ian Blenkinsop sat in silence as he was driven down what he presumed were dark and empty roads. He presumed, because he couldn't actually see. He was wearing a blindfold, a leather strap pulled tightly around his head, but with a cotton wool pad fitted over each of his eyes to prevent any possible chink of vision. It wasn't uncomfortable, but it was unnerving, as was the presence of the two men who sat one on either side of him.

They never spoke, except to make the odd laconic comment about other road users, or the state of the towns and villages they passed through. Noticeably, they never once put a name to any of these places. Neither did they name each other. They were clearly aware that Blenkinsop was listening.

Not that he had much interest in their conversation at present.

He was physically weak, drained of energy and emotion. He was also nauseous; his gut tightened progressively until soon the muscles in his back and sides were tense and aching. His mouth had gone dry; his throat was constricted, and chill sweat bathed his cheeks. The motion of the car wasn't responsible: it glided smoothly, without as much as a jolt. It was also air-conditioned, its interior fragrant of leather and felt.

'Excuse me, I'm sick,' he finally said. 'Can we stop the car?'

'Funny how so many of them want to be sick on the way back,' one of the men remarked.

'I'm serious. I'm going to throw up.'

'Wait a minute.'

Slowly, the vehicle eased to a halt. There was a click as the handbrake was applied but the engine was allowed to continue running. Blenkinsop felt cool air as the door on his left-hand side was opened. Feet clumped on tarmac as one of the men climbed out.

'Lean over this way, Mr Blenkinsop. And don't even think about taking that blindfold off.'

Blenkinsop wasn't used to taking orders from anyone, but now he did exactly as instructed. The man on the right-hand side took hold of him by the collar of his coat, so that he wouldn't fall out of the car completely.

'Okay, let it go,' the first man said.

Blenkinsop felt a surge in his belly, as though everything inside him was about to explode out of his mouth in a torrent. But to his surprise, it was only a trickle, and it felt frothy, light. It didn't even taste of vomit. Rather disgustingly, he realised, it was the champagne he'd drunk earlier; that was all he'd taken into his system in the last few hours. He retched again – another trickle, this one even thinner than the first. The next one was a dry-heave.

'That it?' the man asked. 'Okay, back in with you.'

Blenkinsop was pulled back into the vehicle. The man climbed in alongside him. The door was closed, and the car moved on.

The journey seemed endless. It had been lengthy when

83

he'd been coming the other way – somewhere between two and three hours by his reckoning; and on that occasion he'd been in a state of eager anticipation. Now that he was riddled with horror and fear, it seemed infinitely longer. They'd first picked him up in a rural lay-by near Tring. In the amount of time it had taken to reach their destination, they could have visited almost any part of southern or central England. Of course, by the same token, they may have taken him no more than a few miles, but had driven round and round in deliberate circles to throw him off the trail.

He tried to put these thoughts from his mind. What did he think he was doing, for Christ's sake: collating evidence? The best thing now was to keep his mouth shut. As soon as they released him, he'd head for home and not look back once. But that would be easier said than done. *That horrendous thing . . .*

Blenkinsop was still shaking with disbelief at what he'd just participated in. At what – for Christ's sake – he'd actually *purchased*. Oh, he was under no illusions about himself: he liked to think that he was a family man, but when it came to sex there were some real quirks in his character. He'd discovered that on umpteen trips overseas on behalf of the bank – to the Gulf and North Africa, to developing countries with unstable governments, where just about anything was available if you were prepared to pay for it. He'd often tried to reconcile these dark inner traits with the knowledge that this was the anything-goes twenty-first century, and that sexual experimentation was no longer frowned upon the way it once had been. But that didn't mean he didn't feel dirty and wretched whenever his lust had been sated – not that any previous experience, no matter how extreme, compared with this one.

He wondered if he was going to be sick again, and

struggled to fight it down. It seemed unlikely that the men in the car would tolerate another unscheduled stoppage.

He had to put it all from his mind. That was the only solution. Time healed everything. Even the most dreadful things faded from importance eventually. Another few weeks and it wouldn't matter to him a jot, he was sure. He could relax again, get on with his life. It was all behind him. But still he had to wrestle with himself, to silence the voice of his conscience that was calling shame upon him, to shut the image of Louise's frightened, child-like face from his mind's eye.

If only they hadn't made him stay behind afterwards.

'Just a bit of extra insurance, Mr Blenkinsop,' the one in the orange mask had said, as the one in purple had laid a body-length PVC bin-bag on the bed alongside Louise's unconscious, naked form, and then produced a coil of what looked like piano wire. Blenkinsop knew he'd never forget the heart-stopping shock of that moment. As Purple unravelled the wire, he'd noticed that it was fitted with wooden grip-handles, one at either end.

Orange had chuckled. 'You being here – *involved*, if you like – means you're even less likely to go telling tales, doesn't it?'

Blenkinsop had been half-dressed at the time and still coming down from the rapture of thoroughly enjoying the woman who had taunted him for so long. But he'd never expected to be made to witness the winding of that gleaming wire around her soft, white neck. He'd never imagined having to listen to the grunting efforts of the man in purple as he used the wooden handles to twist and twist and twist, exerting incredible pressure. Most of all, he'd never expected the inert body to start moving slightly, the leaden limbs jerking and twitching.

'Amazing how they do that, isn't it?' Orange had remarked.

'Out for the count, but there's still something inside that's aware she's about to snuff it. Still, kinder than if she was fully conscious, eh?'

The contents of Blenkinsop's gut lurched into his mouth again, but again – thankfully – there was nothing there of note, and he was able to gulp it back.

When she'd finally gone limp – had just flopped down lifeless – that was probably the most horrible part of it. Of course, he'd seen that a dozen times in the movies: a body fighting to survive for torturously long moments and then abruptly giving up the ghost; but in real life it was the most numbing, hair-raising thing he'd ever seen. Even then it had felt unreal – probably because at some subconscious level he couldn't bring himself to accept what he was seeing – though now, in retrospect, it seemed naive to have expected the situation with Louise to be resolved any other way. They always undertook to ensure the crime would go unreported. That was their firm guarantee; they had dozens and dozens of satisfied customers who were still free men, who were at no risk of losing their liberty, and if he asked no questions about how this was brought about, he'd be told no lies – so he hadn't asked. Of course he hadn't. And even now, appalled again by the memory of Louise's final, futile death struggles, he didn't think he'd necessarily have wanted them to take a different course of action. He hadn't known the girl well enough to like her, much less care about her, but he wouldn't have wished such a fate upon her – that was never his intention, and he needed to keep reassuring himself of that; it had never been his plan to . . . *murder* (yes, like it or not, that was the word). And yet, loath to admit it though he was, it suited his purpose. Now there was absolutely *no* danger she would talk – you could never say that about someone you'd paid off or simply threatened.

Oh, it was hideous; there was no denying it – her eyes

frozen in a lovely face turned purple and disfigured; her body, once young and supple, now cold, broken, stiffening, being wrapped in soulless plastic, bound with fishing twine like some demonic Christmas package – but it was for the best. Louise Jennings was now gone. It was over for her. But for him, life must go on.

Somewhere inside a distant voice berated him for attempting to rationalise it in this way, but he wanted to shout the voice down as if it wasn't his own (good Christ, was he going mad?). He hadn't *sought* this outcome, he reiterated to himself, but in all honesty how else could his freedom be guaranteed? Alright, there was no doubt it hadn't been too clever getting himself into this mess in the first place, but you couldn't roll back time . . . and Jesus you didn't want to do or say anything that might antagonise men like this. No Sir, not in any shape or form. You had to *approve* of men like this. He almost cackled, he was so frightened, and again he wondered if shock had driven him mad.

The car now slowed to another halt, disrupting his thoughts.

A door opened and one of the men – by the sounds of it, the driver – climbed out. Blenkinsop knew what this meant, and at that moment it seemed like the greatest relief in his life. When they'd picked him up previously, black tape had been used to mask the vehicle's registration mark. No doubt, once they'd blindfolded him and put him in the car, they'd stripped it away again. Now they were probably re-applying it. When the driver returned, Blenkinsop was told to climb out.

The two other men went first, one of them lending him a hand.

Initially, his legs were shaking so much that he could hardly stand up – but he'd manage it, because *nothing* was going to keep him here. It was over and he was out of this, and at last he could get away from these people and the terrible thing he'd done. Slowly, they removed his blindfold. It was now dark, there wasn't even a streetlamp nearby, but he still had to blink until his eyes adjusted.

To one side, he spotted the vehicle he'd just driven in; it was the same white Range Rover with tinted windows that they'd collected him with earlier. But he pointedly didn't look at it – that was the last thing he wanted; to know any more about these guys than he knew already. In any case, his own car, a new model Audi, was sitting alone in the lay-by. It was in a slightly different position from where he'd left it earlier, but that didn't surprise him. He'd had to surrender his keys so that they could move it; a car like that left for half the day in a place like this would attract attention. Beyond the Audi, the fields were hidden by the night. The narrow country lane curved off into opaque shadow.

Two of the men now faced him. Despite everything he knew and had already seen, he drew a sharp breath. The hair on his scalp prickled like wildfire.

They were masked again. He hadn't seen their faces once, which was exactly how he wanted it, but those masks themselves had become a thing of horror – made from orange and purple wool respectively – yet fearfully implicit of violent crime. It wasn't just the masks: their bodies were solid, bulky, powerfully built, and clad in overalls. Their hands were gloved, their feet no doubt booted, perhaps with steel toecaps; the final perfect touch for the modern-day hoodlum's killing outfit. How often he'd seen figures like these on television or in the newspapers: serial murderers, gangsters, terrorists – and, of course, rapists, a heinous club of which he was now a paid-up member.

At least, he assumed he was paid up.

When the man in the orange mask next spoke, he confirmed that this was the case.

'Apparently we're in full receipt of the cash, Mr Blenkinsop,' he said, slipping a mobile phone back into his overalls pocket. 'It's all cleared. So as far as we're concerned, our transaction is complete. You'll never hear from us again, except in the occasional discreet mail drop, which is the only way you'll be able to request our services a second time.'

Blenkinsop nodded. The mere thought of getting involved with these characters again was enough to make him faint. Just having them in such close proximity to him, and knowing what they were capable of, made him want to turn and run for his life.

'You can drive home from here, yeah?'

Again, Blenkinsop nodded. 'Yes . . .' he whispered. 'Yes, I'll be fine.'

'And your wife won't ask any questions?'

Good Lord, Yvonne! Blenkinsop hadn't thought about her once during today's activities. Even now that it was all over, it was agony to do so.

'She's . . . er, she's abroad with my daughter,' he said.

'Course, it doesn't really matter whether she does or doesn't,' the one in the purple mask added. 'It doesn't matter if anyone asks you any questions. You know the answers you need to give.'

'Yes.'

'You're a client of ours, Mr Blenkinsop,' Orange added. 'And we respect you for that. Not many men would have the bottle to do what you've done. But we're not in the liking or trusting business. Bear this in mind – you don't know anything about us, but we know an awful lot about you. Where you live, where you work, where you socialise. And it's going to stay that way. From now on, we'll be keeping you under covert surveillance. Not all the time obviously, but you'll never know when we're there and when we're not. This is another of those insurance things, I'm sure you understand.'

Blenkinsop couldn't speak; he simply nodded again.

'If there's any indication that you . . . shall we say, even feel tempted to discuss things that you shouldn't be discussing – with anyone at all – then be prepared to suffer a very severe repercussion.'

Blenkinsop would have swallowed, but he had no spittle left in his mouth.

'That's not a threat, by the way. It's just the way things are. So don't go off disliking us. After all, you're a man after our own heart.'

Blenkinsop smiled weakly, then lurched around and marched to his Audi. Climbing in, he found the keys in the ignition, switched the engine on and drove away. It was only ten miles from here to London. At this late hour, it should be plain sailing. Yet he already knew it would be the darkest, loneliest road he'd ever taken.

Chapter 11

When Heck woke that morning, the first thing he thought
was that he was being hit over the head with a plank. The
next thing, he was bewildered to hear the sound of someone
clattering around in his kitchen. He squinted with pain-fuzzed
vision at the bedside clock; it wasn't yet eight, but there was
no doubt there was somebody else here. He got up shakily
– slightly nauseous, his mouth lined with fur – and stumbled
down the hall, which was filled with the scent of grilled
bacon.

'Morning,' Gemma said from in front of the range, where
she was juggling pots and pans.

'What are you doing here?'

'You don't remember?'

'I, er . . .' Slowly and sluggishly, his memories of the
previous night began to return. 'Oh, yeah . . . ouch.' He
touched his forehead delicately.

'How's your head?' she asked, opening and closing the
cutlery drawer seemingly as loudly as she could.

'This is one of those occasions when I think I could live
without it.'

'You smell like a camel.'

He glanced down and saw that he was still wearing his jeans, t-shirt and socks from the night before, all rumpled and sweat soaked. 'You put me to bed?'

'Who else?'

'Didn't bother getting me undressed then, eh?'

'Making you comfortable wasn't a priority. If I was going to sleep on your sofa, I had to get you out of the lounge.'

'You slept on the sofa?' Heck could scarcely believe it.

'How do you like your eggs?'

'Erm . . . poached.'

'Okay, coming up. Bacon, beans, sausage?'

Only now did he notice the food items arrayed along the worktop. Some were still in packages. 'Where's this stuff come from? I haven't got any of this in.'

'I've been round the corner to the supermarket.'

'So this is the condemned man's last breakfast, is it?'

'Just get a shower, Heck, get dressed, and present yourself in a fit state for duty.'

'Correct me if I'm wrong, but I'm actually at home here . . . on holiday?'

She glared at him. 'You've stolen a mountain of police evidence. You're lucky you're not enjoying an extended holiday at Her Majesty's pleasure. Now do as I say.'

Heck did, taking a long shower and climbing into a clean pair of shorts and a vest. When he wandered back, their two breakfasts were on the table, along with a round of toast, a jug of orange juice and a pot of coffee.

'Just like the old days,' he said, sitting opposite her.

'Nothing like the old days,' she corrected him. 'Eat, while it's hot.'

'Only you could make an invitation to breakfast sound like an order from a concentration camp guard.' But feeling refreshed and suddenly hungry, he tucked in.

She watched him as he ate, barely picking at her own

food. 'First of all, let's hear what you've got,' she finally said.

He regarded her over the rim of his coffee cup. 'What do you mean?'

'After all these months and months of backbreaking work, with no tangible results, what reason is there to persist with this enquiry? You must have a reason.'

'I've got thirty-eight reasons.'

'Thirty-eight *possible* reasons.' She sighed. 'Heck . . . we have to face the truth. There's no guarantee these women haven't gone off on purpose. There are all sorts of explanations why someone might want to disappear. We don't know what goes on in people's lives. Look . . . remember back in the 1980s, there was the case of the Oxford don? He was about to be awarded a professorship and made head of his department. The kids from his first marriage were all grown-up and successful in their own right. He had another kid on the way courtesy of his second wife, who was a lot younger than him and hot as hell. I mean, this guy had everything to live for. Yet, the morning after the award ceremony he vanished. They found his car in a lane off the M40. The keys were still in it. His wallet was still in it. There was even a solid gold watch, engraved, that his family had bought him in honour of the award – it had been left on the dashboard. Aside from that there was no trace. Then, about six years later, he was found – working under a false name on a sheep farm in the Outer Hebrides. And living rough. I mean, this guy slept in a croft with a peat sod roof.'

'Remind me why he did that.'

'I don't know why. Some kind of breakdown. The point is it happens.'

'Gemma, that was a one-off. We're talking nearly forty people . . . '

'None of whom you'd class as vulnerable.'

'Exactly.' He took another swig of coffee. 'There are no children on our list, no OAPs, no mental patients. The youngest was eighteen, the eldest forty-nine. More to the point, they're mostly professional types, organised, able to look after themselves. Like it or not, that's a pattern. I mean, it's an unlikely one, but it's still a pattern. Not only that, all our women vanished during routine activities . . . while they were doing something they did every day. None were taken while on holiday for example, or on day trips to other parts of the country . . .'

'Heck . . .'

'If you're going to abduct someone, and not make a complete bollocks of it, you've got to watch them, memorise their patterns of behaviour. I hate using this analogy but, in nature, predators hunt along game trails. Because then they know exactly when the prey animals are coming, and exactly how many or how few of them there'll be. After that, all they have to do is pick their moment and intercept . . .'

'*Heck!*'

He clamped his mouth shut.

'Funnily enough,' she said, 'I read your comparative-case-analysis. You know . . . the one you left in my in-tray and covered with red marker pen "More urgent than anything else you're doing today!" I'm fully aware why you fingered these particular cases and clumped them together. But it's still too thin. Apart from the circumstantial stuff, there's no evidence of abduction, let alone abduction by the same individual.'

'So what are we doing here? Why are we having breakfast together?'

For a few moments, Gemma looked as if she didn't know. She pushed her plate aside, even though it was still full. 'Tell me about this new lead you've got. The one you mentioned yesterday morning.'

'Oh, yeah . . . that.'

She jabbed a warning finger. 'Don't you dare tell me that was a lie!'

'It wasn't, don't worry. Look . . . you go through to the incident room. I'll finish getting dressed.'

While Heck got dressed properly, Gemma took their dirty dishes into the kitchen, scraped them and shoved them into the dishwasher, before drifting through to his so-called incident room. She peered again at the faces ranked on its far wall. So often in her career, she'd perused photographs of victims of violent crime. On first viewing, they nearly always enraged and appalled her. Only later on was she able to click into 'professional investigator' mode, and treat them as just another part of the job.

As she'd insisted several times, there was no guarantee that this particular bunch actually *were* victims, but somehow, seeing them all together like this, linked if nothing else by so much painstaking analysis, she began to suspect that they probably *were*, and it had a melancholy effect on her. In almost all cases, they were smiling or laughing, having been photographed among friends and loved ones. The majority were family snapshots, taken on holiday or at functions. How happy they'd all been while posing for these pictures, how bright their world had seemed. How terrified they'd have been to know the darkness that awaited them.

Heck reappeared in jeans, pulling on a sweater.

'Well?' she asked.

He started sifting through papers. 'I actually had two new leads I was going to run with.' He found a bulging buff folder, checked it was the right one, and then sat on the desk, indicating that she could have the chair. 'First of all,' he said, opening the folder, 'you accept that in some force areas these disappearances were treated as abductions?'

'Which is why they were passed to us.'

He nodded. 'Two summers ago down in Brighton, a lady called Miranda Yates dropped out of sight while loading shopping into the boot of her car. Both the car, which was left with its boot open – I'm guessing the abductor hadn't closed it properly and the wind caught it – and the car park, were treated as crime scenes. This photograph was taken later in the day.'

He handed Gemma a glossy, which depicted a mass of bystanders held back by police tape. She assessed it. It was common practice to take covert photographs of crime scene onlookers. Astonishing as it seemed to police officers, some perpetrators actually *did* return to see if anyone was appreciating their handiwork.

'Which face are we looking at?' she asked.

Heck pointed out a young man in the front row. He was in his early twenties, with neatly combed dark hair. His vacant expression was not wholly visible because he was turning slightly, plus he was wearing a pair of sunglasses. Aside from that, the only noticeable thing about him was his slightly overlarge forehead.

'I've sent copies of this to every local intelligence officer in England and Wales, and it's a non-starter,' Heck said. 'As his features are partly obscured, no facial recognition has been possible thus far. But have a good look at him, and now check this other photo.' He produced a second glossy, also depicting a crowd, though on this occasion gathered against a row of skeletal trees. 'This was taken in Aberystwyth last March. Julie-Ann Netherby, a student at the university, was last seen in the basement of her hall of residence, doing her laundry. This picture was taken outside the hall, the following day.'

Gemma scanned the picture and almost immediately spotted someone who might have been the same man. Even less of this second chap's face was visible – he was standing behind someone else, but aside from having shorter hair and a thin, wispy moustache, he was undoubtedly similar. He even had the same prominent forehead.

'I suppose it looks like him,' she said.

'Agreed, but I know what you're going to say. It isn't *definitely* him.' Heck took the photos back and filed them. 'I admit this one's a long shot. At present I'm referring to him as "the Kid". He's a suspect, but until we find out who he is – and all enquiries at the uni drew a blank – there isn't much more we can do on that.'

'So what's the other lead?'

Heck dug out three more photographs. 'Do you remember in one of my previous reports when I mentioned a suspect called Shane Klim?'

Gemma nodded. 'The sex offender from Birmingham?'

'Correct. Let me refresh your memory. Last January, a Newcastle estate agent called Kelly Morgan failed to report for work and subsequently wasn't seen again. What really bothered the other girls in her office was that a couple of times over the previous weeks, she'd said that she thought someone was stalking her. She'd only seen him in daytime, and initially thought he was a jogger. But when she kept on spotting him, in different parts of the city, she became concerned. She said he was heavily built and that he always wore a hood. That in itself proves nothing of course. However, if you recall, a hooded figure was also captured on CCTV passing the front door of Annette Connor's house in Liverpool. She disappeared a year last April. Here's the still.'

Gemma checked it out. It was a black and white image-capture, very grainy, clearly taken at night. It showed a bulky man, wearing a dark leather jacket and, underneath that, a hoodie top with the hood pulled up. He was only photographed side-on as he strolled head down along the pavement.

She shrugged. 'And I'll say again what I said last time – that could be anyone.'

Heck nodded. 'Could be. Probably a million men walk past that house every year. But remember Margaret Price, another one who disappeared doing the shopping? She was one of our South London girls, and she'd also confided in a friend that someone had recently alarmed her. She was coming home from work one misty autumn night, when she saw a man jogging past her house. She thought it was strange because he didn't seem the jogging type – he had a heavy build and was puffing hard. Apparently, he was wearing a hood. And a horror mask.'

Gemma sighed. 'Not this again . . .'

'It's important, ma'am,' Heck said. 'Margaret Price glimpsed his face as he passed, and he was wearing a horror mask. At least that's what she thought.'

'And if I recall correctly,' Gemma said, 'your contention was that it wasn't a horror mask? You wondered if it was his actual face. First of all, Heck, we haven't got a statement from this Margaret Price – so it's all hearsay. Secondly, it was almost Halloween, so if it *was* a horror mask, there could be a perfectly innocent explanation. Thirdly, we've discussed this already . . .'

'Suppose that what Margaret Price actually saw was a mass of scar tissue?' Heck argued. 'That might explain why he was hooded all the time. Look, it's partly a hunch, I admit . . . but Shane Klim would be an excellent fit.'

He'd brought Shane Klim, a repeat rapist from the Midlands, to his superiors' attention previously, on the basis that while escaping from Rotherwood high security prison on the Fylde Coast four years ago, Klim had been attacked by guard dogs and had had his face very badly bitten (in fact 'torn to bits' was how one witness described it). Though Klim killed two of the dogs and got clean away, it was deemed highly likely that his face would be disfigured afterwards. The problem was that Klim had not been seen since, so no one really knew how badly he'd been scarred.

Gemma pondered what little they knew. 'And you're absolutely sure there's no one else in the system with that extent of facial damage?'

'No one matches that profile at all,' Heck said.

She assessed the most recent image they had of Klim; a custodial mugshot taken before his escape from Rotherwood. It portrayed a brutish man with wide cheekbones, heavy brows, a broken nose, piggy eyes, a shaven head and jughandle ears. 'Do you have any info on his whereabouts yet?'

'Not yet, but I soon will.' Heck handed over the third and final picture. 'Because this is our next new lead. I only came up with it the other day, but I think it's a goer. Take a look at Ron O'Hoorigan, a habitual house-breaker. He was in Rotherwood prison at the same time, and I've now learned that he shared a cell with Klim for nearly two years.'

O'Hoorigan didn't look quite as mean as Klim, but Gemma knew how looks could be deceptive. He had a lean hatchet-face, with thick, dark sideburns and longish dark hair which hung to his shoulders in a greasy mop.

'You think he may know something?' she asked.

'Cons talk, especially when they're banged up together twenty-three hours a day.'

'Heck, you seriously think Klim told O'Hoorigan he was planning to escape?'

'It wouldn't be the first time that happened.'

'Even if he did, he's hardly likely to have told him where he was going afterwards, or what his plans were for the continuation of his criminal career once he'd got out.'

Heck looked frustrated. 'We won't know unless we ask O'Hoorigan, will we?'

'Is O'Hoorigan still inside?'

'No. He was released eight months ago. As far as we know, he's now on his home patch in Salford, Manchester.'

'That's your old hunting ground, isn't it?'

'That was a long time ago,' Heck said. 'But I know the area, yeah.'

She handed the photo back, saying nothing.

'So what do you think?' he asked. 'I know there are a few assumptions here, but have we wound things up prematurely, or what?'

'Come on, Heck, this is a hundred to one.'

'Yeah, but if I'd given you this lead a few weeks ago, wouldn't that have changed things?'

'Not necessarily. Look . . . at the end of the day it's about money. There's nothing here to justify so much further expense.'

'Have I ever been wrong about stuff like this before?'

'On other cases, no, but on this one it's different.'

'All respect, ma'am, but we can't say that yet. Look, this one isn't finished. Not as far as I'm concerned.'

She got up and walked agitatedly around the room. Finally she rounded on him. 'If I'm going to play ball with you on this, and write your leave down as a front so that you can continue undercover while you follow this new lead, you're not going to disappoint me, are you?' She fixed him with so intense a gaze that at first he barely heard her. 'I mean, you're not going to let me down, Heck?'

'Are you serious?'

'Well you're not leaving me much choice. The other day I said you looked knackered, and I meant it. You still do. You look shot. But I know you, Heck . . . you're not going to let this drop under any circs, you're going to press on regardless, despite it being the most flagrant breach of procedure I've ever known. So if you don't get killed because you've got no back-up, you'll probably end up losing your job. Either way, I'll finish up without the services of one of my most experienced detectives. And that's something I can't afford right now. Not that I appreciate being blackmailed like this.'

'What about Laycock? He'll never sign off on it.'

'Need-to-know basis.'

'You're going to go over his head?' Heck was astonished.

'There is no over Laycock's head. Not in NCG. I'll have to go behind his back.'

'Yeah, but that won't last. How're you going to justify me being in deep cover? I mean, deep cover from whom? Someone else in the job? That's how he'll see it.'

'Leave me to worry about that.'

'I'm serious, Gemma.' Heck got to his feet. 'He'll have to know about this at some point, and then what's he going to think?'

'Just make sure we've got a result to show him. Then he won't have any gripes.'

Heck mulled it over. The stakes were suddenly drastically high. Much higher than he was close to being comfortable with. 'And no one else is going to know about this?'

She shrugged. 'If I have to, I'll let Des know . . . but aside from him, no one. You report directly to me, okay?'

He nodded.

'Promptly and regularly,' she said.

'And you'll do the paperwork?'

'I'll do the paperwork.'

'That's always music to my ears. But you know . . . I wouldn't rush to put anything on paper just yet.'

'You mean in case this goes belly up?' She stared at him. 'Don't let it.'

'You'll lose deniability.'

'We're not all rule-bending maniacs, Heck. I can't live that way.' She grabbed her car keys. 'Now look . . . just this one lead, okay? I'm serious. You run this new lead to ground and you do it low key. And after that, zip, kaput, it's over.'

He nodded, but said nothing.

At the door, she turned and looked at him again. Briefly the domineering force was absent. She seemed concerned, but also a little disappointed. 'You realise this is more trust than I've ever put in anyone, Heck? And the irony is that you're one of the least trustworthy people I know.'

Leaving him with that thought, she turned and descended the stairs. Heck watched her from the top, until she'd left the building. Then he went back into his flat, closing the door behind him.

Chapter 12

When he went into work that morning, Ian Blenkinsop felt as if he'd just got up after a night of heavy drinking. His stomach was hollow, his head throbbing.

On arrival, he was greeted cheerfully, as always, by his secretary Sally, which made him feel positively nauseous. It wasn't Sally's fault. She was forty, but very well kept, with a sizeable bosom, slick, chestnut red hair and handsome, feline looks. Many was the time he'd nursed an erection in the lavatories while thinking about her. He'd once had similar designs on Sally to those he'd had on Louise; in fact he'd told himself a couple of times – usually in his cups – that should the 'thing' with Louise go okay, he'd generate a plan for Sally. Now the mere thought of that was unbearable to him.

He closed himself into his office, which was not his custom – normally he'd leave the connecting door open between his and Sally's work areas. Then he walked to the window, which ran floor to ceiling, and opened the blind, admitting the morning sunshine that was breaking through the thin wash of clouds in ethereal shafts.

From this side of the building, the dome of St Paul's

cathedral dominated the skyline. To Blenkinsop's mind it was still the most majestic structure in London. Born from the ashes of the Great Fire, it had withstood everything the centuries could throw at it: time, the elements and of course Hitler's aerial onslaught, which had flattened so much of the surrounding city. He realised that he'd taken its magnificence for granted until now. What a dauntless symbol it was: of man's fearlessness in the face of tragedy, of his devotion to the might and mystery of God – things that Ian Blenkinsop felt hugely distanced from at this moment.

There was a tap on the door and Sally came in with his coffee. She seemed a little subdued. He wondered why. Was it because he'd been abrupt with her on his arrival, or could it be that now he knew he was a brute on the inside, it was starting to show on the outside? That was nonsense, of course. Even Dr Jekyll, when he'd become Mr Hyde, hadn't manifested as a physical monster.

Jekyll and Hyde.

There'd been times in the past – poring sweat-soaked over some particularly lurid and illegal pornographic imagery, or being driven back to his hotel in downtown Lagos or Sana'a, or wherever it was, in the early hours of the morning – when Blenkinsop would consider himself in these terms. But it was no solace to think that way now. These things – especially the thing he'd engaged in last night – weren't nearly as romantic as Robert Louis Stevenson's famous romp. The popular image of Hyde was a wicked but likeable rogue, who flitted among the ladies of the night in a dapper suit, a topper and a cape, winning them over with his wolfish smile, and then abusing them in masterful ways that might, in some cases, leave them begging for more.

Sexy anti-heroes of that nature were rarely to be found in real life. And they weren't to be found at all in Ian Blenkinsop.

He stared out at the City, at its towers and temples of commerce. Would this wonderful view ever be the same to him? Would he ever again feel part of this frenetic, good-natured hive that he so loved, knowing what he now knew for certain about himself – that he was a beast, an aberration? He tried to remind himself, as he had tried many times since yesterday, that this wasn't as wholesome a place as it appeared on the surface; that there were numerous individuals walking these streets right now who had dark and deadly desires. But how many of them actually converted those desires into reality? How many were so driven by lust that they could destroy the lives of others at a whim?

Only a small few shared that inclination – a marginalised few, a reviled few.

But was he really one of *them* – because of one incident?

To all intents and purposes, he was normal. He was honest, he worked hard; he engaged in philanthropy when the mood was on him. And yes, alright, there was that other side to his personality, that secret side, but he only unleashed that when he visited foreign shores where such deeds were a form of currency, where they might not be approved but were tolerated so long as they were out of sight and out of mind, where the other participants – if not always willing – were at least prepared to endure it for the sake of their families. It was hardly what you'd call 'vanilla sex', quite the opposite in fact, but at least it put money in their pockets and bread on their tables, at least they benefited in the long run.

But that wasn't the same thing.

For all the 'experiments' he'd indulged in while overseas, all the taboos he'd broken, all the cruelty and brutality he'd inflicted, there'd always been that all-important factor of consent. And of course, never before – never once – had it ended in murder.

Murder.

Once again, the magnitude of that simple word was immense. Rationalise it though he may try, deny it if possible – and he'd tried that too, reminding himself over and over that it had never been his intent to kill – it still haunted his every thought. He'd barely slept a wink last night even though he'd taken tablets to try and knock himself out. When he did manage to sleep, it had filled his dreams. And it would certainly never diminish in *this* environment. Even as he stood in his office, he heard a snippet of conversation from the next room, where Sally was speaking to someone on the internal phone: 'No, that's Louise Jennings's department. But I don't think you'll get her today – apparently she's off. No, I don't know whether she's reported sick or not, I just know she hasn't come in for work. Strange really, because you know how dependable she is.'

He continued to gaze down through the window – and his heart almost skipped a beat.

A City of London police car was prowling along Cornhill. It clearly wasn't coming here, because it headed off along Leadenhall and vanished from view, but was this now something else he'd always need to be wary of – the law? Would he quake with fear every time he saw a police uniform?

It still amazed him how, in one fell swoop, the orientation of his entire world had changed around, and how there was nothing he could do to restore it. That was the worst part of it: if he could only have the choice again . . .

'Mr Blenkinsop,' Sally said, sticking her head in. 'I have Mr Rylands from Newline Exports to see you. You've an appointment with him at nine-fifteen.'

Blenkinsop glanced around, and nodded. She regarded him with puzzlement, and he realised that he hadn't even taken his coat off yet, and was still holding his briefcase.

'Two minutes, Sally.'

'Are you alright? Under the weather maybe?'

'I'm fine.' He stripped his coat off, sat at his desk and forced a smile.

'You work too hard, Ian. Should've gone on holiday with your family.'

'Rarely have truer words been spoken.'

When she closed the door, he had to struggle to fight back tears. That wouldn't do – someone was about to come in and chat with him. But the tears flowed anyway, and as they were mainly tears of self-pity – for the mess he'd got himself into, and the fear and insecurity he'd ushered into his fami-ly's life – he hated himself all the more for it.

Chapter 13

Heck began to suspect the van was following him when he spotted it on the M6 motorway. He'd first observed it on the M1, about sixty miles further south, where it had appeared to be keeping a steady pace a hundred yards behind him. It was a hire van, a transit, high-sided and brown in colour, but so covered in oil and grime that no insignia was visible on its bodywork.

The first occasion he noticed it, he thought nothing of it. It was now midday on a Monday, and the traffic flow from south to north was, as usual, heavy and relatively slow moving. In addition, there was nothing in the vehicle's demeanour to make him suspicious. It was proceeding along the motorway like so many others – what else was there to say? But when he spotted it on the M6 as well, still close behind, having passed numerous slip roads that it could have turned down, he had his first misgiving.

He pulled into the slow lane and reduced his speed to about forty m.p.h. The transit van cruised slowly past. It was impossible to see who was driving it or how many there were, but soon it was a significant distance ahead. He relaxed and eased his foot back onto the gas. However, ten minutes

later, he saw that the van had also pulled into the slow lane
– for no apparent reason, as there were open spaces in front
of it. Once he'd overtaken it, it slid casually back into the
middle lane and began to speed up, as though to keep up
with him. Initially, Heck wondered if Gemma had given him
a guardian angel. But he soon dismissed that idea. She would
have told him; it would serve no purpose for her not to. He
picked up his mobile and was about to tap in her number,
to enquire – but then decided that if she'd had nothing at
all to do with this, she might be panicked to learn that his
cover had already been compromised, and pull the plug.

The next possibility was that Commander Laycock
suspected he might be up to something. Heck dismissed this
idea too. Laycock would consider that he had far more
important things to do than keep tabs on a damned ranker
like Heck, and even if he didn't, had he the slightest inkling
that the enquiry might be continuing, he'd have called Heck
to his office by now and demanded an explanation.

Of course, there was still a chance that the brown van
was completely innocent. By two o'clock in the afternoon,
Heck was in Cheshire, and about forty miles from the junction with the A580, the East Lancashire dual carriageway
connecting the motorway with Manchester and Liverpool;
the brown van was still an ominous presence at his rear. As
the traffic at last began to break up, he got his foot down
– he didn't race away, but accelerated slowly and purposefully. The dingy brown shape fell further and further behind,
making no obvious attempt to hurry in pursuit.

Even after he'd lost sight of it, Heck continued to accel-
erate. When he reached the A580, he swerved down the exit
ramp, gunning the engine hard to get through the traffic
lights at the bottom, and circled the large roundabout, finally
peeling off and heading east towards Manchester. He still
wasn't sure whether or not somebody had been tailing him,

but if they had been he felt that he'd lost them now – not that this incident was something he could dismiss as unimportant. Ten miles later, he pulled into a petrol station to fill up and buy himself a bottle of water. It was only when he'd got back into his Fiat and was inserting his key into the ignition that he glanced across the forecourt and saw the brown van parked near the station entrance.

Heck was tempted to get out and walk over there, but he resisted. He appraised it. Again, its driving cab was too filled with shadow for him to work out who was in there, though someone was clearly sitting behind the steering wheel.

Casually as he could, Heck started his engine and pulled back out onto the dual carriageway. He drove at a steady fifty for three miles, but at the next junction pulled off onto a B-road, entering Highworth, one of several Greater Manchester townships he remembered from his youth; former coal-mining districts that were now heavily unemployed and run down. At this time of day, there was still plenty of traffic and Heck was forced to slow down to accommodate it. He continued to watch his rearview mirror, and it wasn't long before the brown van reappeared. Now he was sure it was following him. He slowed until it was about thirty yards behind. At the next island, he halted, giving way to traffic from his right. When he finally pushed forward into the flow, the brown van followed. They halted at the next 'give way' line together, the brown van directly behind him.

This time vehicles came piling past from the left. Heck would normally have nosed his way out carefully, but he waited until a minuscule gap approached, and suddenly rammed his accelerator to the floor, screeching out into it. A blue Toyota had to break sharply and tooted with annoyance, but the purpose was served. Heck accelerated hard as he swung right the way around the traffic island, and then braked again. Their positions had been neatly reversed; now he was sitting behind the brown van.

Its reaction pleased him. A split second later it had the opportunity to pull out into the traffic, but it simply sat there, its engine chugging, as if the driver was uncertain about where he was and what he should do next. Heck waited patiently. At length, the van pulled right, taking a town centre road, moving carefully and slowly – too slowly. It stopped at each set of lights, its handbrake applied, and then set off again, always keeping a steady pace, making no attempt to turn – being driven without aim or direction, Heck realised. As the town centre fell gradually behind them, a sixth sense made him check that his seatbelt was secure.

Up ahead there was open land. Several drab-looking housing estates stood to the left, but on the right lay the grey hummocks of slag heaps. The traffic was thinning quickly. From sheer instinct, Heck felt for his pocket where, under normal circumstances, there would be a police radio by which he could inform Comms that he was about to embark on a chase; finding nothing there was an ugly reminder that he was going it alone. They cruised on for a mile before halting at the next set of lights – and that was when the van suddenly lurched forward, rocketing through the red, causing cars to scream to standstills both from left and right.

Heck sped after it, following a road that was suddenly open and half empty, which was massively to his advantage. His Fiat, though ancient and battered, was more than a match for a ramshackle old hire van. He hadn't hit seventy before he was close behind it. Frantic, the other driver swung across the opposing carriageway without indicating – causing yet more vehicles to scream to halts, a couple sliding off the tarmac onto the grass verge – and then bounced and jolted its way down an unmade track, which ran straight as a ribbon across the spoil land.

Heck wasn't able to follow immediately. There was a confused blaring of horns as the opposing traffic tried to force its way past. Seconds ticked by while he watched the brown van slowly diminish, drawing a trail of dust behind it. Swearing, he finally worked his way through onto the dirt track, where he too jolted over ruts and potholes, each one a crashing impact beneath his feet. Despite this, he was gaining ground fast. He saw the van spin left onto another unmade track. However, this one was so bad that it was barely distinguishable from the surrounding clinker. The van swayed dangerously, rubble spurting from its wheels. Heck veered after it. Up ahead there was a dead end; what looked like an old car park attached to a row of prefabricated industrial buildings, all derelict and blackened by fire. The van screeched into this area and tried to pull a handbrake turn, in order to double back as Heck came dashing in after it. But if the van had *ever* been designed for such manoeuvres, it was now way past them. It tipped spectacularly onto its nearside wheels – briefly resembling a stunt vehicle in a Bond movie – and then crashed over onto its roof, rolling twice before coming to rest in a cloud of dust, smoke and debris.

Heck slammed his brakes to the floor, skidding sideways, a stench of melted rubber filling his nostrils. He leapt out. As he did, a lithe figure wormed its way through the van's shattered windscreen. It was clad entirely in black – black gloves, black boots, black combat trousers, and a black 'hoodie' sweat top with the hood pulled up.

'Police officer!' Heck shouted, running forward. 'Stay where you are!'

The hooded figure tried to dart for the line of derelict buildings, but whoever he was, he was limping and Heck quickly caught up with him, leaping onto his back – only to be flipped forward over the guy's shoulder and land heavily in the dirt.

Heck was winded, but still managed to roll away and scramble up into a crouch.

The hooded figure backed off slowly, but the hood had now come down to reveal that *he* was actually a *she*. In fact, *he* was the girl from The Raven's Nest, the dusky-skinned, mini-skirted beauty who'd whupped Heck at pool.

She was in less sensual mode now, breathing hard, her face shining with sweat as she retreated. When Heck got to his feet, she snapped a flick knife open, its long, slender blade glinting like ice.

'I told you I'm a police officer,' Heck warned her when he'd recovered from his surprise. 'You stick that thing in me and I die, you'll get thirty years minimum.'

'You think I've come all this way because I want to kill you?' she panted.

'Okay . . . so put the knife down.'

'Uh-uh.' She shook her head. 'I'm not being arrested.'

'If you knew how many times I hear that in the average day . . .'

'Just back off! I don't want to hurt you.' But she winced as she retreated, her right leg almost folding beneath her.

Heck shook his head. 'I knew Bobby Ballamara was way down the list when they were giving out cerebella, but I never thought he'd be stupid enough to hire an amateur like you.'

'I'd have told you last night, if you'd given me a chance . . . I don't know anyone called Ballamara.'

'Sorry love, but that won't cut it. Whatever you say, or don't say, all they'll need to do is find evidence that you were on his payroll, and anything that happens to me will come back to haunt *him* in a big way.'

'Look . . . I just want to find my sister.'

Heck stopped. 'What?'

'If you'd listened in the pub there'd be no need for any of this.'

'Your sister?'

'My name's Lauren Wraxford. Does that ring a bell?'

'Should it?'

She gave a wry smile. 'Yeah, it should. But it's no surprise it doesn't.' She was still breathing hard and warding him off with the knife, but she now knuckled at her right cheek. To his surprise, he realised that she was trying to wipe away a tear. 'If you don't recognise "Lauren Wraxford", maybe you recognise "Genene Wraxford"?'

'Genene Wrax . . .' *That* name was definitely familiar. Heck placed it: on a mis-per file – one sent down to Scotland Yard at his request by the West Yorkshire Police. It had featured a colour snapshot of a beautiful black girl posed in a graduate ceremony gown, holding a law degree.

'Went to Leeds Uni?' he ventured.

She nodded; her eyes were now brimming with tears.

'There seems to be a resemblance,' he said.

'Genene's my older sister.' She wiped irritably at her cheeks.

'Alright, I understand. Lauren . . . drop the blade, okay? Right now.'

She swallowed, finally closing the knife up and pocketing it, but making sure to keep a distance of several feet between them.

Heck made no further effort to approach. 'You're telling me that all this is because you're trying to find your sister?'

'I was only shadowing you. I wasn't doing anything wrong.'

'Until now. Now you're hampering a police investigation.'

'I thought the investigation was closed.'

'So why were you shadowing me?'

She shrugged. 'I didn't know what else to do.'

114

Heck mopped sweaty hair from his brow. 'If I remember rightly, Genene disappeared three years ago. Why's it taken you this long to get excited about it?'

'I've been away.'

'Away?'

'Afghanistan. Before that it was Iraq.'

'You're a soldier?'

'Was. Until recently. Royal Ordnance Corps, Combat Support Division.'

'That explains a lot.' Heck's side was hurting where she'd thrown him.

'Look, I'm sorry this has happened,' she blurted. 'I've been trying to get information through normal channels, but no one seems to know anything. Or they don't want to talk about it. You any idea how difficult it is for a member of the public to even speak to a copper these days? The small parts of police stations you're actually allowed into are operated by civvy nobodies who think that, just because they've got uniforms on, they can lord it over you.'

Heck dusted himself down before turning back towards his car.

She cautiously followed. 'It took me ages just to get your name.'

'Yeah, well I'm sorry, but like I said last night, you wasted your time.'

'Why? Is the investigation on, or isn't it?' She ran to catch up, snatching him by the arm. '*I'm talking to you!*'

Heck spun around. '*Hey!* Now you've stalked me all the way from London so you can threaten me with a knife. You carry on like this . . . ex-army or not, I'll throw your arse in jail.'

Her dark cheeks had coloured, her eyes shone. She wasn't crying now, he noticed. And she didn't release him.

'You're not just going to walk away from me!' she hissed.

'Look, my sister's been missing thirty months and now it's not a case that you can't tell me anything . . . now it's a case that you *won't*? Are you having a laugh?'

Heck yanked his arm free. 'I'm not answerable to you. I'm sorry about what's happened to your family, but I'm not going to divulge sensitive information to you or anyone else. To start with, I don't have the first clue who you really are. For all I know, you could be the bloody kidnapper.'

'You bastard!' she shouted, as he walked on.

'If you've got a complaint, take it to New Scotland Yard.'

'If you're not going to find her, I am . . .'

He reached his Fiat and opened it. 'I'd be more concerned about how you're going to get home, if I were you. That van looks like a write-off.'

'What . . . you think I can't make it out of here on foot? I used to deploy on ten-day patrols, for Christ's sake . . . through the most godforsaken mountains you've ever seen.'

'Good practice for getting back to Yorkshire, then.' He climbed in, closed the door and switched the engine on.

She limped up to his open window. 'I suppose you'd rather spend your shift dragging out paperwork? Or maybe nicking hard-working citizens for being impolite to their drug addict neighbours?' Heck put the car in gear. 'You just get on with all that,' she added. 'I'll go look for Genene. I'll start with this character Ballamara.'

Heck glanced round at her.

She smiled as she retreated. 'If I can find you, I can surely find him.'

'Miss Wraxford . . .?'

Despite having hurt her leg, she moved quickly away, stopping first at the wrecked van and pulling a heavy Bergen backpack out of it.

'Hey, Miss Wraxford!'

She ignored him, hoisting the pack onto her back and starting to walk.

He spun the car around after her, but she deliberately veered off the lot onto broken ground, crossing it diagonally towards the unmade track that had brought them here. It was several minutes later before he could pull up alongside her again.

'You are not to go looking for Bobby Ballamara!' he said through his window. 'You understand me?'

'What is he?' she scoffed. 'A gangster? You think that scares me? You think anyone in London scares me? I come from Leeds.'

'Just forget Bobby Ballamara. He's nothing to do with this case.'

'Let's see what *he's* got to say about it . . .'

'You'll be putting yourself in extreme danger . . .'

She laughed loudly. 'The time for playing it safe is over! We've been waiting three years to hear from you lot. There hasn't been a damn peep, so now my family has trusted *me* to get some answers. With or without your help.'

Before he could reply, she cut back across the spoil land, heading towards the main road. She was still limping, but covered the ground quickly, 'yomping' army style. By the time he reached the main road, she was on its verge, thumbing for a lift.

'You're more trouble than you're bloody worth!' he shouted, pulling up.

'Yeah?' She shifted away from him. 'Disappointingly, you've been no trouble at all.'

He jumped from the car. 'Do I have to arrest you for taking that transit van without its owner's consent?'

She looked surprised. 'I hired it.'

'And now you've dumped it.'

'I'll phone them and tell them where it is.'

'I can still take you in.'

'Go on then.' She folded her arms and waited. 'I won't resist. Only you didn't lock me up when I threatened to knife you . . . what's changed this time?'

Heck couldn't at first respond. In truth, there wasn't an answer he could give her.

'Get in the car,' he finally said.

'Aren't you supposed to be reading me my rights?'

'You're not under arrest. Just get in the car.'

Warily, she did as he asked, sliding into the front passenger seat.

Heck sighed as he walked around to the driver's door. He wasn't quite sure why he was doing this. But there was more truth in what the girl had said than even she might realise. Besides, he wasn't much of a tough guy when it came to human suffering. Too many cops turned a blind eye to it – either as a defensive mechanism to stop it upsetting them, or because they were heartless shithouses who genuinely didn't care.

'What's going on?' she asked, as he climbed in.

'First, I want proof that you're who you say you are.'

She felt under her sweat top and produced a driving licence. From the ID and photograph, she was indeed Lauren Wraxford.

'You've got bottle, Lauren, I'll give you that,' he said, as he switched the engine on and pulled away from the kerb. 'You've also got a grievance. I reckon the very least I can do is buy you a cup of coffee.'

Chapter 14

Heck pulled off the A580 on the outskirts of Manchester, into a bustling lorry park, where he halted, climbed out and headed on foot to a scruffy café sandwiched between a mountain of old tyres and a dilapidated shed with a sign over its lintel reading 'TOILET'. Lauren got out as well, and leaned against the bonnet of the car as she watched him.

In his jeans, sweater and leather jacket, her chaperon didn't look much like a cop, though she supposed he was a little more presentable now than he had been the previous night, when he'd been drunk and dishevelled and acting like a smartarse in that crappy London pub. Mind you, she supposed she'd looked a bit of a sight herself, dolled up like a teenage hooker.

She glanced over her shoulder into his car. A mass of paperwork had spilled from a zip folder on the back seat. It would be so easy just to stick her head in there and have a quick scan through it – but he might catch her and she didn't want that. For the moment, she needed to keep him on side. Last night, she'd even have let him take her back to his pad and screw her, if that was what he'd wanted. She'd believed that firmly at the time, and she still believed it now. That was how desperate she was to learn more about his investigation. Hell, it might even have been a pleasure. He wasn't unfanciable, in a rumpled, hard-bitten sort of way, though in truth Lauren rarely had time for love. Even when things were going well – and it was a long time since she'd been able to say that – sex was a purely mechanical process for her, designed to satisfy an urgent physical need. She'd had several lovers before, even a couple of proper boyfriends, but if there'd been anything deep and meaningful there, it had slipped past her.

'How's the leg?' Heck asked, returning with two lidded Styrofoam beakers.

Lauren realised that she'd been rubbing at it. 'It'll be okay. Banged my knee on the steering column when I crashed.'

He handed her a coffee. 'Seriously . . . you'd better report that van stolen as soon as you can, or you're going to get locked up.'

'Won't they check for prints, and see there are none there but mine?'

'They won't swab an old donkey-wagon like that for a minor offence like TWOC.' He glanced at her. 'I mean . . . so long as there's nothing in it that shouldn't be there.'

'Don't worry, there's nothing.'

He leaned next to her on the car, sipping his own drink, watching the afternoon traffic shunt noisily past. 'So your family sent you to find your sister?'

Lauren sighed. 'Not really. My family is basically my mum, Angel.'

'That's her name?'

'Yep.' Fleetingly, Lauren almost sounded scornful. 'Angel by name, angel by nature. She didn't want me to come at all. She said we should leave it to you lot.'

'Sounds like a sensible woman.'

'Oh, she's dead sensible, my mum.' Lauren sipped at her

coffee. 'So sensible that even though she's white, she married a black bloke back in the 1970s. Any idea what that meant back then – living in East Leeds?'

Heck pondered. 'Can't have been easy. But what does your dad think about this adventure you've embarked on?'

'Nothing. He was killed in an accident working on the railway . . . six years after they got wed. Left my mum to bring up two mixed-race kids on her own, on one of the roughest estates you've ever seen. And with no help from either side of the family, who, surprise-surprise, didn't want anything to do with her anymore.'

At one time Lauren would have been too embarrassed to elaborate on some of the things she'd experienced in her earliest youth: seeing her mother have to clean words written in excrement off their council flat door every morning. At the time the words had held no meaning for her, but the little girl had been able to read them and had stored them in her memory until she was older, and now there was no doubt in her mind about what phrases like 'white niggers' meant.

'You know,' she said. 'One day we received a letter put together with clippings of newspaper type. It went something like: "Watch out, because next I'm getting a wog or a wog lover. Signed . . . the Yorkshire Ripper." Mum took it to the police, but they told her to ignore it, saying it was nothing more than a joke. A joke . . . for a single mum and two young daughters living on their own in that wasteland. Some joke, eh?'

'Pretty grim,' Heck acknowledged. 'No wonder you and Genene were close.'

'Well . . . we weren't as close as we perhaps could have been.'

'Whatever, your Genene did very well to get to uni after a start in life like that.'

'That was Mum's doing.' Again, Lauren almost sounded resentful. 'She set us the best example she could. After Dad died, she took on two jobs – sitting on a supermarket till all day and checking coats at a nightclub in the evening – just so we didn't want for anything. She pushed us at school as well. Insisted we be polite and ladylike, that we ignore the taunts and hatred around us. I freely admit Genene managed it better than I did . . .'

Lauren's words faded, and this time she declined to elaborate further, not mentioning how when it was her own turn to be encouraged to attend school on time, to look smart in her uniform and deliver her homework promptly, Angel Wraxford had aged prematurely, stress and chain-smoking turning her into a pathetic shadow of the creature she'd once been; and how, as such, there hadn't been quite as much support for the younger sister as there had for the older.

'Anyway,' Lauren said decidedly. 'Enough of this boring crap about me. It's Genene I'm interested in. You're saying there's absolutely nothing about this you can tell me?'

Heck shrugged. 'Only that the disappearance is being investigated.'

'Just by you, or by others as well?'

'Every case has an adequate number of investigators attached.'

'So where are the rest of them?'

'We all have different duties . . .'

'Can't you give me a straight answer?' She was visibly struggling to stop herself getting irate again. 'All you're doing is taking me round the houses.'

'Look . . . I wish I could tell you there was a whole team of us.'

She nodded, having suspected this all along. 'And why isn't there?'

'Finance, politics.' He sipped tiredly at his coffee. 'All the

122

usual reasons that have absolutely nothing to do with fighting crime.'

'And what's your gut feeling? I mean, you're at the heart of this. Do *you* know what happened to Genene?'

'No.'

'She can't have just vanished.'

'People vanish all the time, Lauren. Police stations up and down the country are crammed with "missing persons" reports.'

'How many of them do you recover?'

'Some.'

'Some?'

'A few.'

'A minority?'

'Okay, a minority. But there are others who come back of their own accord.'

'And how many of those who never come back are the victims of foul play?'

He shrugged again.

'All of them, maybe?' she wondered.

'Possibly.'

'And what are we talking here? Per annum, I mean. Hundreds? Thousands?'

Heck shook his head. It was probably closer to the latter, not that he wanted to tell her that. He drained his beaker, and tossed it into a nearby waste bin.

'Why do I get the feeling there's something else you're not telling me?' Lauren asked.

'What do you mean?'

She eyed him carefully. 'Is there something about Genene's case that makes it different from all these others?'

'You know I can't tell you that.' He fished the car keys from his pocket.

'If Genene's case *doesn't* bother you more than any of the others, it should,' Lauren said. 'She's not the sort who'd just

123

disappear. She wasn't in debt or on drugs or being abused. She'd just got a degree, for God's sake. She'd started a job with one of the top legal firms in West Yorkshire. She had everything to live for. She didn't even take a change of clothes with her the day she disappeared, or her credit cards or driving licence. All she had was what she was wearing that morning on her way to work, and a briefcase with a few papers in it.'

This reminded Heck why he'd first requested to see the case file on Genene Wraxford. 'It's time for you to go home,' he said abruptly.

'What?'

'I've told you it's being investigated, and that's it.'

'That's it?'

'Finish your coffee.' He opened the car door. 'I'll give you a ride to Salford station. From there, you can get a train to Piccadilly, where you can pick up a connection to Yorkshire.'

Lauren shook her head. 'I'm not going anywhere. I came here because I want to help you.'

'Don't be so ridiculous.'

'You've already admitted you haven't got a team with you. That means you need help. If nothing else, I can do all the legwork.'

'Lauren . . . this is a police enquiry and you're a civilian.'

'You saying you don't use civilians? I know that's bullshit.'

'You're not qualified in any shape or form.'

'I'm an ex-combat soldier.'

'That isn't qualified and, to be frank, that would worry me more than reassure me.' He indicated the car. 'Hop in.'

'Look . . . just let me tag along.'

'No. Now get in the car.'

She folded her arms defiantly. He shrugged, jumped into the driving seat and switched the engine on. As he nosed the vehicle forwards, she rounded the bonnet and clambered in alongside him. He had to suppress a grin as he pulled back out onto the A580, but Lauren sat in sullen silence – all the way to Salford railway station, where rush-hour commuters were bustling back and forth. Heck pulled up on the cobbled taxi rank beneath the station's heavy concrete canopy.

'You must know that I can't have you with me?' he said, turning to face her. 'I mean, you're an adult, a grown-up . . . you must realise that?'

Lauren stared directly ahead. 'What am I going to tell my mum when I get home?'

'Tell her we know what we're doing. We're professionals . . . we're pretty good at this sort of thing.'

'Why should we trust you now? After three years of hearing nothing.'

'Because we're all you've got.'

She gave a scornful smile. 'That's what I thought.' She climbed from the car, humping her pack onto her shoulder. 'Why should the law-abiding community tremble, eh?'

'Don't forget to report that hire van stolen,' Heck called after her.

She gave him the finger, before limping off towards the station steps.

Heck drove away. It was quite an irony, of course. Given the job that lay ahead of him, if there was one thing he really could have made use of right now, it was a wingman.

Chapter 15

In police terms, Salford was a legendary district.

Existing as a city in its own right, but enclosed by the larger Greater Manchester conurbation, it was regarded as one of the toughest beats in Britain outside London. It fell within the Greater Manchester Police's F-Division, described to Heck on his last day of basic training, when he'd learned that he was being posted there, as: 'A big, dark, noisy, chaotic, rain-soaked, urban hell!'

Heck had done two years as a cop in Manchester before transferring down to London. It wasn't a long time in reality, but it was long enough if you were working on as busy a division as 'the F' to get to know every one of its nooks and crannies. Once a manufacturing hotbed and busy dockland on the Manchester Ship Canal, Salford had endured severe unemployment since the mid-twentieth century and, as a result, had come to suffer some of the worst social and housing problems the northwest had ever seen. Modern regeneration schemes had spruced up certain parts of it – Salford Quays saw the creation of attractive and costly canal-side residences, but other parts of it were still agonisingly depressed. The Industrial Revolution-era slums had been cleared away en masse in the 1960s, and replaced with austere, high-rise architecture, which had very quickly degenerated into slums of a different sort. Some sections of the town were now wastelands of graffiti-covered tower blocks, boarded-up shops and rubbish-strewn subways.

Heck arrived in one such locality around six o'clock that evening. His Fiat, already old and beaten-up, was additionally dirty from the chase across the spoil land, so no eyebrows were raised as he prowled between rows of identical concrete maisonettes that were more like World War II bunkers than dwelling places.

Ron O'Hoorigan supposedly lived at fourteen, Lady Luck Crescent, a spectacularly misnamed cul-de-sac. On one side of it lay the maisonettes, on the other a row of poor quality council houses. The gutters were scattered with litter and broken glass, there was scarcely a gate or fence left intact, and those remaining were covered in spray paint; the burnt hulk of a car occupied the turning circle at the far end.

Identifying number fourteen as one of the maisonettes, he cruised to a halt some three buildings down, where he considered how best to play it.

At length, he decided that the easiest option was to introduce himself as a police officer and invent some imaginary crime that he could claim he was looking into. He checked again through O'Hoorigan's print-out. O'Hoorigan, whose lean hatchet-face glared up at him from the attached glossy, was a professional burglar – mainly small time, though his last offence had involved the tying up of two terrified householders. On arrest, he'd thus been charged with aggravated burglary, which was the reason he'd finished up serving seven in Rotherwood high security unit. Another such conviction and he'd likely go down for twenty, which gave Heck quite a bit of leverage. He'd make something up and demand an interview. O'Hoorigan would be eager to clear himself and, that way at least, Heck could get a foot in the door and start asking questions about Klim.

He climbed from the car, locked it, and walked back along the pavement and up the path to number fourteen. The tiny front garden was an unkempt mass of weeds. The front window had what at first glance looked like drawn curtains, though at second glance these turned out to be hanging bed sheets.

Heck knocked on the red, soft-board door and waited. There was no response. He knocked three times in total. Still there was no response. Eventually, he crouched and peeked through the letter flap. A musty smell, like old sweat, exuded out from it. Nothing was visible inside except vague outlines and dust. He moved away from the front door, and peered down a side passage cluttered with rubbish. An iron gate had once barred access to it, but this now hung from rusted hinges. He pushed his way through, wincing as the corroded metal squealed, and then advanced warily. When an empty emulsion tin clattered away from him, he froze – but there was no sign that any of the neighbours had heard, or cared if they had.

At the end of the entry was a small garden, though its grass was thickly overgrown, and the scabby thorn bushes along the fences to either side were hung with rags and waste paper. An old fridge had been dumped in the middle; its open door yawned on mouldy blackness. The windows at the rear of the maisonette had also been covered from the inside, one with stained sheets and another with newspaper. There was a back door, but it was firmly closed. The window panel in it contained frosted glass, so he couldn't see through.

Heck then heard the squeal of the entry gate again.

He listened as echoing footfalls sounded in the passage. There was a familiar clatter as another foot clouted the emulsion tin. He tensed, moving away from the back of the house, onto the more open ground of the garden.

A figure rounded the corner into view.

Heck couldn't believe his eyes.

'So who lives *here*?' Lauren asked.

'*What the bloody hell are you doing?*' he hissed, dashing forward and glancing past her down the entry; there was nobody else there. '*Well?*'

She shrugged. 'I told you, I'm not just going home.'

'I put you on a sodding train!'

'No, you didn't. You kicked me out of your motor. It wasn't difficult getting a taxi outside a railway station. I think the driver was quite chuffed when I said "follow that car".'

'For Christ's sake, Lauren, this is not a game!'

She looked irritated. 'You're telling *me* that? My sister's been missing for . . .'

'I'm sick of hearing about . . .'

'You're sick of hearing about her?'

'I didn't mean it like that. Look, Lauren . . .' Her gaze burned into him as he made a succession of helpless gestures, only his concern for discretion keeping him from shouting. 'Lauren . . . criminal investigation is a serious business. You can't play at it like this.'

'I want to know what's happening,' she said firmly. 'I want to know what leads you've got.'

'Do I really have to arrest you?'

'Try it. And I'll tell the first inspector I meet that you advised me to report that hire van stolen. That you were covering up a crime. In fact, I'll go one better than that. I'll tell your own boss. What was his name . . . Commander Laycock?' She smiled when she saw his startled expression. 'Ahhh . . . you wouldn't want *him* to know, would you?'

There was no way Heck could answer that without

revealing that he didn't even want Laycock to know he was here in Manchester. He turned stiffly and walked back up the entry to the road.

Lauren followed. 'It doesn't have to be this way, though.'

'You must be out of your mind,' he replied, shaking his head but talking more to himself than to her. It defied all logic how he'd ended up in a situation like this. He'd planned this trip so carefully. He emerged onto the pavement in a daze.

'I can help you,' Lauren insisted.

He swung around to face her. 'You'll get yourself killed. And maybe me with you . . .'

'You looking for Ron?' someone asked.

They turned sharply. A man they hadn't previously noticed was seated on a deckchair in the garden opposite. In contrast to O'Hoorigan's, this garden had no vegetation at all – it was bare dirt. The man was youngish, but pale and rail-thin, and had hair dyed bright pink. He wore a vest and a pair of cut-off khaki shorts; he was smoking, and drinking from a tin of lager.

'I said are you looking for Ron?'

'Ron?' Lauren said, crossing the road towards him.

'Ron O'Hoorigan?' the man said. 'That's his house.'

'Yeah mate, that's right,' she agreed. 'We're looking for Ron O'Hoorigan.'

Heck crossed the road alongside her, just about managing to hold his tongue. The man eyed them. With Lauren in her dark army-surplus gear and Heck in jeans, trainers and leather jacket, they didn't look out of place for this neighbourhood.

'He owe you money or something?'

'Something like that, yeah,' she said.

The man nodded as if this was a familiar story. Up close, his face was pinched to the bone. There were matching sets

130

of needle bruises on both his pipe-cleaner arms. 'You're not the only ones. He hasn't been round here for a bit.'

'So where's he living now?' she asked.

'Couldn't tell you. Try the Dog & Butcher round the corner. It's his local, or was. He used to spend every day there.'

'Cheers.'

The man took a drag on his cig as they moved away, before adding: 'Give him a kicking for me, when you find him, yeah. Our Shaz let him shag her and the bastard never coughed up for it.'

'See,' Lauren said, when they'd got back in the car. 'We make a decent team. I presume this Ron O'Hoorigan is involved?'

Heck rammed his key into the ignition and banged the handbrake off. 'I'm taking you back to the railway station. And this time I'm going to make *sure* you get on a train.'

'One problem. I don't have money for a train.'

'You had money for a taxi.'

'That's why I don't have money for a train.'

'No worries.' He started driving. '*I'll* pay for your ticket.'

'And like I say, I'll ring Scotland Yard. I'll ask for Commander Laycock and tell him you've been covering up crimes in Manchester.'

'You really think this is the way to win my friendship, by trying to blackmail me?'

'I'll do anything necessary.' They'd now turned into the next street, and, as the pink-haired man had told them, the Dog & Butcher came into view at its far end.

'Let me at least help you find this character, O'Hoorigan,' Lauren added. 'Look at this place. You're not going to be asking questions round here on your own, are you? I'm an ex-squaddie. I'll have your back.'

Heck shook his head as they slowed to another halt. He felt completely helpless.

The Dog & Butcher certainly seemed the sort of place someone like Ron O'Hoorigan would hang out. It was one of those one-level pre-fab constructs typical of the 1970s. In a district where tower blocks marched every skyline, it looked more like a shoebox than a building. It was difficult to imagine that any civic architect could seriously have designed something like this without intending it as a joke, yet hostelries of this sort had sprung up all over Britain as part of a grand plan to regenerate the inner cities. Those few that remained, like this one, now stood as monuments to soulless functionalism and intellectual arrogance. It was clear what the locals thought of it. It only had a few windows, all high up and letterbox shaped, and filled with reinforced glass, but even so, many were cracked or broken. Its pebble-dashed walls were daubed with various substances: mud, chewing gum, dog shit.

Heck was unsure what to do next. Obviously, he had to take Lauren back to the station, but what if she really called the Yard and tried to reach Laycock? In addition, Salford station was a good fifteen minutes' drive from here, now through rush-hour traffic. Driving there and back again would use up valuable time, and might make his Fiat noticeable to anyone round here who happened to be keeping an eye out for unusual comings and goings.

'Can I trust you to stay in the car?' he asked, though it tightened his chest just thinking about the risks this entailed.

She shrugged. 'If that's what it takes for you to keep me in the loop, sure.'

'This doesn't mean you're part of the enquiry.'

She shrugged again. He eyed her, looking for signs of deceit, but she seemed a lot more relaxed than she had done earlier. He could always produce his cuffs and fix her to the steering wheel, but that really would draw attention to them. Instead, he got out and sauntered towards the pub, glancing up at the licensee's name as he approached.

It sounded a tad well-heeled for this neighbourhood. Heck glanced back at the car. Lauren waggled her fingers at him through the windscreen. Swearing under his breath, he turned and went inside.

The Dog & Butcher was a dingy, shadow-filled den. Grey light filtered through its grimy windows, showing a stained carpet, Formica table-tops, and, dotted here and there, punters – some in groups, some alone – all of whom looked either tired, miserable or menacing, or a combination of the three. Though it was cloudy outside, it was hot and therefore humid indoors. Flies buzzing back and forth added to the squalid atmosphere.

Heck approached the bar. The man behind it was bare-chested under a faded denim waistcoat, and broad as an ox. He was bullet-headed, with a boxer's battered face; his brawny arms and shoulders bore myriad tattoos.

'Yeah?' he asked, mopping the counter top.

'Pint of bitter please,' Heck said.

The man moved to the pumps. Heck glanced around. Having studied O'Hoorigan's photograph until he'd memorised it, it was evident the guy wasn't in here. But there were actually two bar counters. Beyond the one he was standing at now, another one opened into a second room, where various men and boys were gathered around a couple of pool tables. The toilet passage probably connected with it.

'I'll not be a sec,' Heck said. 'Paying a visit.'

The barman nodded indifferently.

Heck went down the passage, but didn't bother with the toilets. He stuck his head into the pool room. There was no sign of O'Hoorigan in there either, so he returned to the first bar, where his pint was now waiting for him.

'Two quid, mate,' the barman said.

'You Mr Ogburn?'

The barman regarded him suspiciously. 'Yeah, why?'

Heck handed him the requisite coins. 'No reason. Always like to know who the landlord is.'

Ogburn didn't reply.

'I don't suppose Ron's been in?' Heck asked.

'Who's Ron?'

'You know . . . Ron O'Hoorigan? He's a mate of mine.'

Ogburn turned his back. Ostensibly, he was arranging notes in the till. But Heck suspected there was more to it than this. The guy didn't want to look round for fear that his facial language would reveal a deception.

'So . . . has he been in?' Heck persisted.

'Don't know who you're talking about.'

'Come on . . . Ronnie O'Hoorigan. This is his local.'

When Ogburn finally *did* glance around, his eyes met Heck's and locked. 'I don't know anyone called O'Hoorigan. You got that?'

'Easy pal, it was only a question.'

'I'm not your pal. Why don't you drink up and get off, eh? I'll be closing soon.'

'Normally close around tea-time, do you?'

'I close when I want.'

'Maybe this'll help.' Heck filched the photograph from his pocket and held it up, along with a twenty-pound note.

The landlord didn't even look at the proffered gift. In fact, he raised his voice so that now the entire pub could hear. 'What's your fucking game, eh?'

'I just want to speak to him.' Heck pocketed the money. 'So why don't you tell me where he is, then we'll have no problems?'

He'd shifted into tough-assed mode. It wasn't what he'd wanted, but collecting information in a place like this wasn't possible if you went at it nervously. All other conversation

134

in the room had ceased. Ogburn was about to say something else when the door to the toilet passage burst open and a man came in, zipping up the fly on his green canvas trousers.

It was Ron O'Hoorigan.

He was taller than Heck had expected, but also leaner. He came to a standstill when he saw everyone looking; his eyes flirted to the photograph in Heck's hand. Whether or not he spotted his own image there was unclear. Perhaps his reaction came through force of habit. Either way, he bolted for the outside door. Heck gave immediate chase, only for someone to stick a foot out and send him flying. He crashed over a table, winding himself. When he clambered back to his feet, several of the punters had got up and were confronting him.

The one immediately in his face, the one who'd tripped him, might have been sixty; he had grey hair, a grey beard and a moustache, but he had a bull neck and a massive body. To his right there was a younger guy, his hair carroty red and spiked up; he had a scar across his top lip, which gave him a permanent sneer. To his left, there was a biker type – long, ratty, black hair hung down over motorbike leathers; he was pock-marked and broken-toothed. Chair legs scraped as other men got to their feet. Heck sensed Ogburn lifting a hatch so that he could come out from around the bar.

Clearly, there'd be no time for explanations.

Close to Heck's right hand, an empty Newcastle Brown bottle sat on a table-top. It seemed an obvious move to snatch it up. The forehead of the burly sixty-year-old with the grey beard was its obvious destination.

The bottle exploded, and the guy went down as though poleaxed. Heck ducked a swinging punch and caught Scar-Lip in the stomach with a left hook, only to take a head butt on the cheek from Rat-Hair. Again, he fell over a table. Figures closed in from all sides. When Heck got back to his feet, he grabbed a chair and swung it full on at Ogburn, who blocked it with a meaty forearm. Scar-Lip came in with a flying kick. Heck caught his ankle, dropping him onto his back and smashing an elbow down into his groin – only for Rat-Hair to catch him with a stinger in the mouth. Heck's head jerked sideways, and two burly arms wrapped around his neck in a choke-hold. He was dragged backward until he overbalanced. Struggling to breathe, he saw Ogburn grinning down at him, his fat, red face beaded with sweat.

The solution was two sharp, upward blows, a thumb striking each eyeball. The landlord shrieked, dropping Heck and staggering away.

Heck rolled over to avoid another flying kick. It was Rat-Hair, his steel-capped leather boot crashing into the wall, hacking out a chunk of plaster. Again, Heck got back to his feet. He grabbed a pint glass, pegged it at Rat-Hair. Another guy threw a punch. Heck blocked it, slamming his knuckles onto the guy's nose. Rat-Hair swerved back into view. He'd pulled off his biker belt, which was heavy with steel. Heck raised a defensive arm, and the belt coiled around it. A shocking concussion then followed on the side of Heck's head.

It was Grey Beard. Though his face was a bloodied mask riddled with glinting shards, he'd got himself a broken chair leg and swung it. When Heck fell, they were all over him. Fists thundered down from all sides, pounding his head and body.

'Kill the fucker!' one of them growled. 'Cripple him! Do his fucking neck!'

They only noticed that Lauren was among them when Rat-Hair was hit so hard in the face that his left eye ruptured in its socket. Grey Beard spun to face her, only for Lauren to flick out her blade and slash him across the face, laying it open to the cheekbone.

136

A circle cleared as the hoodlums fell back. Lauren pivoted around, blade at the ready. Heck lay at her feet in a groggy heap.

'Who wants it next?' she challenged them.

'You black bitch,' someone snarled.

'Ooooh, that hurts. White pussy arseholes! You're a fucking joke!'

It might have ended there; an alley might have cleared towards the doorway. Heck clambered dizzily back to his feet, anticipating this. But then a new problem arrived. It – or rather *they* – came in from the next bar.

The pool players, maybe twelve of them, filed in from the toilet passage. They were an even worse crowd than the first lot; they were younger, meaner, noticeably fitter. Those of them that weren't carrying pool cues were carrying socks clicking with pool balls. Heck smeared blood across his face with his forearm. He glanced towards the door. A couple of guys shuffled in front of it. The stale air was suddenly foul with the stench of sweat, blood and bad, beery breath.

The mob was about to charge in – when two of them disappeared under a table, which was slammed down on top of their heads from behind. The guy who'd done it was someone nobody had previously noticed. He'd been sitting in a corner, reading a paper. But now that he was standing at full height, he looked as wrong for this place as Heck and Lauren did. He was about six feet three, and of trim, athletic build. He was also handsome and sunburned, with a mop of blond hair. His clothing consisted of a green sweat top cut off at the elbows, a pair of tracksuit pants and training shoes. He was wearing gloves, and both his wrists, which were thick and powerful, were banded with leather.

There was a stunned silence at this intervention, before the louts twirled around to face him. But he'd already grabbed a pool cue, and now laid it on them with brutal force. Skulls were smacked like baseballs, arms were broken. When the cue snapped, Grey Beard tried to grapple hand-to-hand with the newcomer, only to be hoisted up by the crotch and throat, and thrown bodily across the bar counter. A deluge of destruction followed as bottles and glass shelves cascaded on top of him.

Scar-Lip lunged at Lauren, catching her with a full-blooded punch, but, though she tottered, she managed to keep her feet, and stepped around his second attack, ripping the blade in a zigzag across his back. Ogburn, his eyes like raw plums, tried to put another headlock on Heck, but Heck caught the bastard with a hard left and a harder right, and as he staggered backward, swung a broken chair frame into his midriff, drawing a shrill squeal from his blood-spattered mouth.

The big blond man was still wreaking havoc. They came at him relentlessly, but he smashed their faces or threw them across the room. Head, fists, feet, knees – he used them all with amazing skill and ferocity. They were a rough crowd in the Dog & Butcher, but it was unlikely they'd ever experienced anything like this bloke. A couple had now escaped, leaving the front door wide open. Heck snatched Lauren by the collar and hauled her towards it.

After the roiling atmosphere inside, the fresh air was almost cold. They toppled across the pavement towards the Fiat. Another of the hoodlums came staggering out after them. Lauren brought him down with a karate kick to the face. He fell into the gutter, gasping.

'That's enough,' Heck shouted, spotting that she still had the knife, which was glinting crimson.

The next person to come out was the big blond man. He wiped his gloved hands on his sweatshirt as he approached.

'You folks alright?' he said with a grin.

Heck was leaning on the car to get his breath. He glanced up. 'We owe you one.'

'Nah, you don't. Spot of useful exercise, that's all.'

'Who are you?' Lauren asked.

He surveyed them, hands on hips. In full daylight, he was surprisingly good looking. His fair hair, bronze tan and trim physique gave him 'film star' appeal. 'Mates call me "Deke". You can too, if you want.'

'That was a timely intervention, Deke,' Heck said, straightening up. 'Any particular reason why you put your neck on the line for us?'

'Hardly put my neck on the line. Chocolate soldiers, that lot.'

At which point, the pub door was kicked open again. Grey Beard was there, covered head to foot in blood and broken glass. The part of his face Lauren had slashed hung off as though it had been unzipped. He swore and gesticulated at them, but he did not come outside.

'Want more, you old fucker?' Deke laughed. 'Put one toe over that step, and I'll teach you a *real* fucking lesson.'

The door banged closed as Grey Beard disappeared back inside.

Deke laughed again. 'See what I mean.'

'You still took a hell of a risk,' Heck said.

'It was nothing.'

'Maybe, but I'm the sort of bloke who likes to know who's saving his life.'

'It's nothing personal. I just don't like seeing shitheads get on top. Never have.'

Heck nodded, not buying this at all, as he suspected Deke knew full well. 'Well, no offence, Deke . . . but we're out of here. Don't want to sound ungrateful, but our business in this part of town is definitely concluded.'

'You were looking for Ron O'Hoorigan, weren't you?'

'You know him?' Lauren asked.

Deke shrugged. 'Who doesn't round here?'

'Do you know where he is?'

'He lives on Lady Luck Crescent, but I don't think he's there very often. Any reason why you're looking for him?'

Lauren glanced at Heck, who quickly replied: 'Just a business thing. Gambling debt.'

Deke looked amused. 'You two collect gambling debts?'

'Yeah,' Lauren said. 'So?'

'Forget it.' Deke chuckled and waved away the explanation, which he clearly regarded as nonsensical. 'Listen, you take care of yourselves.' He edged off. 'But when you're collecting in future, don't go barging into places where the debtors are likely to outnumber you ten to one. Oh, and if it helps . . . try sixty-nine, Regina Court.'

'What?' Heck called after him.

Deke was walking away, but he glanced back over his shoulder. 'Gallows Hill flats. It's a squat where O'Hoorigan used to buy gear. I think he kips there now and then.'

'Gallows Hill,' Heck said to himself.

'You know that place?' Lauren asked.

'I'll say.'

He glanced after Deke again, but the guy was now out of hearing range. Meanwhile, a crescendo of angry voices was rising inside the wrecked pub. Heck moved to the car, and ushered Lauren inside. As they pulled away from the kerb, the beaten-up rabble, newly armed with staves and pool cues, came spilling out onto the pavement. Heck watched them in the rearview mirror as the Fiat cruised away. Glancing left, he spotted Deke sauntering down into an underpass, vanishing from view.

'Who the hell was he?' Lauren wondered.

'Dunno. But he can kick arse like I've never seen. You okay?'

'Yeah.' She dabbed at her bloodied nostrils with a handkerchief.

'Par for the course in the Royal Ordnance Corps?'

'Not exactly. Chapeltown maybe.' They pulled off the desolate estate and rejoined the main road network. 'We going to this Gallows Hill place now?'

'*We're* not going anywhere. *You're* going back to the railway station.'

'In this state? They'll think I'm a right yob.'

'If the cap fits . . .'

'I just helped you out in there! Big time!'

Heck couldn't argue with that, so he didn't try.

'Look, Heck . . . it's okay if I call you that?'

'Yes, you can call me "Heck".'

'Heck . . . you can't force me to go anywhere.' She shook her head adamantly. 'I don't care what you say, this is a free country. You can't make me get on a train to Yorkshire.'

'Okay, that's true. But if you've got no money and you're not prepared to go home, where are you going to spend the night?'

'I'm not exactly new to sleeping outdoors.'

'Up to you. You certainly won't be alone in this town.' He drove on, circumnavigating a series of concrete roundabouts.

'What about this Gallows Hill place?' she said. 'If O'Hoorigan used to buy drugs there, it sounds a bit rough.'

'You're telling me.'

'So . . . are you going to call back-up?'

If only he could, he thought. As things were, he wasn't even planning to report what had just happened. He wanted to; he knew he ought to. But the moment Gemma learned he'd been involved in a bar room brawl where civilians had been knifed, her kneejerk reaction would be to pull him back in. She might pull him in anyway, if the word reached her from other sources.

'Well?' Lauren asked again.

'We're not going to Gallows Hill just yet. I don't fancy another fight straight away. Do you?'

'Suppose not.' She dabbed at her nose again. 'So where *are* we going?'

Heck followed signs towards the motorway junction. 'Somewhere we can get patched up.'

'Who is this O'Hoorigan guy, anyway?'

'He may know something.'

'So we've *got* to speak to him?'

'Correction. *I* have to speak to him.'

'And while *you're* getting patched up, what if he moves on?'

'Then he moves on. It's not like I haven't learned anything.'

'Eh?' Lauren looked baffled.

'You think we just got lucky Deke intervened when he did?'

'He wasn't being a good Samaritan?'

'You don't find many of those in that neck of the woods.'

'He didn't sound local, I must admit.'

'More East Anglian, I'd say.'

'Still doesn't tell us much.'

Heck shook his head. 'It tells us that we're onto *something*. Trouble is, at the moment I'm not sure what.'

Chapter 16

The house was on Cranby Street, a small terraced row, at least half of which had been demolished as part of some long-ago clearance scheme. It wasn't exactly cobbled, but to Lauren's eye it didn't look as if it had changed since George Orwell's day.

Every house was built from the same red brick, though a couple had received 'stone-cladding', much of which had now deteriorated, making them look grotesque. All their doorsteps had been fastidiously scrubbed, but here and there a lower portion of front wall bellied slightly. There was even a canal at the far end, with a lock-gate visible, and on the other side of that an area of reclaimed spoil land where playing fields had been marked out and rugby posts erected.

It was early evening and the street quiet, when they parked. The heavy cloud cover was in the process of clearing, much of it tinged pink by the setting sun. Both Heck and Lauren were now feeling their extensive cuts and bruises. The shock of the fight was seeping through them. Lauren climbed tiredly from the car as Heck approached the front door. Bradburn – from what she'd seen of it – was a typical South Lancashire backwater, but not massively different to many parts of Leeds.

Located twenty miles north of Manchester, it wasn't the sort of place you'd even notice if you passed it on the motorway: a minor blot on a bleak, post-industrial landscape. Since the collapse of the coal and textiles industries, it had clearly tried to throw off its 'muck and brass' identity, but had found nothing to replace it with. Its central streets were now interchangeable with those of every other stagnating provincial town in the UK; lined with the same boring shops, delineated by soulless, monolithic structures of glass and concrete, which passed for malls. Its outskirts were even worse; a grid-work of uniformly drab housing estates, punctuated here and there by short rows of purpose-built retail units which usually consisted of a greasy chippie, a tanning salon and a boarded-up pub.

At least Cranby Street retained some old-time character.

Heck's sister, Dana, lived at number twenty-three. She answered the door in flip-flops, cut-off jeans and a sleeveless blouse, an outfit which suited her. Aged in her early forties, she was very attractive, with long, dark hair and a slim, shapely figure.

Her eyes initially lit up at the sight of her brother, but then her mouth dropped open in shock. 'Good God, what's happened?'

'Is Sarah here?' he asked.

'She's . . . she's in France with school.'

'Good. That means we can come in?' He shouldered his way inside, awaiting no invitation. 'This is Lauren. She's helping me with a case.'

Dana, still looking stunned, turned and followed him in. Lauren brought up the rear. They entered a small, neat lounge, where a television was tuned to one of the satellite movie channels and a half-drunk glass of wine sat alongside the remnants of a salad.

'What happened to you?' Dana asked, switching the TV off. 'You had an accident, or something?'

'We ran into a spot of trouble.'

Dana glanced at Lauren, who'd cleaned her face with her sleeve, but had found it impossible to hide the dried blood spattered down the front of her sweater.

'You sure you aren't better off at casualty? You both look terrible.'

'If it's any consolation,' Heck said, 'you should see the other lot.'

Dana shook her head as she went fussing into the kitchen, returning with a first-aid kit and handing them each a wad of antiseptic wipes.

Heck peeled off his jacket. 'Don't suppose you're expecting company this evening?'

'Yeah, by nine I'll have gentleman callers queuing down the street.'

He nodded, ignoring the sarcasm.

'Do you want to tell me what happened?' Dana asked again.

'No.'

'At least give me some clue. You never even said you were coming north this week.'

'It's nothing important.' He handed her his jacket. 'Trust me.'

She held it at arm's length, gingerly. 'This is ruined. In fact all your clothes are ruined. I can wash and iron them, but they won't be ready by morning.'

'Doesn't matter, we've got spares in the boot. We were planning to be up here for a couple of days.'

'And you weren't going to tell me?'

'There was no need to involve you.'

'You mean until you got so beaten up that it became obvious a hotel wouldn't let you past the front door?' Dana glanced around at Lauren, who couldn't meet her gaze.

The atmosphere was far more awkward than the ex-squaddie had anticipated when Heck had told her that they were going to his sister's house. Okay, even where members of family were concerned, it wasn't the done thing to turn up unannounced and battered to the point where you were almost unrecognisable. But there'd been no apology from Heck, or even a reasonable attempt to offer an explanation.

'I don't suppose it really matters,' Dana said. 'I'm guessing you're staying over now?'

'If it's convenient,' Heck replied.

'At least I get to see you again. What's left of you.' She glanced back at Lauren. 'Lauren, is it?'

Lauren nodded, smiled.

'Nice to meet you. I'm Dana Black, Mark's sister.'

'Hi,' Lauren said.

'Why don't you go and get yourself a bath?' Dana suggested. 'There's plenty of hot water, and fresh towels in the airing cupboard on the landing.'

Lauren nodded and moved gratefully into the hall. Heck followed her out. 'Go on up,' he said. 'I'll get the stuff from the car.'

When he came back indoors, carrying Lauren's backpack in one hand and his own holdall in the other, Dana met him in the porch. 'You two together?' she asked quietly.

'What?'

'You know . . . *together*?'

'Oh . . . no.'

She looked disappointed. 'She a police officer too?'

'A witness.'

146

Dana's disappointment changed to visible concern. 'And this is why you were attacked?'

'It's a bit more complicated than that.'

'It always is.' She followed him to the foot of the stairs. 'Tell Lauren she can have the spare bedroom. You can use Sarah's. But make sure you have a bath first. I don't want her coming home from holiday and finding blood everywhere.'

He nodded and made to ascend, but Dana stopped him with a hand on his arm. 'Just out of interest, Mark . . . are you going to keep punishing me forever?'

'Don't know what you're talking about.'

'Don't give me that. Never responding to my calls, never getting in touch – not even at Christmas. You're only here now because you've nowhere else to go.'

He gently detached himself from her hand. 'I haven't got time for this.'

'No, you haven't got time for anything. Not even your own niece.'

He'd put a foot on the bottom stair, but now swung around. 'I always send Sarah a card and money on her birthday.'

Dana smiled cynically. 'Correction. You *sometimes* send her a card and money. The years when you forget, I give it to her and say it's from you. That's why she still adores you . . . not that *you'd* notice.'

Heck shrugged. 'I just don't like living the lie that everything between you and me is okay.'

'No, but you're happy to live the lie that you're right and everyone else is wrong.'

He grinned to himself. 'Hell of a time to have this conversation, Dana . . .'

'Well, you kind of limit the opportunities, Mark.'

'What do you want from me, eh?'

'I want you back.' Her voice softened, became unusually plaintive. 'I want my little brother back.'

'If you want your little brother back, you should have been more of a big sister when he needed you.'

She looked shocked by that, and not a little hurt. 'You think you're the only one who's suffered all these years?'

'I've never said that . . .'

'And you think you're completely blameless for what happened? I've said I'm sorry, but you haven't. And whose side do you think Tom would have been on?'

Heck had again tried to head upstairs, but once again turned sharply to face her. 'That's a low blow, Dana.'

Many faces from the past haunted Heck's dreams at night: not just the dead ones, but the living ones too – bereaved spouses and families; the innocent victims of rape, robbery or violent assault, unable to make sense of or even comprehend the dreadful things that had been done to them. But none were quite like the face of Tom, his older brother, who the last time Heck had seen him, had been more etched with angst than it seemed possible for a human being to experience and survive – which, of course, Tom hadn't.

When Heck spoke again, it was with shaking voice. 'I did what I did to try and get justice for Tom.'

'Surely it doesn't surprise you that not everyone saw it that way?'

'*What does it matter!*' he shouted, before realising that he was shouting and hurriedly lowering his voice. 'We can't change the past.'

She laughed. 'Are you telling me you would if you could? I don't believe you.'

'Well . . . you're right there, Dana. Because frankly, this crap has been going on for so long that I can't imagine any other way of life. Which is why I'm not interested in having this discussion. Not now, not ever.' This time he did head upstairs.

'How noble of you, Mark,' she called after him. 'Accepting a lifelong penance. It's less noble of course that you're condemning me and Sarah to the same thing.'

On the upper floor, he heard the bath running. Lauren came along the landing, carrying towels, wearing only her vest and knickers. There were bruises on her arms and legs; sticky red trickles streaked her shin from the knee she'd hurt in the crash. By her agitated expression, she'd heard some of the commotion below.

'You sure you're okay?' he asked.

She nodded, taking her bag from him. 'If your sis would rather I wasn't here, that doesn't bother me. I can find a bed and breakfast.'

'A bed and breakfast?' He chuckled. 'In *this* neighbourhood?'

'I'd sooner sleep under a motorway bridge than somewhere I'm not wanted.'

'Forget it. That rumpus was about something else.'

'Don't get on with her, eh?'

'There's a history there. But it's nothing for you to worry about.'

'I'm not exactly worried, Heck. But I'm surprised. Perhaps you don't know how lucky you are.'

'Come again?'

She eyed him coolly. 'To have a sister you can still talk to. I'm guessing you've never lost anyone close.'

He returned her gaze for a long moment, and said simply: 'You're wrong.'

Then he carried his holdall into Sarah's bedroom, closing the door behind him.

Lauren didn't see him for another hour. First, she had a long soak in the tub, which was just what the doctor ordered. Once she'd put some fresh clothes on – a pair of jeans and a black t-shirt, she checked her room out; it was neat but basic. Before going downstairs, she peered from the window.

Rows of rooftops led off in all directions, beneath tangles of television aerials. Immediately below, there was a small paved yard with a brick outhouse next to the gate, which had probably once been a toilet. Over the other side of that lay a narrow backstreet cluttered with council wheelie-bins. Again she was reminded of Leeds, this time specifically of Chapeltown. And like Chapeltown, this place was a relic; a throwback to an era that was now forgotten. Hearing movement on the landing, she stuck her head through the door. The bath was running again, and Heck, stripped to his shorts, was standing by the airing cupboard, helping himself to some towels. Like hers, his lean, pale body was bruised all over. He looked tired and sallow-faced. When he finally went into the bathroom, he was limping. He was hardly the heroic knight of medieval fable, she thought as she went downstairs – suddenly feeling warmer towards him. But at least he was doing something to help her.

In the living room, Dana was seated in an armchair. She'd cleaned the remnants of her meal, turned off the television, and was reading an evening paper.

'Sorry we just turned up like this,' Lauren said from the door.

'I'm glad you did.' Dana folded her paper and stood. 'I don't see enough of Mark.'

Lauren remained at the door. 'There'll be no comeback for you, if that's a concern. No one's going to follow us here, or anything.'

'Never entered my head that they might. But if you guys are in trouble, maybe there's more I can do to assist than put a roof over your head for the night?'

'We're fine, honestly. This whole thing actually looks a lot worse than it is.'

Dana shrugged. 'Well, Mark's a police detective and a pretty good one, so I have to trust that he knows what he's doing.'

'I think he does.'

An awkward silence followed. Then Dana produced some car keys. 'I haven't got much food in. I mean, I wasn't expecting anyone. But I can always nip down to the supermarket . . .'

'You mustn't go to that trouble.'

'You need to eat.'

'Is there a take-away round here?'

'Two or three.'

'That'll do, I'm sure.'

Dana pocketed the keys. 'I'll go and put the kettle on for you, at least. You must be desperate for a brew.'

'Yeah . . . that'd be great, thanks.'

Dana smiled and went out into the hall. A short while later Heck came down, clad in a blue tracksuit. Lauren had now moved to the mantelpiece. An old-fashioned clock sat in the middle; at either end there was a framed photograph. The first portrayed a pretty young teenager with a pixie-like grin; no doubt this was Heck's niece, Sarah. The second showed an elderly couple, both dressed smartly as though at a wedding. The man was burly, with granite features and dark, slicked hair. The woman was pretty but mousy, grey curls jammed under her tidy little hat.

'I suggested we get a take-away for tea,' Lauren said. 'Save your sister cooking.'

'Sure. Tim Chan's is just round the corner. It's always been good.'

'You know your way around here?'

'I ought to. I was born here. This is the family home, or the closest thing we ever had to one.'

'Dana seems nice.'

'Most of the time she is. Stunning to look at when she was young. Phone never stopped ringing for her.'

'She's not so bad now.'

'Bossy as hell, though. That hasn't improved with age.'

'That's a big sister's prerogative.' Briefly, Lauren sounded wistful. 'So . . . where's Mr Dana?'

'Gone. Long ago.' Heck grabbed the newspaper. 'And no one's missed him.'

Lauren nodded. 'I seem to remember Genene always had some useless idiot in tow.'

Heck didn't comment, but flicked through the paper. Family matters were clearly more than just a minor problem for him.

Lauren indicated the snapshot of the elderly couple. 'This your mum and dad?'

'Yeah. Before you ask, both dead. Mum a few years ago, dad a few years before that.'

'Ahhh . . . sorry what I said about you not having lost anyone. Stupid comment.'

'It's alright. Older people die, don't they. It wasn't them I was . . .' He shrugged, waved it away. 'Perhaps we should focus on the situation at hand?'

But before they could, Dana came in with a tray on which there was a teapot, three china cups, a small jug of milk, a bowl of sugar and a plate of biscuits. In the midst of all this chaos, it was so dignified a gesture – so like something Lauren's mother would have done – that it nearly brought a tear to the ex-army girl's eye. The two women sat, but Heck stood by the window, watching, his hands stuffed into his pockets.

Dana eyed him as she poured. 'You get kicked in the pants as well?'

'What?'

'Why don't you sit down and join us?' Almost reluctantly, Heck sat on the sofa. His sister handed him a napkin. 'You've got blood on your lip,' she said.

He wiped it away. 'Couple of teeth got knocked loose.'

'Should get along to a dentist.'

'I'll be fine.'

'Sure you will. If you don't mind having a mouth like a chimpanzee.'

Heck glanced at Lauren. 'What did I tell you – about how bossy she is?'

'Like I said,' Lauren replied tartly, 'a big sister's prerogative.'

This broke the ice a little. They made idle chat – about the weather, about world events. And okay, it was only small talk, but at least it was talk. Fifteen minutes later, Heck announced that he would go to the Chinese and pick up the take-away. Once he'd gone, Dana took the empties through to the kitchen-diner to wash up. Lauren went through to help her, but when she got in there was surprised to find that the kitchen table had already been laid for two, and that a candle had been lit. A bottle of wine and two glasses sat on the nearby sideboard.

'You shouldn't have done this,' Lauren said, a little embarrassed.

Dana was busy with the washing up. 'It's no problem. I like things to be nice.'

This was evidently true. The kitchen was yet another part of the interior that belied the house's shabby exterior. It was new and clean, designed in the cottage style, with modern low-key lighting and décor done in pastel shades.

'This place is a credit to you,' Lauren said.

'There's only me and Sarah now, so it's not difficult.' Dana busied around the sink in her brisk, cool way. 'How long have you and Mark known each other?'

'Not very long. But we've been through a lot already . . . so it seems like a while. I don't think it's true to say that I *know* him though. I don't feel as if I do.'

Dana half-smiled. 'You probably never will. He's a bit of a loner.'

'So I've noticed.'

'And he doesn't like situations he can't control.'

Lauren had noticed that too, and wondered if it extended to *people* he couldn't control. Maybe that was the cause of the problems he had with his 'bossy' sister.

Dana was still talking. 'I don't mean that in a childish sense . . . I don't mean he wants his own way all the time. But he doesn't trust people. He reckons nobody else in the job is anywhere near as good as he is. Used to drive Gemma crazy.'

'Gemma?'

'One of his work colleagues. They had a thing going at one point, but it didn't last. Afterwards, he said he'd only been in it for the sex. But Gemma was a real high flyer, and that probably put the mockers on it.'

'So Mark isn't a high flyer?'

'Never been interested in that.' Dana shook her head at the folly of youth. '"It's the front line, or nowhere", he says. "I'm a copper, I catch criminals – and that's it." Not interested in politics, not interested in promotion. And certainly not interested in baggage.'

'"Baggage"?'

Dana sighed as she arranged the dried cups on the kitchen shelves. 'It's a long story. Mark joined the Greater Manchester Police originally, but that didn't work out because there were family issues . . . so he got a transfer to London, where he could isolate himself from everything except his job, which, I have to say, he's done to some tune.'

Lauren was mildly amused by all this. Clearly these

154

unsought-for revelations about Heck's past were Dana's sisterly way of sounding out the new girl's interest in him. She opted to play along. 'It clearly didn't isolate him from Gemma.'

'No.' Dana shook her head again. 'That would have been nice . . . but they were chalk and cheese, especially when Gemma started climbing the ladder. There was no way Mark could be loved-up with her at night, and take orders from her during the day. One or the other would have had to give.'

'So what you're basically telling me is that Mark's a typical self-centred bloke?'

'In a nutshell . . . yes.'

Heck was back a short time later with chicken fried rice for himself and beef in black bean sauce for Lauren. When he saw the table for two in the kitchen, he gave Dana a long, withering stare, but she responded by smiling pleasantly and absenting herself when they sat down to eat.

'Your sister's concerned that I'm trying to get my grubby little mitts on you,' Lauren said, as they tucked in.

He nodded as if this was only to be expected. 'Since Mum died, she's got protective. Don't be offended. She's probably not concerned as much as hopeful.'

'Trying to get you fixed up, is she?'

'She knows better than to try that.'

'I've had it chapter and verse about your last relationship.'

'That proves it. She's trying to interest you.'

'Or put me off. Sounds like this Gemma bird was a very fine swan indeed.'

'Well you're no ugly duckling, you don't need to worry.'

Lauren glanced up at him, but he was now concentrating on pouring them each a glass of wine, so she let the remark pass. Once they'd eaten, they returned to the living room and sat with Dana to watch evening television. More small talk followed; polite, almost convivial, though between Heck and his sister it was all rather stiff, if perhaps a little loaded. When a news item concerning a male skeleton found in an inner city flat in the Midlands mentioned that the occupant had been a misanthrope who had lived alone by choice, as a result of which nobody had noticed he was missing for over three years, Dana commented: 'What a strange thing to do. Cut yourself off from all your loved ones to the point where you barely exist to them anymore.'

Heck didn't look round, but replied: 'Maybe he didn't have any loved ones.'

'Maybe he did but just didn't realise it.'

'I think the fact that he'd rather be a pile of bones than be part of their social network meant he realised it all too well.'

After several such brief, acidic exchanges, Lauren was thankful when the evening finally ended, and she and Heck went upstairs together, leaving Dana to lock the doors and turn out the lights. When they reached the top of the stairs, both their bedroom doors stood open, awaiting them. Lauren pondered Heck's 'ugly duckling' comment. She knew he'd liked what he'd seen when she put everything on show for him in the pub, but with the high stress of the last day his priorities had no doubt changed. Though that afternoon's fight paled compared to the shoot-outs she'd experienced in Afghanistan, you never got used to a confrontation as intense as that. Whoever those bastards in the pub had been, they'd been determined to beat the crap out of them, to hammer them into the dirty, beer-drenched floor. God knows where it could have ended. Heck was still pale, still bruised, but he'd cleaned up nicely – more nicely than she had. Of course, men could carry cuts and bruises as a mark of their masculinity. And Heck, now that she was *this* close to him, seemed more masculine to her than at any time so far. But if he was having similar thoughts about her, he kept them hidden.

'I still don't know what I'm going to do with you,' he said. 'Are you going to keep this stolen van thing hanging over me all through the enquiry?'

'Only if I have to.'

'It's not that big a deal, you know. I could shake you off like a flea if I really wanted.'

'So why don't you?'

He shrugged tiredly. 'Perhaps the thought of going to Gallows Hill alone isn't too attractive.'

'I don't understand why you don't just call your office.'

'It's called deep cover. You can't break it just because you get scared.'

'You don't have a handler . . . a manager?'

Heck thought on this. Time was ticking by and for the last hour he'd again felt guilty about not updating Gemma, though at present it was still the case that what she didn't know wouldn't hurt her. Resignedly, he shook his head.

'The main thing is you're still going after O'Hoorigan?' Lauren said.

'He's my best bet.'

'You said he knows something . . . you mean about Genene?'

Heck didn't see it could do any harm to give her a little bit of information. He owed her that much, at least. 'O'Hoorigan knows someone called Shane Klim. They were in jail together, but Klim escaped and went to ground. He's now one of my suspects.'

'In Genene's disappearance?'

'Possibly.'

'So will O'Hoorigan tell us where this guy Klim's hanging out?'

'He may.'

'Shit!' she said. 'I can see why you want to speak to him.'

'On the other hand, O'Hoorigan may know nothing.'

'So it's tenuous?'

'Tenuous is the name of this game, Lauren. As each lead crops up, you have to follow it as far as you can. If I had a hundred detectives, I could be doing a hundred other things at the same time. But I haven't.'

'Do you at least feel we're getting somewhere?'

Heck shrugged. 'O'Hoorigan ran away from us – which likely means he's got something to hide, so it's promising. But I'd like to know more about this guy, Deke. Did you notice he never took his gloves off once in that pub?'

'Probably because he didn't want to bust his knuckles.'

'Or because he didn't want to leave any prints. It's August. Why would he be wearing gloves?'

Lauren pondered. 'Perhaps he'd been working on a site somewhere?'

'What, and he was still wearing them in the pub? Did he even look like he belonged in that place?'

'Okay, I admit it. Deke's a mystery man. But he's not the guy we're after.'

'True,' Heck agreed.

'Which means we've no choice but to go to Gallows Hill?'

He nodded, but looked discomforted by the prospect. 'I hear it's unoccupied these days, which is probably a good thing.'

'Where is it?'

'Just off the M602 motorway. It was built as a series of apartment blocks, but it always looked more like a prison to me. Except . . .'

'Except what?'

'Except that no prison was ever so bloody grim.'

Chapter 17

City of London bars were rarely busy on weekday evenings. The old days, when the City had purely been a place of work, and when tomb-like silence had filled the glass and concrete canyons after nightfall, were long gone. These days there were almost as many wine bars and restaurants as there were financial institutions. But Monday nights were not really the time for socialising, especially late on.

As such, by half past eleven, Ian Blenkinsop found himself almost alone at the bar in Mad Jack's. Anyone who knew him would say that he cut a dishevelled, rather mournful figure. He was still in his daytime suit, but over the last few hours it had become crumpled. His tie was loose, his collar undone. His briefcase lay at his feet, while his coat was draped messily over the bar alongside him. He was pale-faced and sweaty, as he ordered yet another large gin and tonic, maybe his eighth of the evening.

'It's just no good is it,' he mumbled.

One of the few bar servers left at this hour was a girl of about eighteen, with short, dark hair and a pretty face. She smiled politely, feigning interest as she placed clean glasses on the shelves.

'Life's so brief,' he added, slurring badly. 'So fragile. You never know when someone's just gonna come along and snuff it out. You know, love, anything could happen to any one of us at any time.' He gazed at her, trying to be profound – and in doing so, his eyes almost crossed.

She continued to feign interest, but said nothing.

'"Out, out brief candle",' he muttered. 'I'm not just talking about death, mind.' He pointed a long, wavering finger at no one in particular. 'You can bugger up your life in any number of ways. One moment of stupidity is all it takes, and nothing will ever be the same again. You might as well be fucking dead. Take me, for instance . . .'

Another bar server appeared; a youngish, Italian-looking chap. He'd been watching for several minutes, and had now decided to step forward.

'Are you alright, Sir?' he asked.

Somewhat relieved, the girl moved further along the bar, to serve another customer.

'Me?' Blenkinsop said, puzzled. 'I'm alright. Well . . . as alright as I can be after what's happened. You wouldn't believe the things that are going on in my life.'

The barman, Andreas, who'd been working here for several years, was not unused to City men staggering in to drown their sorrows after losing their companies a fortune, so he did what he usually did, which was exactly what the girl had been doing: smile and nod, as if interested, and all the while have his mind on more important things, like who Arsenal were playing that coming Saturday.

'Take me,' Blenkinsop said again, trying to pick up the thread that he'd left hanging a few seconds ago, though to him those seconds seemed like hours. 'Take me . . .'

'Do I have to?' the barman replied with a chuckle, trying to make a joke of it.

Blenkinsop stared at him, fuddled. As he did, his eyes

again shifted out of focus and he swayed, almost falling off his stool. 'No, I'll . . . I'll have another of these.' He pushed his empty across the counter.

'You sure about that, Sir?' Andreas asked.

'Listen, you're on . . . you're on good money working here. Yeah?'

'Am I?'

'Now listen, I'm paying your wages. If I want a drink, there's no reason why I can't have one. I've earned that right. Understand me? I earned it – it wasn't my fault the way things worked out.'

'Anything you say, Sir. Double G&T is it?'

'Erm . . . better make it a treble.'

'A treble?'

'That means three.'

'Okay. If that's what you want, Sir.' Andreas moved away.

'Take me,' Blenkinsop said again, loudly. 'I've . . . I've really blown it, you know. I mean . . . life may get back to normal, but I don't know when. And all through one crazy moment of uncontrolled . . . *desire*.' He stressed the word 'desire', almost growled it. 'That's what it's all about: lust, wanting . . . course there's always a fucking woman involved . . .'

There was a sudden rattle of paper, so sharp that it even cut through Blenkinsop's blurred thoughts. He glanced to his right.

The man the barmaid had gone to serve was sitting on a bar stool a couple of feet away. He had a pint of lager in front of him and was reading a copy of the *Standard*. He was no one familiar, but Blenkinsop was puzzled that he hadn't observed the chap before – it was like he'd materialised from nowhere.

'Erm . . . are we acquainted?' Blenkinsop asked.

The man turned to look at him. He was in his late

twenties, and of stocky build. His complexion was swarthy, his hair cut very short. His eyes were dark, unblinking. He didn't say a word.

'I was just saying,' Blenkinsop mumbled, 'how easily life can unravel. You know, if you make . . . bad choices.'

Slowly and deliberately, the man folded his newspaper, running his thumb and forefinger along the top crease, leaving it razor sharp. He laid the paper down. His eyes never left Blenkinsop's confused face.

The barman now returned – thankfully, because for some reason the attitude of the newspaper-reading man had become a little unnerving, even to someone in a semi-stupor. Blenkinsop fumbled for his money and banged it on the counter. He took a big gulp, and sighed with relief. 'Nectar . . . believe it or not, I needed that.'

But the barman had gone again, heading for the till. Blenkinsop glanced to his right – and it was a cold shock to see that the newspaper-reading man was no longer there. One or two punters were still in the pub, small huddles of them in distant corners, but the chap with the paper had vanished.

For some reason, Blenkinsop found this even spookier than having him at his shoulder. Had he just seen a ghost – one of London's many pub-dwelling spectres?

He tried to snigger, but his throat had gone dry. An icy memory was stirring inside his head. A string of words, uttered to him the previous night, were now uttered to him again, this time in a disembodied but equally menacing voice: 'From now on, we'll be keeping you under covert surveillance. Not all the time obviously, but you'll never know when we're there and when we're not.'

Suddenly Blenkinsop's brow was damp with sweat. He yanked at his collar; another button popped open. He stood up quickly, too quickly – almost overbalancing again.

162

'I wasn't . . .' he said aloud, his breath coming in short gasps. 'I wasn't admitting to anything, I . . .'

Of course there was nobody listening. He glanced back across the bar. The barman and barmaid now appeared to be cashing up. He looked at his drink; at least half of it remained, but he no longer had the stomach for it. In fact, he desperately needed fresh air. He grabbed his coat and briefcase and stumbled across the room – only to hesitate before going outside. As befitted the pub's gin palace origins, the glasswork in the inner door was misted with ornate designs. Beyond it in the porch, a dark shape was waiting.

Blenkinsop peered at it, his heart knocking on the inside of his tightened chest. 'I didn't,' he whispered, 'I wasn't . . .'

Fleetingly, he was fixed to the floor; he could go neither forward nor backward. At the same time the effects of intoxication were fading with extraordinary speed. He looked around and behind him. A couple of women seated at a nearby table had stopped their gabbling and watched him curiously. He gave them a feeble half-smile, and slapped around inside his jacket, pretending that he was checking for his wallet. When his hand alighted on it, he nodded to himself, looked again through the patterned portal, and seeing no figure in the porch now, ventured into it.

The pub's front door was ajar, and, tentatively, he stepped out through it onto the pavement. Intermittent traffic was moving, but when he glanced left and right, there were no other pedestrians around. Lights were still visible in the upper floors of some of the higher buildings, but the rest of them were in darkness, while down here at street level a mist had formed, creating an eerie sodium-yellow gloom. It wasn't unusual in this part of London, only a couple of miles from the river, but it was the last thing Blenkinsop wanted. He was still breathing hard and fast. He glanced again left and right, then across the road to Goldstein & Hoff's impressive marble entrance – and to the narrow alley alongside it, which wound off towards the company car park. That alley, a routine cut-through during the day, now looked as dark and sinister as any passage he'd seen. The mist hung in its entrance in twisting, silvery strands. He gazed at it. It was impossible to imagine there wasn't somebody there, just out of sight, gazing back at him.

He wasn't sure how long he remained in this mesmerised state before he was distracted by the sight of a black cab trawling along with its green light showing. He signalled for it, and it pulled up in front of him.

'Hampstead,' he said, jumping in and closing the door.

'Ohhh . . .' the cabbie replied doubtfully. 'Long way for me, guv, at this time of night.'

'I'll pay you triple the fare.'

'Triple?' The cabbie sounded amazed, but quickly put the car in gear. 'Didn't want to go to bed yet, anyway.'

Blenkinsop glanced out through the window. A figure had emerged in the misty entrance to the alleyway; a man. It was difficult to make out who he was, let alone identify him as the man with the newspaper. But as the cab pulled slowly away, the figure stared after it intently.

Chapter 18

Lauren gazed dully at the dashboard clock. It wasn't yet six in the morning, but the Manchester traffic was already swarming around them.

'Dana won't be pleased that you left without saying goodbye,' she said.

'She won't be surprised, either,' Heck grunted.

'You guys really don't see eye to eye, uh?'

'We see eye to eye as much as we need to.'

He was preoccupied with driving, so she said no more on the subject. It was nothing to do with her. And it wasn't as if they didn't have other things to think about. Her eyes flicked again to the Manchester A-Z in her lap; they'd almost reached their destination.

If there was any part of Salford that twenty-first-century modernisation still hadn't reached, Gallows Hill was surely it. Lauren immediately saw what Heck had meant when he'd described it as looking like a prison. It sat with its back to the deep cutting through which the noisy M602 motorway ran, and was basically a giant horseshoe, consisting of five U-shaped, six-storey tenement blocks, all built from drab grey concrete. To make matters worse, they were now derelict. The vast majority of their windows had been boarded over, though many of these boards had been removed to allow what was presumably nighttime access for vagrants and drug users.

When they pulled off the motorway and approached it from the front, first having to thread through a network of terraced but equally depressed streets, they saw that the entire plot had been surrounded by a corrugated steel fence, which suggested that everything on the inside was earmarked for demolition. Parking about two hundred yards outside this perimeter, in a narrow alley behind a shop with caged windows, they made their way back on foot. Slipping through one of several gaps broken in the fence, they followed an overgrown footpath, which wound its way around the exterior of the abandoned project, before finally joining an access road leading into the heart of it. Regina Court was down at the farthest end of this road, and they felt increasingly exposed as they walked towards it, having to pass the entries to Hascombe Court, Goodwood Court, Merlin Court and Windermere Court.

Like Lady Luck Crescent, all of these places belied their attractive sounding names. They were gaunt, empty edifices, covered with filth and graffiti. Regina Court itself lay under a sea of rubbish; and not just household rubbish, *real* rubbish – as if people had been fly-tipping here. Once in the middle of it, they regarded the high galleries encircling them, the many doorways smashed and gaping like entrances to caves.

'Take you back a bit?' Heck wondered. 'To Leeds, I mean?'

Lauren didn't reply. She was too tense, and she could tell from his tone that even Heck was feeling subdued by the eeriness of these surroundings.

'No offence intended,' he added. 'Just my attempt at levity. Would it be cowardly of me to suggest we stick together while we're here?'

166

'Uh-uh. This place has got "ambush" written all over it.'

'Just remember, I'm in charge,' he said, reiterating the terms she'd agreed to that morning if she was to accompany him today.

She nodded.

'I mean it, Lauren . . . you don't do a damn thing unless I say it's alright.'

'Got it.'

'Good, because . . .' He squinted towards one of the high galleries, where he imagined he'd spotted movement. There was nothing up there now, but had a figure just ducked out of sight? Again, he felt unconsciously at his pockets, where under normal circumstances he'd have a radio. He knew that he shouldn't be here without support. The incident yesterday had been risky enough; in fact, this whole thing, which had started out as a simple plan to continue asking questions and perusing evidence until something – anything – came to light, had taken a turn for the extremely serious. That Lauren, a civilian, was involved was an even bigger concern, though there was no denying – it was fortunate she'd been there yesterday.

'Once we're out of here, you're gone,' he said quietly. 'No questions this time. At present, you're a concerned citizen helping an officer investigate a crime. But I can't be responsible for your safety indefinitely. So when we're done here, you're off back to Yorkshire or London, or wherever you want to go.'

'Heck, you need back-up—'

'I'll have plenty. As soon as I can speak to O'Hoorigan and get him to tell me everything he knows about Shane Klim . . . what plans he was making while he was inside, where he intended to hide when he broke out . . . I'm reporting it in.'

'And suppose he knows *nothing*? Like you said.'

Heck's grimace suggested he didn't want to consider that

possibility. 'I'm still reporting in. Something tells me I'm getting into this too deep to keep flying solo.'

Lauren didn't bother to argue anymore. She could tell he was serious.

The nearest entrance lay about thirty yards to their left. It was tall and arched, and the numbers etched into its concrete lintel read: 20-80. Once inside, they lurched to an involuntary halt. A tall man in dark clothes, wearing a dark hoodie jacket with the hood pulled up, was standing against the far wall. His hands were in his pockets and his head was bowed forward so that the peak of his hood formed a goblin-like point. However, a second glance revealed that this was merely an optical illusion. Someone had once lit a fire against that wall, creating a human-shaped burn mark. Even so, it had given them both a shock from which they didn't quickly recover.

The rest of the small lobby was bare. Dead leaves and used condoms littered the corners. Sometime in the past, a wheelie-bin had been dragged in and knocked over, vomiting a pile of foul refuse, which had now coagulated.

They ventured forward.

Beyond a row of bars, a stairway led up. The barred gate that allowed access to this hung from badly oxidised hinges. When Heck pushed the gate open, its protracted creak echoed in the passages above.

'Think O'Hoorigan will have heard that?' Lauren said. 'If he really is in sixty-nine.'

'I'd be amazed if O'Hoorigan was anywhere near this place,' Heck replied. 'Okay, he's a scumbag, but who in their right mind would want to doss here . . . even rent-free?'

They ascended warily. On the first landing, on the facing wall, someone using blood-red spray paint had slashed the words:

All we have to sell is fear

'They're selling it well,' Heck murmured, glancing to where a door to what might have been a store room or lock-up stood ajar. Dense cobwebs – the sort you'd expect a gigantic spider to weave – filled the darkened recess behind it, fluttering in a breeze that neither of them could feel. Straight passages led off in two opposing directions, lit only intermittently by patches of daylight, though this was sufficient to show strewn rubble. The doors to numerous flats hung open. The silence was palpable.

'As a British copper, do you ever wish you were armed?' Lauren asked.

'I *am* armed. I've got you.'

But even Lauren, fearless and efficient as she'd proved to be in the bar fight, was visibly unnerved by this environment. As they proceeded up to the second floor, the front door felt as though it was falling further and further behind them.

'I'm serious,' Lauren said. 'What if O'Hoorigan's pals from the Dog & Butcher are waiting up here for round two?'

'If there're any of them fit to walk,' he said.

But she'd made a good point – even if the men from the pub weren't here, Deke had mentioned that O'Hoorigan had used this place to buy drugs, which could mean there'd be junkies around, and though junkies, as a rule, weren't tough opposition, they might be carrying syringes. He fished about before picking up a heavy piece of wood; a ceiling lathe with cement caked around one end of it.

They continued. At the midway point where each flight of stairs switched back on itself, a tall, narrow aperture in the outer wall gave a restricted view into the courtyard below. Each time, more by instinct than logic, they peered down – as if to check that hostile forces weren't gathering at their rear. They never saw anyone down there, though when they reached the stair between the fourth floor and the fifth, they thought they heard a harsh male voice shouting something.

They stood and listened for a while, but heard nothing else.

Again Heck wondered about this guy, Deke – what did he stand to gain by telling them where O'Hoorigan was hiding? *If* that was what he'd done. It didn't compute that Deke was in cahoots with O'Hoorigan and trying to send them the wrong way, not after he'd just beaten the hell out of the burglar's friends. But to have casually given them the location of O'Hoorigan's hide-out, when others were prepared to lose teeth to protect it, suggested that his motives amounted to more than personal dislike. Deke, whoever he was, clearly wasn't a Salford lad – that much was evident from his accent. But the role he was playing in this affair was still a mystery, and the more Heck thought about it, an increasingly ominous one.

When they reached the top floor, extensive weather damage was visible. The ceilings were decayed and, in many cases, dripping water. They moved through a fire door onto an outer gantry. It was good to get back into the fresh air – the fetid stench of the stairwell had been cloying – but again they now felt exposed to prying eyes. The courtyard, which looked a long way down, still lay empty.

They advanced, Heck checking off the door numbers as they passed, which wasn't easy as most of the doors had either been kicked down or burned. The interiors beyond them were opaque with shadow. Halfway along, a metal plate hung over an entrance to their left; it bore the numbers: 60-70. They passed beneath it, entering another internal passage, though this one turned out to be a cul-de-sac and was about two inches deep in water. A grime-coated window occupied its far end. No doubt this looked down on the motorway, but the light it admitted was pitiful, seeming to dwindle as they advanced.

'You smell something bad?' Lauren whispered, wrinkling her nose.

'You mean worse than everything else we're smelling in here?'

She sniffed at the air, shaking her head. 'I thought . . . it doesn't matter.'

The next few doors were intact, though covered in paint. But then they came to number sixty-eight, which was missing entirely, and in the entrance to which three supermarket trolleys had been jammed together, creating a near-immovable obstruction that jutted out and half blocked the passage. The light was now so poor that they had to grope their way past this, though both were acutely aware that the next apartment was the one they wanted, and they moved with extreme stealth.

When they got to it, they saw that this door too had been removed – there was no sign of it, either in the doorway itself or amid the soaked trash that littered the passage. Like all the others, this flat was pitch dark inside.

Initially they flattened themselves against the wall and waited. But they heard nothing. Heck glanced into Lauren's face. In the dim light, her brow shone with sweat, but her lips were set in a defiant frown. There was no denying it; he was glad to have her with him at this moment.

'You ready?' he mouthed.

She nodded.

He counted down in his head – three – two – one. Then he hefted the cudgel, and spun around, going straight through the entrance. Lauren followed.

If it ever had been a proper squat, it didn't appear to be being used for that purpose now. The central corridor was cluttered with masses of shattered crockery and clumps of soggy plaster, which had dropped from the ceiling. Two doors opened immediately to rooms on the left and right. The one on the left had once been a kitchen but was now a gutted shell, black with filth and reeking of damp. The room on the right might have been a bedroom: a slashed, stained mattress lay in the middle, swamped on all sides by chip wrappers and food cartons – which suggested that someone *had* been staying here in the recent past. But in neither case was anyone present now.

'He'd have to be absolutely desperate to lie low in here,' Lauren said, revolted.

'Or absolutely terrified,' Heck replied.

They moved towards the room at the end. By now, Heck would normally have raised his voice to let the occupants know this was a raid and that police officers were on the premises. But of course none of that was possible.

When they reached the end room, he hesitated before going in. Lauren had been right, there *was* a smell – and it was vile. He glanced round at her. Her eyes were wide, almost rabbit-like. He pushed on in – but then stopped again, so abruptly that she blundered into the back of him. Neither was really sure what they'd been expecting to find in there. Perhaps they'd only been half-expecting to find Ron O'Hoorigan.

But they certainly hadn't been expecting to find him like *this*.

They could tell it was O'Hoorigan because of his green canvas trousers, but that was the only way. He'd been suspended upside down from the central light fitting, his ankles tied with a coaxial cord, which had then been drawn behind his back and used to bind his wrists as well. He hadn't been dead too long: the blood spattered all over the walls looked relatively fresh. And his intestines, which had been yanked out from his stomach in oily red and purple ravels and left to hang over his chest and face, were still glistening with moisture.

This latter detail explained the nauseating smell.

It wasn't decay – it was offal, ordure, human bowels ripped brutally open, their fecal contents allowed to drain onto the floor.

A cloud of bluebottles exploded from O'Hoorigan's belly cavity, and from the pool of filth underneath him. Heck and Lauren fell back choking as the droning horrors swept around them, getting into their faces and hair, even into their mouths.

They staggered out of the flat together, gagging. Heck, despite having attended countless murders before, had to lean on the facing wall to fight down queasiness. Lauren, though she'd fought on the real battlefield, wasn't in a much better state – she crouched alongside him. Both were gasping for air.

'Christ,' Heck said. 'Jesus Christ . . .'

'Heck, I . . .' She hawked and spat. 'I . . .'

'That guy was clearly an arsehole, but he never deserved . . .'

'Heck, I've seen this before. I mean the *MO*.'

He glanced round at her. 'What . . . *where?*'

She stood up, mopping her mouth with her sleeve. 'Iraq.'

She glanced back into the flat and down its central corridor. Now that their eyes had adjusted to the murk, the ghastly shape could still be seen hanging beyond the open door at the far end.

'Tell me about it,' Heck said.

'It can't be relevant to this . . .'

'I'll decide whether it's relevant or not.'

'Okay.' She still looked sickly. 'It had been done to three Arab men, insurgents who were believed to have been planting roadside bombs. Their killers were never apprehended.'

Heck pondered this – but his thoughts were interrupted by the screech of a vehicle skidding to a halt.

173

It was difficult in the dank passage to judge which direction the sound had come from. The motorway lay just beyond the end window, but there was an ongoing rumble of traffic from that direction, and it was muffled. What they'd just heard had been loud and clear. Heck lurched back towards the gantry overlooking the courtyard. As he did, he heard another car screeching to a halt. He reached the balustrade and looked down. Two police cars were parked below. An officer had got out of each. As Heck watched, a third police vehicle – this one looked like a dog unit – came thundering through the courtyard entrance.

Lauren joined him. 'Timely arrival,' she said, relieved.

'Timely arrival – nothing!' Heck retorted.

He glanced down at his training shoes; they were bloodied. Lauren's were the same. Two trails of reddish footprints were visible on the gantry walk behind them. He glanced at his sweatshirt; perhaps inevitably, blood was also smeared there – along its left sleeve.

'We've been set up,' he said slowly.

'What do you mean?'

A fourth police vehicle hurtled into view. It was another dog-van. Seconds later, the two dog-handlers, their animals straining at the leash, were picking their way through the rubbish towards the entrance Heck and Lauren had used to get up here.

'We're going to carry the can for this,' Heck said.

'Don't be ridiculous.'

He stared at her, amazed that she could be so naive. 'We've been looking for Ron O'Hoorigan, haven't we? Asking anyone who'd listen. Not only that, we've beaten the crap out of some guys who didn't want to help us. Now we're at his murder scene and we've got his blood all over us!'

It still took several moments for the import of this to dawn on Lauren, as though she was dazed by the speed of events. Heck took her arm and dragged her back from the balustrade. Only one copper was now visible in the courtyard, talking animatedly into his radio. Already a yelping of dogs could be heard from inside the building.

'We obviously can't go out the way we came in,' Heck said.

'We're running?'

'Of course we're bloody running! There must be a fire exit.'

He raced back down the internal passage. Previously, they hadn't gone right to the far end. Now they did, and found, as Heck had hoped, a fire escape, though its metal door was badly corroded. When he tried to push the bar down, it wouldn't budge.

He threw his whole weight against it, but it still didn't move.

Lauren joined in – they hit the metal together, and there was a *clunk* as the bar finally shifted. The door opened, but only about an inch before it grated to a halt. Lauren stepped back and aimed a flying kick. The door didn't so much open now, as break from its hinges and go crashing and banging down the spiral stairway on the other side.

Wind and traffic noise assailed them as they peered down. The stair descended to earth via a straight concrete shaft, which was open to the air on the motorway side. Whether or not the coppers in the building heard this racket was unclear, but the dogs sounded a lot nearer – they were barking excitedly.

'Come on,' Heck said.

But the spiral stair was as rusty as the door had been. As they started down, it shuddered alarmingly. In some places, the bolts holding it to the building wall had visibly rotted through. From this terrible height, it was easy to imagine that, should the thing collapse, they'd fall clear down to the

M602. The foot of the stair rested on a small paved area, only about ten yards by ten; a low wooden fence separated that from the dirt embankment plunging steeply to the motorway, along which an endless procession of cars and lorries was roaring in both directions.

'This is suicide,' Lauren said, a dizzying sense of vertigo causing her to sit and try to go down on her backside.

'So's the alternative.' He pulled her to her feet.

They reached the level of the fifth floor, clinging to the hand rails, but now the stair wasn't just shuddering, it was groaning and creaking. In fact it was swaying, as though it had come loose at the top and was only anchored at the bottom.

'Heck, we're going to be killed,' Lauren wailed, grabbing at his arm with a hand that was almost a talon.

'Just keep going.'

'This is crazy. We've found a crime scene. We should preserve it.'

'We'll get locked up, and that will bollocks everything.'

They were now about halfway down, the decayed steel groaning ever more loudly. Of course, with each level they passed there was another exit-door connecting to the building. At any moment, an officer could burst out from one and intercept them, though most likely the cops would be following the dogs, which were on a different trail.

By the time they got to the second floor, the drop wasn't quite so perilous. They were now close enough to the ground to see that the door they'd knocked loose above had flattened a section of fencing. But Lauren's fear had been replaced by anger.

'This is lunacy,' she said. 'Even if we get away, we're going to become fugitives.'

'If that's what's necessary.'

'That's ridiculous! Heck, for Christ's sake, what are we doing?'

They were still twenty feet from the ground, a sufficient distance to break them both in half if they fell, but Heck stopped and turned so sharply that she almost crashed into him and sent them both tumbling.

'This is not just about the investigation anymore, Lauren . . . *this is about our lives*!' He paused to let that sink in. 'Someone has set us up. We've been green-lit. And when you've been green-lit, the last place you want to be is in prison or a detention centre!'

She shook her head. 'You're a cop, we'll be protected.'

'I don't want to be protected! I want to catch the bastard who's doing this!'

He continued down almost recklessly fast. She followed, more carefully.

They at last reached the bottom, and exited Gallows Hill via the hole the escape door had made in the fence. They scrambled down the embankment until they were on the motorway hard-shoulder. It was narrow, and juggernauts rocketed past them with only two or three feet's clearance. The noise of this, exacerbated by the cutting's canyon-like geometry, was deafening.

'Alright!' Lauren shouted. 'But if my life's on the line as well, that means you've got to take me along. Right to the end.'

'I've no bloody choice now.' Heck beat the dirt from his hands as they headed east.

Several hundred yards along, when they were well away from the derelict estate, they cut back uphill, climbed under some barbed wire and found themselves amid sheds and allotments. Beyond these, now watching out for police cars, they threaded their way back through the dismal streets to the alley where they'd left Heck's Fiat.

'Who's supposed to have set us up, anyway?' Lauren asked. 'You think this guy Deke?'

'Who else?'

'I don't get it. If Deke doesn't want us around, why didn't he just let those dickheads in the pub beat us up?'

Heck didn't reply until he'd climbed behind the wheel, where he stopped to regain his breath. 'Because getting us beaten up wasn't enough. Whoever Deke is, he saw an opportunity to kill two birds with one stone: O'Hoorigan – who for some reason we don't know about yet, may have been in his sights all along. And us.'

'But he didn't try to kill us.'

'No,' Heck agreed, 'but like you say, I'm a copper. Killing me would have caused a big stink. This way was better. It would have covered his back, and put us out of the game permanently.'

'But who the hell is he?'

'I don't know.' Heck switched the engine on. 'But one thing's sure . . . he knows who we are.'

Chapter 19

He'd thought it was called a 'beta site'. Blenkinsop had no technical understanding of that term, if it was a *real* term. As far as he was aware, 'beta site' referred to a website without a name, just a string of randomly chosen numbers and letters – mainly because it wanted to remain beneath most people's notice. There could be any number of reasons for this, but none of the ones Blenkinsop could think of were particularly edifying.

He scrubbed a hand through his uncombed hair.

This was the second day running that he'd come to work so untidy that fellow employees had commented. Sally had asked him if he was feeling no better and if he wanted a paracetamol. He'd grunted a curt reply before closing himself in his office.

Beyond the window, radiant mid-morning sunshine bathed the dome of St Paul's. Directly below, Cornhill and Threadneedle Street were packed with cars, the pavements thronging with City types. It was the throb of business, the pulse of commerce, the arterial flow of the world famous Square Mile. As yesterday, however, the vibrant scene did little to uplift his spirits. In fact now it was even worse, because now he wasn't just riddled with guilt, now he was touched by fear.

A 'beta site'.

That was what he believed it was called. There were probably hundreds of them, thousands, millions. Yet he doubted any could be as abhorrent as the one that had so quickly come to occupy his every waking thought.

What a two-edged sword the internet could be.

On its first arrival back in the 1990s, he'd considered it a porn explorer's godsend. Online, you could get anything you wanted – literally *anything*. Talk about a refreshing change after the days of his youth, when in straight-laced, buttoned-up Britain you'd had to content yourselves with girlie mags containing nothing more than tits, bums and snatch. It didn't matter what your kink, the net could cater for it. Nothing was too extreme or bizarre, and of course it was all completely clean and non-judgmental. There was no stern-faced shop lady to stare after you as you scuttled out of the newsagents, your new purchase stowed in your briefcase; no visit was required to a dingy back alley and seedy shop, where the odious old men in raincoats and the stains on the video tape covers made you feel soiled simply for being there.

But in recent years, after some of his trips abroad and with his developing interest in getting 'hands-on' in such matters, these frolics in cyberspace had come to seem tame. The worst thing about this blasted summer had not been that his wife, Yvonne, and his daughter, Carly's annual two-month pilgrimage to the Med would leave him on his own, but that his scheduled trip to the Gulf in early September had been cancelled. The next one was only due in February – six months away. Until then he'd have to make do with the sanitised fantasies of the internet.

At least, this was what he'd thought – but then, two days

after Yvonne and Carly had embarked for the family villa in Italy, the card had arrived.

That was all it was: just a square piece of white card inside a brown envelope, delivered with the morning post. Blenkinsop's name and address were printed on the front in a basic typeface. Not surprisingly, there'd been no return address. Junk mail, he'd presumed, and when he'd ripped it open, intending to throw it away after a single glance, he'd been right – in a way.

'Dear Ian,' it had said in that same standard type, 'here is something that will interest you.' And underneath it was that fateful line of letters and digits – which he'd identified as a web address, as a beta site.

It was a mark of how enthralled he was to the 'thrill-seeker' side of his personality that he'd immediately gone online to check it out. He'd known instinctively that it would be a sex site of some sort, but instead of feeling alarm that these people, whoever they were, had made contact with him at his home (he'd written that off as an inevitability of having used his credit card to join so many sites in the past), he'd been excited and rather absurdly, he now realised, he'd regarded it as the commencement of a summer of online adult adventuring that might be a little bit more interesting than usual.

Despite all that had happened since, it seemed incredible to Ian Blenkinsop that a man at his station in life could ever be described as credulous, gullible, naive. And yet . . . he glanced across the office to his desk, where his laptop was sitting open, its screen blank. Again, fear gnawed at his innards. There was no reason at all to assume that the person who'd been eavesdropping on his conversation in Mad Jack's last night had been . . .

But of course there was reason.

There was *every* reason.

And there was even more reason to be afraid because of it.

He took a diary from his overcoat pocket and thumbed through its pages until he reached the back. There, sandwiched between two of his many legitimate contacts, was that string of digits; he'd destroyed the original card, and this reprint here was scribbled lightly in pencil in case he ever had need to hastily erase it. All he had to do now was go over to his desk, sit down, type these in – and he was there again. But it was a horrible prospect: seeking a meeting with them, trying to explain himself, all the time wondering what they might do to him. And just suppose they hadn't been following him last night? Suppose that man in Mad Jack's had been no one of consequence? If that was the case, yet now he emailed them and blabbed that he'd been drunk and depressed and hadn't deliberately been endangering their operation – wouldn't that have the very opposite effect of the one desired? Wouldn't he himself be alerting them? And yet, if he did nothing, would he spend the rest of his life glancing over his shoulder?

He slumped into a chair. If only he'd never gone onto that beta site.

The Nice Guys Club.

At first there'd been nothing on screen except a poorly shot movie of a young woman with a shoulder-bag walking up and down a railway platform. By the looks of it, it had been filmed with a hand-held camera, possibly from a car parked on the other side of the tracks. She'd been a nice-looking woman, wearing a pink sweater, a short denim skirt and high heels. Then words had appeared, streaming across the bottom of the screen like the end-credits to a TV show.

They'd read: 'Ever wondered what it would be like to do it even if she says "no"?'

Blenkinsop had sat up, his attention caught.

The image had then switched; it was another crude, home-made movie, but this time the subject was a slightly older lady clad in an indecently small bikini and splayed out on a lounger in the privacy of her back garden. This one appeared to have been shot via a zoom lens from a vantage point some distance away.

'Who is it, we wonder?' the words had continued. 'Your co-worker, your neighbour, that bitch in the corner shop who always taunts you by showing her stocking tops when she climbs the step-ladder to the high shelf? Why waste time dreaming when you could be sampling the real thing?'

By this time, Blenkinsop had been captivated. What appeared to be on sale here were simulated rape films. Of course, if he'd been less engrossed it might have struck him as odd that there'd been no warnings on the website about legalities, age restrictions, or any other items that would indicate this was mainstream entertainment.

'Join the Nice Guys now,' it had said, the 'now' highlighted as a link.

So he'd done it. Not joined up as such – not there and then. But, with inhibitions blunted by excitement, he'd hit the button and entered the site properly.

More movies had followed: an attractive woman crossing a dual carriageway bridge carrying shopping bags; an Asian schoolgirl waiting at a bus stop; a lady vicar, for heaven's sake, saying goodbye to parishioners at the church gate. One after another, they'd followed, each one occupying the screen alone but then retracting into a small thumbnail and finding its place in a vast electronic mosaic. And now, only slowly, had it begun to occur to Blenkinsop that what he was looking at here were not teasers for movies that someone had scripted, directed and performed, but fragments of *reality*. These were actual shots of real women going about their everyday business, in each case completely unaware they were being observed.

Another stream of words had then appeared: 'We can arrange it for you to rape any woman, anywhere, any time.'

His hair had actually prickled at that point; his flesh had goose-bumped.

'Age, race, creed – they're no concern to us. It's your choice. We only have two stipulations: a) Women only – we don't do guys or transsexuals (though if that's your bag, we know someone who does); b) UK only – you aren't going to pay our travel exes, so we aren't going abroad.'

An email address had followed, something embedded in a bogus website somewhere – Blenkinsop knew that much about the internet. So he'd mailed to it. Why not? He'd been left alone here while everyone else was on holiday; why couldn't he have some fun? Damn his fucking rule about never doing this kind of thing at home. Why not, if it was all safe and secure? He'd felt no guilt as he'd made contact, only keen anticipation. And, almost immediately, they'd replied with answers to his questions, and strong reassurances about his privacy should he decide to do business with them.

Looking back on it, how ridiculously easy it had been for something so heinous.

But he mustn't email them again, they'd told him. They would email him, but only after checking him out. After that, it had been plain sailing. The following day they'd contacted him from a different email address – and this time had given him the works, the whole picture. All he had to do was name the woman he wanted and state where she was to be found. It was that easy. They would do all the hard work and take all the risks. The only pain for him would be coughing up seventy-five grand, payable to a certain

Swiss bank account, the details of which he'd receive in due course. But was that a problem when such a prize was in the offing?

Blenkinsop had been hooked, dazzled by the ease with which something so desirable could so quickly be his. The mere recollection of it, and its ultimate terrible outcome, made him sick with self-repugnance – and of course with terror as well. How was it possible for such an organisation to exist online? Yet it happened all the time. Terrorists used the internet to recruit, poisoners to advertise their wares and services, and then there was the kiddie porn network – he hadn't thought there could be anything worse than that. But this took his breath away.

Any woman he'd wanted. All he'd had to do was name her and pay the cash.

Any woman – no matter who she was. Imagine that!

Once the ball was rolling, he'd never gone back to the Nice Guys website, as per their strict instructions. All further information, very carefully worded so as to be non-incriminating – would be delivered to him from email addresses that would immediately be negated afterwards, or via snail-mail. But whatever happened, he should stay away from the website. That was their explicit command. He wasn't sure why or how this might affect their security. Presumably the site existed on a machine located in a banana republic somewhere, or was being run from some completely innocent person's computer, which had been hacked and, unbeknown to its owner, was now being used as the host – again he had no technical know-how where this was concerned, but even a layman like him had sufficient under-standing of how it might be done and how it could there-fore be protected.

He walked across the office and stared at his laptop screen.

Under no circumstances, they'd said. The website was for first contact only (in other words the bait, he thought bitterly). From that point on, *they'd* be in charge of communications. Of course, the situation had radically altered now, and as he hadn't been given a customer-care number – he laughed at the very thought – this was the only way he knew to contact them.

He sat at his desk. The muscles tightened in his neck and down the middle of his back. There was a slow pounding in the base of his skull that he knew would soon become a full-blown headache.

He assessed the stream of pencil-drawn gobbledygook in his diary. Then he reached out, typed it in – and hit 'send'.

Nothing happened.

The address was not found.

He tried again, to make sure that he hadn't mis-keyed.

It was the same result, nothing. Frantic, he tried to Google it. Immediately, hundreds of other beta sites were listed for him, and below many there were all kinds of disgusting hints about what they might contain: 'Scat, farm sex, amputee fun day, teen smokes donkey dick . . .' But none of them struck a bell of familiarity.

The back of Blenkinsop's throat had gone so dry that it was hurting him. The tension in his neck intensified to the point of no return, detonating inside his skull in a fiery migraine, but even this was of no immediate concern. Lines of irrational thought began to scramble in his mind.

Had they disbanded, ceased to exist? For a few seconds he was ludicrously hopeful.

But then he realised that they'd simply changed the address, as they no doubt did every time they snared a new customer. It was a simple but foolproof way to prevent him causing trouble for them in the future. Whereas they, of course, from their position of complete anonymity, could cause an awful lot of trouble for him.

Chapter 20

They drove at increasing speed along the A57, swinging south down the A5063 and crossing the Ship Canal at the swing-bridge. Trafford, the next borough, was a massive complex of industrial estates and lorry parks, so there was a bit of a slowdown there. But they finally got out of it via the A518, and headed south again, steadily picking up speed. It was now mid-morning so the traffic was at low tide and, by the time they entered Sale, they were belting along.

'Where's the fire?' Lauren asked.

'Behind us,' Heck replied. 'You mean you hadn't noticed?'

'We got away.'

'Yeah . . . for how long?' They hurtled into Altrincham, where the M56 motorway would hook them up with the M6. 'We've got to get back to London pronto. At least then we'll be on home turf. And I can ditch the car.'

'Why do you want to ditch the car?'

'Because Salford CID will have the registration mark by midday today.' She shook her head, clearly not believing him, but he was adamant. 'From this point on, Lauren, don't use your mobile. In fact, keep it switched off. Mine is. If you must make a call, use a landline, a payphone.'

'Heck, much as you applaud your own craft, you're surely not serious that your lot are going to be onto us so quickly?'

'I'm certain of it. An expert has created this fit-up. Someone who won't have left anything to chance. If the police don't draw the correct conclusions from what they've already got, he'll just drop them another clue.'

She checked the dashboard clock. It was ten-thirty; on a good day they'd be back in London by two. But Heck now stated that he didn't intend to stay on the motorway for long. If an APB was put out, there'd be traffic patrols on the bridges, looking out for them. South of Birmingham, he intended to use the back roads.

Lauren groaned. 'This is a serious overreaction.'

'Have I been wrong once so far?'

'I'm not sure you've been right once.'

'You think people like Ron O'Hoorigan get killed that way every day?'

She had no immediate answer for that. It was probable that scrotes like O'Hoorigan got bumped off more regularly than normal people. But in that particular fashion? It seemed unlikely.

'And doesn't it seem a hell of a coincidence that it happened as soon as we made contact with him?' Heck added.

Lauren had to admit that it did.

'On the subject of which,' Heck said, 'you mentioned something about seeing a similar murder in Iraq.'

'That's true.'

'So?'

'I'm breaking the Official Secrets Act, if I tell you.'

'It's about time you justified your presence on this enquiry, so bloody break it!'

She glanced uneasily at him, though this was more to do with the memory of the incident than the breach in protocol. 'Three guys had been killed, all in identical fashion to the one we saw this morning. They'd been hung upside down and gutted while they were still alive. I was in the patrol that found them . . .'

She hesitated to continue. Even now, several years later, the stench re-assailed her. It had been much worse than that at Gallows Hill because southern Iraq's oven-like heat had commenced the putrefaction process more quickly. The buzzing of flies had been so loud as to deafen even ears like hers, which had become accustomed to the roar of artillery. Just thinking about it again made her gorge rise.

'It was in a ruined town on the outskirts of Basra. Initially, it was assumed to be the work of sectarian Iraqis. But later on evidence suggested the victims were insurgents and that occupation forces might be responsible. Like I said, no one was ever prosecuted.'

They drove on in silence, both wondering how these things might be connected. To Heck it seemed doubtful. Exemplary punishments were enacted in criminal circles in every corner of the globe. There were numerous overlaps in style and method.

'Why did you refer to him as an *expert*?' Lauren asked.

'Who?'

'Whoever's supposed to have set us up.'

'Because he clearly knows what he's doing.'

'You think he could be ex-military?'

'What are you driving at?'

She sat up straight, a new idea taking root. 'You think this guy Deke is the one, yeah?'

'For the moment. He certainly fought in that bar as though he'd been trained.'

'You noticed he was wearing leather wrist-bands?'

'Sure.'

'Were they an affectation, do you think, or to cover

something up? Because when I was in Iraq, there was this shadowy group we used to hear about. A British commando outfit called the Special Desert Reconnaissance unit. They carried out covert operations, sabotage, counter-terrorism, that sort of thing. They also had a rep for being ultra-ruthless. I mean – these hanging-disembowelments, they'd have been typical of the SDR.'

'Were they investigated over the Iraq killings?'

'I don't know. That would have been classified. But the main thing is . . . their nickname was "Scorpion Company".'

'Cool. But how does that help us?'

'It was vanity on their part, a kind of tradition of the outfit since World War Two. SDR troops always had a scorpion tattooed on the inside of each wrist.'

'And that's what the wrist-bands were concealing?' Heck said.

'They could have been.'

They were now passing through Bowdon, two or three minutes from the motorway junction. Heck eased his foot off the pedal, pulling away down a narrow side street.

'What're we doing now?' Lauren asked.

'Just a quick diversion.'

'What happened to us getting back to London?'

'We will do. But you can't beat good intel.'

They parked in a lot attached to a small, prefabricated building, which looked like an annexe to a suburban infant school but was actually the local library.

'You want me to come in with you?' Lauren asked.

'Best if you don't.'

'Danger round every corner here as well, hey?'

'No, but local plod will be looking for you too by now.'

'Me?' she said, surprised.

'You're ex-services, Lauren. They'll have your prints on file.'

'I didn't leave any prints at that crime scene. I made sure of it.'

'But you might have done during the bar fight.'

'Heck, this is ridiculous . . .'

He opened his door. 'Don't underestimate cops, Lauren. It's easy these days to read the newspapers and believe they're a bunch of politically correct do-gooders, who spend every shift at diversity seminars rather than fighting crime. But that isn't the case. They're as smart and efficient as they ever were. If they're looking for me, they'll very likely be looking for the black chick who's with me. Better if you stay here.'

'Alright.'

'There's one thing you could do for me.'

'What?'

'Got any spare change?'

'Change?'

'Yeah, you know . . . as in shrapnel, cash?'

She handed him all the silver she had, and waited in the vehicle while he sloped across the car park to the library entrance. Inside, there was a photocopier/fax machine, which the librarian – a curt lady with glasses on a chain – said he could use so long as he paid twenty pence per sheet. Outside the main room, in the lobby, he found a payphone and put a call through to the CID Admin office at Deptford Green Police Station. To his relief Paula Clark answered.

'It's Heck,' he told her nervously – not sure what kind of reaction he would get.

'Oh hi,' she replied. Clearly she wasn't yet aware that anything was amiss. 'I thought you were on leave?'

'I am, sort of. I want to clean up some paperwork first.'

'Okay, well . . . what can I do for you?'

'If you've got a spare minute, I'd like you to access CrimInt for me. Just to check someone out.'

'Can't you do that yourself?'

'Not at this moment, no.'

In fact, Heck could have. The library also had a computer with an internet connection, but if he'd accessed the Metropolitan Police's main criminal intelligence network with his own password, they'd trace it back to the terminal he'd used, and that would be another clue to his whereabouts.

'Is this important, Heck?' Paula asked. 'Only I'm a bit busy.'

She'd never been the most cooperative woman, even when officially his secretary. Well aware where her responsibilities began and finished, she rarely did anything beyond those limits, so it was probably expecting a lot of her to help him now.

'It would be really useful to me if you could do it,' he pleaded.

'The thing is I can't. Can you call me back a bit later?'

Heck bit his lip. There was never any point antagonising civilian employees. They could make your life hell. Unimpressed by your police status because they worked alongside you every day, to them you were just someone else in the office. In addition, they always seemed to have the ear of the top brass, especially if they were female (usually this was because the top brass in question, who were nearly always male, thought they might get a bit in return).

'Paula,' Heck said, in his most insipid voice, 'I would take it as a personal favour if you could do this for me.'

'I've told you I can't.'

He knew full well that she could. She could access the CrimInt network via the computer that was sitting right in front of her. It was a couple of button pushes away. At the most, this request would take two or three minutes out of her day.

'Look, please . . . I'm trying to progress something. And I can't get any further unless you help me out with this.'

'I thought you were clearing up paperwork?'

'I am. You know what a pain that can be.'

She'd agree with that. Even civilian employees in the police were overwhelmed by paperwork these days.

She sighed melodramatically. 'Okay, okay. What is it?'

'I want a quick search on any faces we might know who served in the British army during the last ten years, specifically with the Special Desert Reconnaissance unit. There shouldn't be too many.'

He waited, listening to her manicured fingernails tapping the keyboard. It went on for several seconds, before she said: 'We've got a hit.'

'Just the one?'

'Yes.'

'Good. That's all I need.'

Lauren had been alone in the car less than five minutes when Heck returned. He crossed the lot quickly, several sheets of paper in his hand.

'Check these out,' he said, jumping in.

He handed her the sheets, which were faxed copies of a computer print-out. The mugshot at the top of the first was very grainy, but it clearly depicted the guy who'd helped them in the bar. She read through the accompanying text.

Heck chattered on: 'That's all the info we've got on a certain Eric Ezekial, thirty years old and, before you ask, a particularly nasty individual. He's got form for assault, demanding money with menaces and threatening to kill. He's also ex-army, a paratrooper who served with Scorpion Company for three years, which included two tours of Iraq and one of Afghanistan. His service record is full of incident, but we'd have to go to the MOD to get that. All we need to know is that he was dismissed from the service three years ago on grounds of mental instability.'

'"Eric Ezekial",' Lauren said, reading aloud. '"AKA . . . Deke".'

Heck put the car in gear. 'We've got him.'

'Christ, you seen this? "Believed active as a syndicate enforcer." What the hell is he doing walking the streets?'

Heck drove out onto the road. 'That suspicion's probably based on intel supplied by an informant. If he's not wanted for anything in particular, there's nothing we can lift him for.'

'Whatever he's doing, it must pay. "Last known address – six, Redbrook Close, Kingston upon Thames".'

'You don't get that kind of bread standing on pub doors in a monkey suit.'

'I wonder what he's been doing up in Manchester?'

'I aim to ask him.'

She glanced around.

'Solves a problem, actually,' Heck said. 'I wasn't sure whereabouts in London we were going to crash tonight. I am now – Kingston.'

Chapter 21

It was late afternoon, and another balmy August evening was in the offing.

Detective Superintendent Gemma Piper was seated in a corner of The Barrow Boy, a narrow brick building tucked away in a nook just off Tothill Street, yet famous the city over for its cosy, wood-panelled interior and diverse range of real ales. She sipped at a glass of wine and, for the sixth or seventh time since leaving the office, tried to place a call to Heck – only to get no response. Frustrated, she laid her phone back on the table. She'd ordered a ham salad sandwich for her tea, but it hadn't yet been delivered. When a shadow fell across her, she glanced up, thinking it was the waiter.

It wasn't. It was DI Des Palliser. He threw his coat over the back of a chair, but remained standing, giving her an unconvincing smile.

'Greater Manchester CID have been in touch,' he said. 'They're a bit confused – as am I, I must admit. They want to know if Mark Heckenburg's apparent involvement in a mutilation-murder on their patch this morning should be registered as a blue-on-blue, or whether they ought to consider him a suspect?'

Gemma was vaguely aware of her jaw dropping. '*What?*'

'Just that. Mind if I go and get a drink?'

When Palliser returned, pint of beer in hand, his boss was still in a state of acute shock. He sat across the table from her, lips pursed as he awaited a coherent response.

'Who's he supposed to have murdered?' she finally asked.

'A local burglar.' Palliser filched some notes from his inside pocket. 'Seems he hung the bastard upside down, slit his belly open and left him to bleed out.'

'And what've they got on him?'

'Well . . . a lot.' Palliser re-read his notes. 'Thanks to Heck's VRM being caught on numerous security cameras and his prints getting left on a broken bottle, he's now been positively identified as someone who went yesterday to the victim's home address, asked questions about his whereabouts, and finally tracked him to a nearby squat, where the aggrieved party was later found hanged and gutted in what might be, quote, "a ritual homicide".'

'The AP . . . he wasn't by any chance a certain Ron O'Hoorigan?'

Palliser arched a disbelieving eyebrow. 'You know about this?'

Gemma shook her head with slow-building fury. 'I'm going to kill him. I'm going to bloody well kill him.'

'Well it can't be Heck, can it? I mean Heck's a pro. If he'd gone to Manchester to top someone, would you expect him to leave a trail of clues as obvious as this?'

'I wouldn't expect him to top someone in the first place!' she hissed.

'Also . . .' Palliser checked his notes again. 'Do we know a girl called Lauren Wraxford?'

'Not as I'm aware. Why?'

'Because a vehicle she rented in Leeds, which is now

overdue to be returned, is currently lying wrecked on some wasteland just outside Manchester.'

'And what's that got to do with this?'

'Good question. Seems she's an ex-squaddie. She's got minor form as a juvenile, but she's been clean for a while. However, she was with Heck yesterday when they got involved in a bar room brawl that left four men seriously injured.'

Gemma closed her eyes and squeezed the bridge of her nose, before taking a long sip of wine. 'What the bleeding hell is he playing at?'

'By the looks of it, he's still following his last case.'

'What've you told Manchester?'

'What else? I've told them he's involved in undercover work for us.' Palliser stared at Gemma accusingly, clearly piqued that she hadn't trusted him enough to keep him in the loop. 'I'm guessing that's the truth. I've also said that we'll bring him in as soon as possible so that we can hear his side of the story.'

'Are they alright with that?'

'Not really. And I don't suppose we can blame them. I mean, they've got a bloke on a slab who spent his last few minutes watching his breakfast drain through his own gizzards.'

'Jesus Christ.' Gemma shoved a hand through her blonde curls, which suddenly looked wilder and more unruly than usual.

'Do you want to tell me what's going on?' Palliser said.

She sighed long and hard, before admitting: 'Heck had a couple of new leads, which he desperately wanted to follow.'

'Good ones?'

'Circumstantial mainly.'

'So why'd you give him the nod?'

'Because I'm weak.' She banged the table. 'And bloody stupid.'

'Laycock's going to love you for this.'

'He doesn't need to know.'

'He'll find out at some point.'

'Let him.'

'He specifically wanted this investigation shutting down.'

'I've run this department successfully for four years, Des. I don't need Laycock's approval for everything.'

'Yes, but if he didn't have much ammunition before . . .' and Palliser laid his notes on the table, 'he does now.'

'Why don't you just drink your beer, and let me think this through?' She drained her wineglass. When her sandwich was placed in front of her, she barely acknowledged it.

Palliser rubbed his beard. 'Possibly a silly question, but have you been in touch with Heck by mobile . . . just to keep a check on what he's up to?'

'I've tried half a dozen times, but it's been switched off. That said, he's only been gone two days. I didn't expect World War Three to have broken out.'

'Whatever's going on, he must realise his job's on the line.'

'His *job*?' Gemma looked amazed. 'Des, the only reason I'm not putting an all-points on Heck right now is because I don't *want* to believe he's responsible for this. Laycock will have no such qualms. I'm not worried he'll sack the bloody fool, I'm worried he'll charge him with murder.'

Chapter 22

They abandoned Heck's Fiat in a multistorey car park in Cockfosters. It was on one of the upper floors, but there was a dank, cavern-like atmosphere, water dripping from the huge arches. At this time of day there were few other vehicles. The dimness of early evening spread between the concrete stanchions.

Before leaving, they again checked the address they had on the print-out.

'Kingston's a good hour from here,' Lauren commented. 'Even by tube.'

'Well we're not going to force entry by daylight, are we?' Heck said.

'We're going to force entry?'

'Unless you want to knock on the front door?'

'Suppose there's someone in?'

'Don't worry, we'll play it by ear.'

They set off down the ramp to the main road.

'What happened to the scrupulous copper I first joined forces with?' Lauren asked. 'The one who didn't even want me with him because it was against the rules.'

'He doesn't want to get hung up by his feet and have his

belly ripped open.' Heck shrugged as if this was all in a day's work, though he didn't look happy. 'It's needs must, okay? I don't like it any more than you, but at present we're flying blind.'

From Cockfosters, they caught a train to Finsbury Park, changed to the Victoria Line, and alighted again at Warren Street, from where they crossed the West End on foot. Heck had decided that, if they went the whole distance by train, it would be easier for their progress to be tracked by station security footage. At Sloane Square, they boarded a westbound Circle Line train, changed to the District Line at Gloucester Road, got off again at Putney Bridge, and proceeded on foot, stopping once at a DIY store to purchase a roll of silver duct-tape.

It was close on eight o'clock when they finally reached Kingston upon Thames.

From Lauren's perspective, this was the first salubrious neighbourhood the enquiry had brought them to. It was a mix of the old and new, handsome Tudor buildings fronting onto the river, alongside restaurants, chic bars and luxury apartment blocks – which was pretty ironic given that both she and Heck were extremely nervous about what they had to do here. They knew from personal experience that Eric Ezekial would be no pushover. Okay, there was no guarantee he'd be here – it seemed unlikely he could have got down to London ahead of them in this short time. But suppose he didn't live alone; what if he had a family, what if there were business associates on his premises?

When they found six, Redbrook Close, it was a white-washed terrace cottage, located in a small, quiet mews. There were no lights inside, but there were in the neighbouring cottages and in the cottages opposite, which meant that a frontal approach was out of the question. As they ventured around to the back, Lauren felt increasingly uneasy about Heck's scheme.

'You sure this is a good idea?'

'When someone's after me, Lauren, I like to turn the tables at the first opportunity.'

'But suppose we've got it wrong?'

He shook his head. 'If we've got it wrong about this being connected to the case, we've not got it wrong about Ezekial.'

'Yeah, but even though we're wanted for murder, your colleagues won't just ignore what you tell them. You can give them enough for them to get a warrant and turn this guy's place over legally. It could blow this thing wide open.'

For the hundredth time, Heck wondered about this. The problem was that he had nothing concrete or conclusive. Even though it was only a hunch that Shane Klim was the scar-faced man who'd stalked some of the women who were later abducted, it was hard fact that beforehand he'd been banged up for two years with Ron O'Hoorigan – ample time for him to discuss any future plans he might have. In fact, it would have been unusual if he hadn't. But taken as a whole, it still looked a little weak. The fact that O'Hoorigan had since been murdered did not prove anything either – it could be completely unrelated to Heck's investigation. And Commander Laycock would not be understanding about that; quite the opposite.

'Perhaps too wide open,' Heck said. 'Let's see what *we* can find first.'

At the rear of the cottage, a long narrow alley meandered away between hedged gardens. Night had now fallen properly, and a single lamppost was visible at the far end.

'I'm just bothered that this business might be distracting us from finding Genene,' Lauren said.

'Has it occurred to you that Ezekial might be the guy who abducted her?'

She looked startled. 'But you said Shane Klim . . .?'

'Maybe they're in it together. It would certainly explain why Ezekial did what he did to O'Hoorigan – to shut him up perhaps? Klim may be inside this building right now.'

She glanced over the hedge at the cottage's darkened rear. 'That's a lot of maybes.'

'For the time being, maybes are all we've got.'

They overcame the hedge easily enough. Heck gave Lauren a leg up and she was nimble enough to do the rest herself, jumping down the other side and opening the gate quietly. He slipped in and they closed it again. As their eyes attuned, they found themselves at the bottom end of a long lawn with immaculate flower beds down either side. They stole forward, passing en route a sun lounger next to a low, wrought-iron table on which there was a pile of newspapers and an empty cocktail beaker with a paper umbrella hanging out of it.

'He's been enjoying the summer,' Lauren murmured.

'Good. He'll have a long, cold winter in Parkhurst to look forward to soon.'

The cottage was about twenty yards in front, and still there were no lights inside. They halted. 'I'd be expecting motion-sensitive bulbs to come on any time now,' Lauren said.

Heck glanced up at the cottage eaves, and at the eaves of the cottage next door. The diminutive shapes of pipistrelles flitted back and forth.

'Maybe not,' he said. 'There's a bat colony there, look. The lights would be coming on and off all night.'

Reassured, they moved forward onto a crazy-paved patio. A French window stood directly in front of them, with the curtain behind it drawn. Alongside there was a recess, and inside that a rural-style door: oak planks painted white with bands of black ironwork.

'I can't see any alarm?' Lauren said.

'There may not be one.'

'Oh, come on . . .'

'Just think about it. If this place gets broken into while he's away, does he really want police activity here? There could be all sorts of incriminating stuff.'

'You're telling me a property like this isn't alarmed?'

'Not in the conventional sense, as in an alarm that makes a loud noise. More likely, it'll have one of those high-tech systems that sends him a text, so that *he's* alerted but no one else is.'

'That still isn't good news for us.'

'Not if he's nearby and can get back quick. But if he isn't, we've nothing to worry about.'

Lauren shook her head; she still wasn't convinced. 'Suppose there's someone living here? A girlfriend?'

Heck glanced at his watch. 'It isn't nine o'clock yet and all the lights are off. It's a fair guess there's no one at home.'

'It's risky.'

'Risks are sometimes necessary.'

They crept past the door recess to a small wash-house window. It was double-glazed, its frame made of PVC.

'Breaking one of these will disturb the entire neighbourhood,' Lauren said.

'Yeah, but *that* won't.' Heck pointed to the floor above, where there was a smaller window with a panel of frosted glass. 'That's a bathroom or toilet. It's our best bet.'

It was far out of reach, though a horizontal stretch of iron guttering was located about three feet underneath it. They might conceivably be able to reach that. 'Okay.' She still sounded unhappy. 'How do we do it?'

He produced the duct-tape. 'Plaster the glass with this, then punch it.'

'You're joking?'

'It works for hundreds of shithead house-breakers every day. There's no reason why it shouldn't work for us. No one'll hear a thing.'

'Who's going to do it?'

'Can you stand on that gutter without ripping it out of the wall? I don't think I can.'

'Christ,' she said, resigning herself to the inevitable.

'Here.' He gave her the roll of tape, then took his sweat-shirt off and handed it to her. 'When you get up there, wrap this round your fist.'

They glanced around once more just to make sure they weren't being observed from the premises opposite. But it was still pitch-black in the narrow canyon between the two rows of cottages. Nothing stirred apart from the bats darting about overhead.

Using Heck's foot as a stirrup, she clambered up his body until she was able to stand erect on top of his shoulders. She wasn't heavy, but after the battering he'd recently taken, he had to lean against the wall for support.

'Can you reach?' he asked in a strained voice.

'Just about.' She yanked down on the gutter with both hands to ensure it was solid, and then used it to lever herself upwards. It was just wide enough for her to gain a purchase with her knees and then reach up and find the window sill. Once standing, she carefully layered the duct-tape on the glass. 'Here goes nothing.'

There was a dull *whump* as she struck it. Another followed, slightly louder, but not loud enough to alert the neighbours. Piece by piece, she handed the sticky tape-coated shards down to him. 'You know we're leaving prints all over this stuff?'

'He's not going to call the police. Don't worry.'

A short while later, she was able to climb in through the empty frame. Heck moved back to the rear door. She opened it from the inside. He stepped through and closed it behind him. Again they had to wait as their eyes attuned, but street lighting filtered in through the front windows, so it wasn't long. The interior was split level in the 1960s beatnik style, the upper floor open aspect with only a carved wooden balustrade to separate the sleeping area from an eight-foot drop. Aside from smaller rooms like the wash room and kitchen, the ground floor was an all in one lounge-diner, modern in look yet with old-fashioned fixtures: a flagged floor, oil paintings on the white plaster walls.

They advanced warily.

'What exactly are we looking for?' Lauren asked.

'We'll know when we find it. There must be something here we can use – I was right about the personalised alarm.' Heck pointed to a corner of the ceiling, where a tiny red light was flashing on and off, and a video camera turning to follow their progress.

'Shit!' She made to dart away, but he grabbed her.

'Don't panic. I want him to know we've been here.' He made a V-sign at the lens.

'This is so nuts,' she replied.

'No. This is psychological warfare. He needs to know that his adversaries are at least as smart as he is.'

'Sounds like macho bullshit to me.'

'Whatever, it works.'

They poked around the downstairs, moving furniture, opening drawers, before Heck headed up to the first floor. Lauren followed, increasingly tense. They'd been here several minutes already, which felt as though they were stretching their luck absurdly. They searched the bedroom shelves but found nothing of interest.

'Know anything about hacking?' Heck asked, eyeing the bedside computer.

'No.'

'Neither do I.'

He tried to access the system anyway, but the password defeated him. While he was thus engaged, Lauren brushed against the wall, only for it to *creak* as though made from flimsy material. Heck heard this and got to his feet. They examined the wall carefully. Now that their attention had been drawn, it became apparent that this portion of wall had been left accessible. There was no furniture against it; it had no skirting board. Heck tested it with his fingers. It creaked again.

'This is just soft-board. Ah hah . . .'

He'd found a tell-tale slit in the paper, which, when he followed it, described a rectangle about six feet tall by three wide. He pushed hard. There was a *click* as a catch was released, and the rectangle swung outward. A bare wooden stair lay beyond.

'What the hell's this?' Lauren said.

'Fifty years ago it would've been Deke's ascent to the gallows.'

The stair connected with the loft, or with a room that had been constructed inside the loft. It was small and square, with only the roof's south-facing slope serving as its ceiling. There were no windows, so Heck felt it safe to flick a switch. An electric light came on, revealing another desk, another computer, a filing cabinet and a wall-cupboard.

'Now we're getting somewhere,' he said.

He opened the cupboard first. Inside it there was a steel rack containing a variety of automatic weapons. Various pistols and revolvers were ranged along the top: Glocks, Brownings, Berettas. Below those, there were heavier-duty items: rifles and submachine guns. Heck recognised a Kurtz, two Armalites, a Kalashnikov, even a high-powered Dragunov sniper rifle.

'Good God,' Lauren said slowly.

Heck turned to the filing cabinet and yanked open its drawers. They were packed with paperwork filed in buff folders. A reference code had been scrawled on each one with felt pen. The codes were the sort you used when listing electronic data and wishing to keep it orderly and chronological; for example, 'a' through to 'z', followed by 'za' through to 'zz', followed by 'zza' through to 'zzz', and so on. There was also a leather-bound ledger. Heck flicked it open. It was filled, page after page, with lists of scribbled notations. At first glance it looked like gibberish, but there were numbers in there with pound signs attached, *big* numbers, each one struck through with biro (possibly to indicate that the full fee had now been paid). On one occasion, Ezekial – because this was evidently a ledger of his accounts – had earned twenty-five thousand pounds for a single job. On another he'd earned forty-five thousand pounds.

Lauren stiffened. She thought she'd just heard movement outside the house.

Heck continued to flick pages. Each separate list clearly referred to a different employer – at least that was the way it appeared. She hooked his arm with her hand. He shook her loose; he was too preoccupied.

'Someone's coming in,' she whispered, dashing to the top of the loft stair. She strained her ears to hear more – a key was turning in the front lock. This time Heck heard it too.

'We've got to go!' Lauren hissed.

He nodded, but his eyes scanned quickly down the very last page in the ledger. At the bottom of the final list, the reference to the most recent job was 'RO'.

Ron O'Hoorigan?

The figure alongside it read ten thousand pounds.

'Heck!' Lauren had been halfway down the stair and now stuck her head back into the room.

He glanced at the top of the list. Whoever these particular jobs had been performed for, he – or they – were referred to simply as 'Nice Guys'.

'Heck, for Christ's sake!'

He nodded, switched the light off and followed her down the stairs.

Just as they did, the cottage's front door slammed open, and yellow streetlight flooded into the darkened ground floor. Lauren dashed across the sleeping area on cat-like feet. She made straight for the bathroom, but Heck didn't immediately pursue. He paused halfway, and moved towards the balustrade. Even the sound of someone blundering around downstairs, and then the loud *clack-click* of what could be a firearm being cocked made no apparent impression on him. He loitered there as though uncertain about something. It took Lauren to hurtle back in, grab him by the collar, haul him into the bathroom and push him out through the window.

They both landed on their feet, and raced down the garden towards the rear gate. As they reached it, full lighting came on in the house behind. They didn't glance back, but crashed out into the alley and raced away into the London night.

Chapter 23

They ran north up Kingston Road, crossed the river at Teddington Lock and only slowed to a walk when they reached Petersham Road. By now they were sweaty-faced and panting. The few late evening pedestrians gave them a wide berth.

'Why did you hesitate like that?' Lauren asked.

Heck shook his head.

'You're not going to start going barmy on me, I hope?'

'He was *there*, wasn't he? Right there, right in our grasp. If we'd jumped him then, it could've been the key to everything.'

'You're kidding, right? You saw the way he beat the shit out of those idiots in Salford. Besides, it sounded like he was armed.'

'Yeah, that might've been a problem. But we could still have nabbed him if we'd been canny. The thing is . . . it's not him we're after. It's whoever's paying him.'

They were now entering Richmond. At weekend these privileged streets would be alive with well-heeled revellers, even late at night. But midweek it was quiet, its jazzy bars and swish restaurants closed and silent. A mist was forming, rolling in from the river. They glanced behind them a couple of times, but there was no sign anyone was following.

'This is a lot bigger than I thought, Lauren,' Heck said. 'This guy, Deke . . . I don't think he's just some brainless bit of underworld muscle. I think he's a hit-man. A proper one, a pro.'

'Yeah?'

'Doesn't it make sense, with the weapons he had? The fact that he's ex-special forces supports that theory.'

'In which case, doesn't it rule him out of *our* investigation?'

'Not necessarily.'

'But we're just looking for a missing woman.'

'Look, Lauren . . .' He mopped his sweat-damp hair from his forehead as they walked. 'There's something you need to know . . . I haven't been entirely straight with you about this. I'm not just investigating Genene's abduction. A whole bunch of women have gone missing in similar circumstances in the last few years. Genene's only one of them.'

She glanced sidelong at him, at first looking as if she didn't quite know how to react. 'You mean . . . you mean this is some kind of serial killer?'

'I don't know. I considered that possibility at first, but we've never found any bodies. You understand that what I'm telling you here is classified? You can't go spreading it around.'

'Who am I going to spread it to, Heck?' She blew out a long, slow breath. 'That's not good news, but I don't suppose I should be any more upset than I was before. All respect to these other birds, Genene is still my priority. But just out of interest, how many are we talking?'

'Upwards of thirty.'

'Jesus Christ!'

'Maybe more.'

'And this Shane Klim is the one who's . . .'

'He's probably not been acting alone. It's increasingly difficult to see how anyone could be doing this alone. And now we know that a professional hit-man is involved . . . I mean, that puts it into a different category altogether.' Heck rubbed at the back of his neck. 'Always assuming I'm on the right track. This is all still theory, I'm afraid. If it's wrong, and we've blundered into some totally different criminal conspiracy, I'm back to square one in a big way.'

'But like you say, you've got to chase every lead right to the end, no matter how slender?'

'Yes.'

Lauren looked thoughtful as they strode. 'Heck . . . just tell me this. If it turns out that you *have* blundered into something else, some other naughty business Ron O'Hoorigan had knowledge of – and it's got nothing to do with Genene or these other women, and you've been barking up completely the wrong tree – you're not just going to give up on them?'

'No. Of course not.'

'You are going to find them?'

'Or find what happened to them, yeah.'

She stopped him mid-stride, fixing him with a near-luminous stare. 'Promise me that, Heck. We're not doing all this for nothing? You're not just gonna give up?'

Heck was quite sincere when he replied: 'That's something I can always promise.'

She nodded, and followed him as he headed into Richmond tube station. 'Where we going, anyway?'

'East,' he said.

'You know somewhere we can stay tonight?'

'I've got a vague idea.'

'It's just that I've got mates all over London. We can crash with one of them.'

He shook his head. 'Our lot'll be after you for sure by

212

now. All your known associates will be under surveillance.'

'So where *are* we going?'

'Leave it to me.'

They caught the District Line and rode to Embankment, where they changed to the Bakerloo and headed south again into dingier districts. At this late hour, the train was otherwise empty, and strewn with the debris of the day's passengers: sweet wrappers, Styrofoam cups, discarded newspapers.

'Won't Deke just move his base of operations now he knows we're onto him?' Lauren asked.

Heck shrugged. 'Maybe. But that's something he won't be able to do quickly or easily. Even if he does, he won't be able to go far.'

'Why?'

'Because we've got *this*.' He reached under his sweatshirt and produced a book – it was the leather-bound ledger from Ezekial's loft.

'Bloody hell!' she said.

'It couldn't be bloodier for him. This amounts to a detailed list of the very, very serious crimes he's committed.'

'So he's going to come after us?'

'He's already after us, Lauren. But now it's personal. In fact, it's more than personal. If he wants this back, it won't just be a simple matter of putting the knuckle on us – he'll have to make a deal.'

'Or alternatively he'll scarper for good. You take that to the law now, and they've got him.'

'Not quite.' They'd now arrived at Elephant & Castle, so Heck slid the book out of sight again and they stepped from the train. 'We stole it during a burglary, remember. It's inadmissible as evidence, and Deke knows it. He also knows that, when push comes to shove, we want his paymasters more than we want him.'

'You really think he'll be prepared to trade them?'

213

'He may have no choice. At present, his arse is in a sling.'

They left the station. Whereas Richmond's sedate streets had been settling down for the night, this part of London – Southwark – was still noisy with traffic, honking horns and belligerent, drunken shouts. They turned left under a brick arch, and followed a narrow side passage.

'I can't believe it'll be that straightforward,' Lauren said. 'We've hurt him bad, and you know what they say about wounded animals.'

'Speaking of which . . .'

The passage now became a tunnel, and led to a tall steel door. A weak bulb illuminated it, showing where blue paint had flaked away, exposing the raw metal beneath. It had the look of a service entrance, as if it had once connected to a warehouse or factory. The bulb over the lintel buzzed and flickered, threatening to plunge them into blackness.

'What's this place?' she asked.

'A drinking den,' Heck said. 'A card school . . . a knocking shop. Hopefully our lodgings for the night.'

He hammered on the metal with his fist. It reverberated deep inside, as though through vast, empty chambers. There was no immediate response, so he hammered again.

Lauren glanced behind them uneasily: the tunnel dwindled off into shadow; a mouse scurried across it. 'Who the hell lives in a place like this?'

'An old acquaintance of mine,' Heck replied. 'Someone you thought you were going to have a chat with yourself at one time. His name's Bobby Ballamara.'

Chapter 24

Gemma read carefully through the print-out that Palliser had just pulled off CrimInt.

'And this is the last thing he asked Paula Clark to do for him?' she said.

'Certainly is,' Palliser replied.

'Eric Ezekial? Not the sort of name you'd forget easily.'

Palliser's office was knee-deep in littered paperwork, most of it having been dragged from the various bags that Heck had brought up from Deptford Green. The larger office beyond the open door, where the Serial Crimes Unit's detectives had their desks, now lay deserted and dark. Gemma and Palliser, both with collars open and sleeves rolled back, were working by the low light of a single desk lamp.

Palliser yawned. A few moments ago he'd had the sudden inspiration to contact Heck's former secretary and see if he'd confided anything in her before 'going on leave'. It had paid dividends, though the woman had torn a strip off him in the process.

'She wasn't best pleased when I rang her up at this hour,' he said.

'She'll be even less pleased when I ring her up again, in

about two hours, to see if there's anything she can add,' Gemma replied. Anyone overhearing this casual comment might have assumed she was joking, but Palliser knew 'the Lioness' better than that. 'This number she faxed it to is definitely up in Manchester?'

He nodded.

Once again, Gemma stabbed Heck's number into her mobile. Once again, there was no response. Sighing, she put the phone away. She laid the print-out on her desk, alongside a similar print-out for Ron O'Hoorigan and a case file photograph of Genene Wraxford; in trying to pinpoint Lauren Wraxford, the girl Heck was in company with, it hadn't taken them long to spot that one of the missing women shared the same surname. But she wasn't their main focus at present. 'This guy Ezekial is obviously the key,' Gemma said. 'Lives in Kingston, I see.'

'Shall we pay him a call?'

'No.' She tapped her teeth with a pen. 'Find out everything you can about him, Des. But don't approach him. Same goes for the Wraxford family.'

'May I ask why?'

She paused, before saying: 'Heck must have a reason for wanting to stay off the radar. Much as it's infuriating me, I feel I've no option but to respect that a little longer.'

By the furrows on his brow, this wasn't what Palliser had wanted to hear.

'You disagree?' she asked.

'His reason may not be a good one.'

'You mean it's because he's a murderer?'

'Of course not. More likely he's continuing the mission AWOL because he doesn't want any crap to blow back on you.' Palliser stood up to go out, but loitered in the doorway. 'That's hardly encouraging, is it?'

'More likely it's because he doesn't want me to interfere,' Gemma argued.

'Probably it's both . . . either way, I'm worried he's out of his depth.'

'I'm concerned about that too. I still want to find him. But in the meantime . . .' and she picked up the Ezekial print-out, 'we're sitting on this lead. At least until Paula Clark feels the urge to blab to someone else, at which point we'll have to come clean.'

'Laycock will go fucking ballistic.'

She slipped the print-out into her briefcase. 'Leave me to worry about that.'

'This is a total fuck-up, ma'am.' Such comments were a measure of Palliser's stress. An old-fashioned type, he rarely used foul language in front of female colleagues, especially not his feisty boss. 'We should have supported Heck in the first place. I don't mean covertly. I mean openly. If we were going to do this, we should have stood up to Laycock and demanded the case be kept open.'

'There were no grounds for that.' Gemma dragged her coat on. 'So don't be so bloody ridiculous.'

'What's bloody ridiculous is that Heck may be in danger, and we're just sitting here.'

'*He's lucky we're sitting here, Des!*' she snapped. 'I sent him out there with a remit to run down a single lead! And to keep me fully and regularly informed. I also told him to keep things low key. For whatever reason, he has disobeyed those direct and explicit orders. I'll never trust him again.'

'You won't trust him?' Palliser said, as she pushed past. 'That's a good one. Have you stopped to think that if he actually trusted *us*, we wouldn't be in this situation in the first place?'

She whirled around and glared at him. But there was no argument. Palliser was being entirely truthful. If not, he wouldn't have stood there and boldly returned her gaze.

217

'I'll leave you to turn the lights out,' she finally said. There was an unusual fluster to her cheek. 'Remember what I said about Ezekial?'

Chapter 25

When the two Greater Manchester Police detectives emerged from the private room attached to the recovery ward, they had a young doctor with them, though it was only the white coat and stethoscope that revealed the doctor's profession. Aside from that, he wore jeans and an open collar shirt, and thanks to the long hours he'd worked, his jaw was covered in stubble. By contrast, the two detectives were fastidiously neat. The detective superintendent, whose name was Smethurst, was a stone-faced, early middle-aged man with cropped, iron-grey hair and a clipped grey moustache. He wore a shirt and tie under his jacket, none of which were even creased despite the lateness of the hour. His compatriot, Detective Inspector Jarvis, was a woman about ten years his junior. She wore flat shoes, a trouser suit, and carried a shoulder-bag. Her hair, which was mouse-brown, was cut almost as severely as that of her boss.

She beckoned to the two uniformed constables – PCs Hallam and Belshaw – who were waiting on the other side of the passage. They were both young men, not long in the job, still probationers in fact, and they came over smartly; after weeks of checking town centre properties and handing out parking tickets, they were eager to get involved with some 'real' policework.

'So what are the chances of us interviewing him tomorrow?' Detective Superintendent Smethurst asked, glancing back into the room, where a blanketed shape lay flat on an orthopaedic bed. One of the patient's arms was attached to a drip, the other to a bank of bleeping monitors.

The doctor shrugged. 'Give it a try . . . why not?'

'So he'll be fit?'

'Possibly, but he suffered quite a beating. Apparently he said something to a nurse about one of your lot being responsible . . .?'

'That's one of the things we want to speak to him about. We didn't manage to get much out of him earlier on. Nothing that made sense, anyway.'

The doctor half-smiled. 'I'm not sure what you expected, given the state he was in.'

Smethurst remained po-faced. 'This is a murder enquiry, Doctor. So all I need from you is a straight answer. Will he be fit to be interviewed tomorrow – yes or no?'

The doctor shrugged again. 'It's hard to say, but I think it's worth your while calling around at some point. The sedatives will have worn off by then.'

Apparently pleased to have been as ambiguous as he possibly could without actually obstructing them, the young doctor sauntered away. Smethurst gazed sourly after him, before moving back into the room to look long and hard at the unconscious patient.

DI Jarvis turned to the waiting PCs. 'What time you two on 'til?' she asked.

'Ten officially, boss,' Belshaw said. 'But we've got overtime 'til three. Nights are taking over then.'

'No nodding off, eh?'

'No problem, boss.'

'I mean it, lads. This bloke may just have come out of surgery, but he played his part in a vicious bar-fight yesterday which was the prelude to one of the nastiest murders I've ever seen. So we're watching him around the clock until he's fit to be interviewed. We don't want anyone coming in to have a word with him, and we certainly don't want him leaving here. You nod off and something happens, you'll be on the dole this time next week . . . clear?'

They nodded, still bright-eyed and bushy-tailed.

'There's a coffee machine down there.' She pointed along the otherwise deserted passage. 'Sup plenty. I don't care if you're pissing for England by morning.'

Again, they nodded.

'I'll say it one more time, lads, this bloke could end up being a *crucial* witness. So no one gets in to see him unless it's one of the nurses or doctors. That's no visitors, no cleaners . . . not even any bobbies unless you know for sure who they are. In fact, even if you are sure, you get on the blower and speak to us first. Whatever time it is.'

Detective Superintendent Smethurst reappeared, car keys in hand. He was clearly uncomfortable about leaving the hospital – even more so when he eyed the pair of youngsters who'd be standing on guard in his absence – but he was nearly fifty, and the extra-long shift he'd put in was finally getting the better of him.

'Sorted?' he asked Jarvis.

'Reckon so, Sir.'

He glanced again at the uniforms. 'If there's anything suspicious at all . . .'

'We'll call it in, Sir,' Belshaw said. 'Guaranteed.'

But once the detectives had left, and despite their genuine enthusiasm, it wasn't long before the two uniforms were starting to wilt through inactivity. It was now close on twelve, and both constables were surprised at how quickly and

221

effectively the hospital – such a hive of frenetic activity during the day – had closed down on itself. A deep quiet seemed to fill the entire extensive building. Most unnecessary lights had been switched off, and there were minimal signs of life down at the recovery ward admissions desk. Occasionally a member of staff would move back and forth down there, but that was all.

PC Belshaw was the first to start feeling the weight of this tedium. He was seated outside the door to the private room, but was already regretting the measures he'd taken to make himself more comfortable. He'd removed his helmet, and then his anorak, draping the waterproof garment over the back of his chair and slumping against it. As a result, sleep was creeping up on him and he constantly had to shake himself and sit upright again. Hallam was posted inside the room, so there was no possibility of lively conversation – not that there ever was with Hallam anyway.

Eventually, Belshaw got up and tried to walk around. He avoided strolling down to the ward-proper. The night staff would be chatty enough – of the two he'd met, one, a young trainee, Nurse Goldenway, was particularly attractive – but he didn't want to get too distracted from what he was supposed to be doing here, so he headed in the other direction.

He passed the vending machine, which stood alone with a single light shining down on it, and reached a T-junction. On the right, the passage ran fifty yards to an exit door, which appeared to be firmly closed. On the left, it receded into dimness, and, aside from a single red emergency light, its farthest end lay almost completely invisible. Several darkened doorways opened off this, but there was no sign of movement. Belshaw was about to head back to his post, when he heard a sound – only brief, like a *click* or *snap*. He held his position, listening. He hadn't been here long enough to apprise himself of the hospital's layout; he didn't know whether anyone was supposed to be down that left-hand passage or not, but the absence of working lights suggested that nothing official was going on.

He advanced slowly, still listening, passing a door on his left, which stood open but revealed nothing except a small bathroom with a toilet and washbasin. Then he heard the sound again, another distinct *click*, followed by a further two in rapid succession. After that there was more silence.

The sounds had appeared to emit from the open door now approaching on Belshaw's right. He moved towards it and glanced through. The room beyond, which was about thirty yards by twenty, stood in deep gloom; most of its corners were hidden in shadow, but its central area was tiger-striped by frosty moonlight filtering through the partly open Venetian blind on a central window. It looked like a treatment area, but was not currently being used: two rows of three empty beds, distinguishable only in vague outline, faced each other from opposing walls.

Belshaw was about to turn and leave, when a flicker of movement caught his eye. He spun around: at the farthest end of the room, another door stood open. This appeared to connect with a small annexe bedroom – his eyes were now attuning to the dimness, and he could just make out the foot of another empty bed in there. As he peered at it, there was more movement: a shadow flickered on the annexe bedroom's wall.

'Hello?' he said, unsure why he was speaking quietly – he was so new to his status as police officer that he hadn't fully acclimatised to it yet; it still didn't come naturally to him to emanate authority. Cursing himself as a rookie, he spoke more loudly. 'Is somebody in there? Because I don't think you're supposed to be.'

There was no response, except for more shadowy

movement on the annexe wall. Unconsciously fingering the baton at his belt, Belshaw walked forward. The shadow moved again – a sharp, flirting motion from one side of the room to the other. There were more sounds: more *clicks* and now *creaks*, as if weight was being furtively adjusted.

The bristles on Belshaw's neck stiffened. They knew he was here. Which meant there was only one course of action.

He approached the door swiftly, drawing the baton from his belt. As he rounded into the room, his other hand clamped on his radio – only for him to find the room empty. He halted, confused. There was nothing in here at all. Not even any side furniture. The bed was just a bare frame, a skeleton. He glanced at the window, the top panel of which was open. Another slight breeze intruded, and the Venetian blind hanging there *clicked* and *creaked* as it swung; more of its shadows flickered across the walls.

Feeling a prize fool, Belshaw backed into the dimly lit treatment area and turned.

Someone was standing directly behind him.

He half-shouted.

In return, the slim, blonde figure in the blue hospital scrubs yelped.

Then she laughed; a delightful cheeky titter. Belshaw also laughed, though in his case more from embarrassment.

'My God, constable,' Nurse Goldenway said. She'd evidently just collected two clean urine bottles from a side cupboard, and hadn't noticed that somebody was nearby. 'My God . . . you gave me a turn.'

'Yeah . . . sorry . . .'

'Like graveyards at night, these places, aren't they?'

'Erm . . . yeah.'

She nodded at his drawn baton. 'And what were you planning to do with that?'

'Oh, nothing . . .'

'You know what I'd be wondering if it was mine?'

'Sorry, what . . .?'

'Where do the batteries go?' She winked, then turned and bustled prettily out, leaving Belshaw feeling strangely abashed.

'Yeah, right,' he said, sliding the baton back into his belt. 'Course.'

If nothing else at least he was wide awake, he thought, as he wandered back to his post. And now he'd ensure that he stayed that way. He stuck his head into the private room, where Hallam was half-dozing in the armchair just inside the door.

'Brew?' Belshaw asked.

Hallam jerked upright, but on seeing it was only his partner, nodded and rubbed at his sallow face. 'Yeah, yeah . . . that'd be good. Ta.'

Belshaw walked back along the passage. Thanks to the light over the top of the vending machine, he was able to find the right change, insert it and then wait patiently while milk and boiling water gurgled into the two paper cups. He took them from the machine – and then noticed that the curtains drawn on an alcove opposite were fluttering.

This time he hesitated before responding, but finally, with a sigh, he approached. He was here to do a job, after all. With two coffee cups in his hands, he had to use his elbows to draw the curtains back. Beyond, he saw the open entrance to what looked like a storage facility. It was a closet-sized room with steel cabinets down one side and a rack of surgical gowns down the other. There was a window in its facing wall, wide open.

Belshaw moved wearily towards it, bending down to peek through. On the other side, he saw a small garden, a little bedraggled – as if it didn't get much attention. On the far side of that, dim lights were visible in other sections of the hospital. Yet again, all was still and extremely quiet. Deciding that now he *was* taking things a little too far, he rose up again and turned – and was hit in the face by a gloved fist that was more like a mallet of flesh and bone.

With one punch, it crushed his nose to pulp and shattered both his cheekbones.

Five minutes later, Hallam was still struggling to stay awake. He continually readjusted his position but it was having progressively less effect. When he finally heard the heavy feet tramping back down the corridor and into the room, he thanked his lucky stars. Hot coffee – that would do the trick. He looked up, smiling, and just had time to glimpse two figures in green surgical gowns, glaring maniacally down at him over masks stretched taut across noses and mouths, before receiving that scalding hot coffee right in his eyes.

Hallam didn't get a chance to scream before PC Belshaw's baton smashed down on his cranium. Not once, but two, three, four times; on each occasion with greater savagery, so that when he finally dropped from the chair his blood crossed the entire room in a thick, flowing stream.

Chapter 26

The men around the table sniggered.

They numbered ten in total, and, as often happened in circles of this sort, there were several types on show: the snivellers – typical Cockney rat-boys with thin features, greased-back hair and suits that looked second-hand even though they probably weren't; the bruisers – shaven headed, scar-faced, and invariably sporting chunky, tasteless jewellery. Then there were the nondescripts, the quiet ones – they could be smart or casual, and their ages could vary from thirty to sixty. They might be soldiers or lieutenants, but these were the ones you had to be careful of. They didn't put on a show, because they didn't need to.

One of these, a youngish chap with a red goatee beard, wearing a blue silk suit and a white silk shirt buttoned to the collar, was the one who'd finally come to the door and let the callers in. He was now back in his seat, checking his hand of cards. As they all were. Heck's unexpected arrival was only a minor distraction to them.

'So let me get this straight,' Bobby Ballamara said slowly. He too was engrossed in his cards, and in smoking a large cigar, but his lips were taut, his eyes lidded – he looked like a lizard about to strike. 'You want me to help you . . . because you have fucked up so much that even your own people are out to nail you?'

'It's only for one night.' Heck stood facing him the way a condemned man might face a deliberating judge.

Lauren had been told to wait in a corner, where she now sat, looking alone and nervous. At first glance, she'd had difficulty working out what the purpose of this room actually was. By the unlagged piping running across its ceiling, and the steel girders in some of the walls, it had once been part of an industrial facility, maybe the ground floor of a warehouse. To get in here, they'd walked through several big, empty chambers with bare brick walls and utilitarian wooden boarding for floors, though this one was a little plusher than those. It had a bar at one end, where more of Ballamara's heavies were lounging. Beside that was a low stage with a steel pole in the middle. An elderly woman in high heels and a leotard was putting two junior strippers through their paces. Music, downbeat jazz – very soothing and romantic, like something from the late 1940s – was playing. It suited the low lighting and rich pile carpet.

'You are aware, Heckenburg . . .' Ballarama said. 'It's okay if I call you "Heckenburg"? I don't have to bother with the "Detective Sergeant" bit anymore?'

There were more sniggers from the rest of the men.

'Heckenburg's fine,' Heck said.

'Because it wouldn't strictly be true to call you "Detective Sergeant Heckenburg" anymore, would it? Perhaps it'd be more appropriate if I called you "Prisoner Heckenburg, 48276983" or whatever the fuck your inmate tag ends up reading.'

'I told you, it's a misunderstanding. I can sort this out. I just need a little time.'

Briefly, Ballamara was too occupied with his hand to reply. He finally played it.

'You see – *Heckenburg,* one of the problems I have is that your usefulness to me only lasts as long as you're looking for my daughter. So if you now can't do that, which you clearly can't – because you're too busy looking after your own arse – then as far as I'm concerned you're a non-person. You don't matter.' He glanced up with those grey, coin-like eyes. 'And you coming here uninvited is a right fucking liberty.'

'I can still find your daughter,' Heck said. 'At least, I can find out what happened to her.'

'I've got six private dicks working on that now. I fail to see how *you* – in your current reduced state – could be a better bet than them.'

'I very much doubt they've even got close.'

'And how would you know?'

'Because I *am* close, and they're not in the picture.'

Ballamara looked at his cards again. 'Three days ago you didn't have a fucking clue.'

'A lot can happen in three days.'

Ballamara played his next hand. For Heck, the delay seemed torturous.

'And this is how you expect to bribe your way into my protection, is it?' the gangster said. 'By teasing me with what you think you've learned . . . after stringing me along for the last two years?'

There were no sniggers from the rest of his crew now. They could sense when their boss was becoming agitated, even though his body language remained calm.

Heck held his nerve – this was always going to have been the tough bit. 'I'm offering a straightforward trade, Mr Ballamara. Refuge for me and Lauren here – for one night. In exchange, I'll give you everything I've got. Down to the last detail.'

Ballamara stubbed his cigar in an ashtray and laid his cards down. 'And what's to stop me having it beaten out of you right now?'

'Feel free to try,' Heck said. 'I'll crack at some point, sure. But how much will I crack? How do you know what I'll be telling you is kosher? How do you know I won't give you the best run-around you've ever had?'

Their eyes locked as Ballamara contemplated this.

'All I'm asking is a bed for the night,' Heck said. 'Is that so steep?'

'I can give you a bed for the night, Heckenburg – and your skirt. But tomorrow morning you'd better be ready to spill your guts.' Ballamara spoke in a low monotone – he was almost droning, but there was no mistaking the intensity there. 'You don't tell me everything I want to hear, I'll make sure that whoever messed your face up yesterday looks like an absolute novice.'

Heck nodded and tried to swallow, but had almost no saliva. 'There's one other thing I could use,' he said. 'A couple of mobile phones – clean ones. I only want to borrow them. You can have them back when I'm done.'

Ballamara said nothing, merely nodded to another of his goons, a black guy in a t-shirt and wraparound shades, with a physique that suggested he bench-pressed with heavy machinery. The black guy ambled away, and the gangsters resumed their game. There was muted conversation as more cards were placed and the money pile in the middle grew larger. One of the trainee strippers approached with a tray, to collect the empties and take orders for another round. She was dressed only in a thong and heels, but she was thin and pale, and had a vaguely Eastern European look – she was sixteen years old at the most. Heck caught Lauren's eye. Neither felt sufficiently comfortable to even imply what they were thinking about their new 'ally'. Heck glanced towards

230

the bar, where the black guy chatted briefly with Lennie Asquith before lumbering back over. He handed Heck two mobile phones, a red one and a blue one.

'Thanks,' Heck said.

'You're welcome,' Ballamara replied without looking up. 'Goodnight.'

More sniggers followed. Heck beckoned to Lauren, who hurriedly joined him. Asquith was now waiting beside an open door, beyond which stairs led upward.

'Oh . . . Heckenburg!' Ballamara called after them when they were halfway there. They looked back. He continued to lay cards. 'Do not be fucking me around.' He took a slug of Scotch. 'Never make that mistake, Heckenburg. I don't forget things and I don't forgive them. You shit on me and I will *seriously* shit on you.'

And that was the end of the conversation.

Asquith led them up the stairs to a first-floor passage that was lit, rather suspiciously, by a crimson light. Numerous doors led off it, but he took them to the one at the end. When he opened it, the room beyond, though plain, was not as seedy as they'd expected. There was one bed, a double – complete with an iron bedstead and duck-down duvet, a writing desk with a chair drawn under it, a sideboard on which a portable television sat, a closet with a slatted door and, besides that, the entrance to a small en suite. The décor was dull – all beige and brown, but at least it was clean. The window looked down on a dismal alley, but they were able to close the blinds and block that out.

'There's no hidden camera in here, is there?' Heck asked Asquith. 'We don't want to end up for sale in one of your gaffer's backstreet DVD shops.'

Asquith almost looked offended. 'Like we could make money out of you two.'

He banged the door closed as he went out.

Lauren shook her head. 'Heck, you're not serious about . . .'

Heck put a finger to his lips, moved across the room and switched the television on, making sure to turn the volume up. 'No cameras, but that doesn't mean there isn't a mike,' he said quietly.

'You let someone like Ballamara into this investigation, and he'll ruin the whole . . .'

'Don't worry. I'll feed him some fictional bullshit. All I needed to do was buy us a night.' He got undressed, stripping down to his boxers.

'Heck, this is a dangerous game we're playing.'

'This firm's like a women's church group compared to the one we're after.'

'That why, five minutes ago, you looked like you were about to cack your pants?'

'Don't worry, I've got it sorted.'

He went through to the bathroom, to wash. Lauren wasn't far wrong though. Despite his bravado, this was a risky strategy. He again considered calling Gemma, not just because the guilt he felt about keeping her in the dark was burning a hole through him, but because her support – in fact any kind of support – would be more than useful. But he was now so far out on a limb that just getting in touch with her would be exactly the wrong thing to do. Even if she believed his theories, she would insist that he came in. She'd probably send units to arrest him. It would be career suicide for her to do otherwise. It didn't matter if the trail went cold as a result of him being taken off the streets. That could never be her priority now.

'In which case I'm still on my tod,' he muttered, as he stared at his battered reflection in the mirror. 'Sorry, Gemm.'

When he returned to the bedroom, Lauren had stripped to her bra and knickers. It struck him as strange how informal

232

they already were with each other after such a short period of time. Of course, Lauren, being ex-army, was probably well used to being undressed in the company of men. Despite this, she was caught on the hop when Asquith barged back in without knocking.

'Bob says there's some sandwiches downstairs if you're hungry.' His eyes rolled appreciatively over Lauren's athletic form.

'We're fine, thanks,' Heck replied, taking a break from checking the two mobiles, to stare pointedly at him.

Asquith shrugged and withdrew. The door clicked shut.

'If I've got a choice, I'll take the red one,' Lauren said, indicating the phones.

'Neither of these are for you, I'm afraid.'

She looked surprised.

Heck was about to explain, when he heard a creak from the passage. He moved to the door, yanking it open. Asquith was still there, but immediately headed off towards the top of the staircase. He glanced back innocently.

'Just keep walking, pal,' Heck said. 'Or the deal's off. And *you'll* be the one who has to tell your boss why.'

Asquith curled his lip in a sneer, but vanished down the stairs. Heck closed the door, just as laughter exploded from below. Immediately, the music changed and became louder. The easy melodies of the 1940s were replaced by black metal – thumping, dark-hearted, the vocals shrieked as if by a madman in a cage.

'We'd have been better on a park bench,' Lauren said, sitting on the bed.

'No we wouldn't.' Heck slid under the duvet on the window side. 'Even if we don't sleep, we need rest. You don't mind sharing, by the way? I don't take up much room.'

She shook her head, switching the light and TV off before climbing in alongside him. It wasn't particularly dark; from outside, an on-off neon glow, green one minute and yellow the next, penetrated the thin curtains.

Lauren chuckled, but there was no humour there. 'Like a movie, isn't it?'

'A bit,' he agreed.

The tone of her voice changed. 'Only you're not much like the cops we see on telly.'

'You mean I'm not as good looking?'

'No, I didn't say that. I mean . . . you've not got some detective buddy who's still on the right side of the fence and is now doing everything he can to get you out of the shit.'

Heck felt her hand on his thigh. He became aware of her proximity. Her trim but feminine curves fitted snugly with his more angular, masculine shape.

He rolled onto his side so that his back was to her. 'We should try to sleep, Lauren.'

In response, she knelt up and reached behind her to loosen the catch on her bra. When it fell away, her breasts tumbled forward.

Heck glanced round at her. 'What're you doing?'

'What does it look like?'

'Okay . . . *why* are you doing it?' He was trying to be tough with her, but her breasts swayed enticingly, and a heat was stirring in his loins.

'I know you like what you see, Heck. I'm not blind. I knew that first night in the pub. You'd have done anything to shag me then.'

'That was then, this is now.'

There was a brief pause before she said: 'Look . . . I don't want to feel alone tonight. Not in here. You don't need to worry; I'm not asking to be part of your life. I don't want to take your control away. I just . . . it's this place.'

Before he could resist – not that he tried very hard – their lips fastened together, their tongues entwining. Hers was sweet, soft and it probed into the deepest corners of his mouth as he wrapped his arms around her and dragged her down onto the pillow.

An hour later, Lauren began to cry – at first very softly, but then with progressively deeper sobs, which she struggled to suppress.

Heck, who'd only been half-asleep, put a hand on her shoulder. 'What's the matter?'

She shrugged him off. 'I don't know . . . nothing, something daft.'

He sat up tiredly. 'Problem shared, and all that.'

'I don't know . . . stupid. Mum would so disapprove of what we've just done. She thinks sex without love is a bad thing.' Lauren sounded embarrassed, though her tears were still flowing. 'Just her generation, I suppose. But it's got me thinking about her . . . everything she's been through in her life, and now *this*. Sitting in that flat all day next to the phone, waiting for good news to arrive about Genene. And *why*? On what basis? I mean I bought my way out of the army to be with her, and I'm not even there, am I? I'm here with you!'

'She knows what you're doing,' Heck said awkwardly. 'You told me that, yourself.'

'I also told you she doesn't approve. You know, she and Genene were so like each other; always pleasant and polite, dead straight-laced, proper ladies even in that shithole. Me . . . I was just a juvenile delinquent who thought the crap I'd suffered meant I could do anything I wanted. I so wasted my school years; hanging out, getting involved with gangs. Genene said I was letting the side down.' Lauren shook her head, fresh tears appearing. 'I was too dimwitted to realise that behaving like a street hoodlum only gave those who hated us even more ammunition. I only went into the army through default,' she said. 'The second time I got arrested for being found in a stolen car was the day it became obvious something had to change. My probation officer said I'd only avoided juvenile prison by a miracle. He pointed me to the armed services.'

'Out of the frying pan and into the fire, eh?' Heck remarked.

Lauren nodded and sniffled. 'That was what Mum said. She was worried sick by it. I mean, there were wars kicking off everywhere. But Genene thought it was a good idea. She said it wasn't as dangerous as the route I'd been following in Chapeltown. Anyway, me and Genene . . . we still didn't see eye to eye on stuff. I almost rejected the idea because she supported it, but thankfully, in the end, I didn't. The army was the first bunch I'd ever met who weren't concerned that I didn't have any grades. They said they'd train me, and not just to fight. They'd find out which disciplines I had an aptitude for, and educate me appropriately. They said I'd come out better equipped to make a go of it on civvy street than most university leavers did . . .'

'Good bit of blarney, if nothing else.'

'They needed bodies, didn't they?' she said. 'They were off to war. Anyway . . . despite that, things went well. Suddenly I had a career, money, prospects.' Fresh moisture glinted in her eyes. 'And all because of Genene, who I never once thanked. Christ . . . Heck, I'd got into some bad habits during my dumb days. One of them was always assuming there'd be time to do things later. You know what I mean? Anything difficult or awkward; anything you don't really want to face up to. You keep putting it off because there'll be time for it later. Except . . . there might not be.' Briefly she couldn't speak. More hot tears dripped onto her breasts. 'Isn't there . . .' She struggled to get the words out. 'Isn't there anything you can say . . . about Genene, I mean? About where she is, what might have happened to her? It was bad enough when I thought some pervert had grabbed her, but now . . . the idea that it's more than one pervert, maybe a bunch of them, who specialise in grabbing women, for God knows what purpose! I mean . . . come on, Heck, tell me something . . . *You're a copper!*'

Heck wanted to put his arm around her shoulders, but felt it would be inappropriate. What they'd just done together had been too quick and functional to entitle him to behave like a boyfriend. Besides, she was seeking comfort, and he had none to give. To most folk, Genene Wraxford was nothing more now than a tattered, peeling face clinging to a few rain-soaked lampposts, and most likely that was all she'd ever be.

'Lauren . . . this is the reality of crime,' he said quietly. 'It's not about Robin Hood, or rebels without a cause, or likeable rogues. It's about evil actions destroying innocent lives. And all we can do as police officers is react to it. Clean up the mess any way we can, wishing as much as everyone else that we'd been there in time to prevent it. I don't know where Genene is or what happened to her. But I've got to be honest with you, it's not good. She's been missing a long time, love.'

Again Lauren mopped her tears away, frowning, the young street-tough trying to reassert herself. 'Why couldn't it have happened to me, eh? I could have dealt with it. Poor Genene wouldn't have had the first clue.'

Heck didn't bother to mention that few, if any, dealt easily with the onslaught of typical urban predators.

She blew her nose, and then, unexpectedly, said: 'You need to be a lot nicer to your sister, Heck. I don't know what happened between you two in the past. But if you intend to make up with her – and I reckon you do, because you don't strike me as the sort of bloke who carries a grudge forever

– you'd better get a move on. One of these days, all of a sudden, she's not going to be there anymore.'

She reclined onto the pillow and rolled over, turning her back to him. 'For the record, I'm pissed off as hell that you've seen me in this state. Bet you were thinking: "She's alright, this one. But no, hang on . . . she's just a soppy girl after all."'

'You think *I* don't cry?' Heck replied.

'Not in front of anyone else, I bet.'

'Only because it's a long time since there's been anyone else.'

'Well don't break down on us yet.' She sniffled again. 'You've got some cases to solve.'

Heck sat up for several minutes after she'd gone back to sleep, pondering her final comments. In truth, he didn't know which prospect he found more onerous – the increasingly dark road along which this investigation was taking him, or the road to reconciliation with his sister.

Chapter 27

Frank Ogburn only opened his bruised, swollen eyes because someone dashed ice-cold water into them. Even then, the anaesthetic was wearing off at its own ponderous pace, so he remained muzzy and nauseous. He knew vaguely that he was supposed to be in hospital, but for some reason the comfortable bed they'd rolled him into several hours ago had been replaced by a crude, wooden frame, which enclosed him tightly from all sides. The warmth of the hospital had also gone; instead, the air was cold, damp and reeked of oil.

'Francis James Ogburn,' said a voice he didn't recognise. 'Landlord of the Dog & Butcher no less.'

'What . . .?' Ogburn felt incredibly weak; his lips dry and sticky. He gasped aloud as a slight adjustment of his posture sent a strap of intense, fiery pain across his middle. 'Where . . . please, where am I?'

'Also known as "Frankie", "Franny", "Oggy" and "Toady",' the voice said. 'Toady? Can't think why they call you that, a good-looking bonehead like you.'

Ogburn blinked hard. His eyes hurt and his vision was unfocused, but a clutch of dark figures seemed to be leaning over him; several standing, one kneeling. Bright lights shone

239

down from high above. He had the impression of a skeletal framework, maybe scaffolding, towering behind them.

Again he tried to move; again the pain across his midriff transfixed him. "Kin 'ell! . . . where . . . where the . . . the fuck am I?'

'One thing at a time, Toady, one thing at a time.'

Ogburn had never heard that voice before. He'd never been likely to, spending most of his life in the rougher neighbourhoods of Salford. It was rich and resonant; sounded educated – like someone on television, which for some reason frightened him as well as baffled him. He tried his damnedest to visualise his captors. None of their features were remotely distinguishable . . . *Good God, were they masked?* He was so alarmed by this that he barely noticed when the one kneeling placed something heavy on his lower legs.

'Looks like someone gave you a real kicking, Toady,' the voice said. Ogburn fancied it belonged to the figure in the middle; whoever he was, he appeared to be leaning on a walking stick. The pain in Ogburn's midriff was intensifying meanwhile, as was the pain in his lower legs – whatever weight had been placed there had sharp, angular edges.

'Some . . . some bastards in the pub yesterday,' he gasped. 'Weird . . . one had a knife, but . . . I think the other might've been a copper . . .'

'Coppers, eh?' The man with the stick tut-tutted. 'You just can't trust them. There you are, an ordinary criminal going about your everyday unlawful business, and some bloody copper comes and . . .'

'I'm not a criminal!' Ogburn blurted, but the pain made him choke.

'There you are,' the walking stick man said, as if the interruption had never occurred, 'going about your everyday unlawful business, pretending you run a pub but all the time fencing stolen goods . . .'

240

'I've not been fencing for ages, I swear! *Oh Christ, it hurts . . .*'

'Funny that. We heard you were Ron O'Hoorigan's fence.'

'Ron who?'

A second weight was placed on Ogburn's legs, this time across his knees – though this one was *dropped* rather than placed. Again it was angled, sharp-edged, and terribly heavy. With a sobering shock, Ogburn realised that it was a breeze-block. It was even more of a shock to now realise that the wooden framework enclosing him was actually the rim of a crate of some sort. *Jesus Christ, they'd laid him in a coffin-shaped crate . . .*

'Let's not play silly games, Toady,' the walking stick man said. 'We've gone to a lot of trouble to meet you tonight, so I'm sure you'll understand that we're quite serious about getting our facts right.'

Ogburn was still semi-paralysed by drugs but suddenly so filled with fear that he could barely feel his injuries. Whoever these men were, they were all wearing dark clothing with peaked hoods pulled up, which cast them in monk-like silhouette against the high lighting – security lamps maybe, on a construction site. The one kneeling was so close that Ogburn could at last see what kind of mask he was wearing: it was a woollen ski-mask, with holes cut for the eyes and mouth.

'Okay, okay, okay . . . I know Ron O'Hoorigan, yeah. Course I do. He's a regular at the Dog & Butcher. But that's all.'

'No, that isn't all, Toady,' the walking stick man replied. 'He's a thieving little scrote. And you're his fence.'

'Ron hasn't done any real jobs in ages. He got sent down for a while – to a real clink, and it scared him shitless. He's only a bit-player now.'

'You're still his mate, though, aren't you?'

'If . . . if you mean does he come into the pub and tell me stuff when he gets pissed, then yeah . . . course he does.' Ogburn tried to swallow, but there was barely any moisture in his mouth. 'Loads of blokes do that.'

'We're not interested in anyone else,' the kneeling figure said in a Midlands accent. 'Just O'Hoorigan . . .'

'That's all I can tell you . . .'

The kneeler slammed another breezeblock down, this time over his groin. Ogburn would have doubled up and screamed had his pain-racked body allowed him to.

'It'll save us all a lot of time, Toady, if you'd stop kidding yourself that you've got choices in this matter,' Walking Stick said calmly.

'You've . . . you've got to take me back to hospital,' Ogburn wept, when he was finally able to make sounds more coherent than agonised whimpers. 'I had surgery this afternoon – on a ruptured spleen.'

'My, my . . . that wouldn't be a nice way to go.' Walking Stick sounded genuinely concerned. 'You'd better tell us exactly the sort of stuff Ron confides in you, and you'd better do it quick.'

'Specifically about the last stretch he served,' the kneeler said. 'In Rotherwood.'

'You said something scared him, Toady,' Walking Stick added. 'What was it?'

'Nothing . . . nothing special. He just doesn't want to go down again . . .'

Another breezeblock was laid on him, this one on his stomach, almost directly over his incision. Even though this one was placed relatively gently, he still gagged at the pain.

'Facts, Toady,' Walking Stick said. 'Not fantasies.'

The next breezeblock was placed on Ogburn's chest; their combined weight was now crushing his wounded body into the crate's hard, timber floor.

'Alright . . . alright,' he said, struggling to breathe. 'All I know is that Ron got told something that spooked him while he was in Rotherwood. That's . . . my understanding from his drunken fucking babbling. Apparently he shared a cell with some bloke who was . . . who was looking to join a real tough firm when he got out. Said they had something massive going, and that he was going to get rich. But if this fella told Ronnie what it was, Ronnie never told me . . . I swear it!'

'Did he say who this bloke was?' Walking Stick wondered.

'Didn't give me a name, didn't give me a description. Nothing.'

'There're lots of hard cases inside,' the kneeler said. 'What exactly was it about this one that spooked him?'

'Whatever job he had lined up, I assume . . . *oh, Jesus God!*' The weight on Ogburn's body was growing worse by the second, particularly over his midriff. 'It . . . it was fucking big apparently. Ron used to be prolific, but like I say, he's small time now. He doesn't want to get involved in anything really heavy. He probably thought that just knowing about this stuff would make him a target for the Old Bill. And it looks like it did . . . didn't it?'

'And *you*, Toady,' Walking Stick said. 'It's made you a target too, hasn't it? You had a chat with some officers from Greater Manchester Police this afternoon at Salford City Hospital, didn't you?'

Ogburn shook his head feverishly. 'They asked about Ron too – what he's been up to and all that. What the fight in the boozer was about. I said nothing. I don't grass people up, ever. I said I felt too rough to talk to them. The nurses showed 'em the door. Check at the hospital if you don't believe me.'

There was a long silence, as if Ogburn's captors were sharing unspoken thoughts. At last, Walking Stick said:

'You sure you're Ronnie's only mate? He doesn't have someone else he may have confided in. Girlfriend . . . boyfriend?'

'He's a fucking junkie as well as an alkie. No one'd go near him normally.'

'So why'd they all jump to his defence back in that shithole you laughably call a boozer?'

'Just the way we are in our neck of the woods.' Ogburn tried to speak with pride, but was in too much agony. 'Some bleeder comes shoving his arse around, we all go in . . .'

'Even if it's a copper?'

'Especially if it's a copper. We . . . we don't like pigs, and don't mind letting 'em know. We don't give a shit. We look after our own . . .'

The kneeler chuckled. 'I hope to Christ you never have to look after me. A job lot of you, and you got fucking leathered.'

'It . . . it happens,' Ogburn stammered. 'Look . . . can I go back to hospital now? Please. I've told you everything I know about Ronnie. I'm not his mate. I'm the only one he talks to these days, and that's only coz I'm the other side of the bar when he's holding it up.'

'Yes, well,' Walking Stick said, 'more the pity for you.'

'Eh . . .?'

The kneeler picked up a heavy wooden lid which was roughly the same rectangular shape as the crate in which their prisoner lay. Ogburn screamed hysterically as the others closed in with hammers and nails, and the lid was slammed down on top of him.

'*What the fuck are you doing?*' he shrieked, hoping his voice could be heard above the deafening blows. '*What the fuck is this? No, no no . . . please no, please no! Don't bury me alive! Please, dear God no, please don't fucking bury me alive . . .*'

The hammering ceased, the lid now fixed firmly on the crate.

'Relax, Toady,' Walking Stick shouted down to him. 'We're *not* going to bury you alive.'

'Oh thank God, thank God . . .'

'Too much like hard work digging a grave. So we're going to bury you in the Ship Canal instead.'

'*No! NO!*'

But the muffled wail sounded for only a few seconds as they manhandled the heavy box across the disused dock, and then, with much grunting and sweating tipped it over the side. It broke the silt-black waters with a thunderous impact, and sank swiftly from view.

Chapter 28

Pat McCulkin was a familiar figure on his home turf of Deptford. But those who knew him would have been surprised to see him walking along Creek Road at six o'clock on a Wednesday morning. As usual, he cut a grumpy figure: he was sixty, with thinning grey hair, and a leathery, shrewlike face. Rings dangled from both his ears and tattoos covered most of his scrawny body, though at present, as he wore a flat cap and shabby raincoat, these only showed on his neck and hands. Even so, they gave him a less than wholesome appearance. It might only be six o'clock, but as he walked sullenly towards Greenwich, he lit what was already his third cigarette of the morning.

Of course, when he got there, the person he was supposed to be meeting – who'd already annoyed him by calling him at home at God knows what hour – was not present. McCulkin stood alone on a bleak stretch of riverside esplanade. There were no other pedestrians around. There wasn't even much traffic on the road. Behind him, the Thames sloshed against the hull of the *Cutty Sark,* the onetime tea clipper now turned museum ship. McCulkin glanced up. The sky was overcast and it was unusually cool for August.

He swore under his breath, coughed, hawked up a lump of phlegm and spat it on the pavement. And to his surprise, a phone began to ring.

He took out his mobile. No call was registering on it. Puzzled, he pivoted around, finally focusing on a waste bin attached to the post of a traffic sign. He wandered over and glanced down. A folded copy of that day's *Guardian* had been left on top of the trash. The trilling of the phone continued; it was emanating from inside the newspaper.

McCulkin glanced furtively around – still no one was in sight. He opened the paper and found the phone. It was red in colour and looked new. He picked it up and answered.

'Yeah?'

'I'm watching you, so don't try anything stupid.' It was Mark Heckenburg again.

'What's all this bullshit?' McCulkin asked.

'Don't talk, just listen. Go straight through the foot tunnel to the Isle of Dogs. No questions, no pissing about. Go now. If I see any sign that someone's following you, you're in big trouble.'

McCulkin pocketed the phone alongside his own and set off as instructed.

The Greenwich foot tunnel was accessible via a spiral stair that descended from under a glazed dome standing only a few yards from the *Cutty Sark*. It was forty-five feet down and, in essence, a steel pipe that ran beneath the river, though internally it was concreted and tiled. McCulkin had never liked it much, always regarding it as a mugger's paradise. There were no hidden places where someone could jump out. It was a straight walk from one end to the other, but that didn't mean some street punk couldn't suddenly come down and confront you when you were hidden from the world above. He scurried across, glancing behind him several times, not just worried about muggers but curious about whom it was Heckenburg expected to be following him, and not a little concerned by it.

At the other end, he emerged in the shadow of Canary Wharf tower and the numerous other skyscrapers that surrounded it. The Isle of Dogs had changed a lot since McCulkin was a lad. In those days, it had been a tangle of wharfs and cranes, studded here and there with blocks of scruffy flats where some of London's poorest residents had eked out a meagre existence. The glittering glass monoliths it now bristled with seemed somehow wrong for the famously deprived borough of Tower Hamlets, though he supposed it was progress of a sort.

The phone rang again. He answered.

'The greasy spoon on East Ferry Road,' Heckenburg said. 'Make it quick.'

McCulkin walked doggedly along the old dockland road. The aforesaid greasy spoon, a small café with steamy windows, loomed into view. He glanced inside. There were a number of men, mainly van and lorry driver types, already in there eating breakfast, but there was no one McCulkin recognised.

A hand tapped his shoulder. He spun around.

Heckenburg was there. He was in casuals rather than his customary rumpled suit, while his face was puffy and cut in several places, as though he'd recently been in a car crash. He subjected McCulkin to a quick but thorough body search, before stepping back and saying: 'You've not heard what's going on, then? I mean with me?'

'Am I supposed to have?'

Heck was pleased. That meant they were keeping it need to know. 'Thanks Gemma, I owe you one. Okay, let's walk.'

They headed north, keeping a brisk pace.

'What about Charlie Finnegan?' Heck asked. Finnegan – a DC in the Serial Crimes Unit, wasn't someone Heck got on with easily, but he was McCulkin's other official 'handler'. 'Has he said anything to you about me?'

McCulkin shrugged. 'Haven't spoken to him for about three weeks.'

Heck nodded, again pleased.

'What's all the cloak and dagger stuff?'

'Tell you in a minute.'

Heck glanced behind them several times, and took one or two detours down deserted side streets, before finally ushering his guest into another tearoom, this one attached to Mudchute DLR station.

'I need some help,' he said, as they nursed cups of coffee and faced each other across a table. 'Trouble is it's got to be off the clock.'

McCulkin pulled a face. 'You mean I don't get paid?'

'You'll get paid. It just won't necessarily come from the grass fund. If I have to, I'll cough up from my own pocket.'

'Sounds a bit irregular.'

'All you need to know is that I'm in deep cover, and that, whoever asks – *whoever* – you haven't seen or spoken to me.'

'That include your lot?'

'Especially my lot.'

'I don't like the sound of this.'

'It's just another job. No different from any of the others you've done.'

McCulkin sipped thoughtfully at his coffee, before replying: 'What do you need?'

'Anything you've got, or can find, on the Nice Guys.'

'Never heard of them.' McCulkin sipped his coffee again.

Heck knew immediately that he was lying. It wasn't just McCulkin's body language – the coffee, which was tepid and rather foul, was subconsciously being used as a shield – it was in his face too, which remained blank but had paled a little. McCulkin had also been way too quick to deny knowledge. His normal form would be curiosity. If he genuinely hadn't heard about a firm with a cryptic name like 'the Nice Guys', he'd almost certainly want to know more, yet he'd asked no questions at all.

Heck was discomforted. Pat McCulkin was his main South London informant, and one of the best in the capital; he'd produced leads that had led to convictions for numerous serious offences. This was a mystery, and another mystery was something Heck didn't need. So he cut to the chase.

'You're a lying little git!'

'Whoa . . .' McCulkin looked taken aback.

'You think I'm on work experience here? Don't jerk me around, Pat!'

McCulkin got to his feet. 'I'm not getting up at this time of the morning to—'

'Sit the fuck down!' Heck shouted, his voice a whipcrack. It was so loud that the girl behind the counter looked around, startled.

Unnerved to see such fury in a man who was usually so affable, McCulkin did as he was told.

'This is a non-negotiable situation,' Heck said, quieter but with the same intensity. 'I need to know who the Nice Guys are, and I need to know where they are. Right now.'

'I've never heard of any Nice Guys.'

'Don't gimme that crap.'

'You're not listening to me!' McCulkin hissed. 'I don't know who they are, and that's my last word on the matter.'

'Yeah?' Heck smiled dangerously. 'Well here's mine – you've had a contract with the National Crime Group for several years now, haven't you? You've done very well out of us. In fact, you've made yourself quite wealthy at the expense of your fellow criminals. Maybe it's time the word got out.'

McCulkin swallowed; working his wet, thin lips together.

'Poor reward for your services, I know,' Heck added. 'But all good things come to an end.'

'You're breaching the rules doing this,' McCulkin replied.

'That should give you an idea how serious I am.'

'You do not fuck around with the Nice Guys Club.'

'So you *do* know them?'

'I've *heard* of them. But only like I've heard of Jack and the Beanstalk or Jason and the Argonauts. It's legend, a myth.'

'Why are you frightened of them then?'

'I'm not frightened, it's just . . .'

'What?'

McCulkin laced his tattooed, nicotine-stained fingers in a tight, tense ball. 'There are red flags all over this, Mr Heckenburg. Any time it comes up in conversation, it's like "you don't talk about this", or "do not even go there".'

'That's Halloween stuff, Pat. It's designed to stop people asking questions.'

'Look, these people are bad news.'

'And I'm not?' Heck leaned forward. 'These bastards are going to find out different. Now you tell me every single thing you know.'

'You really going to spread it that I'm a snitch?'

'Just watch me.'

McCulkin clawed at his brow, which was suddenly glazed with sweat. He looked tortured by indecision, which impressed Heck no end. Among other tough outfits, McCulkin had once grassed on a team of blaggers who'd been doing banks and post offices across southern England and had killed at least twice, and on a car-ringing operation that had involved the import into London of high-end motors stolen from all over the UK. If he wasn't frightened of firms like these, just what level of threat did the Nice Guys pose?

'What do you think is going to happen?' Heck asked him. 'Nothing will come back to you. It never does.'

McCulkin shook his head. 'You'd better keep Finnegan out of this, because he's got a gob on him when he's pissed.'

'At present there are only two people on earth know about it – me and you. And that's the way I'd like to keep it.'

McCulkin took his cap off, ran a hand through his greasy hair. 'Look, I don't know 'em, myself. But I know someone who might.'

'Who?'

'No names. Not at this stage. But I can set up a meet with him.'

'Okay. The sooner the better.'

'This afternoon?'

Heck nodded. He indicated the red phone that McCulkin had found in the waste bin. It was one of the pair that Ballamara had provided the previous night. 'Use this phone to call. Don't call me on any number except the one I rang you from earlier.'

McCulkin nodded worriedly. Before he left the tearoom, he glanced back. 'You've started playing dirty, Mr Heckenburg. That isn't like you.'

'We all reach our breaking point, Pat.'

'Well I'm glad you've reached yours when you have. From what I've heard about the Nice – about *these people*, you're going to have to play it even dirtier.'

Chapter 29

Des Palliser had been at his desk half an hour, and was checking and signing off on a pile of reports, when the phone rang.

'Serial Crimes Unit,' he said, picking up and cradling the receiver under his jaw.

'Detective Inspector Palliser?'

'That's right. Can I help?'

'It's Paula Clark again, at Deptford Green.'

Palliser straightened up. 'Yes, Paula. What can I do for you?'

'DS Heckenburg's still on leave, I understand?'

'Erm . . . one second.' He jumped up and closed his door on the bustle of activity in the main detectives' office. Retrieving the phone, he sat down again. 'That's correct. He's on leave until December.'

'Maybe you could leave a note on his desk, or something?'

'Of course.'

'Or maybe you might want to do something with it, yourself, I'm not sure.'

'I'll do whatever I can, Paula.'

Her tone was perfectly normal – there was nothing nervous

or conspiratorial about it. Whether she'd got wind that something was going on because of the brief contact they'd had with her the other day, enquiring about Heck, he was unsure.

'I was wondering,' she said, 'have you heard anything about a mis-per called Louise Jennings?'

'That name doesn't ring a bell.'

'I see. Well, she's a secretary in the City. Seems she's been missing since last Friday night. As I understand it, Thames Valley are dealing. I only read about it on force bulletins this morning. But it strikes me that her circumstances are very similar to a number of those missing women that DS Heckenburg was investigating.'

Palliser grabbed a spare piece of paper and picked his pen up again. 'Can you elaborate on that, Paula?'

'I only glanced at it, but well . . . she's not the type, if you know what I mean. Apparently, she's nothing to run away from. She's got no lover that anyone knows about, she hasn't fallen out with her husband or her family. She hasn't got drugs, drink or mental health problems. She's got a wide circle of friends and relatives, and none of them have the first idea where she could be.'

'I get the picture.'

'It's probably nothing, but I just thought it seemed very similar to the other cases.'

'That's great, Paula. Thanks very much for drawing this to our attention.'

'No problem. Always glad to help, as you know. Is Mark alright?'

'Oh yes, he's fine. Having a right old time of it, I understand.'

'Mmm.' She probably knew Heck too well to believe *that*. 'Okay, well, you know where I am if you need me. Bye.'

She hung up, and Palliser sat there for several moments,

pondering. Paula was right; it was probably nothing at all to do with the case, but then again . . .? He wondered if he should go down the corridor and speak to Gemma, but finally, deciding that discretion was the better part of valour, he picked the phone up and spoke to Janice, one of his unit's own secretaries.

'Hello love,' he said, checking the brief details he'd just scribbled down. 'Get me Thames Valley, please.'

Chapter 30

The Nice Guys *Club*.

They were a club?

That was what McCulkin had said.

From Mudchute, Heck had taken the DLR to Canary Wharf, then the Jubilee to London Bridge, where he switched to the Northern Line. He was now riding south back towards Elephant & Castle, and puzzling through this latest revelation.

A club obviously meant more than one or two, which he'd already figured. But it could also mean *several* more than one or two, maybe *many* more. In a way, that made sense. Given the complexity that had to be involved in these abductions – ordinary, everyday women snatched from view while doing ordinary, everyday things, and not a trace left behind – it was certainly more than a couple of offenders could manage. And then there was the hit-man factor. This whole thing was getting the whiff of organised crime, yet how did a load of disappeared women who weren't whores or drug addicts fit into that picture?

Heck was now working on the basis – though he hadn't told Lauren this yet – that Deke was onto them because, whoever the Nice Guys were, they'd been following the progress of the enquiry, and had ordered the hit-man to intercept as it was getting too close for comfort.

Did that mean there was a leak inside the National Crime Group?

Heck didn't even like to consider that possibility, though it was difficult to see how it could be otherwise – who else would have known that he'd been pulling files on Shane Klim?

All of this was supposition of course, that police sixth sense that finely tunes itself over the course of hundreds of investigations.

The missing link in all this was the motive. Why would an organised gang abduct ordinary women without making ransom demands? It didn't compute. Heck remembered rumours he'd heard back in the 1980s about Satanists, and how they were responsible for thousands of disappearances all over Europe and America, the victims having been sacrificed in unspeakable rites. Few detectives at the time had believed it mainly because there was so little physical evidence; for the same reason, he was ready to dismiss similar ideas now. There'd been no hint in recent times that dangerous cultists might be at work in the UK – and yet perhaps the real answer wasn't a million miles away from that. He thought again about McCulkin's reaction to the mere mention of the Nice Guys. 'Unadulterated fear' was the only way to describe it. It wasn't as if he'd been asked to grass on gangsters or hoodlums – and Lord knows, they could be dangerous enough – but on something much darker, much more evil. This wasn't a pleasant line of thought when Heck considered the missing women, many of whom he felt he'd come to know personally thanks to his in-depth analysis of their lives and relationships. One thing seemed certain: the answer – when he found it – was going to be extremely unpalatable.

He returned to Ballamara's private club before ten o'clock, but found the gangster, Lauren and several ape-like henchmen in a pub just across the road. Aside from these, there were no other patrons. Ballamara himself was standing behind the bar and looking unusually less than dapper, without a tie or jacket and with his shirt open at the collar. The others were around a table, where two or three heavies were mopping up egg and beans with hunks of bread. Lauren, who was crammed into a corner from which there was no easy escape, sat stiffly with her back against the wall. She glared at Heck as he sauntered in, but no more so than Ballamara did.

As always, the gangster's eyes were flat, grey metal.

'You little shit,' he said. 'We had a deal.'

Heck nodded. 'We still do. I promised I'd deliver, and I will. But I need a couple of days.'

'Pity. You haven't got 'em.'

Ballamara signalled to two of his men who were seated near the door. They closed and locked it, then began to draw blinds on the windows.

'Neither have you,' Heck replied.

There was something in the way he said this – something bold, unafraid, which meant it wasn't just bluff or bravado. The pub fell silent.

'I've been busy this morning,' Heck said. 'Among other things, I've written and posted a letter to my solicitor, which is only to be opened in the event of me being found dead, or not being found at all within a certain time period. In it, I name you and your firm as my abductors and murderers.'

Ballamara snorted scornfully. 'Being sniffed at by the filth is not exactly a new experience for us.'

'They'll do more than sniff this time. Because guess what, I was busy last night too. And when they come and turn your pad across the road inside out, they'll find numerous

258

personal items that I secreted, any one of which will serve as proof positive that I was being held there.'

The silence that followed was ear-pummelling. Ballamara's gaze was so intense that even Lauren, who'd seen the maniacal faces of Taliban killers up close, found she couldn't look at him.

Heck remained undaunted. 'Course, you can go over the place with a fine-tooth comb if you want. But you know you'll have your work cut out. And even if you find some stuff, you'll never know if you've found it all.'

Ballamara's knuckles turned white as he clenched them on the bar top.

'That's called being *owned*, Mr Ballamara,' Heck added. 'And in front of your own team. However, I'm not one to gloat. I'm going to stick to our deal, but the terms have changed. I'll give you the info I promised as soon as I've got it to hand – and hopefully that won't be long off. But in the meantime, me and Lauren are going to walk out of here unmolested. Not only that, we're going to walk out with twenty grand of *your* money in our pocket.'

This was too much for certain members of Ballamara's crew. Loxton leaped up, his chair flying. '*You fucking what?*'

Heck ignored him, and continued to address Ballamara directly. 'I'm a fugitive, wanted for murder. That means they'll be watching my bank accounts. I start making withdrawals around London, and it won't take them long to join the dots. But I can't live on air, can I? Don't worry, you'll get your cash back – it's a loan, not a gift. You can even charge me interest.'

'*Can you believe this bastard?*' Loxton shouted.

'Dale,' Ballamara said tightly, 'shut – your – sodding – trap!'

'I'm not ripping you off, Mr Ballamara,' Heck added. 'I guarantee it. I've done a lot of spadework on this enquiry, but now at last we're getting somewhere. This afternoon I'm seeing someone who can finally put me on the right track.'

'In which case we're going with you,' Ballamara replied.

'No.'

'Yes.'

'*No!* Look . . . the guy I'm seeing is a grass. One of my best. You lot show up, and not only is that relationship fucked, but word'll get out that I can't be trusted, and my relationship with every other grass in London will be equally fucked.'

Ballamara did not like to be wrong-footed, but it was plain to him that Heck had covered every corner. He pondered this darkly, his brow furrowed.

'You won't be kept out of it,' Heck assured him. 'You've got my word.'

'Your word? That's supposed to make me feel better?'

'Think about it – I may actually *need* you. You already know that whoever took your Noreen might have taken a number of other women. I don't know why, or where. But you'd better prepare yourself for the worst.'

Ballamara's anger seemed to ebb a little. 'I've already done that some time ago.'

'Good. But the point is . . . whoever did it, they're not going to come without a fight.'

Again Ballamara pondered this.

Heck produced the blue phone. 'You've even got a number you can get me on any time you need an update.'

Fifteen minutes later, Lauren still couldn't believe that Heck had pulled it off, even as they sat facing each other on a Northern Line train headed north. She watched in bemused admiration as he filched a bundle of crisp new twenty-pound notes from a brown envelope, and began to count them.

'I just don't know how you did it,' she said.

He winked. 'Seventy per cent of being a good bobby is the ability to bullshit.'

'So none of that stuff was true?'

'Not all of it.'

'I should've realised . . . and I'm totally stunned that Ballamara didn't.'

'He probably did. But why take the chance?' The twenty grand was all there, so Heck pocketed the envelope again. 'What's he really got to lose? The only way he's going to get to whoever nabbed his daughter is if I lead him to them. Now . . .' and he checked his watch. 'You've already had breakfast, haven't you?'

'Have I?'

'What were you doing earlier on in the pub?'

'Sitting watching those lunatics stuff their faces, while *my* stomach was turning inside out.'

He shook his head. 'Ballamara's own boozer, and he didn't even treat you?'

'Actually he offered to. But I hardly felt like eating, did I?' Her voice hardened. 'Not knowing what was going to happen to me and all that! You *are* going to keep me a bit more informed from now on, yeah?'

'Sorry to leave you sleeping, but you had to stay behind as a kind of insurance – to convince them I'd come back.'

'*I* wasn't convinced you'd come back, never mind them.'

'Then you don't know me very well, do you?'

'Anyway, the answers are "no" and "yes",' she said sullenly.

'Uh?'

'No, I haven't had any breakfast yet, and yes, I do want some.'

'Okay.'

They dismounted the train at Bank, and rode into the

261

West End via the Central Line, where they found a small diner. Heck ordered scrambled eggs, toast and coffee. Lauren had pancakes with syrup.

'The team we're looking for call themselves the "Nice Guys",' he said while they ate. 'But I don't know too much more about them.'

Lauren glanced up, her mouth full and cheeks bulging. 'They're the kidnappers?'

'It's possible. They were mentioned in Deke's ledger. Whoever they are, it looks like they paid for the job he did on O'Hoorigan. Not to mention a few others.'

'What did you do with the ledger?' she asked, suddenly noticing its absence.

'Parcelled it and posted it.'

'Where to?'

'My home address – safest place I could think of.'

'I thought you said your lot would be sitting on that address?'

'They're only looking out for me. I doubt they've got a warrant to check the mail yet.'

Before she could ask him anything else, the blue phone rang. Heck glanced at the number on its tiny screen.

'Ballamara already?' she wondered.

He shook his head, before answering. The following conversation was mumbled and inaudible to Lauren, even though she was only on the other side of the table. When Heck eventually hung up, he was frowning – partly with concern, but also with puzzlement.

'It's a bloody good job we've got twenty grand to spend,' he said. 'We've got a hell of a taxi drive coming up.'

Chapter 31

Heck didn't want the taxi dropping them off in the exact spot in case 'things turned nasty'. So instead they jumped out in Allhallows-on-Sea, which was little more than a rural hamlet with a few holiday homes dotted around it, but busy enough in August for them to arrive unnoticed. Once the cab had set off back, they walked, leaving the village and heading along a coastal road that led into what seemed like an infinite distance.

'What do you mean "in case things turn nasty"?' Lauren asked.

'Dunno.' He shrugged. 'I'm getting less and less sure about this as the day goes on.'

It wasn't just the stiff sea breeze that was making him uncomfortable. A good thirty miles from London, they'd alighted on the northern edge of the Hoo peninsula, and were now surrounded on four sides by salt marsh and mud flats. When they finally stopped at the lone payphone that McCulkin had specified to Heck, the only buildings in sight were a few weather-boarded boathouses down at the edge of a narrow creek. Gulls and other seabirds swooped noisily, unaccustomed to the arrival of strangers in this remote place.

'This isn't exactly the normal spot for a rendezvous of this sort,' Heck said.

'Who is it we're hooking up with?'

'Now that we haven't got some eavesdropping cabbie to report back on us, I suppose I can tell you.' So he did – about McCulkin, and the agreement reached with him. As he spoke, they proceeded down a path that circled round the derelict boathouses and ran for hundreds of yards along a low dyke.

'Okay, so this McCulkin is your grass,' Lauren said. 'Is he reliable?'

'He has been up until now.'

'But there's still something about this you don't like?'

'It's always good to exercise caution, but *this* . . .' Heck indicated the desolation around them. 'This smacks of over-kill to me.'

They were on the north Kent coast, a scenic but notori-ously bleak and empty district. Somewhere ahead of them, still a couple of miles off, was the Thames estuary. On the far side of that sat the massive petrochemical complex at Canvey Island. There wasn't likely to be anyone closer than that – at least, no one engaged in legitimate business.

'If we've got reservations about this, why are we keeping going?' Lauren asked.

Her own reservations owed more to the gradual sinking of the dyke and the disintegration of the footpath. It was still vaguely visible, beaten through the weeds and tussock grass, winding gamely on ahead, but it was now requiring them to skirt around ponds and leap over ditches. The creek they'd spied was a dozen yards to their left, but was broadening out and filling with water; its banks looked dangerously swampy.

'Because we haven't really got any choice,' Heck said. He grimaced as his foot plunged to the ankle and spurted brackish water up the back of his jeans. 'All I can say is – the bastard had better be here, or I won't be impressed.'

The path turned west and they followed it for another mile before it brought them down into a shallow bay. The Thames now lay in front of them, though they didn't feel that they'd arrived on a riverbank so much as at a point where land ended and the sea began. From this last piece of soggy ground, they could see clear across to the Canvey Island oil and gas terminals and, looking east, to the distant open spaces of the North Sea.

Heck checked his watch; it was five past three, which meant their contact was late.

Almost on cue, they heard the throb of an approaching engine and, glancing left, spotted a small outboard chugging towards them with a solo figure at its helm. It was McCulkin, still dressed – now incongruously – in his overcoat and cap, which had somehow remained on his head despite the coastal wind. He cut the motor about thirty yards from shore and let the vessel glide the rest of the way in, though he stopped it with a paddle ten yards short.

'Can't risk letting it run aground,' he shouted. 'Sorry, you're going to have to get your feet wet.'

'Bit off the beaten track, aren't we?' Heck called back.

'Yeah, but I knew you'd find me okay. You never disappoint, Mr Heckenburg.'

'I don't see any sea fort.'

McCulkin pointed. 'Just round that headland.'

'Sea fort?' Lauren asked.

'Who's she?' McCulkin said.

'A friend.'

Heck waded out, Lauren following, which was difficult with the river bottom deep in soft, slimy sediment. When they reached the boat, McCulkin had to help them aboard.

'Your friend?' he said testily. 'This isn't a daytrip we're on, you know.'

'Stop moaning,' Heck replied. 'I need my back watching just like everyone else.'

'You said only you and me would know about this.'

'I lied. Don't act surprised – you told me I had to play dirty.'

McCulkin regarded Lauren warily. 'You trust this darkie?'

'Hey!' she said.

'Don't point your finger at me, girl,' he snapped. 'After sixty years having to live among you lot, I've earned the right to call you what I want.'

'Which you won't be doing while I'm around,' Heck interjected. 'This lass has done as much good in the last few days as you have in your entire career, and she hasn't asked for a penny in payment. Now let's keep it friendly, or there'll be less work coming your way in future.'

'I'm not sure I want more work if this is the way you're going to play it,' McCulkin said. 'It's bad enough one of you knows about this, but two of you . . . I'll be looking over my shoulder for the rest of my life.'

'And the people you'll be looking for will be rotting in prison. That's the whole idea, isn't it?'

McCulkin didn't seem convinced. 'I asked if you trusted her?'

'Implicitly.'

'And no one else knows about this meeting at all? Especially none of her lot?'

Lauren glowered at him, but said nothing. The average white person had no concept of the sort of casual racial prejudices that 'her lot' still encountered in Britain even in the enlightened twenty-first century. But to meet overt and unashamed examples like this was now quite unusual. Unfortunately they needed this bitter, shrewish little man; otherwise she'd be tempted to chuck him overboard.

'No one,' Heck confirmed.

Reluctantly, McCulkin started the engine and they set off again, turning a wide circle and heading towards the aforementioned headland. Heck and Lauren sat on a low wooden bench at the stern. Bilge sloshed around their feet. Much of the vessel's metalwork was corroded, its paint flaking off in scales. McCulkin had to stand up to control it; where his chair should once have been, only rivets were visible.

'Where'd you get the boat, Pat?' Heck asked.

'Meaning did I nick it?

'Put it this way, if you didn't, you were robbed.'

McCulkin hawked and spat overboard.

'Where the hell are we going?' Lauren whispered. 'A sea fort?'

'Blacksand Tower,' Heck replied. 'It's basically a fortified gun-emplacement. They built a number of them to fire at German aircraft navigating towards London along the Thames. They were called TESDUs, or Thames Estuary Special Defence Units. Most of them are now gone, but a few remain. They're all derelict, of course.'

She stared past his shoulder, focusing on something that had just come into view. He turned to look. The fort had appeared around the headland. It was located maybe three miles from shore, and from this distance it was a lowering mass of rusted girders and weathered, moss-eaten brick. But the closer they got to it, the more they were able to distinguish. It consisted of four towering edifices, the nearest one a massive stone cylinder, which was something like the tower of a medieval castle but lacking the crenellations at the top. Heck guessed that this would once have served as the fort's admin section and barracks. The other three towers, which were probably the gun-towers, looked more representative of the modern world; they were octagonal steel superstructures sitting on top of massive concrete legs. Each was of a uniform height – about ninety feet, Heck estimated – and all were located about fifty yards apart, connected to each other by high steel catwalks.

Heck watched closely as they approached. The whole thing was a scabrous ruin, streaked with dirt and seagull crap, but it was impressive all the same.

'Who is it we're meeting, Pat?' he asked. 'Surely you can tell us now?'

'He used to work for them,' McCulkin replied.

'Worked for who?'

'You know.'

'You mean the Nice Guys? You don't even like saying their name, do you?'

McCulkin clammed up as he steered them towards the concrete tower. A landing platform was visible on its south side, a timber raft held to the mighty structure by chains. The lower section of the tower, up to about ten feet in height, dangled with bright green river weed. Above this there was a tall aperture that might once have had a door fitted in it. A steel stair ran up to this.

'I don't see any other boats,' Lauren said. 'You sure this bloke's here?'

'He's here,' was McCulkin's grunted response.

They were now far from shore, and the wind was stiffer and colder. This close, the fort cast an immense shadow. Waves slapped against its foundations; the cries of gulls and guillemots echoed eerily from its parapets. McCulkin cut the motor and again the boat glided the remaining distance. He brought it hard against the timber raft – there was a dull *thud*, then he jumped out and roped it to a hook.

'Bit of an expert, isn't he?' Lauren observed.

'When you're brought up in the docklands,' Heck replied.

'This is it,' McCulkin said, rather unnecessarily.

He tilted his cap back and stood waiting for them, tensely.

'You nervous about something?' Heck asked, climbing out.

'Are you not?' McCulkin replied.

Lauren jumped up beside them. The platform rose and fell – this part of the Thames was strongly tidal, and the swell came straight from the North Sea. They glanced up the stair towards the entrance. Rusted bolts hung at regular intervals down the pillar on its left-hand side, revealing that there had once been a door there. But access to the interior was still restricted: masses of barbed wire might have made an impassable barrier had someone not gone at it with a pair of clippers, clearing a narrow path to the room beyond.

'After you,' McCulkin said.

Heck went cautiously up the stair, which was not anchored down and shifted under his weight. At the top, he peered through the chopped wire into a dark, dripping interior.

Lauren appeared at his shoulder. 'You sure you trust this guy?'

'Why?'

'You've already said this arrangement is abnormal. Even I'm getting that now. I've got to tell you, Heck, I don't like this at all.'

'Me neither.' He pressed forward, sidling along the path and entering a surprisingly confined holding space, its cement floor puddled with oily water, a few empty barrels occupying one of the corners.

To their right, a metal ladder ascended into dimness. They gazed up, and as their eyes attuned, made out hanging chains and dangling strips of canvas. The underside of the floor above was composed mainly of riveted steel, though there were some gaps in it. Heck moved to the foot of the ladder. Twenty feet overhead, it passed through a hatch and vanished, but light was visible up there – probably daylight filtering through the grimy first-floor windows. He tested the ladder, which seemed sturdy, and began to climb it, acutely aware that the clanks of his footfalls were probably sounding all the way to the top of the tower. When he was about seven feet up, he glanced back – Lauren was standing down there alone.

'Where's McCulkin?' he asked.

She looked around. 'Don't think he even came in.'

An engine growled to life outside.

'Shit!' Heck yelled, jumping back down, racing for the door. He skirted through the wire and descended quickly to the timber platform, but it was too late. The boat was already motoring away, a good thirty yards distant. McCulkin was hunched over the wheel, but he glanced back towards them nervously.

'You arsehole!' Heck shouted. 'What the hell are you playing at?'

Lauren jumped down onto the platform alongside him. 'He can't seriously be leaving us here?'

'McCulkin! You think this is going to solve anything, you little shit!'

But McCulkin was already out of earshot.

Heck dragged the blue phone from his pocket and bashed in the number of the red one. Rather to his surprise, it was answered.

'What the goddamn hell do you think you're playing at?' he demanded.

'I . . . look, I'm sorry,' was all McCulkin could say. 'I didn't . . . I didn't want this, I . . . I had no choice, I mean . . . when your family are under threat . . .'

The words ended mid-sentence. There was a *thump* in Heck's ear as the phone at the other end was dropped into the bottom of the boat. He gazed out over the water. The small outboard was still close enough for him to see McCulkin stagger to its gunwale, his head shapeless and lolling, his hair a glinting crimson mass – and topple over the side.

A second of stunned silence followed.

The boat continued towards the distant shore, now under its own volition. McCulkin's body was briefly visible, bobbing like a buoy, before it sank, leaving his cap floating on the surface alongside a blurred red stain.

'Fuck,' Heck said slowly. 'Fuck . . . *he's been shot*!'

Lauren's eyes bulged in shock. 'How was he, but who shot . . . I mean, out here?'

The answers to these half questions were provided in short order.

Heck had no sooner tapped 999 on the blue phone when a second shot was fired – presumably from a weapon fitted with a silencer, because they didn't hear its report. The phone was smashed from Heck's hand, scattering in fragments across the landing platform. He snatched his hand back; the bullet hadn't penetrated his flesh, but had struck a stinging blow, which felt as if it had come from overhead. Disbelievingly, he peered up towards the topmost parapet of the tower.

Something gleamed up there.

It was the sun. On the barrel of a sniper rifle.

Chapter 32

Heck ducked backward, dragging Lauren with him. A silenced slug impacted on the spot where he'd just been standing. The plank footing was punched clean through.

'Quick!' Heck charged back up the stairs. Lauren was only a yard behind him, but another shot ricocheted from the stair's handrail alongside her, hammering it out of shape.

'Who . . . who the hell is it?' she stammered as they plunged back inside the tower.

'Who the hell do you think?'

'Deke?'

'Murdering bastard lured us here. But what really worries me is how he got to McCulkin.'

The full import of this didn't immediately strike Lauren. Their initial predicament was terrifying enough. Inside the base of the tower, they were sheltered from the parapet above. But of course they were stuck here. There was nowhere else to go, and it surely wouldn't be long before the sniper descended. Gradually however, the meaning of what Heck had just said dawned on her.

'What do you mean, "how he got to McCulkin"?'

Heck mopped sweat from his forehead. 'I've been worried

there might be a leak in my department. Now I *know* there is. McCulkin was our confidential informant. No one outside the National Crime Group could possibly know about his connection to me.'

'But that's ridiculous; why would some copper . . .?'

'Because whoever he is, he must be involved with the Nice Guys.'

'Heck, you can't be serious.'

'It's the only explanation. It explains a few other things too.' He glanced out through the entrance. McCulkin's outboard was a distant dot headed towards the smudged, brown coastline. The bloody traces of McCulkin himself were no longer visible on the rippling waters. 'Lauren, how good a swimmer are you?'

'You're suggesting we swim?'

'Not to the shore. Round to one of the other gun-towers. It's only about fifty yards.'

'Swim in the Thames? What about the current?'

'The alternative is waiting here until miladdo comes down. There's nowhere to hide that I can see, and we've got no weapons. We'll be like fish in a barrel.'

Even as Heck said this, there was a *clang* from somewhere overhead. Then another, and another – heavy feet were descending a metal staircase. Glancing up, they saw shadows of movement flickering through the gaps in the ceiling. Despite this, Lauren was still struggling with Heck's suggestion.

'Swim . . .?'

He took her hand, and met her eye to eye. 'This guy's coming down here to kill us, Lauren. Both of us. Even if we swim, I reckon we've only got two or three minutes to make it to one of the other towers before he gets us in his cross-hairs.'

Slowly, unwillingly, she forced a nod. 'Okay . . . okay.'

It was late afternoon, so the incoming tide helped them. Not that an exhausting effort wasn't required. The nearest of the gun-towers, which was the west one, seemed a nightmarish distance away. Ploughing towards it fully clothed, through ice-cold water, was an ordeal neither of them was prepared for. All the same they swam, shoulders aching, wave after briny wave slapping them in the face and mouth. They constantly craned their necks to look back, to see if a tall, blond-haired figure had appeared on the landing platform behind them, but it was difficult to tell. The stone tower was receding, and the path they were following curved away from it. As the platform was on the south side of the stone tower, it would soon be only partially visible. That was the good news. If the killer didn't spot them straight away on arriving there, he might not spot them at all. This goaded them to greater efforts, and now at last, the colossal, skeletal structure of the west tower was approaching. Again, the cries of gulls echoed down. The sun glinted red on its rust-covered sides.

'Heck!' Lauren tried to shout, coughing out water. 'Heck . . . there's no landing-stage. How do we get onto it?'

Heck didn't answer, just grunted his way forward, arm over arm.

The four concrete legs of the tower projected outward and down from the huge superstructure on top. They had no visible base, and descended straight into the river. But in the very middle of them, a switchback stair hung swinging and creaking in the wind. It came almost to river-level, but whether they'd be able to reach it and climb up, Heck didn't know. He trod water as he looked back over his shoulder. The stone tower was now forty yards behind them, and any figure on the landing platform would have to be standing at its southwest corner to see them. From this distance, Deke would be a matchstick man. But if he was equipped with a high-powered rifle – Heck thought again about the Dragunov he'd seen in the house at Kingston – he'd still be able to pick his targets off, especially if they were clambering wearily up this ladder and thus framed against the sky.

The river current seemed to be strengthening; it pushed them past the southeast leg of the west tower and in fact was pushing them towards their target. But now there was a danger it might push them too far. The foot of the hanging stair was about fifteen yards ahead. Its lowest rung, which again was green and slimy with algae, hung a couple of feet above the surface. It was going to be desperately hard just getting onto the thing, let alone climbing all the way to safety. What was worse, with the current at their back, they'd only get a couple of grabs for it, and then they'd be driven past and would be out of reach. Beyond the west tower, of course, there was nothing but the open waters of the estuary.

'Christ, Heck,' Lauren whimpered.

'We're almost there,' he tried to reassure her.

The current was carrying them leftward of the stair bottom, and they had to swim hard against it, which sapped more of their depleted reserves. The stair was now almost directly overhead, zigzagging up to the octagonal underside of the superstructure, which seemed a dizzying distance away.

'Heck, we're going to die here,' Lauren squealed.

'No we're not.' He extended his arm, knowing he'd only get one shot at this. 'If you miss getting hold of it, grab me,' he said, hoping that she was close enough behind him.

It was a hell of a lunge. Heck managed to grab hold, but almost immediately his fingers slid on the greasy metal. The effort he exerted through that one wrist and hand, through those ten crooked fingers, was indescribable. Still he was sliding loose. But then Lauren reached out and caught it as well, and with her other hand she snatched the back of

Heck's collar and shoved him closer. Soon he was clinging on to the stair with two hands. They were both now gasping for breath, shivering violently.

'Can . . . can you get up?' Lauren asked through chattering teeth.

Heck said nothing at first, just hung on as he attempted to regather his strength. He glanced back in the direction of the stone tower. Still the tiny figure he was expecting had not appeared. But it could only be seconds before Deke realised which way they'd gone.

'Because I think *I* can,' she added. 'Just hang on.'

Heck winced as she began to climb up him, digging a knee into his back, planting one hand onto his shoulder to lever herself higher.

'Christ almighty,' he groaned.

At last she was off him and onto the stair itself, which rattled violently – so much that at first they thought it might break loose at the top and collapse onto them.

'Here.' She took his wrist and pulled him up, though it was a mammoth effort for them both; their clothing was waterlogged, their limbs felt like lead.

If the fire escape on the old building in Salford had felt flimsy, this one was all that and worse. It didn't so much shudder beneath their combined weight as swing. They clutched on to it, gazing at each other like frightened rabbits. Again Heck glanced towards the south tower. Deke still hadn't appeared.

When they ascended, the stair was only wide enough for them to go single-file; its treads remained treacherously greasy and even though it had safety bars to either side, it continued to swing – soon they felt safer going up on their hands and knees. They'd passed the first switchback and were about twenty feet up, when an invisible object whipped past them.

276

Lauren, the combat veteran, noticed it first. She froze; spun around. Heck followed her example. It was Deke. His diminutive shape garbed in black but distinctive for its blond head, had finally appeared at the end of the south tower landing platform. He was in the process of taking aim at them again with his rifle.

'Hurry!' Heck shouted.

They scrambled up to the next switchback, regardless of the groaning, twisting metal, and, on reaching it, threw themselves flat. A slug ricocheted with a screaming whine.

The underside of the superstructure was now only thirty feet overhead. From here, they could see that it was webbed with barbed wire. Seconds ticked by, followed by minutes. There was no sound, just the wind and the gulls. Gradually, as nothing else happened, they began to feel the cold.

'Why doesn't he keep firing?' Lauren whispered.

'He could be having second thoughts about potting us on this ladder. McCulkin's body will wash up downstream somewhere, with a head wound. If we do that as well, there'll be a major enquiry. He won't want that.'

'Okay, so what do we do?'

Encouraged by his own line of thinking, Heck risked crooking his neck up to look. He could just see the south tower and the corner of its landing platform. Deke was no longer there. 'On the other hand, he could be trying to lure us into the open again.'

'Either way, we can't lie here forever,' she replied.

Heck rolled onto his back so that he could peer directly up the remaining flight of steps. Some ten feet below the superstructure it reached a horizontal catwalk suspended by steel rods and running across the underside from the north-east corner to the southwest. At either end, an additional ladder rose to join with the catwalk that ran around the exterior of the superstructure itself. It looked an easy enough ascent after what they'd already been through, if it hadn't been for the coils of barbed wire cocooning the top three or four feet of the stair they were currently on.

'Maybe it'd be easier just to drop over the side and let the river take us where it will,' Lauren suggested.

'And if the tide takes us out to sea, what do we do then?'

'Surely we can make it to the shore?'

'It's several miles off, Lauren, and when we get there – *if* we get there – that shore is likely to consist of tidal mud and/or quicksand. We'll drown.'

'So what do we do?'

With a sudden recklessness, he stood upright and scaled the remaining steps.

'Heck!' Lauren hissed.

No shot was fired.

He didn't look round, just kept going. She jumped to her feet and scrambled after him. Still nobody fired. Heck had now reached the barbed wire. Lauren joined him, throwing another nervous glance in the direction of the south tower.

'What's he doing?' she wondered.

'Well, he won't just be letting us go. Come on.'

Progress up those last few feet was only possible with extreme caution. The wire had been woven around the metal stair in what was basically a large, single coil. It was possible to insinuate yourself carefully through it via a central passage, but time was now a factor – which was why Heck had no qualms about thrusting himself through quickly, even if it meant plucking both his clothes and his flesh.

'Watch yourself,' Lauren said, but he didn't respond.

He was crawling just ahead of her, and for the third or fourth time she saw him draw blood. When they reached the top, they were able to climb onto the catwalk through a circular manhole. But Heck had to fight down a growing sense of panic.

278

'Quickly,' he urged her.

'Okay, I'm coming . . . *ow, shit*!'

'Don't worry about that, for Christ's sake!'

'I'm doing the best I can!' she snapped, climbing up alongside him. She'd snagged her arm and the left side of her face; both were bleeding freely.

The catwalk, which had been exposed less to the elements, felt a lot safer than the stair. Heck led the way along it towards the southwest corner. They scaled the last ladder to the superstructure's outer catwalk, which seemed to be little more than a viewing parapet, a three-foot-wide ledge with a low safety barrier. Heck still urged Lauren on. 'We've got to get inside now,' he said.

The parapet floor was metal grillwork, which *bonged* like a bell as they rushed along it, rounding corner after corner, passing numerous portholes in the superstructure's rusted bulkhead. Just ahead lay the entrance to the bridge connecting with the south tower. A figure in black had already started across from its far end.

'Oh Jesus,' Lauren said slowly.

'That's what I was worried about . . . *QUICKLY*!'

Directly facing the entrance to the bridge was a door. It was made entirely from steel, but again had rusted with age. It stood partly ajar, but when they tried to force it further, it grated on hinges that had all but locked with disuse.

Dum – dum – dum – Deke's approaching feet grew louder.

Flattening their bodies, Heck and Lauren managed to slide inside. As they tried to shut the door behind them, they saw Deke stop in the middle of the bridge and take aim. There was a gunflash and an ear-popping *CHUNG!* The door crashed wide open, a massive indentation in its central panel. Heck threw his shoulder behind it to try and close it again. Lauren saw Deke resume running. The bridge vibrated alarmingly, but he came on at pace. Even from this distance, she could see the red tinge of his angry face.

With a *crunch*, they got the door closed. There were two bolts, again caked with rust. With colossal efforts, they rammed both home. Then they backed away, panting.

A second slug struck the other side of the door; another huge dent appeared.

'So much for us thinking this guy might be prepared to trade,' Lauren said.

Heck shook his head. 'That was before we knew he had someone on the inside. Whoever his police contact is, they'll bury that ledger the moment it gets filed as evidence.'

They glanced around. The room was dim, lit only by a single porthole with dirty glass in it. The light eddying through showed nothing but dust, decay and scattered seagull feathers.

'Where do we go now?' she asked.

'There'll be another bridge on the other side, probably leading to the north tower.'

'Yeah, and there'll be one leading from that to the east tower, and one leading from that back to the south tower . . . Jesus Christ, Heck, he's just going to chase us round in a circle 'til he gets us.'

There was a thundering *crash* against the bulkhead door – it sounded like the impact of a rifle butt. They retreated across the room towards another door, hesitant to go into blind flight – this place was old, rickety, likely to be full of danger. But when two further blows bashed through a corner of the damaged panel, and a gloved fist appeared holding a hand-grenade, they turned and ran for their lives.

There was a cacophonous explosion in the room behind them, made all the louder by the drum-like confines of the superstructure.

They staggered down a long, straight passage, which was lit at its far end by another bulkhead door standing ajar. Various rooms led off from this, looking as if they'd once been offices, though there was a particularly large one on the left into which light streamed from two different sources: an open trapdoor in the middle of its floor, which presumably dropped clear down to the river, and a similar hatch in the roof, accessible by a single wooden ladder. The steel frames of bunk-beds were also visible in there, alongside a row of green lockers. This had once been living quarters, but now the pervading smells were of oil, damp and mildewed metal.

'Go onto the next bridge,' Lauren said with sudden decisiveness.

'What?'

She began to rip her clothes off. 'We can't keep running, Heck.'

From somewhere behind, there was another deafening *boom*. It sounded like the bulkhead door finally being blown from its hinges.

Lauren nodded that Heck should do as she said. By the determined look on her face, the frightened girl had gone and the squaddie had returned.

'I hope you know what you're doing,' he said.

'Just don't go too far – keep me in earshot.'

He nodded, lurched back into the passage and kicked his way out through the next bulkhead door onto the viewing catwalk. The wind tugged at him; once again the drop to the river was precipitous. Ten yards to his right, the next bridge led off towards the north tower. He backed towards it, his eyes fixed on the doorway he'd just vacated.

Lauren meanwhile had stripped down to her vest and knickers. This was a desperate ploy, but she was counting on Deke's professionalism. He was unlikely to dash madly in order to catch up with them. He'd figure that his prey were tired and cold and couldn't keep running indefinitely – so he'd follow warily, expecting an ambush.

She clumped her sodden clothes into a ball, squeezed them until they were dribbling river water, then crossed the room, making sure to leave a trail behind her. When she reached the bottom of the ladder, a patch of sky was visible above the ceiling hatch. That would be the roof, the old gun platform. There'd be nowhere else to go once you were up there – which was why she intended to stay down here. She squeezed her bundle again, and tossed it up through the hatch, ensuring that drips and splashes appeared on the rungs of the ladder. She herself backtracked across the room, climbed into a locker and closed its door to a crack. It was hellishly claustrophobic; tight as a coffin. A loathsome, multi-legged horror landed on her shoulder and scuttled down onto her breasts. She brushed it off with a barely suppressed shriek.

The door to the bunk room opened.

She froze.

Through the slender gap, she saw a tall figure slide in and brace itself against the wall next to the door. It was Deke; he was clad in heavy, dark combat gear, and rigged with a black bandoleer to which a large knife, another grenade and numerous rounds of ammunition were attached. A Glock was visible at his hip, and he held the Dragunov across his chest, one finger hooked on its trigger.

He scanned the room carefully, presumably giving his eyes time to adjust to the gloom. Then he glanced downward. She'd been right – he was following the water trail. He advanced slowly, cautiously, weaving his way towards the ladder.

Lauren held her breath. Deke had clearly realised that Heck's flight to the next bridge, which would have left its own trail of droplets, had been a feint; the question was would he fall for this double bluff? When he reached the bottom of the ladder, he paused to listen. Then, with the Dragunov barrel pointed upward, he began to climb – very, very slowly, his eyes trained unwaveringly on the hatch above.

He was halfway up when Lauren attacked.

She broke cover like a whirlwind, hurling herself across the room and leaping onto him from behind. She was already shouting for Heck as they hit the deck together.

Heck was hovering on the viewing catwalk, wondering if he'd have the courage to drop ninety feet into the river should Deke suddenly appear, when he heard her shouts. He dashed in through the bulkhead door, raced down the corridor and into the bunk room.

Deke had got to his feet, but Lauren was clamped to his back like a crab, legs wrapped around his hips, arms around his neck. He held the Dragunov in his left hand, while slamming his right elbow back repeatedly. She cringed with each blow, but hung bravely on. Only when he drove his head backward, mashing it into her nose and mouth, did she weaken and slip off. Heck was now halfway across the room – Deke swung his rifle like a bat, but Heck ducked it and kicked him hard between the legs. Deke half doubled. Heck kicked again, this time knocking the rifle from his grasp – it clattered across the floor. Clasping both fists together, Heck brought them down hard on the back of the hit-man's neck. But Deke rode the blow and barrelled forward, catching Heck in the midriff, shoving him backward – only to be rugby tackled from behind by Lauren. He fell full-length, and she clambered onto his back. He drove his right forearm back, smashing it against the side of her jaw, sending her sprawling. But as he got back to his feet, Heck swung his right foot, kicking him in the face. Again, incredibly, Deke rode the blow and this time went for his pistol. Heck grabbed his arm, only to be smacked in the jaw with a rocketing left hook.

As Heck wheeled away and dropped, Deke straightened up, spat crimson phlegm, then released the catch on his hip-holster and drew the Glock. And stopped rigid.

'Drop it!' Lauren barked, jamming the muzzle of his Dragunov all the harder into the side of his head. 'Drop it now, or your brains are graffiti.'

Deke's hand opened and the Glock fell to the floor.

'Mitts where I can see 'em!'

For several taut seconds they were motionless, Lauren and Deke bloodied, sparkling with sweat, Heck groggy, only vaguely aware what was happening.

'You need me alive,' Deke said, raising his empty hands.

'Don't bank on it.'

'Okay.' He gave a fluting, crazy kind of laugh. '*I* need me alive.'

And he lurched away quickly, throwing himself across the room in a spectacular dive. He'd aimed for the trapdoor in the floor – and he cleared it by less than an inch, disappearing from view.

'Shit!' Lauren screamed, darting after him. But before she'd reached the aperture, she heard a strangled groan of pain, followed by profuse curses.

When she looked through the gap, Deke was a foot or so underneath her, suspended upside down in a web of barbed wire. Blood leaked from numerous gashes in his face and hands.

Heck, still unsteady on his feet, appeared alongside her. 'Well, well,' he said. 'Seems the Angel of Death has had his wings clipped.'

Lauren watched Deke down the barrel of the Dragunov. 'What do you say, Heck? Shall we snatch total victory from the jaws of certain defeat?'

Deke stared up at them. Despite his predicament, he chuckled. 'Do you people have the first idea what you're dealing with here?'

'You're going to tell us,' Heck said.

It wasn't easy dragging the hit-man back up into the bunk room. Heck did most of it, lugging him by the feet, while Lauren kept the rifle trained on him.

'Just gimme a reason,' she kept repeating, and by the wild glint in her eye, Heck suspected that she wasn't kidding. Deke had hurt her of course: had beaten her, had tried to kill her; they'd been chased from pillar to post, they'd roughed it, been scared half to death – and to top it all, she was still no nearer to finding her sister. Or so she felt.

They tied Deke's hands behind his back with a piece of rope they found hanging from a girder, and knelt him up to face interrogation. Lauren put the rifle aside, and grabbed the Glock. She pointed it straight at the prisoner's face while Heck did the talking. They'd already searched him thoroughly, removing his one remaining grenade, his knife and his ammunition belt, before removing a second, even sharper knife, which they found in his boot. In one pouch they discovered a coil of high-tensile wire, doubtless a garrotte, in another a tube of capsules which Heck guessed were cyanide pills.

'Filthy tools for a filthy trade,' he said.

Deke smiled, unconcerned.

'I know you're working for a group called the Nice Guys,' Heck added. 'And that you and they have been following my investigation. Which means that someone must have been tipping you fellas off about my progress.'

Still no reply.

'It would be in your interests to answer.'

'That shows how much you know,' Deke said.

'You think we won't beat the crap out of you, if we have to?' Lauren retorted.

'Give it your best shot.'

Lauren clenched a fist, but Heck led her to one side. 'He's ex-special forces,' he said quietly. 'He's probably been worked over by experts – and that's just in training. Let's chill out and think this through.'

She scowled but nodded.

Heck turned back to the prisoner. 'You've tied yourself in with some bad people, Deke. People who are only going to one place. You really want to go with them?

Deke still seemed indifferent.

'We have something you want,' Heck added.

'No you don't.'

'Something that will implicate you in a number of extremely serious crimes.'

'That'll be taken care of.'

'How?' Lauren demanded. 'How will it be taken care of? Who's the bent bastard copper who put you onto McCulkin?'

'Ease off,' Heck warned her.

'Look at the smug bastard!' she snapped. 'He thinks we're not tough enough to make him talk!'

'Whoever your police contact is,' Heck told him, 'he's not going to help you now. He can't. You ought to think about your future, what there is left of it. The time for being a good soldier is past. You'll never receive money for murdering or brutalising people again. You'll never receive money for *anything* again. There's no reason to show loyalty to people who'd now rather you were dead than alive.'

Deke smiled to himself.

Heck continued: 'It's very simple. I want to know who the Nice Guys are and where I can find them.'

'And just out of interest,' Deke asked, 'what do I get in return?'

'How about your freedom?'

'*What?*' Lauren said, stunned.

Deke sneered. 'You're not in a position to make that kind of deal.'

'But I am in a position to leave you on this fort alive and unguarded.'

Deke laughed. 'And how do you propose to do that? You can't even get off this fort yourself. Going to swim again? The last time you tried that, it nearly killed you.'

Lauren butted in, grabbing him by the lapels. 'This is not a debating society, you arrogant shitehawk! Give us some answers or I'll punch your fucking lights out!'

'Sorry, but I don't like the smell of her breath,' Deke said calmly. 'Get her out of my face, or this conversation's over.'

Lauren cracked Deke across the temple with the Glock. 'This bastard's taunting us, Heck.'

'It's nothing but bravado,' he said, hauling her away. 'Now cool down, okay?'

Heck swung back to Deke, whose face was running with fresh blood.

'As you can see,' Heck said, 'trying to be clever will prove unprofitable. Thanks to your handiwork in Salford, we're not exactly operating inside the law here. There could be plenty more where that came from, and at some point I'll get pissed off too and will stop trying to prevent it.'

Deke shrugged. 'Enjoy your sense of power while you can. Whatever happens here, you're both going to die soon. And it won't be over quickly.'

'Shit, this is a waste of time,' Lauren said.

'And this jungle-bunny bitch is going to go just like her sister did.' Deke eyed Lauren contemptuously. 'Raped, sodomised, tortured. Of course that was *before* she was dead. You can't imagine what was done with her afterwards.'

Lauren's eyes dilated. 'You son of a . . .'

He laughed. 'You weren't entertaining childish fantasies

that she might still be alive, were you? Or that she died easily?'

'You fucking son of . . .'

'Lauren!' Heck shouted, but it was too late.

She'd already put the gun to Deke's forehead and fired.

Chapter 33

Given the frazzled state of his nerves, Ian Blenkinsop was less than calm when late that afternoon his secretary buzzed through and said that there was a police officer to see him. There'd been police here for the last couple of days, seeking witnesses to Louise Jennings's last movements. They'd spoken to quite a few members of staff, Blenkinsop included – but only as a matter of course, they'd insisted; just trying to establish if Louise had said or done anything out of the ordinary on her last day in work. But Blenkinsop broke into a heavier than normal sweat when he heard that this particular officer – a certain Detective Inspector Palliser – was here from the ominously named National Crime Group.

When Palliser was shown in by Sally, he wasn't quite what Blenkinsop had anticipated. He was elderly to the point where he was surely close to retirement, and thin of physique, with scraggy grey hair and an even scraggier grey beard. He wore an anorak over his rumpled brown suit and, before sitting at Blenkinsop's desk, shook hands and gave a benevolent, almost fatherly smile. He smelled strongly of tobacco.

'Can I get you a tea or coffee, inspector?' Sally said.

'No thanks, my love, I'll be fine,' Palliser replied.

'Can I take your coat?'

'Oh yes, ta.' He stood up, shrugged off his anorak, handed it to her, and sat again.

'So how can I help you?' Blenkinsop asked, waiting until the door to his secretary's office had closed, and doing his level best to suppress the growing fear that this venerable old policeman instilled in him.

'Just a few questions, Sir.'

Blenkinsop was even more unnerved to see that the visitor had already opened a notebook and produced a pen. 'You say you're from the National . . .'

'National Crime Group, yes. The Serial Crimes Unit, to be exact.'

'Serial Crimes . . .' Blenkinsop struggled to keep the quaver from his voice. 'I thought the Thames Valley Police were looking for Mrs Jennings?'

'Funny you should mention Mrs Jennings, Sir. *I* didn't.'

'Is that not why you're here?' Blenkinsop tried not to sound too hopeful. 'Sorry, it's just that there's been quite a lot of police activity here in the last few days . . .'

'Yes, that *is* why I'm here.' Palliser continued to smile, making no apology for the semi-deception.

'I see.'

'Do you know Mrs Jennings well?'

'I know who she is, she knows who I am. That's about it, really.'

'Do you find her attractive?'

'I'm sorry?'

Palliser shrugged. 'Simple question, Sir. Do you find her attractive?'

Blenkinsop's lips had dried and tightened to the point where he thought they might crack. 'Who wouldn't? She was a very good-looking woman.'

'*Was?*'

290

'*Is* . . . I mean *is*, obviously. Look, inspector, I don't see what this . . .'

'Mr Blenkinsop, we've interviewed quite a few staff here at Goldstein & Hoff already.' Palliser checked his notebook. 'I understand that you're one of them.'

'We've all helped in any way we can.'

'Hmm. Was it mentioned to you when you were interviewed that, several times in the recent past, Mrs Jennings confided in friends that she felt you might have amorous intentions towards her?'

Even with everything else, Blenkinsop was stunned by that. 'What? No!'

Palliser tut-tutted. 'An oversight by the detective who spoke to you, obviously. Sorry about that.'

'It's ridiculous.'

'Mrs Jennings apparently told a couple of her colleagues in the Compliance department that she thought you, quote, "fancied her".'

'I don't know how she could have got such an idea.'

Palliser eyed him. 'But you've just told me you find her attractive?'

'There's a difference between that and making an approach to someone.'

'I didn't say you'd made an approach.'

For the first time in several days, the outrage Blenkinsop felt was genuine. He was quite sure that he'd never said or done anything to give anyone this impression. He had of course fancied Louise Jennings – to such a degree that he'd been willing to turn his life upside down in order to 'have' her – but there was still enough of the self-righteous citizen left inside him to be affronted by the notion that he might have lacked sufficient self-control to keep this concealed.

'Inspector Palliser, I'm a married man. I never signalled

291

anything of the sort to Mrs Jennings, who, as I told you, I barely knew . . . I mean *know*.'

Palliser mused. 'Maybe you did it unconsciously? I mean, women have an intuition for this sort of thing, don't they?'

'They may think they have.'

'Well that's a good point.' Palliser closed his notebook. 'It may be that Mrs Jennings was just flattering herself.'

'Inspector, may I ask . . . am I under suspicion for something?'

'Not really, Sir. But you must understand, we have to cover every possibility, no matter how minor or unimportant it may seem.'

'Minor and unimportant? And that job's been given to a detective inspector from the National Crime Group?'

'If you don't mind my saying, *that* seems to be bothering you rather a lot, Sir.'

'Not at all . . . it's not bothering me in the least. Well, I mean obviously this sad business is. I hope it sorts itself out and that you catch whoever abducted Mrs Jennings as soon as possible.'

Palliser raised an eyebrow. 'It's your opinion that she's been abducted then?'

Blenkinsop cursed himself. Everything he said put him in a worse light. 'I assume that's what it is.'

'As you probably appreciate, Sir, we can't afford to make such an assumption. As yet, there's no evidence that she's been abducted.'

'Maybe she's just run away from home.'

'We can only hope that's the case.'

'Wasn't she supposed to be in her car at the time?'

Palliser nodded. 'We've traced her movements to Gerrards Cross railway station, where we believe she left the car park in her own vehicle.'

Blenkinsop tried to sound as if he was encouraged by this. 'If her car vanished too . . . maybe that's a good sign?'

'Maybe.'

'You haven't recovered her car then?'

Palliser stood up and pocketed his notebook. 'I can't really comment on details of the investigation.'

'No, of course not.'

'Well, thanks for your time. Sorry to have bothered you.' Halfway to the door, Palliser stopped. 'Just out of interest, would you be agreeable to providing us with a sample of your DNA?'

Blenkinsop went cold. 'What?'

'You wouldn't need to go to a police station. I can have an officer come and do it here.'

Blenkinsop was stumped, not to say horrified. Surely they wouldn't ask for his DNA unless they had something? 'You . . . you said I wasn't a suspect,' he stammered.

'I'm not *requiring* you to provide your DNA, Sir, just asking. It would help eliminate you from the enquiry.'

'Why should I need to be eliminated?'

'It doesn't matter.' Palliser waved it aside. 'Thanks for your time, Mr Blenkinsop. No doubt we'll be in touch.'

'Erm . . . right.'

Blenkinsop almost stumbled as he followed Palliser across the office. They entered the next room in time to find Sally quickly hanging up her phone – almost too quickly. And why not? Blenkinsop thought bitterly. A girl had gone missing and the police seemed to be interested in *him*. The tittle-tattle machine would be working overtime. That was all he needed. Not that it was the worst of his problems at present. Once the policeman had put his coat on and left, Blenkinsop went back into his office – and had to make a beeline to his private bathroom, where he copiously vomited into the toilet bowl.

*　　*　　*

Palliser left the building with mixed feelings.

He'd learned about Blenkinsop supposedly fancying Louise Jennings through a statement taken by Thames Valley from one of her fellow secretaries in Compliance. It had been a throwaway comment, a nothing piece of intel – Blenkinsop had no reputation for being a creep or a stalker. But Louise had apparently *thought* that he kept a more than friendly eye on her as she strolled the company corridors. In itself this was valueless as evidence, but taken with Blenkinsop's apparent unease at being questioned – he'd been like a cat on hot bricks from the start – it might be worth someone looking into. The request that Blenkinsop provide a DNA sample had been an on the hoof masterstroke, because it had been refused and why would an innocent man refuse? Of course, this wasn't Palliser's case, and to some extent he was breaching protocol getting involved at all. But it wasn't irrelevant – far from it. What he'd found particularly disconcerting was Blenkinsop's response to the involvement of the Serial Crimes Unit – that genuinely seemed to have freaked him, and to Palliser's mind made it seem even less likely that Heck's theory about multiple connected abductions had been wrong. He would certainly write a report and file it with the mis-per department at Thames Valley, and the Lioness would need to know as soon as he got back to the Yard, but he didn't think it was significant enough for them to take to Commander Laycock.

Ten minutes after Palliser had left the City, Blenkinsop emerged from Goldstein & Hoff, his face grey, his hands jammed in his coat pockets. He'd told Sally he was leaving early because he wasn't feeling well. Now, he headed with unsteady steps down Cornhill towards Leadenhall. En route, he called at a newsagent and bought himself a packet of cigarettes, the first in fifteen years. He lit one as he continued walking. At Gracechurch Street, he headed south, coming at last to the river, where he sat heavily on a wrought-iron bench close to London Bridge, and gazed, glassy-eyed, across into Southwark. The world was closing in around him, and that was a definite – quite clearly it was no longer his disturbed imagination. Even if the police weren't onto him as such, they were clearly close. What did he do now? What *could* he do?

He threw the half-smoked cigarette away and lit another one. His hands were shaking as he put it to his lips. Clammy sweat lay in a fine dew across his forehead. Suddenly he realised he was going to vomit again. He staggered forward, hooking his body over the balustrade. He heaved two or three times before ridding himself of the last vestiges of lunch. When he'd done that, he tottered back to the bench and slumped down. His head was starting to ache, in fact to pound.

That was when he realised that somebody else was sitting on the bench as well. They must have sat down while he was throwing up.

He peeked sideways. It was impossible to tell whether it was a man or a woman – they were wearing a waterproof with the hood pulled up, and reading a copy of *The Times*. Okay – it was nothing to get upset about. There was nothing unusual in this.

But of course there was.

It was a free country, and you could sit anywhere you wanted. But this was a riverfront path with several empty benches dotted along it. Would you really choose the one right next to a man who was being violently sick?

Blenkinsop stood stiffly up and walked east. Only when he'd gone thirty yards or so did he risk a glance back. The hooded figure was still on the bench, still reading the paper. That was a relief – but it was only a temporary relief. For now he felt that someone else was watching him. As he turned into Billingsgate Walk, he spotted an unmarked van parked on the other side of Lower Thames Street. There was no obvious reason for this. Nothing was being unloaded; no one was in the process of climbing in or out. But the driver, who was no more than a shadow in the dim interior of the van's cab, seemed to be observing him. Blenkinsop couldn't swear on this, but he felt certain it was true.

He was sure those eyes followed him all the way past the Custom House and up Byward Street. He was now bewildered as well as terrorised. How had his life come to this so quickly? By the time he reached Tower Hill, Blenkinsop was running. He didn't know where he was running to. There was nowhere he *could* run to. But he ran all the same, blindly, tears and sweat mingling on his pallid cheeks.

Chapter 34

With the sun setting behind the isolated fort, its shadow lay long and twisted across the surface of the estuary. On the north shore, the fiery glow of the Canvey Island chemical plant was already leaking into the indigo sky. To the south, the mud flats lay spectral beneath a blanket of mist.

Heck stood on the viewing catwalk and absorbed all this without really seeing it. When Lauren appeared behind him, she'd climbed back into her sodden clothes. There was a worried look on her face, but her eyes flashed with defiance.

'What else could we have done?' she said. 'Your plan was to leave him here on this island. He'd have got free and come straight after us again.'

'That's hardly the point. He was our only lead.'

'He was a mercenary scumbag. To think of all the squaddies I knew who were killed in Iraq and Afghanistan. Good men and women trying to do a difficult job. And a piece of trash like that manages to make it back.'

Heck glanced round at her. 'Nice attempt to change the subject, Lauren. But the reality is that you've totally fucked us. One hour ago, we were *this* close. Now we've got nothing. Not only could Eric Ezekial have led us to the Nice Guys, he could have led us to their grass inside the NCG. And let's not talk about the fact that you've just murdered a man in cold blood . . .'

'You can't count him as a man, an animal like that!'

'You think a court will see it that way?'

'Heck, we shot him in self-defence.'

'We – sorry, *you* – shot him while he was tied up. Any way you cut it, that's not going to look good.' Heck shook his head. 'But I suppose it's my fault. I should've known better than to involve someone like you in this.'

'What do you mean "someone like me"?'

He jabbed a finger at her. 'Don't even think about playing the race card with me, darling. You know exactly what I mean. Someone who flies off the handle, someone who's too emotional for their own good.'

'I didn't see any sign that he was about to help us.'

'Yeah, well now we'll never know.'

He went back inside. She followed. They surveyed Deke's corpse. The sticky crimson pool around his shattered skull was already cooling.

'Look, I'm sorry,' Lauren said.

'Sorry? That's great, that makes it all okay.'

'What else can I say? He was going to kill us. Emotions were high. If we hadn't managed to secure him, and he'd been coming at us with a gun, are you saying you wouldn't have shot him?'

'The point is he wasn't.'

'But he might've done. Heck, there was every chance once he started hunting us that we were going to have to kill him. You surely must've allowed for that possibility?'

Heck shook his head. 'I hoped we wouldn't have to, and, as it turned out, we didn't.'

'And like I said earlier, what else would we have done with him? You weren't serious about leaving him alive here?'

Heck's expression turned solemn. 'When we get off this fort, Lauren, we're going our separate ways. You understand?'

'But I want to . . .'

'There're no buts. Not anymore. You shouldn't even be here anyway. And I certainly can't do this with Calamity Jane in tow.'

'You think I'm just going home, putting my feet up?'

'Erm, no. Not before you've helped me sort out this bloody mess that you've made, however the hell we're going to pull that off.' He paused to think. 'I need one of his knives. And that hand-grenade he had left.'

'Why?'

'Why, she says. Try to engage your brain, girl.'

'Look, we just chuck him in the drink. It's no big deal.'

'Of course it's a big deal.' Heck finally got angry, finally began shouting. 'He'll be found! And if he's been weighed down, there'll be serious fucking questions to answer! But even if he isn't, we can't afford for him to just disappear! We need to account for all this! How we got here, the ledger, who killed Ron O'Hoorigan!'

'Okay . . . so we leave him here and make it look like we shot him in self-defence.'

'Forensics tell no lies, Lauren! There'll be striation marks on his wrists, clear evidence that he was shot while he was bound and helpless! Like I said, try to engage your brain!'

She glared at him, but bit her lip and sloped away. When she returned, she had one of Deke's knives and his remaining hand-grenade. Heck took them both, then gazed down at Deke's face, which lay side-on. It was fascinating the way death so quickly dehumanised a human visage. The hole in the hit-man's forehead was relatively small, no bigger than a two-pence piece, with a thin black stain around it; but his face might have been made from wax – it was white, slack, pudgy; it looked as if you could meld it with your fingers. The cavernous exit wound at the back of the skull completed the picture.

It was no big deal, she'd said. Killing someone was no big deal. Perhaps it wasn't for an ex-soldier who'd seen heavy combat – and in that respect maybe he was being a bit hard on Lauren. But Heck was uncomfortably aware that he'd already strayed far from the traditional police path in what he was doing, and that this might be the final nail in his coffin. Okay, the son of a bitch had got exactly what he deserved, but it was still cold-blooded murder. This grim reality outweighed any elation Heck might have felt that Deke's final words about Lauren's sister had *proved* they were on the right trail.

He cut Deke's bonds, tossing the rope and the knife out through the trapdoor.

'What exactly are we doing?' Lauren asked.

Heck arranged Deke's hands so that they were cupped in front of his stomach.

'The only thing I can,' he said. 'Shattering his hands and wrists, preferably blowing them off completely. That should remove the evidence that he was tied up. It'll also make it look like the grenade went off while still in his possession. That way, at least no one will be able to *disprove* self-defence.'

Lauren backed towards the door. Heck took a breath, then pulled the pin, dropped the grenade into Deke's grasp and dashed after her. They were out in the next corridor when it detonated, the entire structure of the tower shaking with the blast.

When they wafted their way back in through noxiously foul smoke, Deke's body had been thrown halfway across the room. It had been reduced to smoking meat, its innards scattered in a glistening red pattern across the wreckage. The two offending limbs were little more than shredded flesh and

300

gristle. Nothing remained of the hands and wrists.

'As you can imagine, I really enjoy doing stuff like this,' Heck said. 'When I first joined up, the oath I swore to serve and protect doesn't contravene anything we've done here at all.'

'Like you said, it was the only thing you could do.'

'I think the phrase you're actually looking for is: "Thank you Sergeant Heckenburg, for making sure I don't spend the rest of my life in prison."'

'How do we get away from here?' she asked curtly.

'I suppose his lordship here had a plan for that. Of course, now that we can't ask him what it was, we'll just have to look around and see what we can find.'

They began by searching through the rubbish in the other rooms, but eventually finished up on the gun platform overhead. It was a broad deck, the size of a modern-day helipad, floored with wooden planks which in their turn had been laid with a gritty tarpaper sheet. The flat surface was broken here and there with pits and rusted steel fittings where the ack-ack guns had once been located. Heck looked east to the distant sea, then west to where the sun was descending in a fiery cascade over the smoke-grey smear that was London.

'There's nothing else on this tower,' Lauren said. 'We need to check the other ones.'

Heck shifted his gaze to the south tower. 'That was where he was perched when we got here. We'll try that one next.'

They crossed the bridge in single file, so physically and emotionally drained that they barely noticed how rickety it felt. As the sun set, the waters below were turning purple. The stiff breeze blew steadily colder.

'You think it's true?' Lauren asked from behind.

'What?'

'What he said about Genene?'

'I dunno.'

'But what do you suspect? Is she dead?'

Heck hesitated before replying. 'Yes. I'm sorry, but you knew there was at least a chance of that.'

'He said she was tortured.'

'We don't know if that bit's true.'

'Why else would they take her?'

Heck couldn't answer that. They kept walking, feet clanking on the aged metalwork. The upright cylinder of concrete that was the south tower was only a few yards away. The bridge entered it through a single black aperture.

'That's another reason why you should call it a day,' Heck said without looking round. 'You're not going to find your sister alive, Lauren. Which means you're only in it now for revenge, and trust me, you don't want that.'

'You can't ask me to leave, Heck.'

'I can and I am doing. Don't worry, I'll keep you informed.'

'And will you keep me protected?'

He was just about to enter the tower, but now he glanced back at her.

'Like you said the other day,' she added. 'We've been green-lit. *Both* of us. You might have been guessing then, but now we know it's true. Deke knew Genene was my sister. That means he knew who I am. That means the Nice Guys know who I am.'

'Oh. So now, when it suits you, you can be a defenceless girl?'

'The same applies to you, Heck. Will Deke be the last professional killer they send? At least together, we can look out for each other.'

It was an ugly thought but nonetheless true. For Lauren's own sake, Heck couldn't really afford to let her out of his sight now, whether he liked it or not. Of course, the stakes had been raised dramatically for *both* of them. The Nice Guys wouldn't yet know that their enforcer was dead; but when they finally put two and two together, how would they respond? Almost certainly with overwhelming force. This had become a shooting match now and any rules, such as there'd been, would almost certainly be dispensed with.

He sighed. 'There may still be ways we can make this disaster work for us. But first we've got to get ashore and back to London.'

Inside the south tower, the floor was a simple steel grille. A stair led up through a hatch onto the roof. They went up there, and found a green Bergen backpack, and alongside it a khaki bedroll and four spent bullet casings. This was clearly the point from where Deke had originally sniped at them. Heck ripped the first section of the pack open and pulled out various bits of survivalist kit: a water bottle, a flask probably containing hot soup, a mess tin, a packet of chocolate, a box of stay-light matches, a mobile phone and a bunch of keys. He examined the keys – one of them was for a Volvo four-track; the others looked as though they might be for a house.

'Look at *this*,' Lauren said. She'd opened another section of the pack, and taken out two further hand-grenades and a fold-out Heckler & Koch submachine gun with two full magazines taped to the side of its short, stubby barrel. 'He wasn't taking any chances, was he?'

'It's all to the good,' Heck said. 'Useful evidence of who and what this guy was. We leave it here, it'll confirm our story.'

'Don't you think we should make use of this stuff?'

'Lauren, we're already up to our necks in illegal crap. We start getting involved in firefights, and we're going down for sure.'

'What about this?' She held up Deke's mobile phone. 'Maybe we can get something out of it?'

'Any numbers stored?'

She checked it. 'None.'

'Should've guessed. He was too much of a pro to bring anything out here that might lead us to them. We'll hang on to it though – at some point we might be able to investigate his phone records.'

The final thing they found – to their relief – was a deflated dinghy with a paddle and a motorised propeller attachment. They carried it down to the landing platform. It was now almost completely dark. The only light was the eerie glow of the chemical plant. Lauren inflated the boat, and, once they'd both climbed into it, they pushed off with the paddle. It hadn't been designed for two, and rode dangerously low in the water. The excess weight also put great strain on the motor, which groaned agonisingly as it slowly propelled them away from the fort. When Heck steered them round in an arc so that they were heading towards the more distant north shore, Lauren was shocked.

'Why are we going this way?'

'We were seen in Allhallows-on-Sea. I don't want us to be seen there again, especially now we're ragged and wet and beaten up. People remember that sort of thing. Besides, I'm looking for this bastard's Volvo. It's more likely to be on one of the Canvey Island car parks. There'll be loads of other vehicles there, so it won't stand out.'

'Come on Heck, we'll never find it.'

'We don't have a choice, Lauren. How else are we going to get back to London?'

'Are we sure going back to London is a good idea?'

'We're not only going back to London, we're going back to Kingston upon Thames.'

'Why, for God's sake?'

'If there's any further clue to the identity of the Nice Guys, we'll find it in Deke's house. He's hardly likely to turn up and disturb us this time, is he?'

Chapter 35

'When were you going to tell me that Mark Heckenburg's in the frame for murder?' Commander Laycock demanded.

Gemma glanced round from where she was loading paperwork into the boot of her BMW. At this late hour, her vehicle was the only one present on the lower personnel car park. Laycock's had to be around here somewhere, though he'd come upon her unawares.

She continued sorting her stuff. 'He's not in the frame for it, as such.'

'Of course he's in the frame for it.' Laycock waved a three-sheet fax with a Greater Manchester Police logo at the top. 'There's more than enough evidence to arrest him right here.'

'Well, for one thing, we don't know where he is.'

'Have you looked?'

'Yes.'

'And yet strangely enough you haven't found him.'

'We're not running the murder enquiry, Sir. GMP are.'

'I know they are. I've had a certain Detective Superintendent Smethurst bending my ear on and off all day. Apparently this isn't just a murder anymore. Late last night they lost a potential witness and the two uniforms who were guarding him got badly hurt.' Laycock looked genuinely angry. His cheeks had paled until they were almost white – but then, as she already knew, he was a consummate actor. 'What's going on, Gemma?'

'I don't know, Sir.'

'You sure of that? Only it doesn't seem to be worrying you a great deal.'

She shrugged, closed her boot. 'What can I say? Heck's a maverick. This incident could be connected to any one of a number of cases that he's investigated over the years.'

'He's been fitted up, you mean?'

'Or it's some kind of misunderstanding.' She moved round to the driver's door, but Laycock followed and put a hand on it, stopping her from climbing in.

'Gemma, I'd really hate to think Heck was still working on this missing women case.' They regarded each other steadily. 'He is, isn't he?'

'He had some new information. I authorised him to check it out.'

'Why wasn't I informed?'

'I didn't want to bother you with it. Truth is, it was next to nothing.'

'Next to nothing? Look where it's led him to.'

'Sir, I don't believe for one minute that Heck is a murderer. Particularly not a sadistic murderer, which is what GMP seem to be dealing with.'

'Either way, he needs to come in and explain himself. The fact that he hasn't is something of an indictment.'

She reached into the vehicle and placed her briefcase in the footwell of the front passenger seat. 'I'm not reading anything into it until I speak to him myself, and get the full facts.'

'Very honourable of you,' Laycock sneered. 'In the

307

meantime, a police officer suspected of murder is on the run, and the department he works for is doing the minimum it can to apprehend him. According to GMP it's actually worse than that. According to GMP, you've not only been unhelpful, you've been downright obstructive.'

'Their failure to close a case is not our responsibility.'

'Damn it, Gemma!' Laycock's voice echoed through the vast reaches of the car park. There was a hint of scarlet in his cheeks. He wasn't acting anymore – he was furious. 'Have you any idea how this will look when it hits the headlines?'

She remained calm. 'Heck's wanted for questioning – nothing more. There's no reason why it should hit the headlines.'

'You and him used to have a thing going, didn't you?'

He leaned uncomfortably close, so close that she could smell his cologne. He'd moved the hand that had been resting on the open door so that it was now resting on her arm. His grip was tight.

'That was over ten years ago,' she said. 'We were both junior detectives at the time. In any case, I don't see how it's relevant.'

'You want to know what I think, Gemma? I think you still harbour feelings for Heck.' She laughed, but he wasn't put off. 'I can't think of any other reason why you'd tolerate his ridiculous antics.'

'He's a highly productive officer.'

'He's a headcase, and you know it. Or maybe you don't know it. Maybe your feelings for him have clouded your judgment.'

'Will that be all, Sir?' She yanked her arm free.

'No it won't.' Still he wouldn't release the door. 'I can read you, Gemma. Too well. You've done great things during your service, you've got commendations coming out of your ears, you *look* fantastic. You're PR gold for the modern police. But there's a downside to that. It means you've never had to bite and scratch for things, you've never developed the fighting skills or the political know-how. This rough, tough relationship you have with Heck – it may amaze and amuse those who don't know you. But I haven't bought it once. Not once.'

She appraised him coolly. 'It's what I suspected, Sir . . . you definitely *do* have too much time on your hands up there in that palatial office of yours.'

'Ahhh, the cat shows her claws. Hit a nerve, have I?'

'This is such crap.'

She made to climb into the car, but he grabbed her by the shoulder.

'You're right,' he said. 'It's a mountain of crap, and it's getting worse by the minute. But I'm not going to let it bury the National Crime Group. Too many men and women in this organisation have worked too hard to let some fucking wayward lunatic sink us all now. Heck's gone. That's it, it's over for him. And I can't say I'm sorry. But I have to tell you, Gemma, it might be over for some others as well. If you know where he's hiding, or if he's passed any information to you about this murder GMP are investigating, and you've withheld it, you are seriously in for the high jump.'

Carefully, with exaggerated distaste, she extricated his fingers from the material of her coat. 'Sir, your cool dude theatrics may intimidate the sort of craven yes-men you normally like to have around you. But don't make the mistake of thinking they frighten me. If you've an accusation to make, or if you want to launch a disciplinary procedure against me, by all means go ahead. But until then don't bore me with your schoolyard threats.' Now she leaned towards *him*. 'And don't even think about putting your hand on me again, under any circumstances whatever. Because if you do, I'll have you up in front of a tribunal so fast it'll make you faint. This is the positively discriminating twenty-first century, remember. Fast-track promotion for women is a hot ticket in the service these days. That means that, sooner or later, I'll outrank you – and then, whether you've done anything wrong or not, it'll be *your* turn for the high jump.'

Two minutes later, as she drove out of the car park, leaving Laycock fuming behind her, she grabbed a phone from her handbag and stabbed in a number.

'Yeah, Des . . . anything regarding Heck? Anything at all? Damn it! I don't care what it takes, Des, find him! And when you do, tell him I'm going to carpet my office with his bloody hide!'

Chapter 36

It was a long haul across the estuary, two hours at least, during which time the motor threatened to give out on three occasions. At length the boat beached itself in silt and mud, and Heck and Lauren had to plough knee-deep for another hundred yards before they found firmer ground. The massive petrochemical complex lowered over them, a futuristic city of pipes and tanks, its numerous flame-jets turning the night sky a vivid molten-red. They clambered through piles of rocks and rubble, and scaled a wire-mesh fence before entering its outer compound.

There were numerous car parks here, but Heck had come inshore in the straightest line possible from Blacksand Tower, hoping that Deke had done the same thing on his way out. It proved a sensible ploy – the only vehicle on this first lot was a black Volvo XC60. They ventured towards it, glancing around. There was no sign of any staff.

'If the alarm goes, leg it,' Heck said, producing Deke's car key.

He pressed the fob button. No alarm went. The XC60's headlights flashed once and its door locks thudded open.

Relieved, they climbed inside. The car was brand new and

state of the art, its lush, walnut-panelled interior fragrant of leather and crushed velvet.

'The murder business pays well,' Heck said, thinking about his old Fiat with its dented bodywork and broken air-conditioning.

He switched the engine on and put the car in gear. The radio hummed to life: the station was tuned to low-key jazz. They headed cautiously up the exit road.

'Think there'll be a checkpoint?' Lauren asked.

'Wouldn't have thought so. Otherwise, how did he get in here in the first place? This is probably just a visitors' car park.'

He was correct. The barrier lifted automatically as they approached it, and soon they were on the A13, driving fast towards the capital. It was another hour and a half's worth of journey, and midnight had been and gone when they entered the main conurbation. They crossed under the river through the Blackwall Tunnel, and worked their way across South London, finally entering Kingston upon Thames at one-thirty in the morning. Heck pulled up at the front of Deke's house. Lauren, who'd been half asleep, opened her eyes, yawned – and then jerked upright.

'This is a bit risky, isn't it?'

'We've got to try and keep things normal,' he said. 'We dump his motor somewhere else, sooner or later it'll be made for a knocker and an investigation will start. We leave it outside his house, it could be sitting here for months before anyone gets suspicious.'

He switched the engine off and brandished the house keys. 'For the same reason, there'll be no more breaking and entering. This time we go through the front door.'

She nodded. It made sense, but it was nerve-racking.

Once inside the house, they closed the door firmly and switched a few lamps on. As before, the security camera tracked their progress. Heck took out Deke's mobile and switched it on. As he'd suspected, an alert text had already arrived.

'What do we do about that camera?' Lauren asked.

'It doesn't matter now. We've entered these premises because we're concerned for the safety of the missing women. I've got full power under the Police and Criminal Evidence Act. That said, I don't want to get filmed making free with the owner's food and drink.' He took a cover from one of the cushions and tossed it over the camera lens.

'We're going to help ourselves?' she said.

'Only to the essentials. I reckon it's the least he owes us, don't you? That, and a bath.'

Lauren glanced in a mirror. They looked like two corpses dug from a graveyard: damp, ragged, their clothes filthy with mud and oil, their faces battered and streaked with blood.

'We'll get some kip too,' Heck added. 'We need it.' He set the alarm on his watch for five o'clock. 'Should still give us time to search this place top to bottom.'

While Lauren went upstairs to the bathroom, he entered the kitchen, checking in the fridge and bread bin. There was sufficient in there to make some sandwiches, which he duly did. There were also several cans of chilled beer. He took it all upstairs to the sleeping area. The door to the bathroom was open. Beyond it, Lauren stood under the shower. Heck placed the tray on a sideboard, and opened a wardrobe. Inside, in addition to an array of designer sports gear and army-surplus wear, there was a wealth of expensive clothing. He selected a few items that he thought might fit him. When Lauren appeared, wrapped in a towel, Heck took his own shower, luxuriating in the hot spray, flexing every aching joint, every strained muscle. When he came out, Lauren had put on one of the tracksuits from the wardrobe; it was black with a white trim, and elasticated at the cuffs and waist so, although it was too big for her, she was able to wear it in reasonable comfort.

'Another four stone and it'd fit you like a glove,' he said.

She nodded and smiled, and tried to slide something out of sight – but she missed her sagging pocket and it fell onto the floor. It was Deke's Glock 9mm. Red-faced, she scooped it up.

Heck towelled himself dry and put on a pair of clean shorts. 'I thought we agreed to leave all the weapons behind?'

She shrugged. 'I heard everything you said, Heck. But sorry, it doesn't make sense that we should keep going into situations where we can't defend ourselves.'

'That gun was used to murder someone, Lauren. And you're still in possession of it. Do you understand what that means?'

'It's just for insurance.'

'Insurance against what . . . us dying or the Nice Guys living?'

'Why don't we face facts?' Her voice rose. 'You're not going to arrest them. You *can't*! You're not a copper anymore, Heck, you're just a bloke on the run.'

'So they have to be punished in other ways, is that it?'

'You heard what that bastard said they did to Genene.'

'I didn't join law enforcement to be judge, jury and executioner. All we can do is make cases for prosecution.'

'That's easy for you to say.'

He held out a hand. 'Gimme.'

'Forget it.'

'I know you're stressed, Lauren. I know you're upset. But you think I haven't felt the same way over the years? You think my heart hasn't bled for the countless victims of crime I've had to deal with – innocent bystanders shot during bank robberies, timid householders beaten up in their own homes, children violated . . .'

'None of that matters, Heck, because they weren't your own!' She glared at him, not just angry now but raging. 'You talk as if you know these women who've been abducted and killed. But you don't! You've never even met them. The day it happens to someone you really care about, to one of *yours* – you'll see things differently.'

'And how do you know it hasn't?' There was a taut silence, before he added: 'You know your trouble, Lauren? You're so wrapped up in how this tragedy has affected *you* that you've not even considered how others are having to deal with it.'

'You've not lost anyone in this case.'

'Not in this case, no. But as good as.' He paused briefly, as if unsure whether to say more. 'You *think* your sister has been raped, tortured and killed. Understandably you're worried, you're distraught. But I know for a *fact* that my brother was raped, tortured and killed. So how do you think that makes me feel?'

'Your . . .?' She was astonished; the anger drained out of her like water from a sieve. 'You never told me.'

'Yeah, well maybe it was none of your business. But seeing as you've more or less demanded to know about it . . .'

He continued to get dressed, pulling on a pair of tracksuit bottoms and a fresh t-shirt.

'Tom was three years older than me, and a bit of a rebel – I mean an intellectual rebel, not a troublemaker. He was doing his A-levels at Bradburn Tech when he first got into drugs. My mum and dad were creatures from another era. They didn't understand any of that. When he got arrested for smoking a joint at a party, they were beside themselves. My dad's response was to severely punish him rather than guide him. There was a complete breakdown in communications, and the next thing Tom's dropped out of college and gone on the dole. Now he was on stronger stuff – pills and heroin. Instead of getting him help, my dad just bollocked the shit out of him, took every penny he got from the social, which of course only made things worse. Eventually, Tom and some junkie friend of his got caught burglarising the park café. It was a nothing crime. It wasn't a residential property, there was no one in there, nothing worth taking. But unfortunately it was just around this time that some nutjob who the newspapers had nicknamed the "Bradburn Granny Basher" was doing the rounds of the town's sheltered accommodation. He'd smash his way in, beat seven colours out of the OAPs living there, and make off with all their savings – usually about two or three quid. The team who'd been put together to bring him down were having no luck. One particularly lazy bastard DI, who was feeling pressured to get a result, decided that by some stretch of the imagination – and I mean a *considerable* stretch – the photo-fit they'd got of the Granny Basher matched the look of this young drug addict currently in custody for burglary.'

Heck cracked open a can of beer and took a long sip. Lauren listened in silence.

'As you can imagine, even with the Police and Criminal Evidence Act in force, it's never been impossible for a ruthless copper to frame a suspect . . . especially if that suspect is a strung-out junkie who'll say anything to get a fix. Well, the inevitable soon happened. Tom got leaned on hard, and eventually confessed. The next thing, he's been charged and convicted. He was eighteen by this time, so he was sent to adult prison.'

Heck paused, sipped more beer. 'He wasn't up to *that*. He only lasted a month, but at a rough guess he must've been raped fifty times before he decided to call it quits. He went to the shower, took a razor and slashed both his wrists and both his groins. It took him two hours to bleed to death, and it was another hour before anyone found him.'

He gave her a long, level gaze. 'You want to know what the most painful part of all that was, Lauren? About three weeks later – three weeks, that's all – the real Granny Basher got caught in the act by two sharp-eyed uniforms.'

He shook his head, and finished the can.

All Lauren could do was stutter: 'I hope, well, I hope your family got some compo?'

'Course we did, but surely you of all people realise how little that actually means?'

'Yeah, I do . . . but hey, *you* then went and joined the police. What the hell possessed you?'

Heck shrugged. 'Exactly what my mum, dad and sister asked. I mean, after Tom's death the police were *personae non gratae* as far as we were concerned. They were the biggest scrotes on Earth. And I just dropped everything and went off and joined them. You ask me why . . . I don't know. It was vague, I suppose. I wanted to redress the balance, put right the grievous wrong that had been done to my family in the only way I could – by joining up and showing the useless bastards how the job *should* be done.'

'Which you've been doing ever since.'

He chuckled bitterly. 'And what a smart move it was. My dad never talked to me again 'til the day he died. My mum tried to understand, tried to forgive, but I don't think she ever really succeeded. And Dana – well, you've seen the way things are between me and her.'

'From what I saw, that's mainly you.'

'That's because she feels guilty about it now.' He munched on a sandwich, but didn't have much taste for it. 'She tries too hard to be all the things to me that she wasn't during the years she ignored my very existence.

Things got so bad that I didn't just leave home, I ended up leaving town – I was in the Greater Manchester Police at the time, but requested a transfer to the Met. I basically gave up my entire world because my family weren't prepared to let me live in it. And Dana played her part, let me tell you.'

'So now you're teaching her a lesson?'

'I don't mean to, but I can't pretend I don't feel resentful. Anyway . . . the upshot is that you're wrong. I *do* know what it's like to lose a loved one to violence. But grabbing a gun so you can fight those responsible in the urban jungle, like some hoodlum, is the worst thing you can do.'

'Heck . . . whether we like it or not, we're already in that jungle.'

Before he could answer, the phone beside the bed started ringing. They peered at it. It rang maybe four times before the answering-machine kicked in.

'Talk to me,' Deke's pre-recorded voice said.

'Deke?' It was a man; by his accent, he was from the Midlands. 'Might I remind you, we were expecting a progress report from last night. Anyway, contact us when you can. In the meantime, it's a special for Alpha-Yankee-Zulu-Zulu-Zulu. Usual terms.'

The caller hung up. Silence followed.

'"A special"?' Lauren said. 'Sounds a bit worrying.'

Heck crossed to the hidden panel they'd found the previous time, opened it and climbed the stair to the attic. When Lauren got up there, he'd already pulled one of the buff files and spread it open. A photograph showed a dark-haired man in his mid-forties. There was a sheet with typewritten information, including the address of the man's home, which was in Hampstead, and his place of work, which was at an investment bank in the City. His name was Ian Terrance Blenkinsop.

Heck showed her the coded tag on the file cover. It read: *Ayzzz*.

'Alpha-Yankee-Zulu . . .' Lauren's words tailed off.

'Looks like we came to the right place after all,' Heck said. 'We've just found our next lead.'

Chapter 37

When Ian Blenkinsop checked in for work that morning, he looked better than Sally had seen in some time: bright-eyed, clean-shaved, wearing a pressed suit. He was even smiling. But she was a little surprised when she saw that he was carrying an overnight bag instead of his briefcase, and especially so when he informed her that he was taking some unplanned leave.

'I'm joining Yvonne and Carly at Lake Como,' he said cheerfully. 'I think I've been overdoing things a little and I need a break.'

'Well . . . okay,' she answered. 'I mean, there's probably nothing in your schedule that we can't rearrange.'

'Good, that's excellent. Because I've got a flight booked for two o'clock this afternoon.'

'I see.'

Sally wasn't quite sure what else to say. This was a little irregular. Even someone as highly placed in the firm as Ian Blenkinsop occasionally had responsibilities that he couldn't just drop on a whim. Of course there was no question that he'd been 'off-colour' the last few days; he'd almost gone through a personality change. This morning, though he'd

320

only been in for a minute or so, he seemed a lot more like his old self.

'I can't wait to see them,' he confided in her. 'It isn't a good thing being left on your own all summer, Sally. I think we'll have to reconsider this arrangement in the future.'

'Absolutely,' she agreed.

'Anyway, I'm just letting you know.' He slipped an envelope across the desk towards her. 'Here's the appropriate paperwork. No doubt, Mr Brahms upstairs will have something to say about it. Just refer him to my mobile if he does. I'll take full responsibility. Oh Sally, there's one more thing . . . if any more police officers come and want to speak to me, I'm abroad but you're not sure where.'

'I'm sorry?' She looked astonished.

'To be honest, it's all becoming a bit of a nuisance. I'm not sure if you're aware, but that chap who was here yesterday, he's from the Fraud Squad. They want me to witness for them in an embezzlement case. I've told them everything I know, which isn't much. But they keep pestering. Frankly, I can't be doing with it.'

Sally still looked astonished. 'Is this wise?'

'Whether it's wise or not, that's what I'd like you to tell them. From this moment on,' and he checked his Rolex, 'I'm officially on holiday.'

'But Mr Blenkinsop, if it's a pending court case . . .?'

Blenkinsop kept smiling, but suddenly his smile didn't reach his eyes. There was a glint of sweat on his brow. 'Sally darling, I don't know anything. And if they need to go to the trouble and expense of tracking me down and sending a summons abroad, I'm sure they'll finally realise that.'

Sally didn't look placated, and he knew why. She'd probably be quite happy for him to take a few weeks off. It would mean she could keep lax hours and that all she'd really have to do was answer the phone and make coffee for herself – but now she might have to divert a police enquiry too. Well, it was tough. She could thank her lucky stars it wasn't *her* disappearance they were looking into.

Blenkinsop left, but only after removing certain items from his desk. He extricated a diary from his top drawer, tore a single page from it and fed it carefully into the shredder. He nodded and smiled to her as he finally departed, but she had difficulty reciprocating, even though she intended to do as he asked. Sally knew which side her bread was buttered on. She was well paid here and Mr Blenkinsop was hardly a demanding boss. If it came to it, she wouldn't be comfortable telling the police a lie. But then of course she'd only be following orders and couldn't possibly be held to account for it. More than likely, as he'd repeatedly assured her before leaving, there was almost no chance the police would come to see him again.

But ten minutes later they did.

Sally descended to the lobby dry-mouthed with worry. It was a different officer from the one yesterday. This one was much younger, and, if he hadn't looked rather beaten-up, he might've been quite handsome. He certainly dressed well. His suit was Armani, his tie by Yves Saint Laurent. He was seated on one of the sofas in the company's waiting area, alongside a young black woman wearing baggy running gear.

'Hello,' Sally said. 'I'm Sally, Mr Blenkinsop's PA.'

The male officer stood and extended a hand. 'Detective Sergeant Heckenburg.'

'What can I do for you?'

'Actually I was hoping to speak to Mr Blenkinsop himself.'

'I'm afraid that's not possible. He's gone abroad.'

'Ah. Whereabouts?'

'I'm sorry, I don't know.'

Heck raised a sceptical eyebrow. 'You're his PA, and you don't know?'

322

'Well, he's on holiday . . . and it's a travelling holiday. He likes to tour the continent with his family. He could be anywhere.'

Sally was rather pleased with that response. She'd come up with it on the spur of the moment, and felt certain it would deflect any further questions. But she was surprised at how frustrated the detective now looked.

'When is he expected back?' Heck asked.

'I'm afraid I can't say.'

'Miss, you're aware this is an official enquiry? Anyone deliberately hindering us . . .'

'No please, you misunderstand.' She spoke urgently, suddenly frightened. 'What I mean is I can't say *for sure*.' This part was true. Before leaving, Blenkinsop had suggested rather vaguely that he might be away as long as three weeks, but he'd offered no specific dates on which to expect his return – which, now that she thought about it, did seem rather odd. 'I would think he'd be three weeks or so.'

'And in the meantime, do you have a contact number for him? A mobile maybe?'

'He has his mobile with him, of course. But all I can do is leave messages, which he'll pick up from time to time.'

'Maybe if you'd give that number to me, I could leave him a message?'

Sally shook her head. 'I can't do that, I'm sorry. But I'll help you any other way I can. I'll ring him every day.'

Heck regarded her carefully.

She blushed. 'I'm sorry, but it's his private number and he *is* on holiday.'

'Thanks very much for your help. We'll be back in three weeks.'

'You're sure there's nothing I can tell him in the meantime?'

'It's fine.'

Looking more relieved that she probably should have

done, Sally turned and walked stiffly back towards the elevators. Heck slumped onto the sofa alongside Lauren.

'You're surely not buying that bimbo's story?' she said.

'It doesn't matter whether I do or don't. As I'm not here in an official capacity, there isn't much option.'

'Maybe we can blag our way up to his office, give his desk a going over?'

'Let's keep this on a realistic footing, eh.'

'Okay, we've got his home address. If he's away on holiday, we'll have all the time we need.'

'You mean to commit burglary again?' Heck sighed. 'I'm getting tired of only making progress by committing criminal offences. You know, Lauren, I've never been much of a churchgoer – not after what happened to Tom. But it would be nice if, just once or twice, we got a spot of help from Him upstairs.'

'Yeah,' came a loud Cockney voice from the Reception counter. 'That's a taxi for Mr Blenkinsop. London City airport, yeah. Soon as you can, please.'

They turned to look.

The concierge, an elderly, ex-military type wearing a green frockcoat with golden braid at the shoulders, was on the telephone. 'Yeah, he'll be waiting in Mad Jack's – you know that place, the pub on Cornhill? Ten minutes, that's great. I'll let him know.'

'Ask and it shall be given unto you,' Heck said quietly.

They crossed Cornhill side by side. As they entered the pub, they again checked the photo they'd taken from Deke's file.

'Think you'd recognise him?' Heck asked.

'I already do,' Lauren said, stripping off her tracksuit top, regardless of the fact she only had a bloodstained vest underneath. 'Look.'

It was only mid-morning, so there weren't many people

in the pub, but one or two men in suits were sitting at tables reading newspapers. One was standing by the bar, with a bag at his feet. He was a dead ringer for the guy in the photo.

'Ian Blenkinsop?' Heck said, using his best official tone.

'That's right,' Blenkinsop said, turning and smiling – only for his smile to fade very quickly when he realised they were people he didn't know. His smile faded even further when he saw Heck's warrant card.

'I'm DS Heckenburg from the Serial Crimes Unit. Can you come with me, Sir?'

Blenkinsop kept a tight grip on his half of bitter. 'What's . . . what's this about?'

'I assure you it's very important.'

'Am I being arrested?'

'I'd rather hoped it wouldn't come to that.'

Blenkinsop shook his head. 'If I'm not being arrested, I'm not going anywhere.'

'Sir . . .' Heck spoke quietly, but leaned close, getting right into Blenkinsop's personal space. 'I'm assuming that many of the punters in this pub are people you do business with. Do we really want to make a song and dance out of this?'

Blenkinsop's face had gone grey and sickly as melted snow. His lips had visibly dried. 'I . . . I need to see your identification again.'

Heck showed his warrant card.

'And hers.' Blenkinsop nodded at Lauren, belatedly thinking it odd that one of these cops should be a young girl in a vest and running suit.

'Everything alright, folks?' Andreas the barman asked, leaning over the counter.

'Everything's fine!' Lauren snapped. 'Back off.'

Heck flashed his warrant card, and Andreas hastily retreated.

'Listen, you piece of shit,' Lauren hissed, crushing herself against Blenkinsop's body. 'Don't fuck us around. We know exactly the sort of people you've been keeping company with and it's all I can do not to waste you on the fucking spot. Now you walk out of this pub right now, or I'll blow your fucking guts out.'

Hardly able to believe what was happening, Blenkinsop glanced down and saw that she'd drawn a firearm. She was doing her best to conceal it with her rolled-up running top, but its steel barrel was pressed hard against his stomach.

Heck added: 'Believe it or not, Mr Blenkinsop, this is for your own protection.'

Unable to do anything else, Blenkinsop allowed them to hustle him from the bar. When he reached down for his bag, Lauren slapped his hand. She picked it up herself, but once they were outside, tossed it into a bin. The bustle of the street suddenly felt ominous. Everywhere they looked the pavements thronged. Log-jammed traffic honked and shunted. The attack, if there was going to be one, could come from anywhere at any time.

'Do you have some wheels near here, Mr Blenkinsop?' Heck asked.

'Look, whoever you people are . . .'

'I've told you who we are.'

'I'm sure this is a terrible misunderstanding . . .'

'I said do you have some wheels?'

'Don't you have some yourself?'

'Answer the frigging question!' Lauren snarled.

He nodded, swallowed. 'My Jaguar's in the company car park. It's just down that passage over there.'

'Take us,' Heck said. 'Quickly.'

'Try anything cute and you'll be dead before you hit the ground,' Lauren added.

They threaded their way through the traffic, and walked

down the side-alley to the multi-storey car park. The pedestrian door stood alongside the main entrance, in which a uniformed security man was standing smoking a cigarette.

'Just keep walking,' Heck advised. 'Don't try and signal to anyone – you'll be getting them in the worst trouble of their lives.'

'Morning Mr Blenkinsop, Sir,' the security man said.

'Morning Ted,' Blenkinsop replied as they passed.

'Fancy QPR's chances this season, Sir?'

'Oh yes, no question.'

Inside the pedestrian entrance, they jumped into an elevator and closed it behind them. Lauren kept the gun concealed as there'd almost certainly be a camera, but jabbed Blenkinsop with it repeatedly, just to remind him.

'It's on Level Six,' he said shakily.

Heck hit the button, and they ascended – only for the elevator to stop three levels short. Its door slid open. Two parallel rows of parking bays, all empty, stretched about fifty yards in front of them. The only illumination came from electric lighting. This gave a stark glare to the concrete pillars and slick, oily floor. The level appeared to be deserted. On a stanchion opposite, a red number '3' had been stencilled. Heck stabbed the button hard, feeling distinctly uneasy. The only reason why they could have stopped at Three when he'd requested Six was that someone on Three had called them first. Yet now there was nobody there.

The next time, they stopped on Six. Again, two parallel rows of parking bays stretched away. The lighting up here was dimmer. Heck saw why: though the bulbs were housed in metal cages, quite a few – each alternating one in fact – had been broken. Scatterings of recently smashed glass strewed the floor. Was that normal? he wondered. Wouldn't a firm like Goldstein & Hoff keep things in good working order? Or had the lights been broken recently? Dim shadows now lurked behind every pillar.

'That's my car down there.' Blenkinsop pointed thirty yards ahead to where a lone vehicle, a black Jaguar, occupied one of the bays.

'Okay,' Heck said, ushering him forward.

They advanced in a tight group.

'Who are you supposed to be protecting me against?' Blenkinsop asked.

'You're genuinely telling us you don't know?' Heck replied.

'Yes . . . and I might say you've got a strange way of doing it. Would you please take that wretched gun out of my . . .'

'Shit!' Lauren halted sharply.

They all halted sharply.

The Jaguar's four tyres had been cut, slashed repeatedly – until they were nothing but shredded rubber and severed ply-cord.

'Shit,' she said again. 'They're already here.'

Chapter 38

Ian Blenkinsop's demeanour had gone through several trans-
formations since they'd taken him from Mad Jack's. Initially
of course he'd been frightened and bewildered. Then, as it
had dawned on him that this was something he'd half-
expected to happen, he'd become less bewildered and much
more frightened. As they'd ascended into the car park, and
Heck and Lauren had still refrained from using violence
against him, he'd become less frightened and more affronted,
almost bolshy. But now that he'd seen what had been done
to his forty-thousand-pound car, he was terrified.

'Surely the security people would have seen that someone
was in the car park?' he stammered as they hurried him
down the emergency exit steps.

Heck had opted to use this stairwell rather than the
elevator. It was only a precaution, maybe an unnecessary
one – he didn't know if it was possible to sabotage a
modern elevator, but he knew that he didn't want to find
out.

'Just keep going,' he said, urging Blenkinsop down.

Lauren had pocketed the Glock, as they no longer needed
it to convince the errant banker that he'd be safer in their

company than out of it. But she was ready to grab it at a moment's notice.

'Wait!' Heck held a hand up.

They stopped, sweating. Heck could have sworn he'd heard the patter of feet somewhere above, perhaps coming down the stairs after them. But now there was nothing. Almost certainly it had been an echo.

'Okay, keep going.'

They continued to descend, passing the fourth level, and the third. Again there were no windows in this part of the building, and when they reached the second level, the last two flights of stairs had had their lights broken. They halted, teetering on the brink, peering down into menacing blackness.

'This way.' Heck steered Blenkinsop through the fire door into the car park proper.

From here, they made it down to the ground floor by the vehicle ramps. The security man who'd been smoking in the entrance was no longer there. Nor was there any sign of him through the portal to his office.

'If we can locate Ted Chadwick,' Blenkinsop muttered, 'he can probably help us.'

'Ted Chadwick will be helping himself into an early grave,' Heck replied. 'Just follow me.'

They re-entered the alley. There was a figure at its farthest end. It looked female, and was carrying a briefcase; perfectly normal for this part of London, yet it was standing in the middle of the alley, staring after them. They only just managed to avoid running as they proceeded the other way towards Cornhill. It was a relief to join the teeming crowds, which seemed ludicrous given the vulnerability they'd felt there only a few minutes earlier.

'Who exactly are we looking out for?' Heck asked Blenkinsop.

'I don't understand . . .'

'Don't mess me around, you understand perfectly! What do they look like?'

Blenkinsop shook his head. He wore a tortured but helpless expression. 'I've never seen any of them – I've never seen their faces, at least.'

'How many are there?'

'I got the impression quite a few.'

Heck started along the pavement, Lauren and Blenkinsop following. They descended the first stairway they came to, which led to Bank tube station.

'Haven't you got any more men than this?' Blenkinsop wondered.

'Just keep moving,' Heck said.

'We making this up as we go along, or what?' Lauren asked.

Heck rounded on her. 'Got a better idea? These bastards have been one step ahead of us for days. Well, I've had enough of it. We'll take trains at random . . . try to throw them off the scent.'

She stood guard while he bought them all a day's travel pass. After that, he ushered them down to the Waterloo & City Line, where they caught the first connection south. At Waterloo they changed to the Bakerloo and headed north. When they reached Paddington, they took the Hammersmith & City east, changing to the Victoria at King's Cross. All the time they watched their fellow passengers, which became increasingly difficult. The ever changing crush of humanity pressed into and out of the confined space of the tube trains; all types were on view – every race, sex, age and creed. On the Victoria, Heck felt concern about a tall black guy standing close to them. He was handsome, dressed in a smart suit and wearing a distinctive pearl earring. He had a briefcase at his feet and was absorbed in a copy of the *Financial Times*.

'See that dude?' Heck mumbled to Lauren.

She nodded.

'I'm pretty sure I saw him riding the Bakerloo in the carriage behind us.'

'There could be a totally normal reason for that.'

'Could be. We'll know in a sec.'

At Green Park, they jumped out, Heck virtually shoving Blenkinsop down onto the platform. Rushing straight to the Piccadilly Line, they took an immediate train north, changing again to the Bakerloo at Piccadilly Circus, and back onto the Victoria Line at Oxford Circus.

'Surely . . . this is unnecessary?' Blenkinsop gasped. They were again crammed in with hordes of fellow travellers, many of them foreign tourists wearing iPods and backpacks. The air was rank, stifling. 'No one's going to try anything down here.'

'No,' Heck agreed, 'but we don't want them following us 'til they get us somewhere where they *can.*'

'Dear God, this is ridiculous . . . utterly bloody ridiculous.'

'Just watch the crowd, Blenkinsop. See if there's anyone you recognise.'

Thankfully, they seemed to have lost the black guy with the earring. When they passed Warren Street a large number of passengers disgorged. There was now some breathing space.

'Do you want to tell us exactly what you've been up to?' Heck asked.

Blenkinsop broke into a puzzled frown. 'Surely you're already aware of that?'

'If I was, I wouldn't be asking.'

'Well if you're not aware of it, I'm certainly not going to tell you.'

The sweat was cooling on all their brows. Blenkinsop was breathing deeply, but now regarded Heck and Lauren with distaste and something like suspicion.

'May I remind you,' Heck said, 'that I'm a police officer? I'm giving you a chance to explain yourself off the record. But if necessary I'll take you to the nearest nick and make it official right now.'

'Isn't that what you're supposed to have done in the first place?'

'I told you not to give us any shit!' Lauren warned him.

'Or what? You're going to shoot me? In front of a train-load of witnesses? What kind of coppers are you two? You drag me out of a pub, you threaten me with a gun . . . now you're running around London not even knowing who's supposed to be chasing you . . .'

She grabbed his collar. 'Listen, fuckhead . . .'

He violently struggled free. 'I don't have to listen to anything . . .'

She switched her hand to his throat, squeezing his larynx. He gagged, eyes bulging.

Heck snatched at her hand, yanking it loose.

'I don't know what you've been up to, Mr Blenkinsop,' he said quietly but intently. 'But I do know that you are involved with some extremely unpleasant people. Now you listen to me very carefully. This business is not going to end happily. You understand that? You saw what they did to your car. Nice bit of knife-work, wasn't it? Trust me, that isn't even a foretaste of what they could do to your flesh.'

'In that case, why *don't* you take me to a police station?' Blenkinsop asked, rubbing at his throat. 'Surely we'll all be safer?'

'Heck!' Lauren hissed.

'What?'

'Six yards away, combat fatigues.'

'Yeah?' Heck didn't risk looking over his shoulder, but could sense that someone was there now who hadn't been there a few seconds ago.

'He's just come in from the next carriage through the emergency door.'

Heck nodded, understanding her suspicion. Unless you were a high school kid trying to reinforce your cool, moving from carriage to carriage was a big no-no when the Underground trains were in motion. It made even less sense on this particular occasion as both carriages were less than half full.

The train groaned to another halt. They were at Euston.

'Let's go,' Heck said, stepping out, following the signs to the Northern Line. 'What does this guy look like?'

'Short, stocky, swarthy.'

'You said he was in combat fatigues?'

'Yeah, yellow and brown. You know what that means, don't you?'

Heck nodded grimly. It meant they were desert fatigues.

'It could be a coincidence,' she said.

'We're not taking any chances.'

On the Northern Line, they headed south.

'This is insane,' Blenkinsop muttered. 'We're going round and round in circles.'

'We'll do it as long as we need to,' Heck replied.

'Can't we at least go up to the surface? I've got to get some air . . .'

'Forget it.'

Blenkinsop stuck a shaking hand in his overcoat pocket, and pulled out a packet of cigarettes. Heck slapped them from his grasp.

'No smoking on the Underground, Mr Blenkinsop. Surely you're aware of that?'

Blenkinsop swallowed a lump of saliva, which, by the grimace on his face, must have tasted like poison. His lips had dried so much that they'd cracked and were beaded with blood. As they headed back into the West End, more and more people piled onto the train, which made them feel less conspicuous, though soon they'd be south of the river and the crowds would dwindle again.

'Where to now?' Blenkinsop wondered loudly. 'The southern leg of the Northern Line? That's bandit country by anyone's standards!'

'Chill the fuck out,' Lauren snapped. 'Panicking won't get us anywhere.'

'Yeah, okay. Like you lot are acting in a level-headed manner.'

They passed Tottenham Court Road, Leicester Square and Charing Cross, and, as they'd expected, passengers began to disperse. Soon they were south of Waterloo and feeling alone again.

Blenkinsop suddenly stiffened, sucked in a tight breath. 'You said there was a chap in desert fatigues on the previous train?'

'That's right,' Lauren replied.

'I can see through into the next carriage. He's in there.'

This time Heck *did* risk a glance around. There was indeed a figure standing just beyond the glass of the emergency door in the next carriage. He had his back turned, but was clearly wearing combat fatigues. Lauren stole a glance too – and almost froze.

'It's the same guy. Shit, Heck, we're still being followed.'

'We should go topside,' Blenkinsop stated flatly. 'Get a cab.'

'We're almost in Stockwell,' Heck argued. 'There won't be many cabs around.'

'You pair of bloody fools! What have you done to me?'

'If it wasn't for us, you'd already be dead,' Lauren retorted. 'Heck, I'll take rearguard.'

He glanced at her, querying such wisdom.

She shrugged. 'It's the only way to stop the pursuit.

Whatever this idiot knows, it's obviously vital. That means you've got to get him away from here. The next station, you two just go for it – I'll cover your backs.'

Heck was far from comfortable with this, but the idea made sense in a risky kind of way. They were either being utterly paranoid here, or a team genuinely *was* tailing them. Either way, the only solution was to engineer a confrontation.

They pulled slowly into Stockwell station.

'Me and Blenkinsop will go straight across to the northbound, and double back,' Heck said. 'You're absolutely sure about this?'

She nodded. 'Don't wait for me. Just go, full speed.'

Heck dug Deke's phone from his pocket and called up its number. 'Can you remember this?'

She read it two or three times.

'It's the only point of contact we'll have,' he said.

'It's all we'll need,' she replied.

'Call me as soon as you're clear.'

She nodded.

The doors slid open, and Heck pushed Blenkinsop out. They headed up the nearest tunnel, which led straight to the northbound platform. It was arched and narrow, and most of its cream tiles were in the process of being replaced, which left much exposed brick and loose plaster. The only light came from temporary bulbs strung along the ceiling. They swung in the warm breeze, throwing shadows back and forth. The northbound was twenty yards ahead – as they approached it a train glided in. Heck grabbed Blenkinsop by the back of the collar and propelled him forward so that soon they were running.

Behind them, Lauren waited alone on the southbound. She peered down the length of the train, which was pulling out again. A couple of people had disembarked further along

336

– an elderly Jewish man, who went straight up the exit staircase, and a short, bullish figure wearing desert fatigues. This latter now ambled towards her, hands in his pockets. He was thickset, with a broad, powerful neck. His hair was cut very short, his face tanned, brutish.

She waited for him. There was still a chance he was an ordinary commuter. But he came straight on, staring at her with such intensity that he might have been seeing through her. When he was five yards away, he took his hands from his pockets – she saw the tattoos on the inside of each wrist. They were black scorpions.

Lauren went for the pocket containing the Glock – only for a hand to tap her shoulder.

She spun around, shocked. She'd been so mesmerised by the approach of the first man that she hadn't thought to check the two or three carriages behind her. The tall black guy with the pearl earring was there. He smiled at her, the teeth bright in his handsome face. He presented his clenched fist – almost as if he was showing it to her, as if it was something he wanted to sell. It was wrapped in a gold-plated knuckleduster. Lauren made a kick for his groin, but he dodged and she only caught him on the thigh. At which point she was hit in the back of the neck, so hard that nausea engulfed her. She'd convulsed into unconsciousness before she'd even hit the floor.

Heck and Blenkinsop travelled up the Northern Line to Leicester Square, before ascending to the surface. They still didn't know if they were being followed, but Heck was now thinking that, with an organised pursuit like this, only the teeming multitudes of the West End could provide an adequate shield. They gulped fresh air as they finally emerged from London's guts – at which point Deke's phone trilled.

Heck snatched it from his pocket and answered. 'Lauren?'

337

'I like your style,' said a soft, gloating voice. 'Letting a woman do the fighting.'

'You bastards,' Heck breathed.

'It was a novel plan, but,' and the voice chuckled, 'just in case you were wondering . . . it didn't work.'

'I'll get you, I swear it.'

'Gonna send another woman to take care of that for you?'

'I know all about you now.'

'Not as much as we know about you. Or rather . . . as much as we'll shortly know. You see, that's what we do, Detective Sergeant Heckenburg. We find out about people. We make it our business to know them better than they know themselves. So very soon – courtesy of this gift you've left us – we're going to know all your strengths and all your weaknesses. Especially your weaknesses.'

The voice chuckled again, and hung up.

Heck had this conversation on the corner of Lisle Street.

Stiffly, like an automaton, he now pocketed the phone, turned to Blenkinsop, grabbed him, twisted his arm behind his back and frog-marched him to the edge of the pavement. Blenkinsop choked with pain and struggled wildly, but, though he wasn't a small man, he was helpless in Heck's street-toughened grasp.

'You're going to talk to me,' Heck said. 'You're going to tell me everything. Or you've got a date with this double-decker.'

He nodded towards a bus picking up speed as it bore down Charing Cross Road towards them.

'For Christ's sake!' Blenkinsop screamed. 'Someone help me, please!'

But the West End crowds, as was their way, only scurried around the bizarre scene, interested to watch it but more interested to mind their own business.

The bus crashed over a manhole lid. It was twenty yards away and pushing forty.

'You think I'm not serious!' Heck shouted, shoving Blenkinsop over the kerb and across the first carriageway.

The bus was almost upon them, the driver staring in amazement, knowing he wouldn't be able to stop in time.

'YOU THINK I'M NOT FUCKING SERIOUS!'

Chapter 39

'It's a rape club,' Blenkinsop told Heck. 'The Nice Guys are a criminal gang who organise rapes for money.'

They were facing each other across a table in the crowded back room of a Covent Garden pub. Both were sallow-faced and nursing treble-whiskies.

'*Say that again*,' Heck whispered.

Blenkinsop, globs of sweat clinging to his brow, stammered out everything he knew: about how the Nice Guys first made contact with him; about how he'd paid them to procure Louise Jennings for him; about how he'd then raped her while she'd lain unconscious. Heck had paled to a deathly milk-grey by the time the story was finished.

'And afterwards? What happened then?'

'They killed her.' Blenkinsop took a long slurp of whisky, his eyes downcast. 'Put a wire round her neck . . . and garrotted her with it.'

Heck paled even more. 'You witnessed this?'

'God forgive me . . . yes.'

'And you didn't do anything?'

Blenkinsop's gaze flirted up. 'Are you kidding? You haven't seen these fellas. I was fucking terrified . . .'

Heck leaned quickly forward. 'Well . . . the law may understand that. But it's not going to understand why you didn't go straight to the police afterwards, you stupid fuck!'

'After what I'd just done? I was as much part of it as they were!'

'Are you genuinely telling me this is their full-time business?'

Blenkinsop shrugged, helpless. 'I assume so . . . it must be. They're totally professional. I mean, everything about them . . . they had masks on, so I never saw faces. They were so organised. They give you this guarantee beforehand that nothing's going to come back to you, that you'll never hear about the incident again . . .'

'What . . . you thought they'd pay her off, or something?' Heck said scornfully.

By the expression on the banker's face, this was exactly what he'd thought.

Heck shook his head. 'You seriously believed a professional woman like Louise Jennings could get kidnapped and raped and never mention it to anyone just because she'd been bribed to keep her mouth shut? Can you just buy *anything* in your world, Ian? What did you think, that you'd see Louise every day at work afterwards and she'd never bat an eyelid because the Nice Guys had made it worth her while? Are you bloody stupid, or what!'

'I don't know what I thought . . . maybe something like that, maybe that they'd put the fear of God into her, maybe a bit of both. It's carrot and stick, isn't it? That's the way you get people to comply. Look, whatever . . . they guarantee it won't mess your life up, and they're so efficient you believe them!'

'Mess your life up?' Heck had to struggle to regain his breath. 'Jesus Christ, I've come across some things in this job . . . I don't know what sickens me more, the fact that they actually do it, or that there are enough callous bastards out there like you for them to make it pay!'

'Look,' Blenkinsop pleaded. 'I genuinely didn't think it would end like that. I feel terrible about it.'

'Some consolation that'll be to the Jennings family.'

'I'm an idiot, I accept that.' Blenkinsop swilled more whisky. 'But I'm not evil. Look . . . when I first saw their website, I didn't even think they were serious. I got in touch with them to see if it was real, and then it was just too late to stop.'

'It's never too late to stop.'

'I lost control, alright? Look . . . I really, really fancied Louise. I knew I wouldn't have a chance to get near her any other way. So I did it. Okay, I didn't think about her or the consequences, and I know that's wrong, but I just had to fucking have her . . .'

'That's going to sound great in court, Ian. You're really going to win the judge over with that argument.'

Blenkinsop hung his head. 'I just . . . I just want things to be back to normal again, back the way they were before.'

'The way they were before?' Of all the things Heck had heard today, this was the peach. 'Ian, we're talking kidnap, rape and murder here! So that's three life sentences you're facing before we even consider the other women!'

Blenkinsop's mouth dropped open. 'The other women? But I didn't have anything to do with those.'

'Not taking action to shop these men makes you their accomplice.'

'That's insane.'

'That's the law.'

'I . . . but I . . .' Blenkinsop looked as if he was going to be sick; he frantically drained his glass. 'Some kind of witness protection, or . . . if I testify. I mean, I can't face . . .'

'The only way we can even contemplate that is if you give me something concrete I can use against the Nice Guys.'

'I've told you all I know.'

This was at least partly true. Heck knew that Blenkinsop's use as a material witness would be limited, even though he'd been present at one of the murders. The same applied to all the others whose personal files resided in that filing cabinet in Deke's house. Every one of them would have been subjected to the same blindfold treatment.

'How the hell did they get in touch with you in the first place?'

'I told you . . . they dropped me a card.'

'What, they just pulled your name off a list of porn subscribers? At random? Sounds a bit risky.'

'Not any old list. Somehow or other they know I've got money.'

Heck leaned forward again. 'It isn't just about the money, you prat! Not every rich man will indulge in a spot of sexual homicide if he thinks he can get away with it. The Nice Guys will realise that even if you don't.'

Blenkinsop shook his head. 'You've got me so wrong . . .'

'*They* didn't, did they!' Heck's thoughts were racing. 'They must pick their prospective clients carefully. There must be something that drew their attention specifically to you.'

'I don't know . . .' Blenkinsop's brow creased as he pondered. 'There's . . . there's one possible thing. Only occurred to me this morning. I mean, it's a long shot . . .'

'Go on.'

'I go abroad a lot. For the bank, you know.'

'Okay.'

'All over the Middle East and North Africa. I'm a director in structured commodity finance. I have to tap up some pretty important people.'

'Very impressive. And what else do you get up to over there? Come on, Ian, you're obviously dying to tell me . . .'

Blenkinsop mopped fresh sweat from his brow. If it was possible, he looked even more embarrassed than he had when admitting his involvement in a rape-murder. 'There are all kinds of services you can obtain in those countries which are not . . . well, not widely available over here.'

'And what's *your* preference, I wonder?'

'I like a bit of the rough stuff.'

'Well, we've already established that, haven't we? You're a fucking rapist.'

'No!' Blenkinsop half-shouted. 'No, it's not rape . . . not over there. It's consensual. They get paid for it.'

'Yeah . . . probably in peanuts.'

'That's not my fault. It's their living, and it's their choice.'

'And are any of these girls actually old enough to have made this choice responsibly?'

'Some of them, yeah.'

'Some of them!'

'Look . . .' Blenkinsop pointed a shaking finger. 'I didn't create the culture of corruption they have in these countries. You know what the Third World sex game's like. Some girls look older than they are. Some look younger. No one cares about it. No one ever asks. I didn't either.'

'You're a real stand-up bloke, Ian. I can't imagine why the Nice Guys homed in on you. Course . . . none of this explains how they knew about these predilections of yours, does it?'

Blenkinsop pawed at his sweaty brow. 'I was thinking . . . the Nice Guys . . . they're so competent, so organised. I could be wrong, but . . . there's something a bit military about them.'

'And?'

'Well, whenever we go abroad . . . I mean on company

344

business, we use security consultants to put us in touch with bodyguards over there. We have to. Some of these places are pretty dangerous, you need escorting everywhere.'

'Bodyguards?' Heck said slowly.

'Mercenaries . . . for want of a better term.'

'Or for want of an even better one, sex-slavers. Is that what you're saying?'

'Not all are like that,' Blenkinsop replied. 'Some are totally legit . . . but there are others who are . . . well, to be frank, are into all sorts. Drugs smuggling, arms dealing . . .'

'Human trafficking,' Heck added. 'Or was that just the firm you were using?' Blenkinsop hung his head again. 'Tell me about them, Ian. Everything.'

'I don't know too much. I first met them while I was over there . . .'

'Friends of friends, eh?'

'Hardly friends.'

'What a pity you've only realised that now.' Heck laced his fingers tightly; despite his playing the heavy, he finally felt they were getting somewhere. 'When did they first introduce you to this . . . other business of theirs?'

'About four years ago. At the end of a night out. We were all drunk. I asked them to take me to a brothel. They laughed and asked what kind of brothel? We took it from there.'

'And you trusted them? Just like that?'

'Sure. They were British.'

'British.'

'Well, some of them. The ones I spoke to. But there were others who sounded foreign, I suppose: American, French, Russian . . .'

'What else do you remember about them?'

'Like I say . . . gave the impression they were ex-military. They'd *have* to be, working over there in security. Probably ex-special forces. Real tough bastards.'

345

'Any names?'

'Only the boss. Mike Silver. "Mad Mike Silver", they used to call him. I thought it was a joke, Jesus.'

'Most likely that name's bogus,' Heck said. 'Description?'

Blenkinsop fingered his damp collar as he tried to cast his mind back. 'Again, British. War veteran almost certainly – that steely demeanour, you know. Mid-thirties, I'd say. Average height. Well built. Well-spoken too. Possibly a former officer. Dark hair, but prematurely greying. Walked with a cane. Said he'd been wounded in action.'

'What's the total strength of this outfit?'

'I don't know.' Blenkinsop was now looking tired as well as drunk. 'I only usually saw a couple of them at any time, and it was always too dark to memorise faces. Look, what's the point in this? They're over in the Gulf. If you're going to trace these fellas, surely you'll have to go through foreign agencies?'

'That can come later. At present, our priority is the cell that's operating here.'

'But it can't be the same people. Why would it be? Over there they're safe. They can do what they want. Look . . . at worst, all they'll have done is sell my name and details to someone else.'

'At worst?' Heck's disbelieving eyes bored into him. 'At worst, Ian, they could have come home. At worst, they could now be running their very lucrative operation in the UK . . . except that over here they can't just buy the victims off, with peanuts or anything else. And they've got another problem . . . over here they've found this rather big fly in their ointment. A fly who works in structured commodity finance at a City investment bank. A fly they're going to have to squish rather quickly.'

Blenkinsop looked faint with fear, but still shook his head. 'This is pure supposition. You've got no evidence that Silver

346

and his team are behind the Nice Guys.'

Heck thought hard. It was true – there was no firm evidence. But Deke, with his Scorpion Company background, was surely more than just a coincidence. It would also explain how such a firm could operate in London and yet evade the radar of a local gangster like Bobby Ballamara. It would explain the commando-like precision with which the abductions had been executed, the Swiss bank account Blenkinsop had mentioned – that was always a sign you were dealing with someone a little more sophisticated than the average British hoodlum.

Of course, the thought that he was dealing with mercenaries here – ruthless and experienced killers with a vested interest in snuffing out the opposition – was more than a little bit scary. Knowing there was a whole bunch on their tail, the danger level felt as if it had risen exponentially. And he hardly dared think what was happening to Lauren at this moment.

'You were once their customer,' Heck said. 'There must be some way for you to make contact with them.'

'I tried,' Blenkinsop sighed. 'But their website no longer exists. At least, I couldn't find it again.'

Heck sat upright, struck by a sudden thought. 'Which computer did you use?'

'My PC at home.'

'Have you still got it?'

Blenkinsop nodded.

Heck finished his drink. 'That's the way we get them.'

'I told you, the website's gone.'

'It won't be gone. They've just concealed it.'

'It could be being operated from anywhere.'

'They sent you a couple of emails as well, didn't they?'

'Those addresses are defunct too. Anyway, I deleted everything.'

347

'There'll still be electronic traces left on your hard drive somewhere.' Heck stood up. 'We've got people who can retrieve them. Come on, we're going to your house.'

Blenkinsop seemed reluctant to move. 'Shouldn't we get some back-up first?'

'I'm afraid that's impossible.'

'For Christ's sake, why?'

'Believe it or not, the Nice Guys have someone inside my department. I don't know who, but as soon as he learns we're onto them, they'll disappear for good.'

'So all I've got is *you*?' Blenkinsop sounded incredulous. 'I mean . . . you alone?'

'Thank your lucky stars. It's more than you had two hours ago.'

Blenkinsop shook his head. 'I'm going nowhere. I'm staying here.'

'Really?'

'You want to go to my house, which, if they're as motivated as you say, they'll probably be watching . . .?' Blenkinsop dropped a front door key onto the table. 'You're welcome to it. But I'm not. I'm staying here and having another drink. No one's going to try anything with me in here.'

There was a taut silence, before Heck swept down across the table, yanking him up by his lapels so hard that glasses flew everywhere. Blenkinsop gasped as Heck forced him back against the wall, constricting his throat.

'Maybe *I'll* try something with you!' Heck hissed. 'You self-obsessed wanker! My friend has been kidnapped by these people. God knows what they're doing to her. And you think you're going to sit here and get wasted? As far as I'm concerned, Blenkinsop, you are rapist scum, no better than the criminal psychopaths who set this operation up. And you can be damn sure that when these killers go down, you'll be going down with them – maybe to the same prison, maybe to the same cell!'

'Please . . .' Blenkinsop was pouring with sweat.

'The only chance you've got of avoiding that fate is by cooperating with this investigation as fully as possible!' Heck snarled. 'Starting now!'

Chapter 40

Blenkinsop's home was a detached, double-fronted Edwardian situated amid extensive landscaped gardens. This area of Belsize Park was almost exclusively residential, its quiet roads and avenues hedged and tree-lined, so now that night had fallen there were many dark niches and shadowed corners from where an ambush might be launched.

It was close to nine o'clock in the evening when a black cab came cruising along.

'Sixteen, Templeton Drive, did you say?' the cabbie asked the two men, on whom he'd smelled booze the moment they got into his vehicle, though they'd seemed a well-dressed pair, so he hadn't anticipated any trouble.

'That's right,' Heck replied.

'Been to a party, have you?'

'Something like that.'

'Finished a bit early then?'

'Been a long day.'

'Can't argue with that,' the cabbie said. 'Sixteen's coming up, by the way.'

'Any chance you can pull onto the drive? Get right up to the front door?' Heck asked. 'My friend has a bad leg.'

'Suppose so.'

Blenkinsop, who was as white and rigid as a waxwork, took the door key from his overcoat pocket and leaned forward to point its fob through the windscreen at the gated entrance they were now approaching. The wrought-iron gates swung open, and the cab was able to pull right up its gravel drive and park alongside the front of the house. The porch had been built portico style, two white Doric columns supporting an ornate wooden canopy. Heck indicated that Blenkinsop should move quickly. He did, leaping out of the cab and dashing up the marble steps to the front door.

'Doesn't look like much of a leg problem to me,' the cabbie said as Heck paid him.

'Between you and me, he's a bit of a whiner.'

'Oh, one of them, eh?' The cabbie touched his nose. 'I get you.'

The cab pulled away and Heck hurried inside, slamming the front door behind them. The hall light had now been switched on and Blenkinsop was in the process of deactivating the alarm.

'System been tripped?' Heck asked.

Blenkinsop shook his head.

'What parts of the building does it cover?'

'Upstairs and downstairs.'

'Motion sensors?'

'Yeah, but we used to have a dog and we got out of the habit of switching them on. All the doors and windows are covered, though. No one's been in.'

Heck was surprised. 'That's better news than I hoped for.'

'I still don't see the point in this,' Blenkinsop said. 'If they'd left a . . . what did you call him?'

'A spotter.'

'If they'd left a spotter, he'll have seen us arriving. Even

351

if he didn't want to take a shot at us because that cabbie was there, what's to stop him calling his mates now?'

'Nothing, but we've no choice. We have to take possession of your hard drive. It's the only evidence we've got.'

Heck surveyed the downstairs hall. It was expansive and tastefully decorated: the floor was of polished black and white tiles; the furniture resembled a collection of antiques. A chandelier hung from the ceiling. Handsome oil paintings adorned every wall.

'The PC's upstairs, you say?' Heck said.

'I'll show you.' Blenkinsop moved to the foot of the staircase.

'Wait. Show me the kitchen first.'

Blenkinsop shrugged and led him through. The kitchen boasted a real brick floor and an immense cast-iron cooking range. Next to the sink, there was a block of kitchen knives. Heck took one. He examined its glinting blade ruefully, as though horrified his job had finally brought him to using a weapon like this, before concealing it under his jacket. They went upstairs. The landing was a long corridor running east to west. Six bedrooms opened off it. All were deep in shadow, which seemed to deepen even more when Blenkinsop switched on a central light.

'It's down this way.' He headed towards the far end of the passage.

Heck blocked his path. 'Let me go in front.'

'But there's nobody here.'

'I'm beginning to find that a problem.' Heck went first, padding stealthily on the thick pile carpet.

'Coming here was your idea,' Blenkinsop said accusingly.

'It was needs must. Doesn't mean I like it.'

They glanced into each room as they passed, seeing only beds outlined in the gloom. There was one minor shock when Heck kicked open a door standing ajar on one of the house's two bathrooms, only to see a body lying in the sunken tub – it took nearly a full second to identify this as a bundle of dirty towels.

'My wife's away,' Blenkinsop explained sheepishly.

They proceeded, now with only two doors remaining; one on the left, which Blenkinsop said was his bedroom, and one directly ahead, which he said was his study. But now Heck saw something that stopped him briefly. The cream carpet on this part of the landing was marked by a thin patina of grey dust lying across it in a near-straight line. He paused to examine it. Blenkinsop went past him to the study, opened the door and flicked the light on.

'It's all here,' he said.

Heck glanced up.

On the other side of the study, a state-of-the-art computer rig was visible on top of a large desk.

'We've beaten them to it,' Blenkinsop added.

Heck glanced down at the dust again. 'Just wait!'

But Blenkinsop had already gone in. The study had once been an extra bedroom, but had now been fully adapted for its current use, its shelves packed with folders. The study floor was of varnished wood, a thin patterned rug occupying its central section.

'*Wait!*' Heck said again.

Blenkinsop looked back, but had now stepped onto the rug – and was most surprised to feel it drop away beneath him.

Heck darted forward, but though Blenkinsop seemed to be falling through the hole cut in the floorboards in slow motion, he was still too late. Both Blenkinsop and the rug were sucked down through the square aperture like waste food going into a disposal chute. At first he gibbered with shock – almost comically, but once below, those gibbers turned to squeals and then to weird, guttural gurgles.

Heck tested the floorboards with his foot before coming to the edge of the hole.

Blenkinsop had dropped into his own garage. But a four-foot steel spike with a heavy concrete base had been placed directly below, and, having landed on it backward, he'd now been impaled through the midriff. At least a foot of shining steel protruded from his belly. He scrabbled at it with weakening hands, his crimson mouth horribly agape, the eyes bugging from a face turning yellow with shock. Blood spattered like tap water onto the concrete beneath him.

Heck didn't get a chance to move or even speak before he heard a *creak* and *clunk* of woodwork. He spun around, but the trapdoor in the landing ceiling had already opened and someone had leapt lithely down – as he no doubt had done once before, which explained the line of dust on the carpet. Heck pulled out the kitchen knife, but the figure, which was dressed all in black, including a black hoodie top, sprang up from its haunches brandishing a more effective weapon – a Colt Cobra .44 revolver complete with silencer.

'Don't you just love these houses where the only security's on the doors and windows,' the hoodie said in a strong Brummie accent. 'I guess these mollycoddled middle-class types never stop to think the roof might also be accessible.'

Beneath the hood was the bland face, wispy moustache and overly prominent forehead of 'the Kid', the young guy caught on the photos taken at the scenes of the Miranda Yates and Julie-Ann Netherby abductions.

'Nasty way to go,' the Kid added, standing on tip-toes to glance past Heck at the hole in the computer room floor. 'Not our normal style. We're usually a lot more discreet. But sometimes examples have to be made.' He chuckled. 'Make a nice piccie to send out with our next mail-shot . . . remind our client-base that it never pays to fuck us around. Glad *you* didn't go in there first, by the way, detective. We've got something much more tasty planned for you.'

Chapter 41

'Looking for this?' the Kid asked.

He produced something flat and shiny, which looked like a sardine can with the wrapper removed. It was the hard drive from Blenkinsop's computer. When he opened his hand, it fell to pieces, having already been dismantled. One by one, he ground its circuits under his heel.

'Oops,' he said. 'Sorry. Oh by the way, drop the blade.'

Heck had no option; he released the knife.

The Kid chuckled. 'Good of you to leave your dabs all over that. That's another murder we can frame you for. I'm a bit surprised actually. You're the one who supposedly outsmarted Deke. Least, I'm guessing you did. We haven't heard anything from him since he was supposed to whack you, and now you're answering his phone.'

Heck shook his head. 'You'll never find out what happened to Deke.'

The Kid shrugged. 'Hardly matters. He was never really part of the crew, just an employee. They come and go. We don't form emotional attachments with any of them.'

'Cold professionals, eh? Except that *you* aren't, are you? I mean *you* personally.'

The Kid grinned and beckoned Heck along the landing. 'I wouldn't press too many buttons if I were you. Just because I'm under orders not to kill you yet doesn't mean I won't get the pleasure later on.'

'The rest of your mob are professionals, but you aren't,' Heck insisted. 'You're the immature one, aren't you? The one who craves notoriety.'

'I'm warning you, pig . . . don't make it hard for yourself.'

'You see, I've seen you before. On crime scene photos from Brighton and Aberystwyth. Those were perfect snatches. Your crew got clean away each time, but *you* couldn't resist coming back to see what was happening. To revel in the misery and fear you'd caused.'

'Every job has its perks.'

'And every job has its fucking idiots who can't be trusted to do it properly. Which is where *you* come in.' Heck knew he was getting to the Kid by attacking his self-esteem; he could see the laugh lines fading from the truculent, youthful face. 'You're the weak link in the chain, son. A social inadequate who's only in it for the thrill of feeling powerful, and as such is going to get his mates bagged and tagged.'

'Enough talking!' the Kid snapped, backing towards the top of the stairs, but now pointing the gun straight at Heck's forehead. By the gleam in the Kid's eyes, he was crazy – he'd have to be to be part of this outfit – but by his own admission he was under orders not to shoot. So Heck took the gamble and continued goading him.

'You know what we call you in the Serial Crimes Unit – "the Kid".'

The Kid's eyes were slowly clouding over.

'That's right,' Heck said. 'As in the young one, the inexperienced one, the *inept* one. Can't build much of a rep on that. Ever heard of a master criminal called "the Kid"?'

The Kid's gun hand was trembling.

'But it gets worse,' Heck said – he knew they were reaching critical mass, and was now watching his captor ultra-carefully. 'How'd you think your mates would react if they knew what you'd been up to? I bet they wouldn't stop at "inadequate" or "inept", would they? I bet they'd slip "dick-head" in there, or "useless prick". How about "brainless fucking pipsqueak"?'

'You pig bastard!' the Kid shrieked, raising the gun and slashing down with it.

Heck blocked the blow with his left, and caught the Kid square on the nose with a right. The Kid's head flew backward, but he kept his feet. Heck clutched at the hand holding the gun and slammed it against the wall. The Kid hung on to the weapon and tried to claw Heck's face, but Heck butted him, drawing a yelp of outrage. They were now at the top of the stairs, the Kid teetering on the edge. Heck threw another right, catching him again on his already broken, blood-spurting nose. The Kid squawked, tottered and fell backward. Heck, not wanting to lose hold of the gun hand, dived down the stairs after him. They crashed all the way to the bottom, breaking spindles, bouncing over treads. The adrenaline that seemed to have been pumping through Heck's veins for several days rendered him almost immune to the many bumps and sprains. Though he was again fighting for his life, it was a less terrifying ordeal than it would have been a week ago. This member of the opposition had plainly never been a soldier of any description, let alone a special forces guy; his combat skills were too inadequate. This boosted Heck's confidence no end – he got to his feet first.

The Kid, who was grovelling in agony on the hall floor, was still clinging on to the gun. Heck stamped on his hand twice. The gun came loose, and Heck kicked it, sending it skittering away across the tiles, its silencer detaching. The Kid tried to stand up – Heck let him, then caught him with another left, followed by a short, crisp right. The Kid crumpled down in a heap, where he lay groaning. Heck turned to look for the gun. There was no sign of it – it had slid away in the direction of a half-open door on the other side of the hall. Heck limped over there.

But the Kid couldn't afford to leave it at this; there was too much at stake. Unexpectedly, he dragged himself to his feet and barrelled into Heck's back, toppling him out of the way, and running past to get to the door first. Heck caught him by the belt and hooked an arm over his shoulder. They crashed into the open door together, blundering through it and falling down yet another stair, this one made from rough wood. The floor at the bottom was cold concrete, and this time Heck got the worst of it. He was underneath and the Kid on top, so it drove all the wind out of him.

The Kid tore himself from Heck's weakened grasp, jumped to his feet and, in the half-light, stumbled over an empty box, hitting a workbench. Hand tools flew everywhere. The Kid swore as he kicked them around, still looking for the gun. Heck levered himself up onto his elbows. The Kid suddenly spotted something, and hunkered down. Winded, Heck tried to get up but knew that he wouldn't make it. His opponent spun around, Colt Cobra in hand, his face a Halloween mask of bloodied, maniacal glee. He fired twice, the detonations deafening.

The first slug hit Heck in the solar plexus with what felt like crushing force. The second took him in the upper right chest, flipping him sideways. He slammed against the bench, sending yet more tools spinning. Both blows had packed sledgehammer power; his innards seemed pulverised.

Reality ebbed before his fading eyes, and then he slumped to the floor.

The Kid came forward, panting.

'Maybe I can build a rep on *that* instead!?' he jeered. 'Not so cocky now, are you, pig bastard!'

He kicked Heck over onto his back, and knelt astride his body to search it. He didn't notice Heck's right hand close on the handle of a claw-hammer. He didn't even notice the hammer – until it was whistling up towards his left temple.

SMACK!

The meaty impact echoed across the cellar.

The Kid dropped like a sack of potatoes, his head striking the concrete.

It took several agonising seconds for Heck to haul himself to his feet. He extricated the gun from the Kid's hand, tucked it into his waistband, and then yanked open the shirt he'd been wearing to check the Kevlar vest beneath. The two flattened slugs were still lodged in it.

'Much as I enjoyed your flash suit, Deke,' Heck said to no one in particular, 'I enjoyed your underwear more.'

He worked the slugs loose and dropped them, though even that was painful – no doubt there'd be bruises the size of dinner plates underneath. He turned back to the Kid, who was still unconscious. 'And just who the hell, I wonder, are you?'

He searched the Kid's clothing, finding, among other things, a mobile phone, which he pocketed, and a leather wallet containing a number of credit cards. It seemed the name the Kid was currently going under was 'Brian Hobbs'. If that was a fake, it was a fake the Kid liked, because not only was that the name on his cards, it was also the name on his driving licence. Heck felt at the Kid's throat, to check the carotid was still pulsing. It was, which Heck supposed was a relief.

He moved away, looking for a light. Finding a cord with a toggle, he pulled it and a bulb sprang to life. The cellar was larger than he'd thought, and quite orderly, apart from the area the two of them had just destroyed during their fight. There was another workbench in the corner, underneath a shelf laden with jars of screws, nails and so on. There was also a hook from which a bundle of rope was suspended. That would do nicely. It was a bit Spiderman-like, but Heck couldn't think of a better outcome than calling this incident in and leaving the culprit bound at the scene of the crime.

He walked over there – and heard a noise behind him.

Yet again, because it was absolutely imperative that the Kid saved this situation, he'd somehow revived himself. When Heck turned, the Kid was halfway across the cellar, a razor-tipped wood chisel raised above his head. He screamed with homicidal rage.

Heck pulled the gun and fired four times.

It wasn't what he'd planned to do. It wasn't even what he'd wanted. It was pure instinct, sheer self-preservation.

The first three bullets tore into the Kid's torso, stopping him as if he'd run into a brick wall, while the fourth – just in case he too was secretly armoured – was directed at his massive forehead, in which it blasted a hole the size of a fifty-pence piece.

The Kid again flopped to earth, this time with blood venting in spurts from his chest, his back, and the right side of his imploded skull.

Heck leaned on the bench to regain his breath. He tried to console himself with the knowledge that he hadn't just done what he'd earlier berated Lauren for doing. This wasn't an execution, it was simple self-defence. But he didn't feel particularly bad about it . . . until about ten seconds later, when he heard the approach of sirens.

He whirled around in a panic. This was Belsize Park of course; not the sort of neighbourhood where gunshots would go unreported.

He took the stairs three at a time, and emerged into the

hall to see a blue spinning light outside the front windows. He dashed into the kitchen, where he halted to think. A sensible patrol officer would have sent his partner around to the back before trying to gain entry at the front, but they'd only *just* arrived. There was still a chance. He grabbed a stool from under the breakfast bar and heaved it at the window over the sink. It exploded outward in a jangling cacophony. They'd hear it, but speed was all that mattered now. Heck vaulted out and sprinted the full length of the extensive rear garden. By the time he reached the far end, he could hear shouting. Torchlight speared onto the lawn. He didn't look back, but scaled the fence and dropped down the other side into a narrow, leafy lane, which he ran off along at full pelt.

Only when he was four or five streets away and thoroughly exhausted, the sweat swimming into his eyes, did he halt and double over, hacking out coughs. Almost on cue, there was a ring-tone from his pocket. It was Deke's mobile phone.

He took it out. By the number on the screen, the call was coming from the same phone that had called him on Lisle Street. He put it to his ear.

'Talk to me,' he said.

'Mark?'

'Ye-yeah, who is . . .?'

'Oh Mark . . . oh God, Mark . . . who are these awful people?'

The voice was cut off as though a hand had been slapped over a mouth. It had been tearful, totally terrorised – but there was no doubt who it belonged to.

Dana, his sister.

Chapter 42

Gemma's eyes snapped open to the trilling of a telephone bell.

She lay confused for a few moments, before focusing on the neon numerals of the clock on the other side of the darkened bedroom. It was just past midnight – she'd turned in relatively early because she'd wanted a quick start the following morning. She fumbled on the bedside table and finally found the offending article.

She put it to her ear. 'Yes, Piper.'

'Ma'am, it's me.' It was Des Palliser.

Gemma sat up. 'Have we got something?'

'Yeah . . . I think we do.'

'Well?'

'How soon can you get over to Hampstead?'

'Hampstead?'

'Belsize Park, to be precise?'

'Belsize Park?' Gemma's thoughts were still fuddled. What on earth could take them to that exclusive neck of the woods? 'This is related to Heck, yes?'

'I think it could be.'

'*Could* be?'

'Ma'am, this is serious.'

Gemma was now fully awake. Palliser's tone was one of suppressed excitement, but she didn't like the sound of that last comment. 'How serious, Des?'

'As in . . . "do you want to check a fresh murder scene yourself before local plod get their dirty paws all over it" serious.'

She leapt from the bed. 'I'm on my way.'

Gemma made it to Belsize Park in record time. She lived in Highbury, but a blue spinning beacon on top of her BMW meant that she could hurtle down Camden Road and up Haverstock Hill without being intercepted by uniforms, and allowed her to pull straight in alongside the crime scene tape now deployed across the driveway entrance to sixteen, Templeton Drive.

'Ma'am?' one of the local detectives said. He'd been standing behind the tape, jawing with a couple of uniforms, and looked astonished to see her.

'Hello Tony,' she replied.

Detective Sergeant Tony Gibbens was close to retirement. His stained tie, scruffy brown mac and cynical attitude indicated that he was a creature from another era. He was balding, with tufts of white hair behind his ears. He scratched at one of these as she approached.

'Fancy letting me take a look, Tony?'

'Yeah, course. Surprised to see you, though, ma'am.'

'What have we got?'

Gibbens turned and regarded the house, every window of which was now brightly lit. 'Well . . . it's a two-hander. Unusual circs. But if someone's called your mob in, they were a bit previous. Lab team haven't even got here yet.'

'Who's Crime Scene Manager?'

'DI Jeffries. When he arrives.'

'Alex won't mind me having a quick shuftie, will he?'

'Don't suppose so, ma'am.' Headlights flooded over them. 'This is probably him.'

But the beaten-up Chevrolet that pulled in alongside Gemma's BMW did not belong to DI Alex Jeffries. When DI Des Palliser climbed out, Gibbens looked even more surprised.

'Something we should be told about, ma'am?' he asked, looking suspicious.

'If there is, Tony, you'll be the first to know. Okay?'

'Sure.' He lifted the tape.

'So what is this?' Gemma asked, as she and Palliser headed up the gravel drive.

'That bloke I interviewed at Goldstein & Hoff?' he said quietly.

'Blenkinsop . . . yeah?'

'This is his house. And apparently he's one of the APs.'

She stopped and stared at him. 'Are you serious?'

He nodded.

'*Come on.*'

They flashed their warrant cards to the uniformed sergeant at the front door, then donned Tyvek coveralls from the sterile container in the porch and pulled on pairs of latex gloves and shoe-covers, before being guided towards an internal door connecting with the garage. Neither of them was quite sure what to expect, but then no officer ever was when he or she first approached a murder scene.

Even to sensibilities as battle-hardened as theirs, the sight of the impaled man was a sobering shock. He was still transfixed mid-way up the steel spike. What looked like several bucketfuls of blood had spilled across the cement floor beneath him, and were now slowly coagulating. The lower section of the spike was crusted crimson. Blenkinsop's waxen face, which they could only see upside down, was a rigid grimace of agony. Gemma glanced to the ceiling, where someone had gone to great trouble to saw out a large square section of boarding.

'Whoever set this up wasn't taking any chances,' she said.

Palliser couldn't at first reply. He'd turned a shade green as he surveyed the punctured body. It was always difficult, even with years of CID experience, to be cool about a corpse, which, a few hours earlier, you'd seen walking around and had engaged in conversation.

'Remind me what it was that bothered you about this fella?' Gemma said.

'Well . . .' Palliser cleared his throat, making an effort to get it together. 'He was way too nervous. Wouldn't even let us take a DNA sample.'

'He's hardly the sort to be involved in routine crime.'

'Nothing routine about this, ma'am.'

'Agreed. Let's have a look at the other one.'

They moved through the house, the uniformed sergeant still chaperoning them, and descended to the cellar. This was a more conventional crime scene: wrecked furniture, and a deceased party who had clearly been dispatched by gunshots. Gemma picked her way as close to the body as she dared. A wallet lay open beside it, and personal documents were strewn around. She crouched to get a closer look.

'Brian Hobbs,' she said, reading the name on the credit cards. 'This a genuine ID?'

'We don't know that yet, ma'am,' the sergeant responded. He'd remained on the stairs, not wanting to trespass on the scene.

Gemma nodded, before beckoning Palliser to the far side of the room, where they were out of the uniform's earshot.

'How'd you actually get onto this?' she asked quietly.

'Force radio. Was on my way home when it came over. Sixteen, Templeton Drive. Remembered it straight away. Blenkinsop.'

'There was no reference in Heck's paperwork to Blenkinsop?'

Palliser shook his head.

'What about this guy, Hobbs?'

'Not as I noticed.'

'Because I think I've seen *him* before. On a couple of crime scene glossies in one of Heck's folders.'

Palliser looked startled. 'Okay . . . okay, now I'm getting excited.'

'Well don't get too excited. Half this fella's head's been blown off. I can't be absolutely sure.'

'On the FR they thought this might be a robbery-homicide.'

'What . . . Blenkinsop killed one of the robbers then fell through a trapdoor they'd prepared for him earlier?' She looked scornful as she turned to the uniformed sergeant. 'Have we found a firearm anywhere?'

'Not yet, ma'am. We won't do a thorough search until the Lab get here.'

Palliser nodded towards the wallet. 'That's what probably gave the first impression.'

Gemma shook her head. 'There's still money in it. Whoever got that wallet out wanted to know who this guy was and where he was from.'

Palliser eyed her. 'Three guesses who that was.'

She crouched again to analyse the spilled documentation – and to check the address on the driving licence, which was fifty-eight, Rentoul Street, Coventry.

She thanked DS Gibbens on her way out.

'You done, ma'am?' he asked, surprised.

'Absolutely, Tony. Thanks very much.'

'That's it?'

'For the moment.'

'See you then.'

'See you,' she said, climbing into her BMW.

Before Palliser jumped into his Chevrolet, he heard Gibbens muttering to the uniforms on the tape about the privileges of special squads, and how 'those lucky buggers will be back in bed before one'.

'I wish,' Palliser said, as he sped away after his boss.

Chapter 43

Heck pinched the motor from outside a council flat in Finchley belonging to a well-known car thief. It was a Lexus LS, and the property of one Errol Buchanan, who, according to observations by Scotland Yard's Organised Crime Division, had been involved in car-ringing operations for the best part of a decade. The Lexus, which would initially have been stolen, was now – on paper at least – Buchanan's property. It would probably have been intended for sale abroad, but Buchanan, a reckless, self-indulgent bastard even by car thief standards, had presumably fallen in love with it and decided to keep it.

This was why Heck had no qualms about taking and driving it away. Not that he'd have hesitated to lift it from a law-abiding citizen if he'd had no other choice.

It was close to one o'clock in the morning and he was bulleting up the M1 motorway. That last telephone message went through his head again and again: he'd been told simply to head north and await further instructions, which he would receive en route. They'd threatened that if they saw any sign the police were following, both Dana and Lauren would suffer unimaginable consequences. There was no gloating this time, no taunting. It had been a quick, straightforward message, delivered in a businesslike monotone.

But to hear Dana's voice – in pain, in terror . . .

It had been bad enough that they'd got Lauren, but Lauren was an ex-soldier who'd lived with fear and violence as part of her profession, and, even if she hadn't, she'd willingly bought into this escapade. Dana on the other hand, was an estate agent and housewife, the mother of his beautiful young niece.

Lauren's words hadn't seemed prophetic at the time, that night in Bobby Ballamara's gaff, about Heck's sister suddenly not being there anymore. But they had remained in the back of his mind and, to some extent, had started him thinking that he needed to readdress his priorities. Only yesterday, he'd decided he was going to see Dana again when all this was over. Try to be a proper brother to her, try to be an uncle to Sarah, but now . . .

Heck had trouble keeping below a hundred m.p.h., but knew that he had to because otherwise he'd pick up a traffic patrol and that would defeat the entire object. They'd be watching his progress, the voice on the phone had said. If he tried to pull anything, the outcome would stagger even a hard-ass cop like him. Heck didn't know exactly what he was headed for here, but it was plain he had no option. He *had* to go and meet them.

The lights and motorway bridges flipped by like speeded-up cine film. At this time of night, the northbound carriageway was almost empty. He passed Luton, Milton Keynes, Northampton. Then Deke's phone rang.

Heck banged it to his ear. 'Yes?'

'Take the M6. Follow it north. Any sign you've got a police tail, on land or in the air, the ladies in your life are carrion.' The line went dead.

Heck hit the M6 north of Rugby, blazing towards

Birmingham. He'd warned Ian Blenkinsop that this thing wasn't going to end happily. There was now a sinking feeling in his gut that he was fast approaching that denouement.

He passed between Coventry and Nuneaton, where he came to a contra-flow, and swerved through it recklessly, barely slowing down. His many cuts and bruises, some of which on a normal day would send him to casualty, meant nothing. Heck had tunnel vision; all he saw was the empty motorway spooling out ahead.

The phone rang again.

'Go into the rest-lounge at Corley service station, and wait. We'll contact you there at exactly two o'clock.'

Heck did as instructed. At Corley, he shot up the access ramp so fast that he skidded across six or seven parking bays before he was able to bring the Lexus to a halt. The engine – which he'd only managed to activate by breaking the housing on the steering-column and inserting a key between the ignition heads – stalled and cut out.

Seconds passed as the vehicle cooled and Heck prepared himself for the ordeal ahead. He glanced across the car park.

Corley services was one of those typically impersonal motorway structures – all sheet glass and bare concrete. There were lights inside, but few people visible. The car park was almost deserted. He climbed out and waited warily. Behind him, there was the occasional *VOOOM* as some other nocturnal traveller rocketed past.

He looked at his watch. It was one-fifty.

Slowly, he walked across the tarmac, his footsteps clicking. As soon as he entered the station, he scanned for suspects. The shop was empty, aside from an overweight young man sitting at the till. Behind the fast-food counter, two girls in uniforms and paper hats had drawn down the trellis and were now tidying things away. There were very few customers: a dishevelled businessman who walked out past Heck, carrying a briefcase; two maintenance guys in steel-capped boots and fluorescent jackets, also on their way out; and in the rest-lounge itself no one at all except an elderly lady in a pinafore, moving up and down with a mop and bucket.

Heck bought himself a coffee, and sat in a window seat. He glanced at his watch. It was one-fifty-five. He sipped the tepid brew, all the time watching the lounge entrance. Bang on two o'clock, three figures came filing purposefully in, and Heck's hand clenched on his mug. But it was two girls and a man, all in their early twenties. They were laughing and chatting. The young man was carrying a guitar. They bought coffee and sat down in another area.

Heck relaxed a little, but continued to watch the entrance with hawkish intensity.

The minutes ticked by. At two-fifteen, they left. Heck crossed the room for a refill, and resumed his seat.

There was a massive crash outside the window, like an explosion of gunfire.

He jumped, whipped around – and saw that it was a lorry unloading crates of foodstuff. He drank his second coffee. It was nearly two-thirty when someone else came into the rest-lounge. Heck regarded him warily. It was a rugged, burly man, wearing a green sweater and green, canvas trousers. He got himself a coffee and sat nearby with his back turned. Heck's eyes locked onto him. Still the minutes ticked by. The man didn't move, even when he'd drained his cup. Heck was shifting into hyper-tense mode, his breathing short and shallow; there was a streak of chill sweat down his back.

The man got up again. He walked across the lounge area. And left. Heck peered out through the window, and saw him climb into a battered old Mazda, which he drove off towards the motorway.

Confusion was now replacing Heck's nervousness. They had definitely said Corley service station, hadn't they? They *had* said two o'clock? He glanced again at his watch. It was almost three. He looked back across the lounge. The only other person in there was the cleaning lady. Even she looked to be leaving. She thrust her mop into the bucket and headed towards the entrance – where she stopped and turned to face him.

And beckoned.

Heck rose unsteadily to his feet.

He followed her out through the lobby into the car park, where she left her cleaning utensils next to a wall, and set off walking towards the rear of the building. She was moving quickly, keeping a good five yards ahead of him, though this was made easier for her because he was following cautiously, constantly glancing over his shoulder. She crossed the slip-road leading to the garage, and took a paved path between two motel blocks. This was lit, but at this late hour the blocks themselves were in darkness. The warmth and light of the service station was falling away behind.

Heck slid his hand under his jacket, seizing the Colt Cobra's grip, but the woman strode on ahead without speaking. She was short and dumpy in stature; from the glimpse he'd had of her, she looked to be in her late sixties. The paved path terminated at a line of bushes, but now another path – this one unpaved – wound off through them. The woman followed it, so Heck had no option but to do the same.

Beyond the bushes there were fir trees. These closed in thickly from both sides, and were wet with dew. The path narrowed and steepened as it descended a slope. Again, Heck glanced over his shoulder – but no one was bringing up the rear. He looked back to the front, and saw that the woman was no longer in sight. Jarred, he lurched forward, hurrying to catch up with her – and emerged on a quiet canal bank. A stretch of black water rippled in front of him. Its

brick-built sides were thick with moss and other rank vegetation.

The woman was waiting there, facing him. She had lank,
thinning hair and a pudgy, wrinkled face, but she was wide-
eyed – almost certainly because she was frightened. When
she spoke, she had a strong Polish accent.

'The man say you go that way.' She pointed west along
the canal bank.

'What man?' Heck asked.

'I never see him before. You go.'

'He paid you to give me this message?'

'No question. I need money. You go! *Go!*' And without
waiting to see if he would comply, she hurried back up the
path towards the service station, vanishing from view.

Heck glanced again over his shoulder. Around him lay
only the blackness of night, the stillness and silence of the
dead hours.

Though every molecule in his body was screaming at him
to do otherwise, he began to edge along the canal bank in
the direction he'd been shown. There was no sound. The only
light came from the moon, just visible through the interlaced
branches above. He'd advanced maybe a hundred yards, before
a narrow-boat came into view, moored on the other side of
the water. Curtains were drawn on its windows, but muffled
lamplight could be seen inside. Then Heck spotted something
else – a stocky figure waiting on the tow-path, just across
from the vessel. A thrill went through him when he realised
that the figure appeared to be leaning on a stick.

'That's far enough,' came a voice. It was clipped, resonant;
Heck remembered what Ian Blenkinsop had said about Mad
Mike Silver once being a member of the officer corps. 'Empty
your pockets onto the path in front of you. Every single
thing you're carrying – weapons, mobile phones, notebooks,
recording devices. Everything.'

Heck hesitated, his fingers caressing the Colt Cobra under his jacket.

'It's up to you how you play this,' the figure added. 'But we hold all the cards, as I'm sure you're aware.'

'Are Lauren and Dana alright?'

'I know no such persons. Now do as you've been told.'

Realising he had no choice, Heck took the gun and both Deke's mobile phone and his own, the latter of which was still waterlogged from the river, and placed them on the path in front of him.

'That's a good chap,' the figure said, slowly approaching – definitely walking with a limp, definitely using a stick. 'But that had better be everything. I'll shortly be searching you. If you haven't done exactly as you were told, there'll be a severe outcome. Likewise, if I find you're wired . . . trust me, that will prove to have been a big mistake.'

The man was now about ten yards away. Heck saw the moonlight glinting on his short, silver-grey hair. It was uncanny the way this fellow fitted the image that Blenkinsop's brief, drink-sodden description had put into his mind.

That was when he sensed movement behind him.

Heck swung around. Two other men had stepped from the bushes a couple of yards to his rear. Both wore gloves, hoodie tops and knitted masks with holes cut for their eyes and mouths; one was purple, one orange. The taller one was armed with a machete, the shorter one with a small submachine gun – it looked like an Uzi. Heck heard a *click* as a firearm was cocked somewhere behind him. The sweat on his brow turned swiftly to ice.

It was the guy with the Uzi who came forward first. He raised the weapon and pointed it directly at Heck's face. As he did, his sleeve cuff slipped away from his glove, and Heck saw the tattoo of a black scorpion on the exposed wrist.

This was the kick-starter. Before a shot could be fired, Heck had thrown himself sideways and dived into the canal.

It was rank, brackish, filled with weeds and floating rubble, but he'd got used to such discomforts over the last few days and didn't surface again until he'd swum clear to the other side. There he pounded on the hull of the narrow-boat and shouted at the top of his voice for help. To his surprise, there was an immediate response. A door banged open and he heard the sound of feet coming out onto the upper deck. A figure gazed down over the gunwale, finally extending a hand towards him. Heck took it, and was hauled up. But then moonlight fell on the face of his rescuer – it was a raddled patchwork of scar tissue. There was no nose; there were no eyelids. The mouth, though crimped in an amused grin, was a monstrous parody of humanity.

'Klim!' Heck shouted, trying to drag himself free.

But Klim wouldn't release him; in his other hand he held a heavy implement, something like a monkey wrench. Heck tried to flinch away, but it was impossible to avoid the crashing blow that impacted on his cranium.

Chapter 44

Heck remained dazed even after he'd regained full consciousness. The top of his head throbbed, his vision was blurred and strands of blood-gluey hair dangled in front of his eyes.

'Detective Sergeant Heckenburg,' a vaguely familiar voice said. 'I must say, I'm impressed.'

Heck jerked upright, so quickly that it made him nauseous. He was briefly blinded by the well-lit room, which seemed to be long, narrow and sparsely furnished. The floor was bare wood; he thought there might be steel shutters over the windows. Gradually, he became aware that five people were standing in front of him. One was the grey-haired man with the stick who'd confronted him on the tow-path. The others were equally recognisable: the tall black guy with the pearl earring – the one he'd seen on the Victoria Line, though now he was wearing a hoodie top and dark overalls; the swarthy, bullish guy in desert combat fatigues, who they'd also encountered on the Victoria, also now in a hoodie and overalls; and Shane Klim – with his hideously scarred visage, dressed in a sweatshirt, jeans and trainers. The fifth person was positioned *behind* them, and she wasn't standing up. She was hanging by the wrists from a hook in the ceiling. She was unconscious and naked; her sleek brown body blotched from head to toe with livid bruises. It was Lauren.

When Heck finally focused on Lauren, he struggled to get up – only to find that he too was naked and fastened into place, though in his case he was seated and bound by his wrists and ankles to an iron chair that appeared to have been bolted to the floor.

'You're part of a police unit that covers the entire country,' the walking-stick man said. He smiled almost benignly: he wasn't as old as his grey hair made him appear from a distance; probably in his late thirties. He could only be Mad Mike Silver. As Blenkinsop had said, there was a steely air about him; he was handsome like an actor – lean featured but with a strong, square jaw, a bronze tan and penetrating blue eyes. His walking stick was of thick bamboo, with an ivory skull for its handle. He was smartly dressed in tan chinos and a crisp, white shirt buttoned to the collar beneath a navy-blue blazer. 'And I can see why, sergeant. You're here, there, everywhere.'

'So are you people,' Heck retorted. 'But personally I'm *not* impressed.'

'You've no need to be. We're nothing special, just a bunch of fellows making a living. It's all about supply and demand.'

'Where's my sister?' Heck said.

'She's not too far away,' Silver replied. 'Don't worry, she's safe . . . for the moment.'

'Why we talking to him and not doing him?' one of the men muttered – it was Klim; he spoke awkwardly as if his disfigured mouth was stuffed with soggy bread. 'He's fucking trouble. Soon as I saw his face, I knew we'd have problems.'

'Says *you*,' Heck snorted.

Silver raised his bamboo on high and swung it down, dealing a hard, stinging slash to Heck's shinbone. Heck just managed to restrain a bellow of agony.

'Mr Klim may not have been one of us originally, but he's more than proved his worth since,' Silver said. 'Even if he did make a few unwise comments while he was in prison . . .'

If it was possible for Klim's mangled features to blush, they did so now. Highly likely, Heck thought, he'd already been made to pay for those comments.

'Not to worry,' Silver added. 'That's now been taken care of. Either way, I won't hear him mocked.'

'No, but you'll see women and girls raped and killed!' Heck gritted his teeth on the lingering pain. 'You fucking animals!'

Silver made an airy gesture. 'Casualties of war . . . collateral damage, and . . . I don't know . . . there are lots of other euphemisms they've invented for those kinds of unfortunates.'

'I can see why they call you *Mad* Mike!'

If Silver was surprised that Heck had identified him, he didn't show it, but neither did he deny that this was his name.

'You might have made this crackpot scheme work in lawless banana republics,' Heck said. 'When you were using tough squaddies that you'd once led in battle. But just because you're back in Blighty you resort to hiring Johnny Handsome here . . .' he indicated the scowling Klim, 'who'd stand out even among the rank-and-file dickheads? Some pro you are!'

Silver regarded Klim's ravaged face almost fondly. 'We value expertise more highly than anything, but sometimes an enthusiastic amateur can be just as useful.'

Heck had pored over many case files detailing the sort of grisly enthusiasms that Shane Klim specialised in. 'You weren't just wounded in the leg, were you, Silver?' He shook his head. 'You've lost your fucking marbles.'

Silver pondered. 'I've had a high-stress career, I'll admit.'

'You're nothing but a cold-blooded murderer.'

'An interesting comment from a man whose own hands are not entirely clean. I'm assuming you killed Trooper Ezekial? There's no other reason why he'd simply drop from sight like this.'

Heck sat back as the ache in his leg eased. 'Hey . . . another of those unfortunate casualties of war.'

'And I'm sure a fair one. After all, Trooper Ezekial attempted to ruin your life by framing you for a serious crime. He got exactly what he deserved, yes?'

Heck didn't reply. Behind them, he saw Lauren's eyes flutter open. They were bloodshot, watery, but when they fixed on him he could see that she was cognisant of what was happening.

'Except that Trooper Hobbs here doesn't share that view.' Silver indicated the guy who'd worn the desert fatigues. Not only did Heck recognise him from the Underground train, but now – having heard the name 'Hobbs' – he recognised similarities in him to someone else. Okay, he looked older, tougher and more rugged than the 'Kid' currently lying dead in Belsize Park, and he was a lot more suntanned, but there was no denying that overly prominent forehead.

'We're a small outfit at heart,' Silver added. 'A tight-knit bunch. Trooper Ezekial wasn't really part of that – he was an outside contractor, who it suited us to use now and then. But he was also a friend. Trooper Hobbs and he were very close when they were back in Scorpion Company – and what kind of skipper would I be if I didn't respect comradeship? So . . .' Silver sighed as if it pained him, 'when all this is over, I'll have to let Trooper Hobbs have the final say.'

Trooper Hobbs moved his gloved hands to his belt and gripped the hilts of two large, hook-bladed knives.

Heck eyed the blades nervously, but still tried to tough it

out. 'He couldn't have been very handy with those when you got run out of town back in the Middle East. What was it, Silver . . . local cowboys turfing you off their patch? Local sheriff deciding he wasn't getting a big enough cut?'

Silver chuckled. 'What a simplistic world you police officers inhabit.'

'Well I'm damn sure you didn't come back here for the climate.'

'There are political tides out there that people like you can't even comprehend, Sergeant Heckenburg, but even you must have noticed that the Arab world is changing dramatically. And we don't do wars and revolutions anymore. So for the last few years we've been gradually catching up with former clients over here. Setting up a new base of operations.'

'One that isn't as dangerous, eh?' Heck scoffed.

'One that pays better too,' Trooper Hobbs blurted out in broad Brummie.

The black guy now spoke up as well. He sounded more educated than Hobbs – he had no noticeable accent, he was almost refined – but his was the gloating voice Heck had heard on the telephone. 'You wouldn't believe how much we earn these days,' he said, 'for taking almost no risk whatsoever. And the job satisfaction . . . well!'

Heck regarded them the way he would the lowest vermin. Despite his attempted boldness, there was only so much that even he could endure. 'What the hell's the matter with you, Silver? For Christ's sake, you and your lads once served Queen and country. You followed an honourable profession. Even when you were mercs – you were doing an honest job. How the fuck . . . *how the diddly fuck did you come to this?*'

Silver shrugged. 'Well . . . I'd like to give you a load of Rambo-type baloney about how tough it is for veterans coming home from foreign wars . . . having to live in the woods and all that because they can't integrate back into society. But I've never been much of a romantic. The facts are simple. When we all left our respective units, we were still very good at what we did. We were a collective, you might say . . . of uncommon skills and abilities. In the light of that, it was always going to be a crime if we were just to spend the rest of our days sitting around hotel lobbies sipping mineral water, or driving armoured limousines up and down the nightclub strip, dodging the paparazzi. I mean seriously . . . would you have let us go to waste like that? Even back here in civilised Europe, it would have been a crying shame.'

'Oh, I see,' Heck said slowly. 'So you're all about making a British contribution to the world?'

'That's a good way of putting it.'

'Except that Ian Blenkinsop told me you had foreigners working for you out in the Gulf. French, Russian, American . . . where are they now?'

'Sergeant Heckenburg, I'm so disappointed.' Silver glanced around at his men, who sniggered at their prisoner's innocence. 'For someone who's astute in so many ways, you're amazingly dense in others. Haven't you heard? We live in a global economy now. There are many more markets than the United Kingdom.'

At first Heck couldn't respond to that. A truly horrible picture was unfolding in his mind of numerous mirror-image operations to this one – abduct-to-order rackets – functioning efficiently in countries all over the world. In only a few years, Britain's own Nice Guys had clocked up nearly forty 'scores'. But what was the figure on a Europe-wide scale? What about if you included Eastern Europe? What about North America?

'I assume you're telling me all this because I won't be leaving here alive?' Heck said.

Silver's expression became regretful. 'Sadly, that's true.'

'In which case, you can presumably tell me what happened to the victims?'

'No I can't actually. At least, I can't give you their exact locations. Put it this way, the sea rarely gives up its dead.'

'The sea?'

Silver indicated the long, narrow room. 'We're on a boat, sergeant. Surely you've noticed that. And most of Britain's waterways connect with the sea at some point.'

Heck hung his head. He almost felt sick at how simple it was. Even when there was a major search for a missing person, he couldn't imagine many police forces thinking to check the canal traffic, not when the boat-owner in question was a bloke with a walking stick, who from a distance looked quite a bit older than he was.

'When you're out at sea, even if it's only a mile or so,' Silver added, 'it's astonishing how useful bin-liners, twine and a few lumps of cement can be.'

'You'll still get found out!' Heck snapped. 'At some point you'll be caught.'

'Maybe. But we obviously have to do everything we can to reduce that possibility. Which brings us rather neatly to you.' Silver produced the two phones, Deke's and Heck's own. 'Your mobile is clearly beyond repair, and we've been through Trooper Ezekial's data from the last few days and found no sign that you've put a message or text out. All of this is in your favour, but you could have made a call from a landline before you left London, and let someone know roughly where you were headed for.' He gave Heck a frank stare. 'So . . . did you or didn't you?'

'You know I haven't contacted anyone at Scotland Yard. If I had, your man inside would have informed you.'

'But that doesn't mean you didn't contact someone else, or someone in a different police department.'

So the insider was *definitely* a member of the NCG. Heck

made a mental note of this. Not that it made a lot of difference at present.

'You see, my problem, Sergeant Heckenburg,' Silver added,
'is that though I'm well aware you're a bit of a chancer, I
find it hard to believe you're so stupid that you'd come after
us entirely alone.'

That was the second time in the last few days he'd been
called a 'chancer', Heck realised.

'Now okay,' Silver said, 'granted . . . whoever your back-up
people are, they aren't very close, or they'd have intervened
when we ambushed you. But I still need to know who they
are, and where they are, and how much, exactly, they know
about our operation.'

'No one else knows anything about you. I knew you had
a man inside. So I couldn't risk spreading the word.'

'You expect us to believe that you don't trust anyone at
all?'

'No, I have friends. But I'm wanted for murder, I'm AWOL
. . . and if I'd gone to them I'd have put them in an impossible position.'

Silver pondered this. 'That has a ring of truth about it,
but unfortunately I can't just take your word for it.'

'You're going to have to.'

'No . . . I'm afraid I don't.' Silver signalled to Hobbs,
who stepped forward again. 'Trooper Hobbs here used to
have a specific role inside his unit. Can you guess what it
was?'

'Never,' Heck said, his body tensing.

'Scorpion Company made great use of him in Iraq and
Afghanistan. Everyone talks in the end, of course. But
Trooper Hobbs made it happen more quickly than most, as
you'll discover. Well . . . you won't discover *personally*.'
Silver turned to Lauren, whose eyes were closed again. 'But
your friend here will.'

Heck went rigid. 'Don't be crazy!'

'Sergeant, we're playing for very high stakes.'

'*Silver, for Christ's sake!*'

Silver merely shrugged. 'Like it or not, everyone's involved – your friend, your sister. Oh, I know what you're thinking. The longer you hold your tongue, the longer you'll hold off the inevitable. With that in mind, I imagine you'd be able to resist us for quite some time. But the inevitable is going to happen eventually, to all three of you. It's only a matter of how.' Silver smiled. 'If we commence it now – on those you care most about, and prolong it and prolong it and prolong it – then you holding out will become rather pointless, don't you think? Especially if I give you my solemn guarantee that the moment you tell us what we want to know, we'll end it very quickly.'

'The inevitable will happen to you too, you fucking maniac,' Heck replied. 'Everyone gets theirs in the end.'

Silver sighed. 'Have it your own way. Mr Klim, Trooper Kilmor, let's leave Trooper Hobbs to work.'

Hobbs drew the two hooked blades from his belt and began to strop them together the way a butcher does before carving a joint.

'Believe it or not, sergeant,' Silver said, as he and the other two moved to a door at the end of the room, 'there are some things even we can't stomach.'

Chapter 45

'You ever seen someone skinned alive?' Trooper Hobbs asked. 'Being slowly peeled, layer after glistening layer?'

'I thought you Scorpion Company faggots liked to work from the inside out?' Heck said, hoping he sounded cooler than he felt.

Hobbs examined Lauren's inert form, sliding both his gloved hand and the flat of one flensing blade across her bruised flesh. Again he was like a butcher, sizing up a piece of meat. 'We can work from the outside in just as well.'

'And what do you expect it to achieve?' Heck said.

'If it makes you tell us everything we need to know – who else is investigating us, how close they are, and all that . . . it'll have achieved plenty.'

'I've already told you there's no one else!'

Hobbs shrugged. 'If you stick to that story, we'll eventually reach a point where we believe you. But we have to put you to the test first. Just so we can be sure. Now, where shall we start?' He put a hand on Lauren's crotch. 'Loin?' He slid it round and gripped a buttock. 'Rump? No, I know where. My favourite – breast.'

He took Lauren's left breast in one hand and raised the knife as if to slice off the nipple.

'How's your little brother?' Heck asked him.

Something in his tone made Hobbs glance around.

'Yeah, that's right . . . I'm talking about Brian,' Heck said. 'He *had* to be related to one of you. That's the only way he could have got involved with an outfit like yours.'

Hobbs regarded Heck cautiously. 'Brian's busy tonight.'

'What happened . . . you bring him in when you came back home? He was clearly no soldier. Fought like a fucking girl.'

Slowly, Hobbs lowered the knife.

'When you say he's busy, I'm guessing you mean he's busy up Hampstead way,' Heck added. 'But haven't you wondered why he hasn't called in yet? I'll give you a clue, Trooper Hobbs . . . he's never going to call in again.'

'You're full of shit.'

'Your Brian's probably lying in a chalk circle now, with police flashbulbs going off all around him. He won't need a tent to cover him, because he's in a cellar. That's where he met his maker, Hobbsy. A dirty, grubby cellar. I bet there are beetles all over him.'

Hobbs slipped the knife back into his belt, took a mobile phone from his pocket and stabbed in a number. No one answered and it went to voice mail. He tried the number again – it was the same result. He tried again – the same. He was now breathing deeply, almost snorting, like an enraged bull.

'Never leave a boy to do a man's job,' Heck laughed.

'You lying shit!' Hobbs shrieked, drawing both blades and rounding furiously on him – which was all the distraction Lauren needed.

Her eyes snapped open and she swung her body up, clamping her muscular thighs around Hobbs's neck. His head was immediately forced to one side; his eyes bugged with disbelief.

Heck struggled with his bonds, but he was held securely. Hobbs buffeted wildly back and forth, but Lauren levered herself upright on top of his shoulders, releasing her hands from the ceiling hook, which enabled her to ball her fists together and slam them down onto his nose, pulping it in a blow. Meanwhile, the choke-hold she had on his neck was clearly killing him. He dropped the knives, and tried to grab her and throw her off. But Lauren was also fighting for her life, which, weakened though she was from the brutality she'd been subjected to, gave her extra strength. They crashed to the floor together. She still wouldn't release him. He was turning blue in the face, his lips slathered with froth.

Heck fought desperately with his bonds, but still couldn't free himself.

Lauren threw her body over. Hobbs twisted with her, but now he was gargling. His eyes were bulging, bloodshot orbs. When she threw herself over a second time, he couldn't match the manoeuvre. With a *crunch*, his neck broke.

There was a brief, breathless silence, and then Lauren grabbed one of the knives and began tiredly sawing through the ropes binding her wrists.

'Bloody glad you were fully conscious,' Heck said. 'Wasn't sure whether you could hear me or not. Nice leg-work.'

'Not going to berate me for taking out another worthless cockroach?'

He shook his head as she cut him loose from the chair. 'I slotted one myself only a few hours ago.'

'That stuff about Hampstead wasn't BS?'

'My scruples are now on the backburner. This is a fight to the death.'

He got to his feet, though initially it was difficult. He

388

was dizzy and there was no blood in his lower limbs. Lauren had problems too. They'd hanged her by her hands for God knew how long. Momentarily, she had to lean against Heck.

He looked towards the door that the rest of the Nice Guys had exited through. No doubt there was a stair beyond it, leading topside. He listened intently. What sounded like a muffled conversation could be heard. There was a creak of wood; but it was directly overhead rather than descending towards them.

'I don't think they've sussed us,' he said. 'But it won't be long. You seen Dana at all?'

Lauren pointed to a door at the opposite end of the cabin.

Heck opened it, and saw a small, luxurious bedroom. Dana was on the bed. She was wearing pyjama bottoms and a t-shirt, but she seemed to be out cold. He approached nervously. Her hair was disarrayed, but there were no visible signs of harm. Her pulse at least was strong. He smelled at her breath, which was tainted with something faintly chemical.

'Gamma hydroxbutyrate,' he said grimly. 'The date-rapist's drug of choice. I hope to God they haven't . . .' A belated thought occurred to him. He spun around to face Lauren.

'If they did I didn't notice,' she said, before he could ask. 'Not that we can rely on that, a set of dickless bastards like this lot. Heck, what the fuck are we going to do?'

'There must be another way off this boat.'

There was one other door in the bedroom, but it only connected to a dressing room filled with gaudy clothes. Heck cursed as he padded back down the main cabin. At the far end, he opened the exit door a crack and listened. The conversation was clearer, but still sounded as though it was taking place on the deck above. He risked a peek. A tight stairway led up, but alongside it there was a recess in which several coats and rain-slickers hung. He climbed into a pair of waterproof pants, threw a slicker over his shoulders and zipped it. He'd have grabbed one for Lauren, but she'd now stripped Hobbs's body and was pulling on his khaki vest and trousers.

'No exit this way,' Heck said. 'We'll have to go through one of these windows.'

There were six in total, three down either side of the cabin. As he'd already observed, there were steel shutters on each one, all fastened with padlocks.

'Don't suppose they've been daft enough to leave a key lying round?' he asked.

'No. But they've left us these.' Lauren picked up one of Hobbs's flensing knives. 'This is sharp enough to stick up a gnat's chuff.'

'Can you make it work?'

'I can try.'

They chose the window farthest from the exit, and on the starboard side of the cabin, which they guessed was the one against the canal bank. Lauren worked feverishly. She couldn't do anything about the padlock, but the shutter was part of a steel frame, which had been screwed into the wooden bulkhead. It was these screws that she went for. Initially nothing happened. She pumped sweat as she strained and twisted the knife. When the point of its blade snapped off, she had to try the other knife, but the first had loosened the screw sufficiently for it to finally give way. With the frame's grip on the bulkhead weakened, and pulled out a little to weaken it further, the second screw came more quickly and the final two were almost easy. Behind it was a curtain, and then a glass window with a movable panel. Lauren flipped the catch and slid the panel open. Beyond it lay the canal bank, the tow-path and a mass of darkened foliage.

Heck had now brought Dana in from the dressing room. He was carrying her, but she was stirring slightly.

'If we can get her walking,' Lauren whispered, 'it'll save us a lot of trouble.'

'Depends how long she's been out for. It can take hours to recover from a stupor like this.' He patted Dana's face a couple of times, but she stayed under the influence.

Lauren shook her head. 'I'll go out first. You pass her up to me.'

Once she'd got out onto the bank, she crouched and listened. Their captors were congregated down at the far end, talking quietly. There were no other night sounds.

'Okay,' Lauren breathed.

With much struggling, Heck passed Dana's comatose form through the aperture, at which point she moaned loudly.

They froze.

There was no response.

They continued at speed. Lauren threw Dana over her shoulder in a fireman's lift, but remained crouched. From this angle, it was difficult to see over the top of the boat to where their captors were. What position were they actually in? Were their backs turned? These questions remained unanswered. It was going to be another big gamble. Heck slid up onto the bank beside her.

'We've got to dash to the undergrowth,' she whispered into his ear. 'It's only a couple of yards, but we'll be fully exposed.'

He nodded, sweating hard. 'You want me to take Dana?'

'I've carried bigger, heavier fellas than your sister out of the battle-zone, Heck. Don't worry, I can handle it.'

They counted down from five to one, before rising to their feet and scurrying towards the bushes. At first it seemed as though they'd made it. But when they entered the wood, it was impossible for leaves not to rustle and branches not to thresh.

'Hey!' came a gruff shout from behind. It sounded like Klim. '*FUCK!*'

Chapter 46

Dana was coming round and no longer a dead-weight, but carrying her between them wasn't easy. When they broke out of the trees, they were at the foot of a long, sloping pasture, with the outline of a house on the ridge at the top. Shouting loudly, they stumbled uphill towards it. Heck and Lauren were both shoeless, the stones and twigs cutting and bruising their naked feet, but fear dulled the pain. They were halfway up when a shot rang out from behind. They ducked as what felt like a high-speed wasp whined past Heck's ear.

'Keep going,' he gasped. 'Just keep going.'

'They can't afford to let us live,' Lauren said.

'Don't worry. We're not the ones who are going to die here today.'

But even before they reached the house on the ridge, they saw skeletal spars where its roof should be, windows that were now empty sockets.

'It's derelict!' Lauren wailed.

'Just get inside. We'll defend it somehow.'

It had once been a farmhouse, but now was a gutted shell. They managed to force open its front door, though the hall passage beyond was partly blocked by rubble. Not only had most of its roof collapsed, but a lot of the upper floor had come down as well. Lauren laid Dana on a mound of bricks, while Heck forced the door closed behind them and tried to wedge it with a fallen beam.

'There'll be a back door too,' Lauren said.

'Go and sort it!'

She hurried off, while he cast around for a weapon, though all he could initially find were lumps of useless rubbish.

'Heck, there are windows in here!' Lauren called.

Heck veered right into what had formerly been the living room. Again it was knee-deep in wreckage: smashed furniture, bottles, cans and a dirty mattress. Grass and thistles grew deep in the detritus. However, the windows were not as big a problem as he'd feared. The building being very old, they were small and set in deep embrasures, and most of them were barred.

'These are easily defensible,' he shouted back.

There was a grating of stone and a *bang* as Lauren forced the back door shut.

Then he heard voices outside. They were low and mumbling, but he could discern the guttural tone of Shane Klim and the smoother, more modulated voice of the black guy, Trooper Kilmor as Silver had referred to him.

'Any knives in there?' Heck asked, as Lauren re-emerged from the kitchen.

'Nothing. Not even any units. It's been stripped.'

'Okay, let's keep it down for a sec, and see what they do.'

'We know what they're going to do – they're going to try and get in!'

Stressed and weary, Lauren's voice rose shrilly, and though he tried to shush her, it was too late. A Browning pistol was thrust in through one of the smaller windows, and fired indiscriminately around the living room. The reports were deafening, bullets careening from wall to wall. They dived and covered their heads, but out in the hall Dana began to moan with fear and confusion.

Heck scrambled to his feet, grabbed a plank, flattened himself against the wall and aimed a blow down at the hand. It was withdrawn at the last second, the plank meeting empty air.

'Shit!' he hissed.

There was a *crunch-crunch-crunch* as feet padded around the exterior of the building.

'What are the kitchen windows like?' Heck asked.

'Like these, small. But someone can get in if we don't guard them.'

'So what are you waiting for?'

She nodded and darted into the kitchen. He hurried back to the hall, where Dana was conscious but very groggy.

'Mark . . . Mark, what's happening . . .?'

'We're in a fix, Dana. But I promise I'm going to get you out of it.'

His eyes were attuning to the starlight, and he now saw a staircase. It led up to nowhere, its topmost section having fallen away with the upper floor. But beneath it there was a triangular door. He opened it on a narrow closet-space. Taking Dana's hand, he lugged her unceremoniously to her feet.

'Mark . . . what're you doing?'

'Get in here, quick.'

'What? No, I won't . . .'

'Dana!' he hissed into her ear. 'There's going to be a fight, and if you don't find a hiding place you'll be caught in the middle of it. And I can't have that on my mind as well as everything else. Now for once do as you're told.'

She might have been dazed, but she knew her brother well enough to know when he was being deadly serious. She nodded dumbly and, stooping down, allowed herself to be pushed into the under-stair cupboard. Heck closed the door quietly.

There was a sudden massive impact on the other side of the building.

'Heck!' he heard Lauren shout. 'Heck!'

He scrambled back through the living room, and turned into the kitchen. Lauren had blocked the back door with lengths of wood, but a full-scale attack was now being launched on it. Heavy blows landed one after another, possibly with the flat of a foot, but no obvious progress was being made.

'Surely he realises he can't *kick* it down?' Lauren whispered.

'He's not trying to kick it down,' Heck said slowly. 'This is a diversion!'

He scarpered back into the living room, just in time to see Trooper Kilmor's head, shoulders and upper body protruding through one of the windows. Heck charged forward, ripping up one of the thistles growing through the layer of rubble. Kilmor shouted a threat, but Heck was already lashing him across his unprotected face. Kilmor shrieked and tried to drag himself backward. Heck lashed him six or seven times before he managed it, but then had to duck as the muzzle of the Uzi appeared in the aperture and blazed off maybe thirty rounds.

'*Shit, my eyes!*' Kilmor screeched. '*The bastard's blinded me!*'

Now another voice was heard. It was Silver. 'He hasn't blinded you, you fucking pretend soldier! Get inside and finish them off like I told you!'

More shots sounded from the kitchen.

'Lauren?' Heck shouted.

'It's okay,' she called back.

He rushed through. They were pistol shots from the Browning. Three more followed, and with each one a moonlit hole was punched in the back door.

396

'He still can't get in!' Lauren laughed.

Another angry kick struck the planks, and then there was silence.

It was ear-punishing.

They strained to listen. Still they heard nothing, but Heck was certain this was only the prelude to a renewed attack somewhere else on the perimeter. He beckoned to Lauren, and they moved.

Aside from the living room, there was a second chamber adjoining the kitchen. This was long and narrow, and ran along the back of the house; it had probably been a dining room at some time. Again it was open to the night, but there were fragments of furnishing left in it: a few broken plant pots, a metal-framed table with a Formica top, the Formica itself having peeled away, leaving mildewed planks underneath. The door at the end of this room connected with the front of the house again. They progressed towards it, and halted there, glancing into the hall. Still there was no sound from outside.

'Think they've given up and run for it?' Lauren wondered.

Heck shook his head.

There was a sudden scraping sound, a scrabbling of loose stonework. They glanced upward – to see a squat, misshapen form balanced on the jagged apex of the outer wall.

'Fuckers are trying to *climb* in!' Lauren shouted.

They dived in different directions as Klim pointed his Browning down and fired, Lauren throwing herself back into the dining room, Heck running clear across the hall, past the cupboard in which his sister was still concealed, and back into the living room. Klim pegged another three shots at them. There were more screaming ricochets, but none of the slugs struck home, which perhaps wasn't surprising given that, from his perspective, Klim was shooting down into a darkened interior.

He tried to improve his position, clambering across the open roof-space by its exposed joists, until he reached the top of the connecting wall between the hall and the dining room, which he perched on like some great, overweight ape. Heck stuck his head through the living room door, only for two more shots to be fired at him. He ducked back, but not before he was able to see that Klim was now directly above the staircase. If he hung by his hands, it was only a couple of feet to the topmost tread.

Lauren, watching from the dining room, had also seen this.

'Heck, the bastard's almost made it!' she shouted.

Heck was helpless to do anything, other than grab a half-brick and hurl it up. It missed by some distance. Klim fired at him, but then swung down from his perch, and, as they'd feared, alighted comfortably on the top of the stair. He again took aim at the living room door, now with both hands, and pumped off three more shots. Each one blew out a chunk of the door-jamb behind which Heck was flattened.

'I'm inside!' Klim bellowed, alerting his confederates beyond the walls.

His eyes too were adjusting to the gloom. He turned towards the front door, and saw the heavy prop that had been used to shore it up. He squeezed off two shots at it. One of them struck, but the prop held firm. Klim ejected his spent clip and slid another into place – only for Lauren to seize the moment and come yelling up the stair towards him. He swung around to face her, but she'd picked up the Formica table and was using it like a shield. All he could see was the flat surface rushing up at him. He fired at it twice before it slammed into him, knocking him backward against the rotted banister, which split loudly. The spindles gave way, and Klim fell headfirst into the rubble below.

It stunned him, knocking the gun from his grasp. But he

knew he had to regain his feet quickly. He did this just in time to see Heck ballooning through the dimness, another half-brick in hand. Klim blocked the blow by taking it full on his forearm, which made him squawk in pain. Heck clamped a hand on his throat and forced him backward. Klim grabbed Heck's throat in retaliation. They wrestled together, but now Lauren came swinging down over what remained of the banister, hitting Klim in the back with both feet. It winded him, and his legs buckled. It was all the opportunity Heck needed. He swept down hard with the half-brick, catching Klim in the mouth. The second blow was even more vicious; it struck Klim's left temple, crushing it inward like sodden cardboard.

A moment passed, and then the criminal fell sideways, his knees bending at one-eighty degrees beneath him. By his glazed eyes, he was dead before he hit the ground.

Heck and Lauren stood panting. Then Heck spotted a dark stain seeping down the front of her vest. 'You're hurt!'

She nodded and felt at the side of her neck. When she brought her palm away, it was bloody. She tried to smile, but it was weak, pained. 'Just a flesh wound.'

'Let me look.'

He stepped over Klim's body, only for another noise to distract them. They spun around. It was just beyond the front door – a *click* followed by a metallic *snap*. Unmistakably the cocking of a firearm.

The Uzi.

The fusillade that followed was furious, and blew the door clean from its hinges. Heck, who was directly in the firing-line, was hit twice – once in the shoulder, once in the left forearm – and was flung down on top of Klim. Lauren wasn't hit, but stumbled backward, suddenly lacking the energy or guile to run. Her strength draining out of her with her blood, she slumped down onto her backside.

The tall shape of Kilmor shouldered its way in through the smoke and splinters, Uzi levelled. Trickles of blood gleamed on both his cheeks. But his pearl-white teeth shone in a demented grin.

'Time's up, folks,' he said simply.

Heck rolled slightly, but couldn't move. Pain was spreading through his body like corrosive acid; he was entirely paralysed down one side. With deliberate slowness, the remaining Nice Guy raised the Uzi in both hands and took careful aim at him.

Only for a *boom*-like detonation to cut him virtually in half.

Kilmor's body jack-knifed forward from the doorway, his offal spattering the whole room. Before he could hit the ground, a second thunderous report tore into him, slamming him against the closet door, which he slid slowly down, leaving a thick, crimson smear on its rotted woodwork.

The silence that followed hung heavy on air tainted with the mingled stenches of acrid smoke and burst-out bowels, and lasted for several torturous seconds.

When another figure finally stepped in through the doorway, he was the last person Lauren had expected. It was dark of course, and at first he only appeared as a silhouette, but then he moved into the moonlight, and there was no mistaking the smart, pinstriped suit and clipped white moustache of Bobby Ballamara. The sawn-off shotgun in his leather-gloved hands smoked from both barrels.

'Better late than never,' Heck said weakly.

'You're alive, aren't you?' Ballamara replied.

Another figure ambled in. It was Lennie Asquith. He too was armed, in his case with a sawn-off pump. He chuckled. 'Had a rough night, detective?'

'What the hell is going on here?' Lauren demanded.

'Sorry . . . didn't get a chance to t-tell you,' Heck stammered.

Seeing how badly hurt he was, she crawled over to him. 'You okay?'

'No worse than you.'

Ballamara kicked at one of the corpses. 'So this is them?'

'How did *you* get here?' Lauren asked him.

'With some luck,' he replied. 'We almost lost Heck at the service station. Had to drive past, and come back on the southbound carriageway to make it look like we weren't following him. Took a while to trace him down here. If we hadn't been on the car park when the shooting started . . .'

'But how did you . . .?'

'I called them,' Heck said. 'From the motorway.'

'But they checked your phone records, I saw them.'

'I used another phone.' Heck winced as his pain intensified. 'Took it off the little bastard I potted down in Hampstead . . .'

'We've got to get him to hospital,' Lauren said urgently.

'And you, by the looks of it,' Asquith sniggered.

'Get someone,' Ballamara told him.

Asquith nodded and moved away, slipping his own phone from his pocket.

'There were only two of them?' Ballamara said.

'There's one back on the canal boat, too,' Heck grunted. 'He's dead as well.'

'Hey!' Lauren suddenly shouted, stumbling to her feet. 'What about Silver?'

Ballamara looked mystified. 'Silver?'

'Their gaffer!'

'Lauren, wait!' Heck said.

But Lauren had already grabbed up the Uzi, pushed past Asquith and staggered out through the front door.

'Lauren, you're in no fit state . . .'

401

'He's not getting away!' came Lauren's fading voice.

'Help me,' Heck gasped.

Reluctantly, gingerly – as there was barely a part of Heck that wasn't sopping with blood – Ballamara offered him a hand, and pulled him to his feet.

'You're telling me there's another one left?' the gangster said.

Heck didn't answer. Nauseated with pain and shock, he had to grit his teeth and was only able to get out through the farmhouse door and along the side of the building by leaning on the wall. When he reached its northwest corner, he peered down the moonlit slope, and saw Lauren hobbling after a stocky shape waddling along by the aid of a stick towards a silver-grey vehicle parked behind a low stone wall.

'Lauren,' he breathed, watching intently.

There was a rattle of gunfire and a strobe-like flash as she fired into the air. 'Stop where you are!' she called. 'Stop or you're dead!'

Heck held his breath as he watched the figure in front of her come to a stumbling halt a few yards short of the wall. Lauren fired into the air again. The figure slowly turned. Even from this distance, Heck fancied he could see that its arms were raised.

Theoretically, there'd be no problem. Lauren was also an ex-combat soldier. She had a gun in her hand, and even if she hadn't, even with that flesh-wound, she ought to be more than a match for this crippled opponent. But there was something about Mad Mike Silver . . . they barely knew him, yet Heck felt instinctively that he was evil to his bones, and clever with it.

'Lauren!' Heck tried to stagger after her, but even cautious progress sent him dizzy.

The two distant figures were now very close to each other. Heck heard Lauren shouting further instructions

– instructions with which Silver apparently wasn't complying. Lauren shouted again; a different tone. Heck's hair prickled as he saw the two shapes suddenly slam together in a fearsome tussle. There was a *smack* of fist on bone, only to be followed by what sounded like a *ripping* of flesh and a piping, half-choked squeal. Desperation gave Heck extra strength. He was halfway down the slope, picking up speed. But one of the two shapes had now slumped to the ground.

'Lauren!' he sobbed.

The other figure climbed over the wall, rounded the vehicle to its driver's door and slid inside. The engine rumbled to life. The headlights came on, spearing along the darkened road. As Heck approached, it rumbled away, dust swirling behind it.

Lauren was seated on the grass, her back against the wall. He dropped to one knee beside her. She smiled at him feebly. One bloodstained hand was clasped to her chest.

'Missed . . . missed the fucker,' she mumbled.

'Don't talk,' he said, moving her hand aside.

Beneath it, a gleaming, fist-sized bauble was visible against the fabric of her bloodied vest, apparently fixed in place. With a thrill of horror, Heck recognised it as the skull head of Mike Silver's walking stick. By the looks of it, it was actually a sword-stick, about a foot in length. The bastard had drawn it and run her clean through with it.

'I thought you said we weren't the ones who are going to die,' she whispered.

'Don't talk, just try and relax.' Heck turned and screamed: '*Ballamara!*'

'Relax? . . . that's a good one. I can't move anyway.'

'Lauren . . .'

'We got most of them, at least? Those bastards who hurt Genene . . .'

403

Heck nodded, helpless. The light in her eyes was fading even as he watched.

'You're going to get that last one, Heck?'

'I'll make it my life's work, I promise.'

Her mouth curved into a smile. 'You're a top bloke, Heck. Just get yourself a girl too. It's a sorry waste, you flying solo . . .'

'Lauren, just . . .'

'Gotta go, I think.'

He couldn't do anything except clutch her hand. Her eyes closed, but then flickered open again. She looked troubled. 'Heck . . . we did right?'

'Yeah.'

'That's just . . . for my mum. I want . . . her to know that.'

'I'll make sure she does.'

Lauren nodded and smiled. When her eyes flickered shut this time, they stayed shut.

Heck held her hand for another couple of minutes, by which time he could hear Ballamara and Asquith advancing down the meadow, mumbling together. Heck was too numbed to pay attention to this; too numbed by pain, by fatigue and by catastrophic blood-loss. He wanted to cry, but couldn't because there was barely any moisture left in his body. When Ballamara finally arrived, Heck too lay silent in the grass.

Chapter 47

The street was quite ordinary in character, part of a typical unassuming suburban neighbourhood. There were nice, quiet families living here. The fathers all had jobs. The children went to school on time, and when playing out in the evening were polite to adults and would keep the noise down if there were babies in bed. Newspapers were delivered. Milk floats made early morning rounds.

No one batted an eyelid about the people who lived on this street.

It was perhaps unusual to see nocturnal activity here. For someone to be placing bags and suitcases in the rear of a car at four o'clock in the morning was out of the ordinary, but then it was the middle of August, and people flew to Spain, Greece and the Canaries at all kinds of ungodly hours at this time of year. Even so, Mike Silver made as little noise as possible as he hobbled in and out of one particular house, ferrying various small items of luggage down the garden path and placing them in the boot of his Citroën C2. It had all been packed and ready, and waiting on the upstairs landing. Not because he'd anticipated having need of it this evening, but because it was *always* packed and ready.

Once it was all stowed in the boot, he made a last trip into the house, not so much to check that everything was locked up or unplugged, as a regular holidaymaker would do, but to ensure that no items of paperwork had been left behind. In truth, there was minimum chance of this. Silver kept only small items of paperwork, and none of it in his own name. But of course, he hadn't been the only occupant of fifty-eight, Rentoul Street, and despite the discipline he'd routinely imposed on his underlings, not everyone was always as careful about cleaning their tracks as he was – though on this occasion, thankfully, they had been.

Satisfied, he pulled a clean anorak over his roll-neck sweater, and turned the lights off one by one. Soon only the hall light remained. The switch for that was next to the front door. He intended to flick it off as he stepped into the porch. But just as he was about to do this, he noticed someone approaching along the garden path. It was a youngish, blonde woman in a light coat, slacks and high-heeled boots. 'Mr Hobbs?' the woman enquired.

'Hello?' Silver replied, standing in the doorway.

'I wonder if you can help us?'

'I'll try,' Silver said, noticing that a white BMW and a battered old Chevrolet parked behind his Citroën, and that a thin, older man with a scraggy grey beard was circling around it.

'I'm Detective Superintendent Piper,' the young woman said, showing a police warrant card. 'This is Detective Inspector Palliser.'

Silver smiled. 'I see.'

'Sorry if we've caught you going on holiday.'

'I've got a couple of minutes. What can I do for you?'

'How long have you lived at this address?'

'Oh . . . all my life.'

Gemma pondered this, wondering why he didn't seem to

406

have a Coventry accent, and then spotting a reddish mark on his cheek. 'Does anyone else live here with you?'

He smiled and shook his head. 'No, I'm resolutely single.'

Gemma glanced past him into the lighted hall, and was surprised when the man shifted sideways and drew the front door half closed, as if to prevent her seeing anything.

'No one else has access?' Gemma asked, distracted by the sound of Palliser's mobile phone ringing and being immediately answered.

The man shrugged. She noticed that the hand with which he clutched the door handle had knotted until its knuckles were white. 'Erm . . . friends call round from time to time.'

'Friends?' Gemma said.

'Ma'am!' Palliser shouted, hurrying up the path, his face graven in stone. She turned to face him. 'Heck's been shot!'

Gemma swung back round to the man, but the front door was already closing. She threw herself forward, smashing it open with her shoulder before the lock could engage. The man staggered up the hall, limping badly, but Gemma followed and brought him down with a tackle that would have made a rugby three-quarter proud.

'You bitch!' he bellowed. 'You can't do this! You've got nothing on me . . .'

'We've got that to start with,' Gemma retorted, indicating a white shirt and a blazer hanging at the foot of the stairs. Both were liberally stained with blood.

Palliser barged into the house behind her. 'Apparently he's alive . . . just.'

Gemma nodded, before twisting the man's hands behind his back and saying: 'Now Mr Hobbs, or whoever you really are, I'm arresting you on suspicion of attempting to murder a police officer. You don't have to say anything, but it may harm your defence if you don't mention when questioned

407

Chapter 48

Detective Superintendent Piper and Detective Inspector Palliser were in morose mood as they watched the television in Palliser's office. On the screen, a Devon & Cornwall Police launch was backing into a rain-swept dock in Plymouth harbour. Visible on board, three prone shapes lay side by side on the deck, covered by tarpaulins. Underwater Recovery officers, still in their wetsuits and oxygen tanks, stood alongside them.

'So how many does that make?' Gemma asked.

Palliser checked his notes. 'Six bodies recovered from Plymouth Sound. Three from the mouth of the Wash. Searches are also commencing off Holy Island in the northeast, off Blackpool and Anglesey.'

'All areas where these maniacs chartered offshore craft?'

Palliser nodded solemnly.

Beyond the glazed partition, the entire rest of the squad, who'd all been called back from their various assignments, scrambled madly between telephones and computer terminals. There was a hubbub of noise; paperwork was being flung everywhere.

'Any IDs yet?' Gemma asked.

'None yet, but I don't think we'll need to look any further than *that*.'

He nodded out into the main office, at the far end of which a large placard had been set up. The array of mugshots on it, and the accompanying sheaves of notes, had all been removed from the makeshift incident room in Heck's flat.

'What about the suspects?'

He consulted his notes again. 'Sonny Kilmor and Tommy Hobbs. Both formerly of the British Army. Exemplary records, bizarrely. Both saw a lot of action, and were decorated many times for bravery. Much involvement with special ops. Believed to have gone freelance about the same time as each other – 2007-ish. Tommy Hobbs actually owned fifty-eight, Rentoul Street. Seems like the rest of the gang used it as a base or a safehouse whenever they were up in the Midlands . . .'

'The rest of the gang being who exactly?'

'Tommy's younger brother, Brian, who was already a registered sex offender when he was a juvenile. Spent his adulthood in and out of institutions. Probably where he hooked up with Shane Klim. Birds of a feather, and all that. Heck's suspicions were right about those two. Looks like they were only brought into the firm when it relocated to the UK. Klim broke out of Rotherwood to hook up with them permanently.'

'If you can't get quality at least get loyalty, eh?' a voice said from the doorway.

They were astonished to see Heck standing there. He wore only trousers and slippers, and was bare-chested under his jacket, which was draped over his shoulders. His entire right arm was encased in plaster and fixed at a right angle, with a sling to hold it in position and a steel bar bracing it across the joint. He was pasty-white in colour, but black and blue with bruising. Much of his hair had been shaved off to accommodate the tram-lines of stitching in his scalp.

'What the hell are you doing here?' Gemma said.

He hobbled in. 'I discharged myself early.'

'That's ridiculous!'

Palliser dragged a seat forward and Heck lowered himself into it.

'Lauren Wraxford, who saved my arse countless times last week, is dead,' he said. 'The very least I owe her is not to waste time lying on my back while her murderer refuses to cooperate.'

'You think I'm going to let *you* speak to him?' Gemma said.

'You could do worse. I hear he's defying all analysis?'

Palliser sighed. 'We still haven't got a clue who he actually is. Not only is he saying nothing . . . we've gone back through military records for the last twenty years, and there's no trace of any British serviceman, commissioned officer or otherwise, name of Michael Silver. CrimInt's got nothing either, nor SOCA, nor SIS. Likewise, there are no comparisons in prints or DNA. We've circulated his mugshot throughout agencies abroad, but no hits so far.'

'We should check the security consultants Goldstein & Hoff use when they send their execs overseas,' Heck said.

'Already have done,' Palliser replied. 'And it's no dice. They're all clean. Seems like Ian Blenkinsop made extra arrangements once he got to the Gulf.'

'What about paperwork?'

'We've found no personal documentation.'

'Come on, Des . . . the bastard had access to different vehicles, different properties!'

'All in the names of his men. Same goes for the boat hire.'

'At least tell me Interpol and Europol are looking into the foreign angle.'

'As much as they can, but there isn't much to go on.'

411

'How much do they need? Blenkinsop mentioned American colleagues, French, Russian . . .'

'But he made no statement to that effect, and now he's dead.'

'Shit!' Heck swore. 'Silver *knows*! He didn't just hint at it, he fucking boasted – said there were other Nice Guys operating overseas. Damn it, we should *make* him talk!'

'And then you'd be just like him,' Gemma said primly. 'A sadistic criminal, a torturer, a psychopath. Look Heck, the main thing is he's going down. If absolutely everything else fails, at least he's bang to rights for the murder of Lauren Wraxford – we got her blood from under his fingernails and from his clothes. His dabs are all over the murder weapon.'

'On the subject of Lauren, has anyone been to visit her mother?' Heck asked.

Gemma nodded. 'I did.'

'Thanks,' he said, subdued. 'I appreciate that.'

'So did she, I think. She sent you this letter.' Gemma handed him a sealed envelope. 'She wanted to express her gratitude personally.'

'Her *gratitude*?'

'For finding out what happened to Genene. And for providing Lauren with a friend when she needed one.'

Heck took the envelope almost gingerly. He didn't think he could face opening it now. 'Never been thanked before for getting someone killed.'

'You didn't strike the blow, Heck,' Palliser said.

'Why do I feel like this then . . . survivor guilt?'

Palliser was about to respond when a detective constable beckoned him through the glass partition. He excused himself and slipped out, leaving the other two alone.

'I'm still waiting for my apology, by the way,' Gemma said, folding her arms. 'Just in case you were wondering.'

'I know,' Heck replied. 'And I'm sorry.'

'Heck . . . I don't actually mind that you broke almost every law you joined the police to uphold while pursuing these people. But what I do mind – what I absolutely revile – is that you lied to me.'

'I didn't lie to you.'

'You promised to keep me in the loop, and you cut me out at the first opportunity.'

'I only left you out when I learned they had someone on the inside.'

'You could at least have told me *that* much.'

'Would you have believed me?'

'You want the truth, I'm not sure I believe you now.'

'Really?' He laughed. 'You mean we coppers are too good to become clients of the Nice Guys? How else did they get to McCulkin, our *confidential* informant?'

'Look, if this guy Eric Ezekial had been shadowing your investigation, he might have seen you setting up meetings with McCulkin about other things.'

'All respect, ma'am, he still must have been getting inside info. Once the Nice Guys learned I was looking hard at Klim – courtesy of their insider – they sent Deke to sit on O'Hoorigan. Obviously they had O'Hoorigan fingered as a weak link. Klim had told him all about this outfit while they were in Rotherwood together, and they couldn't trust him not to tell us if he ever got lifted for something. Deke was shadowing O'Hoorigan rather than me, but when I turned up in Salford he had to act quickly. O'Hoorigan had to go and so did I.'

'Well, as both Deke and O'Hoorigan are dead, we can hardly prove that.'

'And what about Dana, how did they find out about her unless some bent bastard in our department told them?'

'Heck, are you seriously saying that one of our lot can afford to lay out seventy-five grand every time he wants a sex-service?'

In a low, wary voice, he replied: 'Someone at the very top could.'

At first she was baffled as to who he could mean. And then it clicked. 'Oh no . . . no, no, no, Heck. No, we're not even going *there*.'

'Someone who did everything in his power to close this enquiry down.'

'Don't you say it!'

'Someone who was once in the military himself. Perhaps that's how he got to know them in the first place?'

'Heck, I'm warning you . . .'

'They used his exact terminology when referring to me!'

'I'm not listening to this . . .'

But Heck was now in full flow. 'Ma'am, you told me that Commander Laycock found out I was still investigating when that detective super from Manchester contacted him the morning after those GMP officers got hurt at the Salford hospital . . . but that it was a full day before Laycock came to see you about it. Why a full day? So he could pass on everything new to the Nice Guys first? So he could tell them who Lauren was – I don't see how else Deke could have known she was Genene Wraxford's sister. How about so that Deke could get to us before you did? . . . that was the same day we got lured out to Blacksand Tower, remember.'

Gemma regarded him incredulously, as if for a moment his crazy assertions were making a kind of sense to her. Then Palliser came back in, and the spell was broken. 'Forget it!' She waved the whole notion away. 'I'm not listening to any of *that*.'

Heck shrugged. 'You don't have to listen to me. Whoever their insider was, his details will be in that filing cabinet in Eric Ezekial's attic.'

Gemma glanced uncomfortably at Palliser.

Heck noticed this. 'What?'

'You haven't heard about that then?' Palliser said.

'Obviously not.'

'Well . . .' Palliser cleared his throat. 'Owing to the . . . shall we say *confused* issue of what exactly happened to Mr Ezekial . . .'

'I fully explained that,' Heck said.

'Yes well, it wasn't as easy explaining it to a magistrate. However, we finally managed it, and the search-warrant for Ezekial's premises was issued this morning.'

'And?'

'The filing cabinet in the attic is empty.'

Heck rose slowly to his feet. 'You are joking?'

'Sit down, Heck,' Gemma said, 'before you fall down.'

'What do you mean it's empty?'

'All these files you described, with the names and coded reference numbers. They've gone.'

Heck slumped back into his chair. 'That *proves* there's some bastard on the inside.'

'Not necessarily,' Gemma argued. 'If there are any more of these Nice Guys knocking around . . .'

'Why would they take the risk of going there?' Heck said. 'They're going to prison for life, whatever happens. The only people those files would have implicated are the dozens and dozens of men who used their services. If we wanted to know who their grass was inside this department, his details would've been right there. So naturally he's got there ahead of us, and pinched them.'

Palliser's doleful expression suggested that he didn't disagree.

Gemma pondered. 'Wasn't there a security camera inside the house?'

'Yes,' Palliser said, 'but Ezekial's hard drive has also been removed. If the camera was still recording at the time of the burglary, it was uploading onto nothing.'

415

'So let's get this straight,' Heck put in. 'Just so we're absolutely clear on the matter. You're telling me that the details of maybe a hundred men guilty of rape and murder, currently living in Britain – have disappeared? Right from under our noses?'

Palliser made a helpless gesture.

Heck banged his one good hand down on the desk, though it wasn't quite that good, and he grimaced in pain.

'Chill out, Heck,' Gemma said. 'This is still a major result.'

'You know something, you're right.' Heck got to his feet and lurched towards the door. 'I *should* have kept you fully informed . . . all the way, about every single thing. Then you could have pulled me off the job the first time you got nervous, and we'd have got nowhere near the Nice Guys. So at least now we wouldn't know what we'd lost.'

'Heck, wait a minute!' she said. 'I want to talk to you.'

'Correct me if I'm wrong, ma'am, but I'm on sick leave until next year.'

'Of course you are.'

'You've seen my doctor's note? I'm not skiving, I'm not malingering – I am completely unfit for duty.'

'So?'

'So, if you want to talk to me, book your appointment for next January.'

'Heck, don't you dare . . .'

But he'd already left the department and was now out in the corridor, which was where he met Commander Laycock. The commander, looking cool and preened as ever, was clearly surprised to see him.

'Afternoon, Sir,' Heck said.

Laycock eyed him up and down. 'Looks like there wasn't a beating you didn't take.'

'All in a day's work.'

'And how's your sister?'

416

'She's recovering. It's mainly shock. Could've been a lot worse than it was. She wasn't physically harmed.'

'That's a relief.' Laycock sounded sincere. 'Look Heck, I'm sorry you ended up going it alone on this.'

'Shit happens.'

'You heard that we've lost all the evidence from the assassin's house?'

'Yeah, well don't worry. I'll find something else.'

'I think you've done enough for the time being. You can leave the rest to us.'

'If only I could, Sir. The problem is there are a lot of men scattered around the UK who are probably thinking that, thanks to the secret dirtball we coppers currently have hiding in our midst, they're home and dry. Well . . . they aren't. And he isn't either. And I already have strong suspicions about who he is. All I need to do now is prove it.'

'Well done anyway,' Laycock said with a bland smile, offering his hand.

Heck took it, and held on to it just a fraction of a second longer than was absolutely necessary. 'You can trust me on that, Sir,' he said intently. 'As long as I'm in this job, someone else in this job is going to need to be looking over his shoulder. Every minute of every day, for the rest of his life.'

Laycock nodded, smiled again and walked away.

He didn't look back.

Can't wait to see what Heck does next? Read on for an exclusive extract from the next in the series, *Sacrifice*.

Chapter 1

The whole of Holbeck should be bombed.

That was Alan Ernshaw's view. Okay, he was a relatively new police officer – just ten months in the job – so if anyone overheard him make such a politically incorrect statement and complained, he'd have an excuse. But the gaffers still wouldn't be impressed. Holbeck, the old warehouse district located just south of Leeds city centre, might well consist mainly of buildings that were now empty shells, its Victorian terraced housing might now mostly be derelict, its pubs and shops boarded up, the few parts of it that were inhabited reduced to grotty concrete cul-de-sacs strewn with litter and covered in graffiti, but policemen didn't take these sorts of things personally anymore. Or at least they weren't supposed to.

Holbeck should *not* be bombed. That was quite out of the question. Holbeck should be refurbished, remodelled . . . *rejuvenated*. Yes, that was it. That was one of the nicey-nicey buzzwords they used these days.

Ernshaw yawned and scratched the dried razor-cut on his otherwise smoothly shaven jaw. He supposed 'rejuvenation' sounded okay, even if it was only a euphemism for flattening shithole areas like this and trying to build something better.

Radio static crackled. *'1762 from Three?'*

Ernshaw yawned again. 'Go ahead.'

'What are you and Keith doing, over?'

'Well we're not sitting down for a turkey dinner, put it that way.'

'Join the club. Listen, if you've nothing else on, can you get over to Kemp's Mill on Franklyn Road?'

Ernshaw, who was from Harrogate, some fifteen miles to the north, and still didn't know his way street-for-street around West Yorkshire's sprawling capital city, glanced to his right where PC Keith Rodwell slouched behind the steering wheel.

Rodwell, a heavy-jowled veteran of twenty years, nodded. 'ETA . . . three.'

'Yeah, three minutes, over,' Ernshaw said into his radio.

'Thanks for that.'

'What's the job?'

'It's a bit of an odd one actually. Anonymous phone call says we'll find something interesting there.'

Rodwell didn't comment, just swung the van into a three-point turn.

'Nothing more?' Ernshaw asked, puzzled.

'Like I say, it's an odd one. Came from a call-box in the city centre. No names, no further details.'

'Sounds like a ball-acher, but hey, we've nothing else to do this Christmas morning.'

'Much appreciated, over.'

It wasn't just Christmas morning; it was a snowy Christmas morning. Even Holbeck looked picture-postcard perfect as they cruised along its narrow, silent streets. The rotted facades and rusted hulks of abandoned vehicles lay half-buried under deep, creamy pillows. Spears of ice hung glinting over gaping windows and bashed-in doors. The fresh layer muffling the roads and pavements was pristine, only occasionally marked by the grooves of tyres. There was almost no traffic and even fewer pedestrians, though it wasn't eight o'clock yet, and at that time on December 25th only fools like Ernshaw and Rodwell were likely to be up and about.

Or so they'd assumed.

'Something interesting . . .' Ernshaw mused. 'What do you think?'

Rodwell shrugged. He spoke in monosyllables at the best of times, and as he was now deep in thought there wasn't much chance even of that.

'Bunch of druggies or something?' Ernshaw added, 'Squatting? If that's it they'll all be dead by now. Must've been minus-ten last night easily.'

Again, Rodwell shrugged.

Kemp's was a former flax-spinning mill, but it had been closed now for nearly two decades and was a forlorn reminder of prosperous times past. Its tall octagonal chimney was still intact, the square windows arrayed in uniform rows across its dingy frontage were largely unbroken, and most of its ground-floor entrances were supposedly chained shut (there was talk that its industrial/gothic exterior might at some point gain 'listed building' status, so some attempts to preserve the place had been made), but, like so many of the derelict buildings around here, it wouldn't be difficult for determined intruders to force entry.

Snow crunched under their tyres as they slid to a halt on the mill's southward-facing lot. The gaunt structure lowered over them against the white winter sky. The red bricks with which it had been constructed were hidden beneath soot so thick it had become scabrous. Those pipes and gutterings that hadn't already collapsed sagged beneath Alpine over-hangs of snow. At first glance there was no movement – no sign of life, but the place was enormous; not just a central block, though that in itself might once have housed a thousand workers, but comprising all kinds of annexes and outbuildings. As the van eased forward at a snail's pace, it dawned on Ernshaw how long it might take them to locate 'something interesting' here.

He put his radio to his mouth. '1762 to Three?'

'Go ahead, Alan.'

'We're at Franklyn Road now. Everything looks okay so far. Any further on the complainant, over?'

'That's negative, Alan. Could be some prat with nothing better to do, but probably best to check it out, over.'

'Received,' he said, adding under his breath: 'Might take a while, mind.'

They drove in a wide circle around the aged edifice, their tyres sliding as they hit patches of sheet-ice. Ernshaw wound his window down. It was bitterly cold outside – the snow was still dry and crisp as powder – but even if they didn't see anything untoward, it was possible they might *hear* it.

That they didn't was vaguely, unexplainably disconcerting.

Christmas morning ought to be deeply quiet, ought to be restful, ought to be hushed by the freshly fallen snow, yet the silence around Kemp's Mill was somehow uncanny; it had a brittle edge, as if it could shatter at any moment.

They rounded corner after corner, gazing up sheer faces of windows and bricks, networks of ancient piping, hanging, rusted fire-escapes. The van's wheels constantly skidded, dirty slush flying out behind. They trundled through an access-passage connecting with a row of empty garages, the corrugated plastic roof of which had fallen through after years of decay. On the other side of this they spotted an entrance.

Rodwell braked gently, but the van still skated several yards before coming to rest.

What looked like a service doorway was set into a recess

at the top of three wide steps. There was no sign of the door itself – possibly it lay under the snow, but from the state of the doorjamb, which had perished to soggy splinters, this entry had been forced a long time ago. A pitch black interior lay beyond it.

'2376 to Three?' Rodwell told his radio.

'Go *ahead, Keith.*'

'Yeah, we're still at Kemp's Mill. Evidence of a break, over.'

'*Do you want some help?*'

'That's negative at present. Looks like an old one.'

They climbed out, gloving up and zipping their padded anoraks. Ernshaw adjusted his hat while Rodwell locked the vehicle. They ventured up the steps, the blackness inside retreating under the intense beams of their torches. At the top, Ernshaw thought he heard something – laughter maybe, but it was very distant, very faint and very brief. He glanced at Rodwell, whose dour, pitted face registered that he'd heard nothing. Ernshaw was so unsure himself that he declined to mention it. He glanced behind them. This particular section of the property was enclosed by a high wall. The van was parked close alongside it, the entrance to the garage-passage just at its rear. Aside from the tracks the vehicle itself had made on entering the yard, the snowfall lay unbroken. Of course, flakes had been falling heavily until about two hours ago; so this didn't necessarily mean that no one had been here during the night.

They entered side-by-side, torchlight spearing ahead, and were immediately faced by three options: directly in front, a switchback stair ascended into opaque blackness; on the right, a passage led off down a long gallery zebra-striped by smudges of light intruding through the ground level windows; on the left lay a wide open area, presumably one of the old workshops. They ventured this way first, their torch-beams crisscrossing, revealing bare brick walls and a high plaster ceiling, much of which had rotted, exposing bone-like girders. Shredded cables hung like jungle creeper. The asphalt floor was scattered with planks and fragments of tiles. Here and there, the corroded stubs of machine fittings jutted dangerously upward. Despite the intense cold, there was a sour taint to the air, like mildew. The scuffling of their feet echoed through the vast building's distant reaches.

They halted to listen, hearing nothing.

'This is a wild goose chase,' Ernshaw finally said, his words smoking. 'You realise that, don't you?'

'Probably,' Rodwell replied, shining his torch into every corner. From the moment they'd received the call, Rodwell had seemed a little graver of purpose than usual, which was intriguing to Ernshaw. Keith Rodwell had been a copper for so long that he generally knew what was what without even having to think about it. The way he was behaving now suggested either: a) that he was bored and was treating this like a real mystery purely to liven things up (though that hardly ever happened – Keith Rodwell was never more content than when sitting vegetating on an uneventful shift); or b) that he genuinely believed something untoward was going on here.

'Okay, I give up,' Ernshaw said. 'What do you *think* we're going to find?'

'Keep it down. Even if this is someone taking the piss, let's catch 'em at it.'

'Keith . . . it's Christmas morning. Why would someone . . .'

'Shhh!'

But Ernshaw didn't need to be shushed. He too had just heard the long, low creak from overhead. They regarded each other in the gloom, ears pricked.

'Take the front stair,' Rodwell said quietly, edging across

the workshop. 'I'll go around the back . . . see if I can find another way up.'

Ernshaw retreated to the door they'd come in through. He glanced at the van out in the yard; as before, there was no sign of movement. He started to ascend, attempting to do it stealthily though the slamming impacts of his feet rang up the stairwell ahead of him. The first floor he came to comprised another huge workshop. Not all the windows up here were boarded, though their glass was so grimy that only a paltry winter light filtered through. Even so, it was enough to hint at an immense hangar-like space ranging far across the building, filled with stacked crates and workbenches, forested by steel pillars.

Ernshaw hesitated, gripping the hilt of his baton. This time last year he'd been an innocent young student at the University of Hull, so he had no trouble admitting to himself that, while it was bad enough being made to work on Christmas Day – only the older, married guys tended to be spared that pain-in-the-arse duty – it was even worse having to spend it trawling through the guts of a eerie, frozen ruin like this.

A loud crackle from his radio made him jump.

The voice of Comms boomed out as it dispatched messages to patrols elsewhere on the subdivision. Irritated, he turned the volume down. Like Keith had said, it was always best to catch them at it – whoever *they* were.

He advanced as his eyes adjusted to the half-light. Directly ahead, about forty yards away, a doorway opened into what looked like an antechamber. For some reason, the rear brick wall of that chamber was lit by a greenish glow.

Green?

A coloured candle, maybe? A paper lantern?

Ernshaw halted as a figure flirted past the doorway on the other side.

'Hey,' he said under his breath. Then louder: *'Hey!'*

He dashed forward, now with baton drawn.

When he entered the chamber, nobody was there, but he saw that the odd-coloured light had been caused by a sheet of mouldy green canvas fastened over a window. A stairway – an indoor fire-escape, all rust and riveted steel – dropped down through a trapdoor; while a secondary stair rose up to the next level, though this was very narrow, scarcely broad enough for an average-sized man to climb it without turning sideways. He peered up, spying a ray of feeble daylight at the top. When he listened, he heard nothing, though it wasn't difficult to imagine that someone was lurking up there, listening back.

'Alan?' someone asked.

Half-shouting, Ernshaw spun around.

Rodwell gazed at him from the trapdoor, in particular at his drawn baton.

'Have you . . .?' Ernshaw glanced back up the stair, listening intently. 'Have you been up here once? I mean, have you been up already and gone back down for any reason?' Rodwell shook his head as he rose fully into view. 'Thought I saw someone, but . . .' The more Ernshaw considered it, the less substantial that 'figure' had seemed. A shadow maybe, cast by his torch? 'Could've been mistaken, I suppose . . .'

Rodwell also glanced up the next stair. Without speaking, he ascended it.

Ernshaw followed. The floor at the top of this had been partitioned into small rooms and connecting corridors. Even fewer of the windows on this level were boarded, but there were less of them, so a sepulchral gloom pervaded.

Before they commenced exploring, Rodwell lifted a dust-caked Venetian blind and peered down into the yard below. It had occurred to them both, somewhat belatedly, that if this was some daft but elaborate ruse to create a diversion by which to steal a police vehicle, they'd be left with an omelette-size egg on their faces. However, the van sat unmolested; the snow around it, almost blinding-white after the dimness of the interior, was unmarked. From this height, they could see further afield into adjacent streets, or what remained of them. Most of the rows of terraced housing on the south side of Kemp's Mill had been demolished, but even with the recent snowfall, the parallel outlines of their old foundations were still visible.

There was no sign of anyone around. The nearest habitations were two blocks of 1970s flats about three hundred yards away, beyond a mountain of snow-covered scrap; only one or two lights – the garish neon of early morning Christmas decorations – twinkled from their windows. The rest were still curtained.

'*2376 from Three?*' the voice of Comms crackled from Rodwell's PR.

'Go ahead,' he said, dropping the blind back into place.

'*Anything from Franklyn Road yet?*'

'No offences revealed at this stage. Still searching, over.'

'*Message from Sergeant Roebuck, Keith. Don't waste too much time there. If it's just some kids messing around, leave it. There are other jobs piling up.*'

'Roger, received.'

'That it, then?' Ernshaw asked hopefully.

'No,' Rodwell replied.

They ventured along a central passage, peeking around the first door they came to, seeing what had presumably once been an office. In the middle of it, weak daylight illuminated a single filing cabinet from which a ton of paperwork had overflowed. Ernshaw entered, scooping up some of the documents: work rosters yellowed by age; dog-eared time-and-motion sheets. He tossed them away, moving through the next doorway into another identical office. Sometime in the past, vandals had scribbled slogans all over the walls in this one. Almost unavoidably, he paused to read – the depths of the perverted imagination never ceased to fascinate and revolt him.

'Kids have been in here, alright,' he said. 'Dirty little buggers too. Seen this . . . "My little sister gave me my first blowjob. She'll do you too for a fiver". There's even a fucking phone number. "Every day I wank into my mum's knickers – now she's pregnant again. Oh shit".' Getting no response, he turned.

Rodwell had not come into the room with him.

Ernshaw went back to the door and glanced into the office with the filing cabinet; Rodwell wasn't in there either.

'Keith?' he said.

A footfall sounded behind him. He whirled around – to find that he was still alone. But on the far side of the room another door stood ajar.

Hadn't it been closed previously?

Ernshaw approached it, suddenly suspecting that someone was in the next room. Hand on baton again, he yanked the door open – entering yet another deserted corridor, the contents of more gutted offices spilling into it from adjoining doorways.

'Keith?'

Still there was no reply.

Ernshaw proceeded forward. At the extreme end there was another stairway, but when he reached this, it was only short and it led up to a closed door beyond which a crack of bright daylight was visible.

'Keith? You up there, mate?'

Again, nothing.

He ascended – slowly, body half-turned so that he could watch both in front and behind. At the top, the door swung open easily and he entered the most spacious office he'd seen to date – a good forty foot by thirty – the sort of palatial residence an MD might once have inhabited. It possessed several large windows, all intact, none covered by planking or sheets of icky green canvas. The walls were even papered, though the floor comprised loose boards, several of which had warped and sprung. It contained no furniture; just a scattering of broken bricks and, in one corner, rather curiously, a wheelbarrow rimmed with hardened cement, with a pick and sledge-hammer standing against it.

But none of this captured Ernshaw's attention as much as the strange object on the farthest side of the room.

He walked forward.

It appeared to be a section of new wall; a seven-foot wide rectangle rising almost floor to ceiling. The paper and plaster had recently been torn away, and the ancient stonework beneath demolished; new, yellowish bricks had been mortared into the resulting cavity. But what *really* caught his eye hung in the middle of this: a sheet of white paper with a message emblazoned on it in startling crimson. The paper was fresh and new; when Ernshaw took it from the wall it had been fixed there with a blob of Blu-Tack, which proved to be soft and pliable – so that was new as well.

The message had been printed by a modern desk-jet of some sort. It read:

Ho Ho Ho

For some reason, Ernshaw's short-cropped hair prickled. This could easily be more empty-headed idiocy from the local scrotes. But there was something about it – probably the fact that it was clearly a recent addition to this neglected pile – that made him think it might be significant. He stepped backward, examining the wall again. It had definitely been constructed recently. At its base, two lumps of tapered black wood protruded through a tiny gap under the bricks; some builder's device, no doubt, to keep the whole thing level.

A hand tapped his shoulder.

Ernshaw spun around like a dervish. 'Fuck me!' he hissed.

'What's this?' Rodwell asked.

'Will you stop sneaking up on people!' Ernshaw handed him the notice. 'Dunno. Found it pinned to the wall.'

Rodwell stared at the wall first. 'This brickwork's new.'

'That's what I thought. Well . . . they'll have done all sorts of jobs over the years, to keep the place serviceable, won't they?'

'Not in the last twenty.' Rodwell glanced at the notice, then back at the wall again. 'This is a chimney breast. Or it was. Probably connected to one of the outer flues.'

'Okay, it's a chimney,' Ernshaw said. 'Bricking up an old chimney isn't much of a criminal offence these days, is it?'

Rodwell read the notice a second time.

Ho Ho Ho

'Jesus . . . Christ,' he breathed slowly. 'Jesus Christ almighty!'

Moving faster than Ernshaw had ever seen him, Rodwell threw the paper aside and dropped to one knee to examine the two wooden stubs protruding below the brickwork. Ernshaw leaned down to look as well – and suddenly realised what he was actually seeing: not wooden supports, but the scuffed toes of a pair of boots.

Rodwell grabbed the pick and Ernshaw the hammer.

They went at the new wall as hard as they could. Neither man was much of a dab-hand at this, so at first it resisted their efforts – but they pounded fiercely, Rodwell stopping only to call for supervision and an ambulance, Ernshaw to

432

unzip his anorak and throw off his hat. After several minutes grunting and sweating, mortar was bursting out with every impact – then they were loosening bricks, extricating them with their fingers, striking again, guarding their eyes against flying chips. Piece by piece, the wall came down, gradually exposing what stood behind it – though it was the aroma that hit the two cops first.

Ernshaw gagged, clamping a hand to his nose and mouth. Rodwell, more used to rotting meat, worked all the harder, smashing away the last vestiges of brickwork.

They stood back panting, wafting at the dust, retching at the stink.

'Good God!' Rodwell said as he focused on what they'd uncovered.

Though it stood upright, this was only because it had been suspended by the wrists from two manacles fixed above its head. It had reached that stage of early putrefaction where it could either have been a shrivelled corpse or a wax mannequin, its complexion somewhere between sickly yellow and maggoty green. It had once been an elderly man – that much was evident from the scraggly white beard on its skullish jaw, plus it was bone-thin, an impression only enhanced by its baggy, extremely dirty red garb. This consisted of a red tunic hanging in foul-smelling folds, trimmed down the middle and around its hem with dirt-grey fur, and red pantaloons, the front of them thick with frozen urine, their cuffs tucked into a pair of oversized wellingtons.

It was not an unusual experience, even for relatively new bobbies like Ernshaw, to discover corpses in a state of corruption. Not everyone handled it well, though Ernshaw usually had – until now.

He laughed. Bizarrely. It was almost a cackle.

'S-Santa,' he stuttered.

Rodwell glanced at him, distracted.

'Fucking Santa!' Ernshaw continued to cackle, though his glazed expression contained no mirth. 'Looks like there was no one nice waiting for him at the bottom of this chimney. Only naughty . . .'.

Rodwell glanced back at the corpse as he recalled those words – *Ho Ho Ho*. He noticed that a red hood with a greyish fur trim had been pulled up over the wizened, hairless cranium. He hadn't spotted this at first because a few futile death-struggles had dislodged it backward.

'Christ save us,' he whispered. The corpse wore a tortured expression, its eyes bugging like marbles in a face twisted into a rigid, grimacing devil-mask. 'This poor bastard was walled up in here alive.'

Chapter 2

If it was possible for a newsagent billboard to shriek, this one did. If it had been printed in huge, zigzagging letters, it couldn't have been any more eye-catching.

Detective Sergeant Mark 'Heck' Heckenburg observed it through the driver's window of his Fiat while he waited at a traffic light. Homeward-bound commuters darted across the road in front of him, huddled and muffled against the February evening. Much of the heavy winter snow had cleared, but dirty, frozen lumps of it lingered in the gutters and on the corners of pavements. Thick wafts of exhaust drifted across the road as the traffic light changed to green.

Heck eased his Fiat forward, glancing continually at his sat-nav. Milton Keynes was a big place; it comprised about two hundred thousand citizens, and like most of the so-called 'new towns' – purpose-built conurbations designed to

435

accommodate the overspill population after World War II left so many British cities in smoking rubble – its suburbs seemed to drag on interminably. After half an hour, the entrance to Wilberforce Drive appeared on his left. He rounded its corner and cruised along a quiet, middle-class street, though all streets were quiet at present, particularly in southern English towns like Milton Keynes, which were close to the M1 motorway. Especially after nightfall.

For the most part, the houses were semi-detached, nestling behind low brick walls or privet fences. All had front gardens and neatly paved driveways. In the majority of cases, cars were already parked there, curtains drawn. When he reached number eighteen, he halted on the opposite side of the road and turned his engine off.

Then he waited. It would soon get cold, so he zipped up his leather jacket and pulled on his gloves. Eighteen, Wilberforce Drive seemed almost impossibly innocent. A snug pink light issued through its downstairs window. A child's skateboard was propped against its garage door. There was even the relic of a snowman on its front lawn; little more now than a sooty, twisted ghost, but it was clear what it once had been.

Heck took his notes from the glove-box and checked through them. Yes – eighteen, Wilberforce Drive, the home of Jordan Savage, thirty-three years old, a married man who managed the local garden centre for a living. The homely environs made it altogether less menacing a scene than Heck had expected. It would be easier than usual to walk up the path and rap on the door here, even to get tough if he wanted to – this wasn't the sort of place where cops normally got their teeth knocked out. But Heck was still nervous that he might be barking up the wrong tree.

Not that he would ever know sitting behind his steering wheel. But before he could open the car door, another door opened – the front door to number eighteen. The man who stepped out could only be Jordan Savage: his solid build and six-foot-two inches of height made him unmistakable; likewise his shock of red, spiky hair. No doubt, up close, those penetrating blue eyes of his would be another give-away.

Savage was wearing jeans, a sweater and a heavy waxed jacket. As Heck watched, he moved the skateboard aside, took a key from his pocket and opened the garage door. There was a vehicle inside; it was too dark to tell for sure, but it looked like a Mondeo Sport. Again Heck consulted his notes. Yes – a green Mondeo Sport. The VRM checked out as well. It was the same car the Traffic patrol had become suspicious of and had stopped that dank October night.

The Mondeo's engine rumbled to life, its headlights snapped on and Savage eased it down the drive. If he noticed Heck seated in the car opposite, he gave no indication, but turned right along Wilberforce Drive, heading for the junction with the main road. When Savage was a hundred yards ahead, Heck switched his own engine on and followed.

Tailing a suspect was never easy, especially when you were doing it unofficially and on your own – but it wasn't hugely difficult either. Heck had performed this task dozens of times and was well aware that you were never as exposed as you felt. Unless the suspect had reason to believe he was being followed and was keeping watch, he most likely wouldn't notice you, particularly if the traffic was heavy.

Heck stayed about three cars behind – not too close to attract attention, but close enough to keep a careful eye on his target. Even so, when the Mondeo suddenly veered left onto what looked like another housing estate, he was taken by surprise. Exercising extreme caution – it was easier to be noticed following someone around a quiet estate than on a busy thoroughfare – he drove in pursuit.

This neighbourhood was less salubrious than the previous

one. Its houses were council stock, some terraced with communal passages between them, some with front gates hanging from broken hinges. But its central artery was called Boroughbridge Avenue, and that rang a bell of familiarity. Heck didn't need to rifle through his notes this time to know that this was where Jason Savage, Jordan's twin-brother, lived.

About fifty yards ahead, the Mondeo stopped outside a two-flat maisonette. Jordan Savage didn't get out, but sat there, his exhaust pumping winter fog. Heck slowed to a halt as well – just as a glint of light revealed that a door to the upstairs flat had opened and closed. A figure trotted down a narrow flight of cement steps.

Even from this distance, the similarities between the two men were startling. Jason Savage, who was a mechanic by trade, wore an old donkey jacket over what looked like black coveralls, but he too was about six-foot-two and had a mop of spiky red hair. He climbed into the Mondeo's front passenger seat, and it drew away from the kerb. Heck remained where he was, wondering if they were about to make a three-point turn, though apparently there was another exit from this estate: the Mondeo drove on ahead until it rounded a bend and vanished.

Heck nosed forward. This was better than he'd hoped for, but it could also mean nothing. It wouldn't be the first time that two brothers had spent an evening playing darts together, or catching a flick. That said, when he swung around the bend and found himself at a deserted T-junction, he briefly panicked.

Trusting to luck that the left-hand route would lead back onto the council estate, he swung his car right and got his foot down. Leafless trees closed in from either side as he passed through public woodland – this didn't look promising, but then it gave way to the high fencing of an industrial park, and about fifty yards ahead a red traffic light was showing and a lone vehicle waiting there. Heck accelerated and, to his relief, recognised the Mondeo. He'd be directly behind them now, but he couldn't afford to worry about that. His police instinct – that old 'hunch' thing honed to near perfection through so many criminal investigations (or alternatively, 'his imagination', as Detective Superintendent Gemma Piper called it), told him he was onto something.

The light turned to green as he pulled up behind the Mondeo, and it swung left. Heck followed, but decelerated a little. They were on another main road, with houses to either side, followed by shops and pubs. More and more vehicles joined the traffic flow. Heck decelerated further to allow a couple to push in front of him. With the relaxed air of a driver who knows his way around, Jordan Savage worked his way across the centre of Milton Keynes, negotiating roundabouts and one-way systems as if he could do it blindfold. There were roadworks in abundance, but he glided through the contra-flows without hindrance. Heck, who wasn't a local and in fact had never even been to Milton Keynes until he'd arrived here as part of the enquiry team some six months earlier, found it more difficult, though thankfully that ultimate bugbear of the covert tail – a traffic light or stop-sign separating him from his target – never occurred. It *almost* did as they approached a bustling inter-section, but Jordan Savage, who clearly (and interestingly) seemed to have no intention of causing a stir, halted at the white line even though, if he'd floored his pedal, he could probably have made it through the break in traffic.

Heck was only one car behind him at this stage. He too slowed and stopped, by chance underneath a large Crimestoppers notice-board. As well as various telephone numbers, including the hotline in the Main Incident Room at Milton Keynes Central, it carried a massive photo-fit of the so-called 'M1 Maniac', a frightful figure with hunched, gorilla-like shoulders, wearing a black hood pulled down almost to his eyes, which in turn were half-covered by a fringe of lank hair, and a collar zipped up to his nose. It was impossible to tell in the yellowish glow of the streetlamps, but in normal daylight those eyes would be a startling blue and that fringe a vivid red. In fact, to emphasise this, the artist who'd constructed the photo-fit had only colourised those sections; the rest of it was in black and white.

Heck followed cautiously as the Mondeo advanced through the intersection, the vehicles between them peeling off left. The Mondeo headed straight on, taking a narrow street between industrial units surrounded by high walls. Past these lay shabby apartment blocks: broken glass strewed their forecourts, ramshackle cars cluttered the parking bays. Heck slowed to a crawl, but still managed to keep the Mondeo in sight. It was about a hundred yards ahead when it turned right, appearing to descend a ramp.

He cruised forward another fifty yards, then pulled up and stopped. He grabbed the radio from his dashboard, switched its volume down and shoved it under his jacket, before climbing out and walking the rest of the way.

The ramp swerved down beneath a monolithic tower block, which, from a rusted nameplate screwed onto a concrete buttress, was called Fairwood House. As Heck ventured down, he kept close to the wall on his right. When he reached the bottom, he halted, waiting until his eyes adjusted. What looked like a labyrinthine underground car park swam slowly into view. Unlit alleyways wound between concrete stanchions covered with spray-paint, or led off along narrow alleys between rows of padlocked timber doors. The occasional niche or litter-strewn corner played host to wrecks: hunks of burned, twisted metal sheeted with cobwebs.

There was no immediate sign of the Mondeo, but given

the state of this place it could be anywhere and Heck wouldn't see it until it was right on top of him.

He walked back up the ramp and climbed into his Fiat, releasing the handbrake. It was tempting to freewheel down there with his headlights off, but if he did encounter the Savage brothers, that would look suspicious in the extreme. Instead, he behaved as normally as possible, switching the engine on and driving down as if he hadn't a care in the world. Once below, he casually prowled, turning corner after corner. There were other exits, he noticed – some were caged off, others stood wide open. His heart sank as it occurred to him that his targets might have exited the place altogether; perhaps they'd sensed they were being followed and had used this car park as a diversion. But then, as he cruised another gallery between rows of padlocked doors, he saw light ahead – and not street-lighting. It was orange, and it flickered.

Firelight.

He proceeded for forty yards, before parking and creeping the rest of the distance on foot. The firelight was reflecting on a wall beyond the next T-junction. But when he edged forward the last few feet and peeked around to the right, he spied a parking bay in which a couple of ragged, elderly men were burning rubbish in an oil-drum. They were bearded and grizzled; one glanced around – his face was weasel-thin, his mouth a toothless maw.

Heck swore under his breath.

He went back to his Fiat. Somehow or other the bastards had eluded him. He slotted his key into the ignition – and bright illumination fell over him. In his rear-view mirror, two powerful headlamps approached from behind.

Heck sank down so low that he couldn't see the vehicle as it passed him slowly by. But when he peered after it, it was the Mondeo. It reached the end of the drag, turning left. Heck jumped out, running back to the T-junction on catlike feet. The Mondeo was now making a second left-hand turn. He scampered after it, sweat stippling his brow. From the next corner he saw that it had stopped some thirty yards ahead, alongside another row of lock-ups.

The Savage brothers climbed out, conversing quietly. Heck flattened himself against the damp concrete wall to listen. He fancied he heard them use the word 'van', which excited him so much that his hand unconsciously stole to his radio, though he managed to restrain himself from grabbing it. He risked another peek. Jason Savage was clambering into the Mondeo's driving seat, switching its engine back on. Meanwhile, Jordan Savage approached the nearest lock-up, produced a key and, opening its narrow side-panel, sidled through into darkness.

Heck felt a tremor of anticipation the like of which he'd never known.

It was several minutes before Jordan Savage reappeared, but when he did he had changed his clothes, or had put other clothing on over the top: black waterproof trousers and a black hooded anorak. He handed something to his brother through the window of the Mondeo – it looked like a pistol. Heck couldn't quite identify it, but a Ruger Mark II had been used in all eight killings to date.

Jordan Savage stepped back inside the lock-up and closed the side-panel behind him, while the Mondeo pulled forward. The lock-up's main door was then lifted laboriously from within. Headlamp beams shot out as a second vehicle emerged. Heck clutched the concrete corner he was braced against with such force that it almost drew blood from his fingernails. When a white transit van rolled into view, he jerked backwards, retreating quickly from the corner and fishing his radio from his jacket.

'DS Heckenburg on Taskforce, to Sierra Six . . . over?'

'*DS Heckenburg?*' came a chirpy response.

'Urgent message. Immediate support required. Underground car park at Fairwood House. Send as many units as possible, block off all exits . . . but silent approach. I also want a Trojan unit, over.'

'*Could you repeat the latter, sarge?*'

Heck tried to keep his voice low. 'Get me a Trojan unit pronto! And get me supervision . . . DI Hunter and Chief Superintendent Humphreys. I'm sitting on two targets I believe to be the M1 murderers, so I need that back-up ASAP, over and out!'

He turned the volume down again as the message went rapid-fire across the airwaves. Lurching back to his car, he unlocked the steering, knocked the handbrake off, and pushed the vehicle forward. As he reached the end of the drag, he yanked the handbrake on and crept on foot to the corner, where he risked another glance.

The white van sat behind the Mondeo, both rumbling and chugging fumes. The two twins were standing together talking. Jason Savage had removed his donkey jacket and put on a similar black hooded anorak to his brother.

If they would just keep the conflab going until the cavalry arrived . . .

'Any change today, sur?' someone asked loudly.

Heck twirled. One of the tramps had come stumbling around the corner and now was standing out in the open with hand cupped. His threadbare garb reeked to high Heaven; grey locks hung in matted strands over his semi-glazed eyes.

Heck glanced back towards the Savage brothers, who were suddenly staring in his direction. A piercing light sprang forward as one of them switched on a torch. Heck jumped back around the corner, but the tramp didn't move except to shield his eyes.

No doubt the Savage boys knew there were human dere-licts down here. No doubt they'd seen them before and had discerned there was no threat from them. But it was plainly obvious to anyone that this particular hobo was interacting with someone else.

'Just a little change, sur,' he said again in fluting Irish, sticking an empty hand under Heck's nose. 'A couple of pounds wouldn't go amiss . . .'

Heck chanced another glance. One of the two brothers, it was difficult to say which, had opened the driver's door to the van and looked set to climb into it. The other was still frozen in place, still peering along the passage.

'Get down, you damn fool!' Heck hissed. 'Get on the floor now!'

'Just a little change, sur.' The tramp tittered crazily. 'An entry fee, if you loike. The price of visiting our little parlour . . .'

Heck lunged forward, grabbing the skeletal figure by the lapel of his coat and dragging him out of the torchlight, hurling him to the floor. At the same time he bellowed: 'Armed police! You're completely surrounded! Drop your weapons and get on the ground with your arms outspread!'

The response was two thundering gunshots, the first kicking a chunk the size of a fist from the concrete corner in front of Heck, the second careening from the opposing wall, whining past his ear. There was an echo of slamming doors.

Heck slid forward to look. Both brothers must have leaped into the transit van, for it was already haring away down the passage, its tail-lights receding. The Mondeo sat unat-tended. Heck raced back to his Fiat, stepping around the groaning tramp.

''Tis a cruel thing to manhandle a fella so,' came a feeble voice.

Heck leapt behind the wheel, slammed his key into the ignition and hit the gas. The tramp, only just back on his feet, gave a V-sign to the windscreen, only to be blinded by Heck's headlights. He toppled backwards as Heck wove the car around him, accelerating past the lock-ups, tyres screeching. Far ahead, the transit van rounded a corner at such speed that its bodywork drew sparks from the opposing wall. Heck took the corner tightly as well. The van was still far ahead; at the end of the next drag, it ascended another ramp into the sodium-yellow glow of the streets.

'DS Heckenburg . . . chasing!' Heck shouted into his radio. 'Two suspects for M1 murders travelling in a white Ford van, leaving Fairwood House car park by what I believe is the east exit . . . no registration as yet! Urgent warning! At least one of the suspects is armed, shots already fired . . . no casualties, over!'

There was nothing more dangerous, nor more discouraged in the modern police, than high speed pursuit of suspects through built-up areas, yet Heck knew he had no choice. For so many months they'd had nothing – no forensics, no CCTV footage, no crime-scenes, no survivors (bar one, who was brain-damaged), no likely suspects at all – and now, suddenly, they had everything . . . just in front of him, by a skinny fifty yards, yet moving at seventy mph through a busy town-centre.

Horns blared and pedestrians scattered, shrieking, as the white van mounted pavements to cut across junctions. Other vehicles swerved and skidded into shop-fronts, lampposts, or each other; panes of glass imploded, splinters of metal flew. Heck weaved frantically through the chaos. Reaching out of his offside window, he managed to throw his detachable beacon onto the roof of his Fiat. He shouted again into his radio, updating the Comms suite as best he could. By the approaching wail of sirens, other units were close by, but it still seemed likely, at least initially, that the target vehicle would escape. He lost sight of it completely when it sped through a stop-zone on red, other vehicles slewing sideways, one crunching headlong into the traffic light, buckling its pole and bringing the signal head down in a mass of dancing sparks. The cars in front of Heck shunted together, while others turned skew-whiff in their efforts to avoid the pile-up. By instinct, Heck shot down a right-hand alleyway, trying to evade the snarled-up junction, only to see the van zip past the end of the alley, now headed in the opposite direction.

'DS Heckenburg to Sierra Six!' he bawled into his radio, swerving into pursuit. 'Target vehicle doubling back on itself, headed west along . . .' He scanned the buildings flicking by, trying to catch a street name. 'Heading west along Avebury Boulevard. The suspects are Jordan and Jason Savage, and they live at eighteen, Wilberforce Drive and fourteen, Boroughbridge Avenue respectively. I repeat they are armed and highly dangerous!'

Just ahead, the van mounted a pedestrianised precinct, sending benches cart-wheeling. Heck mounted the precinct as well, but the van slid to a halt about forty yards in front, smearing rubber as it pulled a handbrake turn, its engine yowling. Heck only realised at the last second that he'd been lured into a side-on approach. He ducked as a gun-muzzle flashed from the driver's window, the projectile punching through the top corner of his windscreen, spider-webbing it.

'Where's that bloody firearms support!' he shouted, back-handing the Fiat into reverse, crashing through heaps of boxes.

A local police patrol, a Vauxhall Astra in yellow and blue Battenberg, came hurtling onto the precinct from the opposite end, sirens whooping. The van responded by lurching forward again, bolting down a side-street and veering left onto another main road. The patrol car made immediate pursuit, litter swirling from its wheels. Heck went next, still shouting into his radio.

'Target headed north along Saxon Gate! Seventy-five plus!'

The van was all over the road as it hit speeds it had never been designed for, sideswiping a litter-bin through a shop window; flying over a controlled crossing, a woman and child running for their lives to get out of its way. The Astra kept pace from behind, only for the van's back doors to burst open and one of the Savage brothers to crouch there and take aim with his pistol. Over the howling engines and shrieks of tortured rubber, Heck barely heard the detonations, but the three rapid gun-flashes were clear enough. Its windscreen peppered, the Astra crashed over the outer-wall of a civic building with explosive force, the footings tearing out its front undercarriage, so that it finished standing on its nose in an ornamental pond.

'Police RTA on the entrance to Portway!' Heck bellowed. 'Ambulance required!'

He wasn't sure that his instructions were even being heard. The airwaves were alive with crackling static and frantic messages. In front of him, the van's rear doors slammed open and closed as it juddered from side to side. The gunman knelt just inside them, apparently slotting another magazine into place.

'Heading east along Portway!' Heck shouted. 'These guys are fucking packed! Get me that Trojan pronto!'

Sirens could now be heard from all directions. A Thames Valley motorcyclist overtook Heck in a swirl of blues and twos. It tried to overtake the van as well, but the van swung right, sending the bike hurtling onto the pavement and glancing along a wrought-iron fence, from which it caromed back onto the blacktop, managing to right itself again – only to flip end-over-end when it struck the kerb of a traffic island, its rider somersaulting through the air.

Heck only glimpsed this in his rear-view mirror as he blistered past. 'DS Heckenburg to Sierra Six! We now have two police RTAs . . . one on Saxon Gate, one on Portway! At least two officers injured! Ambulances essential! Still pursuing!'

Ahead, flashing blue lights were clustered across a bridge. He hoped this meant that a stinger unit had been deployed underneath, but the white van rocketed through unhindered. Two more police vehicles, a Vectra and a Vivaro came surging down the slip-road; not soon enough to intercept the target, though they managed to block Heck's progress. He shouted and swore as he took evasive action.

The gunman in the van's rear opened fire again, concentrating first on the Vectra. Two holes the size of hubcaps were torn in its bonnet. A third slug missed, and ricocheted from the road surface, blasting Heck's offside mirror to shards.

The Vectra promptly lost speed, pouring black smoke. Heck accelerated into the gap, he and the Vivaro running neck and neck. On an open, empty road there were manoeuvres they could attempt, boxing the van in, bringing it to a forced halt. But too many members of the public were around. A Royal Mail vehicle spun out of control as the target rear-ended it, trying to ram it out of the way. Heck swerved again to avoid a body-crumpling collision. The Vivaro wasn't so lucky: it slid across the opposing carriageway, hitting a row of bollards, jerking around on impact, steam boiling from its mangled radiator. The van hastened again as it found open space, the gunman in the back falling from left to right, unable to get a shot off at his one remaining pursuer, Heck.

The two vehicles tail-gated each other as they blazed across a flyover, beyond which signposts gave directions to the M1 motorway.

Heck swore volubly – that was the last thing they needed.

It wasn't so much that the van, now brutally battered, could outpace the police on a high-speed road, but there would be many, many more road-users on the motorway – and these guys had shown no interest in preserving innocent life.

Before they reached the motorway they hit another round-about. Here, more police patrols – Traffic unit Range-Rovers – were waiting at the turn-offs. They seemed more interested in holding back the public than in attempting to intercept the target, thus allowing it to roar around the circuit unimpeded, spewing black fumes. Possibly, Milton Keynes Comms were issuing orders for officers to stand off. But Heck had received no such instruction; maybe because his radio reception was breaking and distorting – either way he continued the chase, bulleting along the slip-road and down the access ramp.

The M1 southbound was busy at the best of times. Now, at the tail-end of rush hour, it was heaving. The average speed was still about sixty mph, but it was like a fast moving log-jam. Despite this, the van played 'weaver bird' as it forged ruthlessly ahead, ignoring the honking horns and shaking fists. When making insufficient progress, it resorted to the old tactic of ramming and shunting. Heck hit his own horn repeatedly, but had to swerve and skid as vehicles were sideswiped into his path.

The bastards were trying to *cause* a pile-up, he realised. Their plan was to create a barricade of car-wrecks. And on top of that they were still armed. He glimpsed more flickering blue lights in his rear-view mirror, but they were far behind. Maybe the local chopper was now on the case. If so, he could fall back and let the fly-boys take up the pursuit, but he could neither hear nor see it, and nobody in the control room seemed to be answering his messages – at which point his quarry suddenly attempted the craziest manoeuvre Heck had ever seen.

There was a double-sided crash barrier down the motorway's central reservation. A fleeting gap appeared in it – and the van jack-knifed into this, attempting a U-turn.

A U-turn! At sixty miles an hour! On the motorway!

By instinct rather than logic, Heck did the same thing. The next junction was a good fifteen miles way. He hadn't been informed that air support was close, so he couldn't take the chance that the race might be lost and the felons would escape.

But even though Heck jammed his brakes on as he turned, slowing rapidly from sixty to thirty, he lost control crossing the northbound carriageway, skidding on two wheels and slamming side-on into the grass embankment with such bone-shuddering force that his Fiat actually rolled uphill . . . before rolling back down again and landing on its roof, its chassis groaning, glass fragments tinkling over him.

The white van had also lost control, but whereas Heck had lost it at thirty, the Savage brothers had lost it at sixty. Their vehicle didn't even manage to turn into the skid, but ploughed headlong across the carriageway – straight into the concrete buttress of a motorway bridge. The resulting impact *boomed* in Heck's ears.

That sound echoed for what seemed like seconds as Heck lay groggily on his side.

At length, in a daze akin to the worst hangover in history, he began to probe at his body with his fingertips. Everything seemed to be intact, though his neck and shoulders ached, suggesting whiplash. His left wrist was also hurting, though he had full movement in the joint so it was likely only a

450

sprain. With an agonised grunt, he released the catch of his seatbelt, crawled gingerly across the ceiling of his car and tried to open the passenger door, only to find that it was buckled in its frame and immovable. For a second he was too stupored to work this out; then slowly, painfully, he shifted himself around and clambered feet-first through the shattered window.

When he finally stood up, he found himself gazing across the underside of his Fiat, which was gashed and dented and thick with tufts of grass and soil. Clouds of steam from his busted radiator hissed across it. Passing vehicles slowed down, the faces of drivers blurring white as they gawked at him. Multiple sirens approached from the near-distance. From somewhere overhead came the distinct *chud-chud-chud* of a rotor-blade.

How about that, Heck thought. *The eye in the fucking sky's here after all.*

Clamping a hand to his throbbing neck, he had to turn his entire body to gaze along the debris-strewn hard-shoulder. Thirty yards away, the smouldering hulk of the white van was crushed against the concrete buttress like an accordion, reduced to about a third of its original length. Heck hobbled towards it, but when he got within ten yards the stench of fuel and rubber and twisted, melted metal was enough to knock him sick.

And so was the sight of the Savage brothers.

Whichever one of them had fired the shots from out of the back had been catapulted clean across the van's interior, bursting through its windscreen, his head striking the buttress of the bridge as viciously as his vehicle had, and splurging several feet up the concrete in a deluge of blood, brain and bone splinters. The driver had been flung onto the steering wheel, and now lay across it like a bundle of limp rags. At a guess, from the crimson rivers gurgling out underneath him, the central column had torn through his breastbone and punctured his cardiovascular system.

Heck tottered queasily away from the wreck.

Other police vehicles were now drawing in behind his Fiat. The first of their drivers, a young Motorway Division officer in a bright orange slicker, came running up. 'Is that him?' he asked, pale-faced. 'The Maniac?'

Heck, who was too nauseated to stand up any longer, slumped backwards onto the grass. 'Let's hope so,' he muttered. 'Bloody hell . . . let's hope so.'

Hear more about Paul and his inspiration
behind the Mark Heckenberg series in
his monthly blog on Killer Reads.

Writing so good it's criminal . . .